WHO'S YOUR DADDY

TEXAS BILLIONAIRES CLUB BOOK #3

ELLE JAMES
DELILAH DEVLIN

To all the women who want a baby but don't want the messiness of a relationship to get one. May you find love ever after and have that baby you so desperately long for.

CHAPTER 1

NUMBER FIFTEEN COULDN'T BE any worse than the first fourteen men she'd tried.

Rachel Taylor pressed the fast-forward button on the screen, skimming past the dating service's introductions before pausing the video at the end of the blur of pink and purple advertisement. A heavily featured, but handsome man, stared back at her from the screen. Maybe things were looking up.

"Yo, babes. I'm Vinnie Fetachelli."

Rachel groaned then glanced to her friend to see whether her reaction to the exuberant greeting was equally disbelieving. Genie's hand had stopped in mid-air, popcorn forgotten. When her gaze met Rachel's, Rachel couldn't help but grin. "Told ya, this would be better than watching The Bachelorette."

The dark-haired, brown-eyed man on the video from the Date-Your-Mate online dating service, continued introducing himself in an abrupt, staccato voice betraying his Bronx-Italian origins.

"Yooze...," he said, aiming his forefingers at his audience, "...should go wit me..." now pointing his thumbs at his chest, "... 'cause I know how to treat a babe right."

"Is this guy for real?" Rachel watched dumbfounded.

"Shhh, shhh, listen," Genie said, shoulders shaking. She wiped tears from the corners of her eyes.

On the screen, Vinnie Fetachelli was looking down at a paper. "Occ-u-pa-tion..." Frowning, he glanced back up and shifted to the side in his seat. He appeared to be looking at something behind the camera. "Yo, lady. What's that mean?"

From out of view of the camera, came a faint female voice. "Job—Mr. Fetachelli—job."

"Oh, yeah, right, I knew dat."

He straightened, and stared directly at them once more.

"Me and my family own a deli, called Fetachelli Deli. Family business, if ya know what I mean." He gave them a sly smile and a wink.

Rachel snorted then surrendered to a fit of the giggles. It was nervous laughter, but it was better to laugh than to cry.

"Oh, my God. Fetachelli Deli, what a hoot." Genie gasped, holding her sides as Vinnie looked once more at the paper.

"Hobby? I like to watch wrestling, boxing and da races. I'm not picky on da type of races. I like horse, car and dog races--anyt'ing I can place a bet on. But don't worry—I rarely lose. And if I did, my family'd take care of me, if ya know what I mean."

"Oh, my God, he's with the Mafia," Genie exclaimed dramatically. "Rachel, what on earth did you tell them you wanted when you filled out their online quiz?"

Rachel frowned and tapped the pause button. "I simply

told them I wanted someone who was healthy and...um, well...healthy."

"That's it?" Genie's voice rose. "You didn't ask the agency to match you with a compatible personality? Or to have them screened for a minimal intelligence level? Rache, you should at least have asked them to check for rap sheets. Heavens, don't they automatically do background checks?"

Sniffing, Rachel raised her chin a notch. "I didn't think it was important for my purpose, and frankly I didn't think about rap sheets."

"Not important—are you nuts? This guy could be connected, 'if ya know what I mean,'" Genie said, mimicking Vinnie's accent. "And you don't think that's important?"

Rachel took a deep breath, striving for calm. "Now, Genie, we don't know that he's Mafia. It's rather nice that he has such a supportive family. You're letting your imagination run away with you. Besides, I think he's kind of cute."

Pressing PLAY, Rachel ignored Genie's exasperated glare and pretended interest in whatever gem of wisdom Vinnie mumbled as he continued his monologue.

"Expectations..."

A female voice in the background prompted him, "What do you want in a woman?"

Vinnie shrugged. "Da chick I go wit has to look good on my arm, so da other guys can see what a babe she is when I take her out."

The computer screen turned black as the interview ended. Rachel clicked to minimize the online video and leaned forward to take two more sheets of paper from the stack sitting on the coffee table. "Here, let's fill out these evaluation forms. After we watch all the interviews and complete the evaluations, I'll enter the information into a spreadsheet."

"I still can't believe you made up an evaluation form to help you choose your date."

"Are you going to help me or not?" Rachel asked impatiently. "We have three more videos to review from the dating service. I want to be as objective about this as possible."

"Okay, okay. Don't get your panties in a wad," Genie wiped butter from the popcorn off her fingers. "Give me that paper." Grabbing a pen, she began to mark the sheet.

Rachel tapped her own pen thoughtfully against her lip as she read through the questions. Some were straightforward questions about physical attributes like hair and eye color, that required an A through D answer. The rest were subjective, and asked for rankings between one and five. Questions like, "Does this candidate appear athletic?" or "Does the candidate give the impression of mental stability?" Rachel congratulated herself on devising a clinical and objective list of questions. They would help narrow the search for the perfect candidate considerably.

Genie slapped her form on the coffee table. "I've gotta hand it to you, Rache" she said wonderingly. "You're the only person I know who could reduce the characteristics of physical attraction to a multiple-choice test."

Rachel grimaced. She knew her friend wasn't about to let another opportunity to nag pass her by. Genie wasn't wild about her plan. One look in Genie's sympathetic gaze and Rachel thought, *Oh boy, here it comes.*

"Rachel, won't you reconsider?" Genie pleaded. "This just doesn't seem right. Your plan doesn't take into consideration the human factors. I mean, just look at all the candidates we've gone through tonight. Tell me there's even one guy you would feel comfortable hopping into bed with, hmmm?"

Dotting the last 'i' and crossing the last 't' on her evaluation form, Rachel delayed answering. Instead, she picked up her planner and checked Vinnie's name off her list then looked at her best friend. "Genie, the simple fact is, I'm determined to have a child. I'm thirty years old, and in all my time on this earth, I've never found a man I would like to be tied to for the rest of my life. I *need* a child, but I don't necessarily *want* the complications of a husband."

"But those can be the best complications in life," Genie said softly, her brown eyes reflecting her concern.

"Maybe for women who have the time and patience. I have neither that I'm willing to lavish on a man. I want to concentrate all my attention on a baby." Rachel searched for the next name on her list. "I've made up my mind. This is the only solution that makes sense for me. Shall we continue?" she asked, without looking up from her notebook. She heard Genie sigh.

"Just let me finish my evaluation of the Italian Noodle."

"The Italian Noodle?" Rachel's eyebrows raised, and she couldn't resist turning to face her friend.

Genie shrugged her shoulders in silent surrender. For now, at least, the subject of the advisability of "The Plan" would wait. Thank goodness. Her friend's resistance was beginning to wear on Rachel's nerves.

"We have to have some way of keeping these guys straight in our minds—so Vinnie's the Italian Noodle," Genie said. "I've given them all nicknames."

"Fine. Good idea." Rachel exhaled in relief, glad her friend was going along with her and letting the subject of single parenthood drop for the moment.

While Genie reviewed her form, Rachel took a gulp from her wineglass and swiped the screen for the next interview. "Here we go."

"No, wait. I'm not ready...and I'm not sure I'll ever be," Genie ended, mumbling under her breath. She grabbed the wine bottle in front of her and topped off both glasses on the table.

Rachel waited patiently while Genie took a deep gulp of her drink and settled back against the couch cushions. "Roll 'em, Rache. I have to admit, this is a lot more fun than watching some Barbie flirt with half a dozen men—damn unfair, that."

Rachel tapped the screen and moved her finger to the right, zipping to the start of the next interview. A hulking specimen of a man appeared on the monitor. She sat forward, her interest captured. He looked like an actor in an ad for exercise equipment, and he definitely looked...healthy.

Wearing a muscle shirt, he stood before the camera with his hands on his slim hips, displaying bulging biceps and broad muscular shoulders. His skin was a beautifully tanned golden brown and glowed with a slight sheen as though he had just applied a layer of tanning oil. His blond hair was cut close on the sides and was spiked on top. He stared out of the screen with a stunning pair of ice blue eyes—directly at them.

"Ooh-la-la!" Genie let out a shrill wolf whistle. "Now, we're talking."

Then the gorgeous hunk opened his mouth...

Genie moaned, echoing Rachel's sharp disappointment.

"Hi, I'm Marion Hohenberger." The man's voice was high, squeaky and totally incongruous with his appearance.

Genie squealed then hiccoughed. "He sounds like a mouse!"

"Who would have thought such a perfect body would be stuck with such a wimpy voice?" Rachel groaned.

"Maybe, too many steroids?"

"Yup, that's my guess." Rachel reached for her glass, sure that a little alcohol might improve her first impression of the muscled wonder.

Genie lifted her wineglass at the same time in salute. "Here's to Mighty Mouse."

"I used to be a little guy...," Marion continued.

"Yeah, right," snorted Genie.

"...until I found the Royal Academy Health Spa. I built this physique, and now own my own franchise with the spa."

"Hmmm, I'll have to keep him in mind," Rachel said thoughtfully. "I have a client who sells weight equipment. Mighty Mouse here would look dynamite in my client's ads."

"But that voice." Genie's incredulous expression caused Rachel to smile.

"You'd be amazed at what they can do to sweeten a voice in a sound studio."

The muscleman turned to the side and curled his forearm toward his shoulder. He posed like a Mr. Universe contestant, displaying his muscles to their best advantage. "Even though I'm thirty-eight, I have the body of a twenty-five-year-old."

"And the brain of an eight-year-old." Genie chortled.

"Genie," Rachel swatted at her friend. "Give the guy a chance."

"Really, Rache, intelligence goes a long way in this

world. You should have stipulated intelligence to that agency."

"You're letting your prejudices run away with you again. He owns his own business; he has to have some smarts."

"I'm an entrepreneur and personal trainer," Marion droned on.

"Surprise, surprise," Genie continued her running commentary.

"My hobby is body building. My expectations in a woman are simple: she should be in good shape, enjoy physical exercise, and she should be a vegetarian and non-smoker."

The image faded to black as Marion's video ended.

Sighing, Rachel handed Genie an evaluation form and automatically began filling hers out. "Well, I only fit his last requirement, non-smoker. I wonder why they even bothered forwarding his link to me."

Genie glanced over at Rachel, who sat on the couch in a pair of shorts and a T-shirt. Eyeing her as if she were a steer at a cattle auction, Genie began to list her attributes. "Oh, I don't know. You keep yourself in pretty good shape. You have toned muscles, not weight-lifter size, but still, you're firm. Your skin isn't sagging anywhere that I can see, so you're aging well for a thirty-year-old hag."

Rachel picked up a pillow and tossed it at Genie. "Okay, okay, you can stop rubbing it in about my age. Just because you're a twenty-nine-year-old baby, doesn't mean you can pick on me. Remember, you'll be thirty next year. If you don't behave yourself, I'll paste your birthday notice on every billboard in town."

"I plan on being twenty-nine the rest of my life, so

there." Genie stuck out her tongue and threw the pillow back at Rachel.

"Just finish the form, while I play the next video." Rachel swiped again, entered another name in her planner, then settled in with her glass of wine to watch the next candidate.

"How do you do? I'm Herbert Molter."

Genie leaned forward, squinting at the monitor.

Curious about what had caught Genie's attention, Rachel leaned closer to view the man in the center of the screen.

"Does there seem to be something funny about that man's hair?" Genie asked.

Rachel froze the picture, and they both peered at the image on the screen to inspect his carefully groomed coif.

"He has hair plugs," Genie crowed.

"Are you sure?" Rachel hated to admit it, but she could see the neat little rows of hair on the man's scalp. It was as if he had a small orchard of miniature saplings sprouting from his head. But Rachel felt compelled to defend him—after all, going through a dating service to find her baby daddy had been all her idea. "He looks nice enough," she said hesitantly.

"But could you imagine running your fingers through his hair?" Genie's face screwed up, and she gave a delicate shudder. "Oo, I'd be afraid of uprooting them."

"Don't be so mean, Genie. Hair doesn't matter, anyway."

"I bet it does to him."

Rachel set the video into motion and sat back on the couch staring at the screen dispiritedly. She could have done without Genie's eagle-eye. Now that she was aware of the man's unnatural hairline, it was all she could see. He could be the most handsome man on the planet for all she knew--but that was lost to her now. Her gaze was glued instead to the dots of brown hair that sprung tightly from his too-perfect crown.

Genie slid another look at the man on the screen and grinned as she sat back, crossing her arms over her chest. "Rachel, you really are desperate, aren't you?"

"Hush and watch."

"I'm a utilities specialist," Herbert said with a small smile. "I read the electric meters for the city."

"Now, that's exciting," Genie's voice dripped with sarcasm as she rolled her eyes heavenward.

"Hobbies." Herb puffed out his chest and preened. "I'm one of the founding members and the current membership chairperson for the local Botanical Society. I have a spectacular rose garden that was featured as the Rose Garden of the Year in the *Southern Horticulturists Review.*"

"Oh, whoopee." Genie tossed her popcorn up in the air like confetti. "I'm impressed."

"Stop that." Rachel slapped at Genie.

"Expectations...," Herbert paused to give the prompt some careful thought, "...my expectations are that my date be female and heterosexual. That is all."

A match made in heaven, Rachel thought wryly. *His expectations aren't any higher than mine.*

The video immediately faded to black.

There was no sound out of Genie, so Rachel looked in her direction to gauge her reaction. She was doubled over and shaking, her face pressed to a throw pillow, and she was clutching her midsection as if in pain. Suspecting that Genie was choking on her popcorn, Rachel placed a hand on her friend's shoulder. "Genie, are you all right?"

Genie waved a hand in the air.

"Nod if you are choking," Rachel instructed urgently.

Genie nodded vigorously and beat her hand against the couch.

Rachel raised herself to her knees, positioning herself behind her friend and circled her midriff with her arms, placing her closed fists against her diaphragm. She jerked her arms sharply inward.

Genie exhaled noisily. "What the hell are you doing?"

"Saving your life."

Genie sat up rubbing her tummy, then burst into a loud fit of hilarity--this time accompanied by the usual snorts and guffaws.

By now, Rachel understood clearly she was incapacitated for another reason altogether.

Eyes streaming with tears and her face a bright red, it took Genie a full five minutes before she calmed down enough to breathe without wheezing.

"If you are quite finished..." Rachel leveled a killing glare toward Genie, then twisted, giving her full attention to the computer monitor. Realizing she was about to click on the last link, she hesitated before touching the mouse. But instead of clicking, she leaped to her feet and hurried to the kitchen, returning a moment later armed with a fresh bottle of wine. As she took her seat, Genie was blowing her nose loudly and scrubbing smeared mascara off her cheeks.

"Are you ready?" Rachel asked in clipped tones.

"Yes, oh yes. Go ahead, put it on. I could use another good laugh." Tossing back another gulp of wine, Genie continued. "I think my favorite, so far, is the last one—Plug Man." She dissolved into giggles again.

Rachel relaxed, and couldn't help but smile. Genie had the gift of laughter. That's why she valued the redhead's friendship so much. Rachel tended to take life too seriously, while Genie thought life was one long comic relief show. Her special spin on life often helped Rachel put things into perspective. "For what it's worth, we don't have any more potential candidates to review."

"No? What about this last video? I promise to try and keep an open mind." Genie touched Rachel's arm, giving her a steady look. "And we don't have to make any decisions tonight."

Blushing, Rachel reached for the remote and held it protectively against her chest. "It isn't another man."

Genie's eyebrows rose. "Uh...I thought the whole point was you needed a man to get you pregnant. Is there something you want to tell your best buddy, Rache?"

Rachel rolled her eyes. "Stop it, silly. It's *my* video."

Genie grinned at her embarrassment. "Start 'er up. I need to see what you're advertising."

Her hand hovering over the mouse, Rachel glared at her friend. "You have to promise not to laugh."

"No can do."

Rachel sighed. "Oh, Genie, you're a mess. I guess there's no use asking you not to laugh. That would be like asking a mudslide to stop mid-way down a steep slope. Oh well, what's it going to hurt?" With a resigned shrug, Rachel punched the play button and sat next to Genie, attempting to view it with a detached eye.

"Hello. I'm Rachel Taylor." Rachel complimented herself on her confident delivery. She also thought the leopard print chiffon scarf looked daring against the deep V of her double-breasted camel-colored coatdress.

"So far, so good. You remembered your name." Genie grinned.

"I own an advertising firm and handle my own accounts."

"Sounds important, maybe a little stuffy—so's that dress."

Rachel frowned, that was one of her favorite outfits. "Genie, I'm an executive, that's what I do, I can't lie about that."

"Shhh. I want to hear what you say your hobbies are."

"My hobbies are...," the Rachel on the screen paused, looking a little confused by the question, "...um, reading...I belong to an investor's club, and I enjoy organizing...things...."

Genie's eyebrows rose with every word until they were hidden in the hair hanging over her forehead. She held her comments until the Rachel on the monitor concluded her interview.

"My expectations in a man are that he be male, healthy, and have a good genetic background, with no mental or physical health issues in his family. He should have at least a high school education, and I will require a copy of his most recent physical as proof that he is free of any infectious diseases."

"Wrong, wrong, wrong!" Genie shook her head. "Oh, Rachel. What are you trying to catch, here? Most men would run screaming from the woman in that video."

"Why? What's wrong with the truth?"

"What's wrong? What's wrong is that it reeks of geek! There's none of your natural warmth and caring reflected in that video. You should be talking bed sheets, not spreadsheets."

"Well, I wasn't very comfortable before the camera, and they only gave me three minutes. I had to make the most of it." Sighing, Rachel could tell her interview made a lousy first impression, but it couldn't be helped now. "Never mind my video, we need to make a decision about the gentlemen we just watched."

"But none of them are right for you."

"Well, then I'll keep looking," Rachel said stubbornly.

"You're kidding, right?"

"No. I'm determined to stick to my plan and find an acceptable donor."

"Rachel, you really need to think about this whole scheme. It just isn't right. You must know someone. You work with a lot of guys, isn't there one you might consider?"

A picture of a tall, lean man with laughing blue eyes, hair the color of butterscotch, and the devil's own smile popped into Rachel's mind, but she squelched that thought immediately. He was a client. Mixing business with her personal life would be a sure recipe for disaster. Besides, he was already taken.

Snatching her planner from the table, Rachel rose from her seat and paced the floor. "You know I'm not searching for a relationship, Genie. I've thought about it for an entire year. I've planned and researched until I know exactly what I have to do. There won't be any strings attached to this baby. It will be all mine."

"But Rachel, where does love and marriage fit into this?"

Rachel closed her planner with a snap. "It doesn't." She walked over to the window and stared out into the darkness. "I've always wanted to be a mother. I've dreamed of holding a child in my arms, someone I could love and who would love me in return, *unconditionally.*"

Turning to Genie, she continued, "It seems that every relationship I get into, the man wants to change me into someone he wants me to be. A baby won't do that. I happen to like who I am, and I'm sure that my child will like who I am too."

"Alright, I understand your wanting to have a child. And since you haven't found Mr. Right, I can see why you aren't looking for a relationship at this late date. So, why not just go to a sperm bank?"

Rachel shuddered. "That would be my last resort. Just the thought of having some mystery man's sperm injected into my uterus gives me the creeps."

"Put that way..." Shrugging away her reservations, Genie watched her friend sympathetically. "I still think you're going about this all wrong, but I'll help you however you want me to."

"Thanks, Genie. I need to continue my search for The Babymaker."

Genie blinked. "The what?"

Blushing, Rachel grinned. "I can use a nickname, too. That's what I'm calling him...whoever *he* is."

"So where are you going to look next?"

"Hell, I'm an ad executive. I'll just write my own ad for my babymaker," she said with quiet determination.

With a resigned look on her face, Genie cringed. "Honey, I don't have a good feeling about this."

CHAPTER 2

FIDGETING, all Rachel could think about was the stack of paperwork awaiting her attention back at her desk. The afternoon was turning out to be endless. Entertaining the customer was all part of the ad business—the unwritten part of the contract, which states you have to humor your client to make him happy, so he'll want to buy more ads from your agency. At the insistence of her client, Rachel stood at the rear of the room, irritated and tapping her toe.

She smothered a groan when the photographer made yet another adjustment to the aluminum shield directing light toward the set. Experience told her this would just be the beginning of another round of minor adjustments before the shot would be "right." Sure enough, Evelyn instructed her assistant to move the section of split-rail fence, which served as a prop behind the male model.

"Jesse, I need you to lean back against the rail," Evelyn said, before looking through the viewfinder of her camera once more.

The photographer's dulcet tones grated on Rachel's

ears. She might as well say, *Jesse, take off your clothes,* so intimate was the suggestion in her voice.

Not that Rachel could blame the woman. She often fought to keep her own poise when those baby blues were trained on her. And drat the man. He certainly knew his appeal.

The model aimed a smile at the photographer and adjusted his stance. As Jesse hooked his thumbs into the pockets of his jeans, Rachel could imagine the photographer's lenses fogging at this slight, but ultimately male gesture. Every female eye was now glued to the bulge framed by his hands at the front of his jeans.

"Is this what you want?" he drawled.

He was a natural at this. The camera loved him, as did every woman in the room. Except for her, of course. Rachel stiffened her spine with the self-admonishment; she had to endure this for the sake of her client. Problem was, the model was also the client.

Jesse Jordan owned a chain of ranch supply stores stretching across south Texas. He had built the chain from a single rundown store that had been in his family for years. In his mid-thirties, he was now a multi-millionaire who lived on a large, sprawling ranch in the Texas Hill Country.

But it wasn't his wealth that was heating up the room. Even the bright light aimed at the cowboy couldn't approach the wattage of the smile he wore.

If only Jesse were fat, dumb and obnoxious.

Unfortunately, he was quite the opposite. Sun-kissed, golden hair curled down to the top of his collar, and his skin was tanned and healthy from hours of working in the outdoors. Those clear blue eyes of his had slight crinkles at the corners from the smile that was quick to light his face.

And that moustache, not too full, and only a shade darker than the hair on top of his head, drew attention to a mouth that engendered wicked fantasies.

Today, he wore a chambray shirt, slightly faded blue jeans, cowboy boots, and a white cowboy hat. Lean and broad-shouldered, with more than his share of sex appeal, he was the cowboy every girl dreamed of riding off into the sunset with.

At their first meeting, Rachel saw the potential of his appeal, and worked hard to convince him he would be the perfect spokesman and model for advertising his own stores. If nothing else, the entire female population of Texas would probably frequent the stores in hopes of catching a glimpse of the gorgeous owner. He'd agreed to model, but only on the condition that Rachel be there at every shoot.

Looking around, Rachel noted with disgust the over-abundance of female assistants present at this particular photo session. Every time Jesse was in the building, there was a flurry of women gathered around him. So why did he insist she be present? He didn't appear to be the least bit nervous. He had enough adoring fans without her to add to the melee.

Refusing to become a part of the crowd of worshipful women, Rachel stood in the shadows and observed. She had a strict policy for herself: *Never* get involved with a client. It just wasn't professional to mix business and personal relationships. She'd worked darned hard to get where she was in this business and one blue-eyed cowboy was not going to put a spoke in her wheels.

"Jesse, honey, could you open the top two buttons of your shirt a little to show off that handsome chest?" Evelyn asked.

Rachel ground her teeth.

"I don't know about that. What are we trying to sell here, ranch supplies or sex?" Jesse smiled, and winked in Rachel's direction giving her a start, before moving his long tanned fingers to open the requested buttons in a slow strip tease.

"If it's sex you're selling, I'll be first in line to buy." The photographer's camera continued to click and whir, even as she spoke.

"How far do you want me to go?" he asked, as his hand paused on the next button.

"All the way," a chorus of feminine voices sang out.

Rachel rolled her eyes. *Oh, brother.*

Jesse laughed and stuck his thumbs back in the pockets of his jeans.

Uncomfortable at the ease of familiarity the photographer shared with Jesse, Rachel refrained from rebuking her. Evelyn was worth everything she was paid. She was one of the best in the business. When a client was also the model in a shoot, she was called on to do the work. The scrutiny and attention to every gesture and pose tended to make inexperienced models nervous and uncomfortable. Evelyn knew how to put them at ease, bringing out their best traits in the finished photograph. Rachel grudgingly acknowledged the sexual banter certainly brought out the sensual appeal of this particular client. She moved further into the shadows to avoid his knowing eyes.

One of the lighting assistants smiled and batted her eyes at Jesse. "Jesse, are you thirsty? Could I get you something? Anything?"

Smiling at her, he replied, "Thank you, Sheila, but all I need is a smile from your pretty face to keep me going."

With an eyebrow raised in challenge, he gave a quick

glance at Rachel--obviously she wasn't as well hidden as she hoped. She stifled an urge to groan. He certainly loved to live up to his playboy image.

Sheila was so intent on smiling and batting her pretty eyes, she failed to notice when her feet caught in a tangle of electrical cords, and she stumbled. Blushing furiously, Sheila righted herself and shrugged self-consciously.

Another one bites the dust, Rachel thought. Lips twitching, she struggled to resist the urge to laugh. Catching Jesse's glance, she noted that he too was amused by the situation. *It's a good thing I'm immune.*

"Rachel, could you come over here for a second?" Jesse motioned to her with a crooked finger.

Startled out of her musings, Rachel walked hesitantly toward Jesse.

"Yes, Mr. Jordan?" she asked, straining her neck backward to look up at him. He was tall enough without the added height of the set platform. This put her eyes level to his crotch. She looked up to avoid staring at that particular part of his anatomy.

"Now I told you before, call me Jesse," he admonished.

"Okay, Jesse, what can I do for you?"

One eyebrow quirked upward, and she blushed, ducking her head to hide the telltale color of her cheeks. Unfortunately, that put her gaze dead center on the long ridge at the front of his jeans. Flustered, her head came up again, sharply, "Yes, Jesse?"

His grin spread so that every pearly white tooth in his head joined the smile. "Just what I like to hear from a woman," he teased. As her blush grew fiery, he relented in his teasing. "I'd like a photograph of me with my favorite account rep."

"What?" she squeaked. Glancing around, she saw they were the center of attention.

"I only want one," he said, grinning. "This is my first time modeling, so I'd like to have a picture of the lady who so charmingly convinced me to do this."

That high voltage grin turned her insides to mush. She fought valiantly to resist. Rachel would not be added to his list of conquests. "I don't know...I've never had a client ask for that before."

His brows rose. "Is it a problem?"

"No, I suppose not, but...." Unable to think of any rational excuse, Rachel shrugged. "I guess it's okay. Do you mind, Evelyn?"

"Not at all. Just stand there next to Jesse while I check the lighting."

Climbing up on the raised platform, Rachel stood a foot away from Jesse, crossing her arms self-consciously, feeling exposed and embarrassed.

He eased closer. "I promise I don't bite."

She jumped at Jesse's softly drawled words, and a traitorous shiver ran down her spine. Realizing the discomfort her posture betrayed, she relaxed her arms to her sides, straightened her shoulders and pointedly ignored his presence.

She was angry at his teasing, and angrier still that it affected her so much. She felt just fine on the other side of the camera. Squelching the thought that it was being this close to Jesse that made her uncomfortable, she reminded herself he was her client. It would be best to ignore this little game he was playing with her composure.

Evelyn held a light meter in front of Rachel's face then turned to adjust the light—again. Rechecking the meter, she backed up, apparently satisfied. "Okay, you two, smile and look natural."

Rachel could feel Jesse's gaze on her. Ignoring him, she smoothed the skirt of her navy-blue suit. She knew she presented an odd contrast to Jesse's casual, cowboy attire. Turning her head toward him, she was dazzled by his smile and felt her heart skip a beat at the twinkle in his eyes.

"No, it's not quite right," said Jesse. Closing the distance, he slid an arm around her waist, pulled her up against his side, then turned to smile happily into the camera. Click.

Rachel groaned inwardly, knowing her expression the camera captured had been one of shocked stupidity. Thinking had not been an option the moment his warm, muscled arm had pulled her close to him. She couldn't have formed a coherent thought to save her life.

"Okay, Rachel, you can step down, now." Evelyn's voice cut through her tangled thoughts.

Rachel started to pull away from Jesse. She was startled when he reached out to snag her hand.

Bringing it to his lips, palm up, he placed a gentle kiss there, his moustache dragging against her skin intriguingly. He folded her fingers around the kiss before slowly releasing her hand. "Save that for later, when you're all alone," he whispered, his voice, low and incredibly seductive. Then louder for the benefit of their audience, he said, "Thank you, Rachel," and he stared into her eyes as if he could see right through to her very soul.

The cheers from the peanut gallery broke through the sensual haze. *The nerve of the man.*

Embarrassed, Rachel responded, "You're welcome, Mr. Jordan," her voice curt. She wiped her palm against the side of her skirt, sending him an unmistakable message: His kiss was not welcome. It was a lie, for try as she might, she couldn't dispel the lingering tingle left by the brush of his moustache.

"Jesse," his voice chided.

"You're welcome...Jesse," she replied through gritted teeth.

Resuming her position in the shadows, Rachel was thankful she was no longer in the spotlight. Her face felt flushed, and her heart pounded. It took until the end of the shoot for her pulse to return to normal.

When Evelyn finally called a halt to the session, Rachel, having fulfilled her obligation, made a hasty escape. Deciding she could do without the confusion his nearness caused, she left Jesse to the adoration of his fans. Her heels clicked on the tiled floor as she walked purposefully and quickly down the hall to the elevator. She was not running away, she assured herself. There was a mountain of work begging for her attention in her office.

Slamming her open palm against the up button, she let out a sigh of relief as the door slid open immediately. She looked back toward the closed doors of the studio and noted with satisfaction she had escaped without notice. Contrarily, as the door slid closed she felt her satisfaction deflate into disappointment.

Back at her desk, in the relative safety of her office, she punched the button on her mouse to reactivate her computer screen. She watched as the picture came into focus. It was the Internet site she'd been browsing earlier that morning. Displayed on the screen was a bassinet decorated with a colorful baby layette.

Reaching out to touch the screen, Rachel sighed. *Focus on the goal, girl. Playboys, no matter how handsome, are not necessarily good sperm donors.* She didn't need this wild attraction to clutter her brain and make her wish for things she didn't have time for. Now, this crib with its rainbow-colored blankets was another thing altogether.

"Rachel, I have some papers that need your attention."

Minimizing the screen, Rachel turned toward her secretary, a blush staining her cheeks.

"Leave them on the desk, Mildred. I'll look at them as soon as I check my calendar for the next appointment."

Mildred placed the stack of papers on the corner of her desk and smiled knowingly before she left the office.

Some high-powered ad executive you are, Rachel. Before you know it, you'll have the entire agency aware you have babies on the brain.

Taking a deep breath, Rachel plunged into the work she had neglected in order to satisfy Jesse's request.

As the photo session wrapped up, Jesse looked around for Rachel. Catching a glimpse of her sexy derriere sliding out the doorway, he hurried to follow her.

"Jesse, could you wait around for a few minutes?" Evelyn's hand on his arm detained him. "I want to make sure I took enough shots so you don't have to come back for a retake."

Suppressing the urge to swear, he stared at the door Rachel had disappeared through and shrugged. "Sure, Evelyn."

Taking a seat, he waited impatiently for the okay to leave, his mind on the navy-blue suit and the pretty executive in it. He smiled when he thought of how uncomfortable she'd been in front of the camera. When he'd put his arm around her, she'd almost jumped out of her skin.

He'd been surprised too. It had felt "right" to snuggle

her up beside him. Her soft brown hair had brushed against his chin, and her heated skin had emitted a faintly musky, wholly feminine fragrance that had almost caused him to embarrass himself. While she wasn't the usual sort of woman he tended to gravitate toward, there was some indefinable quality that pulled at him.

Captivated from the first moment he'd walked into her office, he was determined to crawl right under her skin like she had unwittingly done to him. Keeping her off-balance seemed to be the key to getting to know the real Rachel Taylor. Her warm blushes betrayed her frosty façade and intrigued him.

"Sorry for the wait, Jesse. I think I have what I need. You can..."

Before Evelyn finished her sentence, Jesse was out of the chair and through the door. Loping quickly to the elevator, he punched the up arrow and waited, oblivious to the admiring stares from passing females. The doors slid open. Stepping inside, he pushed the button for her floor. Before the doors closed completely, a small manicured hand inserted itself through the opening, causing them to part once more to admit a short, red-haired woman.

"Oh, hi. I'm so glad I caught the elevator. I'm already late and waiting for the next one would just make me all that much later. You don't mind, do you?" She stopped to catch her breath, and then grinned up at him flirtatiously. Her eyes widened as she gave him a long encompassing stare.

It was impossible for Jesse to hold back a grin at the vivacious redhead. "No, ma'am, I don't mind at all," he drawled. Flirting with a woman--young, old, homely or melt-your-bones-gorgeous—was as natural to him as breathing.

Reaching to push a button, her hand stopped in mid-air, "Well, isn't that nice? At least I won't hold you up again by stopping on a different floor. We're going to the same place." Sticking out a crimson-tipped hand, she introduced herself. "Hi, I'm Genie O'Connor."

He took her hand. "Jesse Jordan. Nice to meet you."

"Do you work here?" she asked, her brows arching inquisitively.

Deciding explanations would take too much time, he replied, "Well, sort of. I just finished a photo shoot for a ranch supply store."

"Oh, so you're a model. I should have guessed."

"Why's that?" he asked in startled amusement.

"Oh, don't be so modest." Genie's gaze ran down his length. "You sure do fill out a great pair of jeans."

Jesse blushed at her flagrant appreciation. "Do you work here, too?"

"Oh, no. I'm here to meet a friend. We're going out man-hunting tonight," she said, grinning at her outrageous statement.

"Man-hunting?" He smiled, and entered the game. "Is your friend homely or something? I can't imagine you needing to hunt for a man."

"Oh no, she's just too wrapped up in her job to take time to meet men. It's up to me to make sure it happens."

The elevator bell rang to announce their arrival, and the doors slid open.

"Well, here we are. It was nice meeting you, Jesse."

"Nice meeting you, too, Genie."

The two stepped out of the elevator, turned in the same direction and laughed.

"I guess we're headed in the same direction still. I'm

going to Rachel Taylor's office. Where are you headed?" Genie asked as she walked down the hall.

"Same place," Jesse said, his smile growing wider. "So, is Rachel the friend you're hunting with tonight?"

"Yes, but don't you dare let her know I told you."

They arrived outside Rachel's office, laughing together.

"Mildred, is Rachel ready?" Genie asked.

The older woman looked up from her computer screen and nodded her welcome. "Hello Genie, Jesse. She's finishing up some paperwork. Genie, she told me to tell you to go right in."

Apologetically, Genie looked over at Jesse. "Did you have an appointment? I didn't mean to jump in front of you."

"No, I didn't. I was just...uh...stopping by...uh..." Looking for a reason, he spied Mildred watching them converse with avid curiosity. "I came to speak to Mildred. That's what I was doing. Isn't that right, Mildred?"

"Huh?" Mildred's eyebrows rose above the top of her granny glasses.

Walking around behind her, Jesse gave Mildred a big hug and leaned down to whisper in her ear. "Go along with me."

"Go where?"

"Go along with my charade," he whispered.

"You want me to go to a parade?"

Blushing, Jesse looked up to see Genie valiantly trying to hide a smile behind her hand.

"Don't let us keep you. I'm sure Miss Taylor doesn't like to be kept waiting." His accompanying smile was more a grimace for his clumsiness.

As she opened the door to Rachel's office, Genie smiled

back over her shoulder. Then she stepped in and closed the door behind her.

"Now, Jesse, just what were you trying to say to me? You know I have trouble hearing whispers," Mildred grumbled, frowning in his direction.

He knew she wouldn't stay mad at him for long. An old friend of his mother's, she had known him since he was a toddler. She'd watched him struggle through awkward teenage years and mature into the man he was today. In fact, she was the one to suggest he use Rachel's agency to promote his business. You could say she was the one who'd turned him on to the delectable Miss Taylor. He hoped one day he could thank her. Right now, it looked like he had a long way to go before Rachel would look at him as anything other than a client.

"So what's she like?" He nodded toward Rachel's office.

"What is who like?" Mildred asked, as she continued to sort through the day's correspondence.

"Miss Rachel Taylor."

"Rachel?" Holding an envelope in mid-air, Mildred paused to think about her answer. "Rachel is a tough business woman with an eye for what pleases her clients. She's intelligent and able to hold her own with any pompous ass in the business, excuse my French."

"No, no, that's not what I meant. What is she like on a personal level?"

Her eyes narrowed at him. "Why do you ask? I hope you're not thinking to use your Casanova wiles on my girl. She's not your kind."

"Mildred, darlin'," he drawled, letting a hurt look cross his face. "Can't you give me the benefit of the doubt? Have you ever thought that maybe I've just been searching for the right woman?"

She eyed him skeptically. "My foot." Putting her right leg out, she shook it. "Here, pull the other leg."

"Won't you please tell me more about her?" He leaned closer and used the wheedling smile, which never failed to bring a blush to the old tartar's cheeks.

"I love that child like she was one of my own. If you cause her so much as a single tear, you'll answer to me," she said sternly.

He let his face grow solemn and held his right hand in the air, three fingers raised as he promised, "Scout's Honor. I mean no harm."

Mildred's face softened as she relented. "Rachel doesn't have any family left, you know, unless you count Genie, the little redhead you just met. Her parents had her late in life and died shortly after she finished college. She has a heart the size of Texas, but the social ability of a skunk. Not that she has body odor—she simply doesn't have a clue how to attract a man. Sometimes, I don't think she even notices y'all even exist. Bless her heart. She's one tough cookie in the boardroom, but I'd lay odds she doesn't have a life in the bedroom."

Jesse's eyebrows rose in mild shock at her blunt response, then he chuckled. These were not the words he would have expected out of his mother's dear old friend, but they were the words he wanted to hear.

So, Rachel was unattached...for now. He perched on the edge of Mildred's desk and raised his hand to his chin, rubbing the stubble, which always began to show about this time of the day. Thoughtfully, he considered why he was still cooling his heels in the office of a woman who'd sooner kiss a horse as give him the time of day. She was prickly, but he felt drawn to her—and it wasn't just the sway of her classy little behind. In fact, he doubted seriously that she was even aware of her physical appeal. He sure would love to be the man to show her just how sexy she was.

"Mildred, what kind of man do you think would appeal to her?"

She gave another of her signature snorts. "I haven't a clue. That woman takes life much too seriously. But I suppose she'd want someone...safe...someone she could pencil into her planner. You know, someone reliable. Although what she really needs is someone who can show her how to let loose."

As he pondered that thought, he heard the sound of Rachel's door opening softly and straightened. It was Genie returning.

"She's still on the phone with a client." She wrinkled her nose, "I'd much rather wait with a gorgeous model than listen to a one-sided conversation about market penetration for spray disinfectants. Blah."

"So, where do women go man-hunting these days?" Jesse asked with the smile his mother told him could charm the snakes out of the trees.

"I usually hang out at the fitness center, but tonight, Rachel and I are going to O'Malley's Bar and Grill."

"You're going to pick up men at a bar? Isn't that kind of risky?"

"No, not really." She glanced back towards Rachel's closed door, before eyeing him speculatively, her voice dropping to a whisper, "You see, Rachel advertised for a man. Tonight, she'll be interviewing the ones who responded."

"What do you mean by advertised?" he asked mildly shocked.

"You know, like putting an ad in the singles column of the newspaper."

Jesse shook his head. "I can't see Rachel doing that. She's a beautiful woman. Why would she need to advertise? I'd think she would have to beat them off with a stick."

Mildred snorted, again. Jesse glared at her. She hadn't heard his whispers earlier, but her ears seemed to be working just fine now.

"Rachel doesn't have time to do things the normal way," Genie explained. "She works twenty-four/seven."

"I see your point." Jesse rose from the edge of the desk.

Never one to question the whim of inspiration, he made a quick decision, ticking through a mental list of errands he still needed to finish. "I have some things to take care of. I'll talk to you soon, Mildred. Say hello to Fred." Dropping a peck on her check, he turned to glance at Genie. "It was nice to meet you. I hope to see you—soon."

With that, he left.

CHAPTER 3

"Rachel, you're hopeless. You look like you're going into a board room instead of on a date," Genie said.

That afternoon, Rachel had spent a considerable amount of time choosing the outfit from her wardrobe, not wanting to appear too easy or too old. She'd thought she'd settled on just the right look for the evening's purpose. She raised a questioning gaze to her friend in the glass above the sink in the ladies' room of O'Malley's Bar and Grill. "Genie, I'm conducting interviews. These are not dates."

"Yeah, but these are *prospective* dates. You want to attract them, not intimidate the hell out of 'em."

"What do you mean?"

"Well, you look so...stuffy. Remember, they're interviewing *you* as well."

"Is there something wrong with what I'm wearing?" Rachel asked, checking her appearance in the mirror. The cut of her navy jacket was a little severe, but tailored to conform to her shape, and the matching skirt was an inch or two shorter than she was normally comfortable wearing. The white silk blouse with the attached ascot, gathered at her neck, was a nice flamboyant touch. She raised her eyebrows in question to her friend once more.

Genie rolled her eyes. "What do guys look for in a woman? Skin. Cleavage. What are you wearing under that blouse?"

"A camisole. Why?"

"Take off the blouse. Hurry. We haven't much time left."

When Rachel resisted, Genie added, "Humor me. Take off the blouse."

Rachel removed the jacket then the blouse.

Genie snatched the blouse away from her. "Now, put your jacket back on."

Rachel complied.

Genie took a step back from her, her head to one side, her eyes narrowing. She stepped up to Rachel and unbuttoned the top two buttons of the jacket, spreading the lapels wider. "Mmmm...that's better."

Rachel stared at herself in the mirror. The lace of her camisole was visible between the lapels, and the broad expanse of her upper chest was bare. "I'm not going out there like this—I'm not dressed."

"There's no time to argue now. Get to your table, and I'll get to mine," Genie said, as she crammed the silk blouse into her oversized shoulder bag and headed to the door. Rachel dragged behind her, surreptitiously rebuttoning one of the buttons on her jacket.

Glancing around the bar, Rachel ensured the table she had chosen provided her the best vantage to observe customers as they entered. She had selected a booth against the wall, opposite the entryway. Genie would sit in the booth behind her once the interviews began. For now, Genie was being Genie, conducting a non-stop commentary effectively calming Rachel's nerves. Her mind wandered back to the conversation.

"I wish you had let me read the ad before you sent it to the newspaper. I could have written something sure to land the right man. Something like the Pina Colada song. 'If you like walking in the moonlight along a deserted beach or running barefoot through wet grass, meet me at the edge of the fishing pier at dusk on Friday. I'll be the one wearing a smile and nothing else.' Now, there's an advertisement with a hook, if you ask me." Genie sighed. "I could have written one to inspire the poets."

"I'm not here to inspire the poets," Rachel grumbled. "I'm here to find a sperm donor."

Ignoring Genie's dreamy mood, Rachel pulled out her day planner to double-check the time and order of her interviews. Snapping it shut, she adjusted the vase containing a single red carnation in the middle of the table. Determinedly, she tamped down the butterflies in her stomach. "Bachelor number one should be here any minute, if he's punctual. You'd better take your place."

"Are you sure you want to do this?" Genie asked. "This seems kind of cold."

"Genie, we're not rehashing that again. I'm sure. I've scheduled this to cause the least amount of disruption to my work. I want to treat this like any other business transaction so I can maintain a distance from the man I choose for the job. It will be easier to make a clean break with no emotional attachments, and most importantly, no likelihood of pursuit."

"I still think you ought to do it the old-fashioned way—fall in love, get married, make babies. You know, the whole happily-ever-after thing." Genie's head tipped to the side, and she sighed.

"Oh, Genie. You're a hopeless romantic. We've been over this before. I don't need a husband. In my hectic life, I only have time enough for one child, not two. And I prefer an infant to a grown baby."

"Have it your way, Rache. I'll be in the next booth, eavesdropping like crazy. Remember, if you feel like you're in trouble, just say the secret code. You do remember the code, don't you?"

"I remember, it's 'when pigs fly.'"

"That's it. Break a leg, honey."

Genie took her position in the booth behind Rachel and motioned for the waitress. Sitting alone, Rachel finished her Vodka Collins with a long gulp and watched the door from the corner of her eye.

Suddenly, she was very nervous. Why? She didn't understand. She'd been involved in much more stressful situations at work. Having hired her entire staff, she was confident with her interviewing skills. But these candidates had her wiping her palms on the worsted wool of her navy skirt and jacket, and dabbing at the perspiration gathering on her upper lip.

I can't do this. Having second thoughts, Rachel rose halfway out of her seat, and prepared to bolt. Just then, a thin man in a neatly pressed suit, wearing round wire-rimmed glasses, walked over to her. "Are you Ms. Taylor?"

Rachel nodded automatically.

"I couldn't help noticing the red carnation. I must be in the right place," the man continued. "I'm Dr. Milton Peebles. I believe we have an appointment?"

Since she was already halfway out of her seat, she rose the rest of the way, and discovered she was two or three inches taller than Dr. Peebles. She was mildly dismayed, since she was only average height herself.

The doctor blinked, owl-like.

Feeling gawky and awkward, she stuck out her hand and grasped his in a firm handshake. "Nice to meet you, Dr. Peebles. Won't you sit down? Would you like a drink?"

She spotted the girl who'd served her a drink earlier and called out, "Waitress." Her nervousness made her voice shrill, and she cleared her throat, heat rising up her throat into her cheeks. Rachel decided to remain silent and regain her poise while the waitress took the doctor's order and replaced her own drink.

"Did you have a hard time finding the place, Dr. Peebles?"

"No, your directions were fine, and please call me Milton. All my friends do." Milton's voice was rather monotone, each syllable spoken quietly and precisely.

"Oh, okay...Milton."

"I found the place just fine. I drove around yesterday just to locate it before today."

"How thoughtful."

"Oh, it was nothing. I just like to be punctual. It bothers me when people are late, especially to appointments."

Rachel took another fortifying swig of her drink. "What kind of doctor are you...Milton?"

"I'm a gynecologist."

Rachel choked, and her Vodka Collins nearly exited her nostrils before she could gain control of herself once more. Milton reached across the table to pat her back comfortingly. Rachel resisted the urge to cringe. Who knew where his hands had been that day?

The waitress appeared at his side with a glass of white wine and set it in front of him. Rachel used the lull to study the man as he thanked the waitress and took a tentative sip from his glass.

He wasn't an attractive man. Small beady eyes blinked nervously, magnified by thick, round wire-rimmed glasses perched on the bridge of his long narrow nose. His hair was mousy brown, sparse, and unnaturally curly. The moist and clammy hand she'd held briefly was soft, narrow and small-boned with neatly manicured nails.

Rachel stared at the bottle-thick lenses and let herself imagine what an intimate encounter with the mousy doctor might be like.

She saw herself, standing in the door of an institutional-green office with an old Naugahyde-covered examining table as its only furnishing. The doctor stood next to the table wearing only his white coat, skinny legs and knobby knees showing from below the hem. Reaching underneath the table, he drew chrome stirrups up and pulled the white paper protector toward him, reeling it to the bottom of the table, nearer to the edge where he stood...

"Have we been drinking just a little too much?" Milton inquired, with a little smile on his thin lips. Rachel shuddered, then jerked back to reality. She made her decision in a moment.

Rising to her feet, Rachel waited for Milton to stand, and then she stuck her hand out to shake his.

"Dr. Peebles, I want to thank you for meeting me here. I'm glad we had the opportunity to get to know each other, but I have another engagement and must be going. I'll call you when I've made my decision. Again, thanks for coming."

Rachel turned to walk quickly toward the ladies' restroom, leaving Dr. Peebles looking a little befuddled by the abruptness of the end of the interview.

She peeked at him from behind the door of the lady's

room. As soon as he left the bar, Rachel came back to her table and sat sideways in her booth to talk with Genie.

"That was short. Well, what did you think?" Genie asked.

Rachel shuddered visibly. "I'm sure he's a very nice man, but I'm not letting him come near me."

"I have to agree; he was kind of dweeby."

"Well, let's hope bachelor number two is an improvement."

Genie raised her glass in a mock toast and quickly returned to her table as a man stepped through the entry. He paused to look at his reflection in the mirror behind the bar. Then, gazing around the room, he spotted the carnation in the bud vase on Rachel's table and walked in a beeline toward her.

He wasn't a bad looking man. Rachel took a deep breath and unbuttoned the top button of her jacket, awaiting his approach. He stood just short of six foot tall and had dark eyes and dark hair, slicked back neatly. His black silk shirt had three buttons opened from the collar, displaying a thick gold medallion nestled in the curly black hair on his chest. Nodding and speaking to everyone he passed, he finally made it to her table.

"Hi. Monte Luett's the name, car sales is my game. You must be Miss Taylor. Glad to meet ya, sweetheart."

Without waiting for a response from her, he slung himself into the seat across the table and whistled to the waitress. "Hey, sugar! Bring me a Jack Daniels on the rocks. And make it quick, will ya?"

Turning back to Rachel, he continued without pausing, "So, what's the game plan? You want to test drive before you buy?" he asked with a leer. "Well let me tell you, this model has all the options. I'm single, only been married twice before. Three's a charm. I have a smooth-running engine, new treads and a fresh paint job, so to speak. This one rides like a tiger. I guarantee it or your money back."

Monte ran a hand carefully over the slick waves of his hair and leaned back in his seat so she could fully appreciate the view.

Rachel's eyes rounded in alarm. A vision of herself standing naked in a used car showroom flickered across her mind. Monte's beringed, sausage-shaped fingers smoothed their way down her sleek back as he extolled the virtues of this particular model to the growing crowd of customers.

Yessiree, folks. This is a hot little number, very low mileage. Purrs like a kitten when you flick that ignition--if you know what I mean, he'd say, with a wicked wiggle of his bushy eyebrows.

He'd pat her bottom. *This twin-cam engine will go from zero to sixty in no time flat. Would someone like to take her for a test drive? If you like, we can open up the hood and check her oil....*

Rachel shook her head and looked into her glass, wondering whether something other than Vodka had found its way into her drink. "I'm sorry, sir, but you must have me mistaken with someone else."

"I gotta be in the right place. What about the carnation? It was part of the set-up."

She feigned a look of wide-eyed innocence. "The flower was here when I arrived. Is there supposed to be something significant about it?"

He frowned for a second then shrugged. "No, I guess not. Well, since I'm already here and so are you, can I interest you in a used car or a drink?"

"No, thanks. I'm not in the market for either. Do you

mind?" Rachel stared pointedly at him. He finally got the hint and good-naturedly vacated his seat, moving on to schmooze a blonde at the bar.

Groaning, she tossed the remainder of her drink down her throat and leaned her head against the back of the seat.

"So, what was wrong with that one?" Genie drawled. "He was nice to look at."

"So *he* thought. There would be a threesome in any relationship with that man. The girl, the man and his ego. No thanks."

"Well, you aren't exactly looking for a relationship, are you? He looked healthy, and he certainly seemed willing."

"I couldn't stand to be in his company for longer than five minutes," Rachel harshly whispered. "How the heck would I ever conceive? I'll keep searching."

"Don't look now, but I think that might be number three coming your way."

Rachel groaned. "Oh, god. I need another drink."

Both women watched in fascinated horror as the man paused in the doorway to the bar. His gaze darted around the room until it landed on the carnation in front of Rachel. As they watched, he slipped to the side of the room, following the perimeter, with his back to the wall at all times.

Rachel quickly buttoned her jacket up to her chin, and crossed her arms protectively in front of her. When the man reached her booth, he stood back from the empty seat and stared around the room nervously.

After he stood there for a few moments without speaking, Rachel cleared her throat and prompted, "Excuse me, are you Mr. Lindeman?"

"Who wants to know?" His gaze jumped nervously.

"I'm Ms. Taylor. Would you care to join me?" She cringed inwardly. *Why did I say that?*

He looked over his shoulder one more time before sliding into the seat, scooting as close to the wall as he could.

Lenny Lindeman looked like the star of a horror movie. His skin was so pale it was almost blue, as if he had never seen the light of day. The dark purple circles under his eyes gave him the appearance of the living dead. Sparse bristles stood straight up from his scalp, and his lips were large and moist.

Containing her rising alarm, Rachel launched into her interview. "So, Lenny, what is it you do for a living?"

"My friends call me Mr. Lindeman. I am an animal reconstructive engineer."

"Animal reconstructive engineer? I don't think I've ever heard of that profession."

"In layman's terms, I am a taxidermist."

"Oh." She gulped, suddenly feeling queasy.

His gaze narrowed on her expression. "The science of taxidermy is a much-maligned discipline. Years of experimentation and study are required to produce professional results. Careful removal and preservation of tissues are needed to maintain the integrity of the desired specimen. It takes a lot of practice to create a natural, life-like expression on the deceased anatomy."

Rachel hoped her drink would stay down. Her eyes rounded with alarm as she visualized formaldehyde-filled specimen jars containing animal parts, and bubbling crucibles over Bunsen burners in a dark cobweb-filled basement. With nervous trepidation, she asked the next question on her list. "What are you looking for in a relationship?"

"I'm looking for a woman who can share my interests. Have you ever removed the entrails of a Canis Lupus, or the gray matter from the skull cavity of a great horned owl?"

A chill went down Rachel's spine. "Can't say that I've had the pleasure."

Anxious about offending her guest, Rachel frantically searched her mind for an effective exit from this delicate situation. Her face lit up and she smiled. "Lenny, I'm sorry to say, but I faint at the sight of blood."

He drew back. "Oh, dear, such a shame. Well, I'm sure you would get used to it in time, Ms. Taylor."

"When pigs fly."

"What?"

Desperately, Rachel repeated the code. "I said, when pigs fly."

Muffled giggles erupted from the booth behind Rachel.

A moment later, Genie appeared at the side of their booth. "Rachel, honey. I thought that was you. When did you get out of the hospital?"

Rachel jumped up from her seat and was immediately enveloped in a hug. "Hospital?"

"I hope you got rid of that nasty rash. It really was quite disgusting, you know."

"Rash?"

Genie smiled at Lenny. "Oh, I'm sorry. Who's your friend?"

Ignoring her hint for an introduction, Rachel said, "He was just leaving, weren't you, Lenny?"

"No, I wasn't."

Genie jumped into the breach, cutting him off. "Well, it was nice meeting you, Lenny. Toodle-loo," she said, curling her fingers in a cutesy farewell, all the while smiling and staring expectantly at Lenny.

Lenny stood, looking at the two women with a confused look on his face, then turned to walk away, shaking his head. When he disappeared through the barroom door. Genie burst out laughing while Rachel moaned.

"Oh my god, Rachel. You had an interview with Jeffrey Dahmer. What the hell did that ad say?"

Rachel lifted her hands. "Oh, I give up. I guess I'll have to resort to Russian roulette with a sperm bank." Rachel downed the rest of her third Vodka Collins. "All I want are the chromosomes to produce a healthy, intelligent and mentally stable baby."

"I still think you ought to do it the old-fashioned way."

"We've been over this before, Genie. I have it all mapped out, and it *will* go according to my plan. All I have to do is find the right donor."

"Well, hell, the pickings were pretty slim with the singles agency, and your ad in the classifieds produced even scarier results. You'd be better off haunting bars and personally scouting the candidates."

"As far as that goes, I may as well choose the next man who walks through the door," Rachel stated wildly.

Both women turned to look expectantly toward the entrance to the bar. Pushing through the door at that moment was a rotund man with his slacks belted tightly beneath his sagging belly. His large jowls quivered as he turned back to hold the door for a reed-thin woman wearing a peach-colored polyester pantsuit.

Rachel and Genie collapsed backward into their seats in relief.

"Well, maybe the next *single* man who walks through the door."

Genie glanced back again hopefully, and then grabbed Rachel's arm. "Rache. Get a load of what just walked through the door."

Rolling her head to the side against the vinyl upholstery of the booth, Rachel's chin sagged as she spotted the object of Genie's fascination.

"Don't just sit there. I don't see a wedding ring. Go get him."

Closing her mouth, Rachel took inventory of the Adonis filling the doorway, starting at the pointed toes of his cowboy boots. She followed the line of his faded blue jeans stretched snugly over his leanly muscled thighs and trim waist. His shoulders strained against the fabric of the blue chambray shirt tucked neatly into those sinfully tight jeans.

Continuing her perusal upward, she noted a strong, square jaw and lips that were meant to be kissed. His nose was straight, and his eyes were a pale color. Rachel guessed them to be blue to compliment perfectly the beautiful rich wheaten hair curling down to the collar of his shirt. Her eyes finally noted the golden moustache gracing his upper lip, and her heart sank as recognition dawned on her gin-soaked brain.

What was he doing here?

CHAPTER 4

"OH GENIE, THAT'S JESSE JORDAN," Rachel whispered.

"Jesse?" Squinting to get a better look, Genie waved.

Rachel grabbed for her friend's uplifted hand. "What are you doing?"

"I'm going to ask him to join us," Genie said, lifting her other hand to attract his attention.

"Oh, please, don't encourage him. He's nothing but a flirt."

"Yes, but he's a really cute flirt, and I like him."

As Jesse made his way through the bar, Genie leaned close to Rachel. "So why don't you go for Jesse? He'd be perfect."

"No way," Rachel said with finality.

"Why not?"

"He's nothing but a playboy. His picture is always in the society news with some blonde bimbo on his arm. Besides, he's a client, Genie, and I make it a rule..."

"I know, I know, not to fraternize with a client. But Rache, he's gorgeous. Couldn't you bend your rule just this once?"

"No, and hush—he'll hear you."

Rachel sank low in her seat. Maybe he wouldn't see her. What could possibly be more embarrassing than having Jesse Jordan catch her 'scouting for prospects' at a bar?

She watched, dread forming a cold knot in her stomach as he drew closer, his gaze searching in the dim light. She grabbed frantically for the menu, tucked between the salt and pepper shakers and the wall, and raised it to her face, crouching lower still in her seat. Hiding behind her shield, her heart racing frantically, she nearly screeched when a softly drawling voice spoke over her right shoulder.

"Hi, Genie."

Rachel grimaced and lowered the menu. There was no escape.

Nodding with a smile for each of the ladies, Jesse asked, "Do you mind if I join you?"

"As a matter of fact..." Rachel began.

"Please do," blurted Genie, before Rachel completed her sentence.

Sliding in beside Genie, he looked straight across at Rachel, much to her dismay. "So, what brings you ladies to O'Malley's tonight?"

Genie looked at him, clearly puzzled. "But Jesse, I told you...ouch!" Reaching down, Genie rubbed her leg as Jesse continued to smile across at Rachel.

"*Girl's* night out," Rachel replied, glaring at Genie. "What are you doing here, Jesse? I thought you'd be tired after a full day in front of the camera."

"Rejuvenated, actually. Nothing like flexing your muscles after having to hold a pose over and over." As if to demonstrate, he rolled his shoulders and tilted his head in a circular motion to work the kinks out.

Anxious to get rid of him, Rachel tried the tack she'd

used on Lenny. "Well, I'm sure you have plans, don't let us keep you."

Jesse wasn't going for it. "No plans. I can think of nothing better to do than spending an interesting evening with two lovely ladies."

Reaching his arm around Genie, he squeezed her shoulders and smiled over at Rachel. Something about him putting his arm around Genie made Rachel mad. Before she could voice her displeasure and embarrass herself, a voice intruded on their little threesome.

"Miss Taylor, I'm sorry to interrupt, but there was something I wanted to give you."

Oh no. Lenny Lindeman was back, standing next to her with a small box in his hands. She caught herself before she rudely jerked away.

"Rachel, won't you introduce me to your friend?" asked Jesse, his face the picture of innocence.

His smile grated on Rachel's last nerve, and she itched to reach across the table to slap it off.

Jesse stood, extending his hand to the man. "Hi, I'm Jesse Jordan. Won't you join us?"

Lenny grasped Jesse's hand, answering as he cringed from the obviously bone-crunching handshake Jesse bestowed on him. "Lenny. Lenny Lindeman."

Jesse released his hand and motioned to the empty space beside Rachel, "Please have a seat."

"I'm sure he has much more pressing things to do, don't you, Mr. Lindeman?" Rachel asked, hopefully.

"No, not really," Lenny offered quietly.

"Then it's settled. Have a seat," Jesse said, motioning for Lenny to sit with Rachel.

"Oh I don't know..." Lenny began.

"Sit!" Jesse commanded.

47

Lenny sat.

Rachel slid as far away from Lenny as possible, glaring at Jesse. *What the hell is he up to? Can't he see the man is mentally disturbed?* Rachel groaned and shrank into the vinyl seat cushions.

Jesse seemed to be relishing his role as a gracious host. "So Lenny, what do you do for a living?"

"I'm an animal reconstructive engineer."

"Oh? What's that?"

"A taxidermist," Rachel and Genie replied in unison.

"That's quite interesting." Jesse's eyes twinkled, and he winked blatantly at Rachel. "Aren't you going to open the box, Rachel? I'd be interested in seeing what Lenny brought for you."

Three pair of eyes turned to Rachel. Trapped, she reached out to peel the brown paper from the outside and eased open the top, afraid of what might jump out.

"Eeeeeeuw," she said, and tossed the box on the table.

"Oh, don't worry, Ms. Taylor, it isn't alive," Lenny said quickly, and added as an afterthought, "...anymore."

Grabbing the box from the table, Lenny lifted out something furry with a small face and bright glassy eyes. "It's a wrist watch covered with the hide of a gray squirrel." Lenny displayed the item proudly.

"Let me see." Jesse reached for the furry treasure. "How interesting. Look, Rachel, you lift the little guy's head to see the face of the watch. Very clever." Smiling at Lenny, Jesse asked, "Is this your design?"

Lenny's chest puffed out, and his wan face suffused with mottled color. "Yes, indeed it is. I found the squirrel on the road. Must have been hit by a car."

"Rachel, really, I think you should model the watch." Jesse held out the gift, his lips twitching.

"No, thank you," she said through tight lips.

Jesse raised his brows. "You don't want to hurt Lenny's feelings, do you?"

"I'm sorry, Lenny, I just don't like fur against my skin."

Lenny's face fell at her rejection. "What a shame."

Still holding the offensive object, Jesse studied it carefully. "This actually looks like it's still alive. You do remarkable work, Lenny."

When Jesse reached across the table to hand the squirrel watch to Rachel, she shook her head emphatically. "No, thank you, Lenny," she repeated firmly. "You keep it. I could never wear it."

"Are you sure?" Lenny's lips turned downward on the corners. "I was certain you would like it."

"It was a lovely thought, but I'm sure there are others who would gladly wear it. You should find one of them."

"So, Lenny, I bet you do a fair amount of business around hunting season," Jesse said.

"Yes, but it takes me away from the bird collection I'm working on."

The two men talked on for thirty minutes about the intricacies of skinning, gutting and stuffing. Rachel was sure she would never eat meat again—ever. Finally, she looked to Genie for deliverance. "Genie, if you want to catch that movie, we need to leave, now."

"What movie...ouch!" Frowning, Genie leaned down to rub her other shin. "At this rate, I'm going to be crippled," she grumbled. Then continuing with a long-suffering tone, "Okay, Rachel, let's go so we don't miss that movie." Genie smiled apologetically at Jesse, then fluttered her fingers in farewell to Lenny.

Rachel never looked back.

As Rachel pulled Genie behind her in a rush for the

door, she heard Genie ask, "Hey Rache, just what *did* that ad say?"

JESSE SAT across the table from his best friends and members of the super secret Texas Billionaire's Club. The club had been formed by four college students back when they didn't have a nickel to rub between them. At their lowest point financially, they'd made a pledge to each become millionaires before they reached the ripe old age of thirty.

And damned if they hadn't made it. Every one of them. Not only had they made their first million, they'd gone on to billionaire status.

Tanner Peschke set his beer mug on the table at the Piki Tiki. "So, why the emergency meeting of the TBC?" He grinned. "Not that I mind coming to your rescue. You're just lucky I was in town between shoots of the show. I left Janine packing for our next adventure into the wild."

Jesse grinned. "Why are you still doing the show? You don't need the money. You made a fortune day-trading, and your business interests are just adding to it."

Tanner shrugged. "Janine loves being a star, and it keeps me from getting bored."

Rip pounded Tanner on the back. "I nearly snorted beer out my nose when that female chimpanzee took a shine to you. I thought Janine was going to kill her with that foam baseball bat."

Gage chuckled. "Never thought I'd see a blond human jealous of a female chimpanzee. I nearly lost it when they played tug-of-war with you."

Tanner frowned and rubbed his shoulder. "That chimp

had a hold on me so tight, I thought she'd rip my arm out of my socket."

Rip laughed. "You're a lucky man. Janine must really love you to take on a wild animal to save you."

Tanner nodded, his lips twitching. "She's amazing, and you're right. I'm a lucky man." He turned his gaze to Jesse. "Which brings us back to our reason for being here. Are we all on track to meet our next goal? I've got Janine. Rip proposed to Casey—by the way, that was an epic proposal, my man. Doing it right there on the radio for all of Austin to hear."

"I want to know if you had a backup plan." Gage shook his head. "What if she'd said no?"

Rip patted his Hawaiian-shirt-covered chest. "How could she say no to this?"

Gage snorted. "Easily."

Rip gave them a twisted grin. "I have to admit, I was sweating it until she said yes."

"So, that leaves two of our group." Tanner turned to face the two men who hadn't secured a woman's love or promise to marry. "Gage? Jess? Where do you stand?"

Gage held up his hand. "I refuse to be pushed into anything as important as marriage. Besides, I'm about to take command of a National Guard unit. I won't have time to date. Women are a huge time commitment."

Tanner held up his hand. "No excuses. We all made promises. You have to at least be trying."

Gage frowned. "I need more time."

Rip crossed his arms over his chest. "You have until the end of this year. We didn't make it as far as we've come by reneging on our pledges."

"I'll work on it," Gage said. "Besides, we're not here to

badger me. Jesse called this meeting. He's the one with the problem."

Jesse shook his head. "Not so much a problem, but a challenge. I've found the woman of my dreams. But I'm struggling to convince her I'm her man."

"How can that be?" Rip waved a hand toward Jesse. "You're the all-American, boy next door with the physique of a model and a killer smile."

"The Austin Enquirer named you Austin's most eligible bachelor," Tanner said. "Shoot, you probably have ladies lining up outside your house day and night, begging you to marry them."

Heat rushed into Jesse's cheeks. "As a matter of fact, I have had a few women show up in my yard, carrying signs."

"I heard you had to call the cops when you found a naked lady in your bed."

Jesse frowned. "How the hell she got into my house, I don't know."

Rip laughed.

Jesse glared. "It's not funny."

"Oh, but it is." Rip chuckled and slowly settled back in his seat. "Hell, you could have any woman you want."

Jesse sighed. "Except one."

Gage leaned forward. "Who is she?"

"If I tell you, you can't go claim jumping." Jesse stared pointedly at Gage. "She's mine."

"Apparently not, based on what you've told us." Gage raised his brows for a moment, and then smiled. "Don't worry. Like I said, I don't have time right now. I've got to get my arms around the new unit, and I'm moving into a house."

"A house?" Tanner stared at Gage. "You're giving up the condo life?"

Gage nodded. "It's not fair to Rambo to keep him at the condo. He needs a backyard to run around in while I'm at work or on a drill weekend."

"And it took you two years to figure that out?" Tanner's lips pressed together. "A dog as big as Rambo needs room to stretch his legs."

"Exactly. Thus, the move." Gage tipped his head toward Jesse. "Her name?"

Jesse cast a glance around the room, took a deep breath and let it out slowly before he said, "Rachel Taylor."

Tanner's brows dipped. "I know that name."

"You should. She's done some marketing for Peschke Motors." Jesse leaned forward. "And thanks, by the way. Her marketing team has done wonders with my chain of ranch supply stores."

Leaning his head to the side, Tanner's frown deepened. "Isn't she the owner of the marketing firm?"

Jesse nodded.

"She wears skirt suits and pulls her hair back in a knot at the back of her head." Tanner tapped the base of his skull.

"That's the one," Jesse said. "And she barely knows I exist."

"How can that be?" Tanner rested his elbows on the table. "You hired her to run your advertising campaign?"

Jesse nodded. "I did."

Tanner tapped his fingers on the sleek wooden surface. "You work with her on at least a weekly basis to make sure the campaign is effective?"

"Is she the one who has you modeling for your own ads?" Rip asked.

Jesse snorted. "I even had it written into the contract that she be present for every photo shoot."

"Then she knows you exist," Gage said. "Did you piss her off?"

Jesse ran a hand through his hair. "I don't think so. Her executive assistant claims she has a strict 'no fraternizing with the clients' policy."

Rip gave a bark of laughter. "A no *what?*"

With a sigh, Jesse sat back in his chair. "She doesn't get involved with her clients."

Gage flung a hand in the air. "Then fire her. Problem solved."

"I can't fire her. She's doing a great job on the marketing, and it would look bad for her business to lose such a big client." Jesse pushed back from the table and stood. Nervous energy set him pacing. "Besides, it's the only way I get to spend time with her."

Gage leaned back in his chair. "Sounds like you're between a rock and a hard place."

"Yeah," Tanner said. "And you want us to help? How?"

Jesse ran his hand through his hair again. "I'm not sure."

"If you're looking for moral support, you know we're here for you," Tanner said.

"You need us to take out the competition?" Rip raised both fists. "We've gotcha covered."

Tanner perked up. "Is there competition?"

"Not that I've noticed. Rachel is a workaholic. Up until the past few days, I didn't think she had time for a relationship."

Rip leaned closer. "But now you think she does?"

"Yeah. She and a friend of hers went to a bar tonight to go—as her friend put it—man-hunting."

"That doesn't sound good." Gage drummed his fingers on the table, his eyes narrowed. "If you want my advice..."

"The man who doesn't have time for women is giving advice?" Rip raised his brows and gave Gage a pointed stare before turning to Jesse. "The big question is, did they take rifles on this manhunt?"

Jesse frowned. "No. But the man Rachel met there wasn't even close to right for her. I don't understand where she found him, or why she would be interested in the guy. He was a taxidermist, for God's sake."

Tanner chuckled. "That's kind of ironic. If they shot him, he couldn't stuff himself, now could he?"

"Seriously," Jesse paced a few steps away and turned back. "Rachel deserves a man who doesn't smell like formaldehyde."

"And ode du horse dung is any better?" Tanner asked.

Jesse dipped his head and sniffed his shirt. "Do I smell like the barn?"

Rip held up his hands. "I'm not getting close enough to find out."

"What's so special about this Rachel?" Gage asked. "Why are you so hung up on her?"

Jesse stopped and stared across the nearby barroom. For a moment, he didn't say anything as all the little impressions of Rachel rippled through his mind, forming one sexy picture of a woman in skirt suit, her long, elegant neck begging to be stroked, her full, luscious lips perfect for kissing. "She's driven."

"Like you," Tanner said.

"She owns a business she built from scratch."

"Like you," Tanner repeated.

"She's smart," Jesse said.

Rip snorted. "Well, two out of three ain't bad."

Tanner backhanded Rip across the chest. "Give the guy a break. He's spilling his guts."

"She has a big heart." Jesse faced the other men. "She doesn't brag about it, but I found out she volunteers at a children's shelter, and she spends her holidays feeding the homeless at a soup kitchen."

"Sounds more like a saint," Rip grumbled, rubbing his hand across his chest.

Jesse smiled, his thoughts shifting to Rachel's firm ass in her form-fitting skirts. "Only if saints can be sexy. I can see her as the mother of my children. And I want at least half a dozen." He sighed and faced the others. "The problem is getting past her defenses. At work, she's all business."

"If you want my advice..." Gage started again.

Jesse raised his head. Normally, Gage was the last one to voice his opinion. Usually the big guy listened, took it all in, making his own decisions before he spoke. "Yeah?"

"It's simple. You need to be around when she's *not* at work. *A lot*," Gage said. "Persistence pays off."

Jesse rubbed his chin, his thoughts spinning. "She does have a friend who might help."

"Female?" Tanner asked.

"Yeah," Jesse answered.

Tanner held up a hand. "Be careful the friend doesn't fall for your killer charm and good looks."

Jesse nodded. "I'll make it clear."

"If you need me to run interference," Rip patted his chest. "I'm your man."

"We're all here for you," Tanner agreed.

"That's right," Gage said. "Now, go get 'er, Tiger."

"And remember," Tanner said. "Nothing can stop Jesse Jordan when he sets his mind to something."

Jesse stood taller. He hadn't gotten where he was by taking no for an answer. Securing Rachel's love should be no different. "Thanks, guys. I was beginning to doubt my own abilities."

"Don't," Gage said. "You've got this."

"Now that Jesse's back on track..." Rip stood and stretched. "Next round is on me. After I shake the dew off my leg." He headed toward the bathroom.

Jesse took his seat and lifted his untouched beer mug. They were right. He hadn't amassed a fortune by giving up. If he wanted something badly enough, he went after it with single-minded tenacity. Going after Rachel, the potential mother of his children, should be no different.

CHAPTER 5

RACHEL SAT at her desk the next day, discouraged, but not defeated. She wanted a baby. When she set her mind to a goal, she persisted until she attained the goal. Failure was not an option.

Sitting on the edge of Rachel's desk, Genie rested her chin on her fist, her brows furrowed. "Why don't you let me write the ad this time?"

"There's not going to be another ad. I'm not going through that again. Who knows what I'd wind up with next?" Rachel's fingers flew across the keyboard as she typed up her notes from her last client meeting into her desktop journal.

Genie shook her head, her lips quirking upward. "How can you hold an intelligent conversation at the same time as you type something completely different?"

"I just do." Her hands never slowed.

"Must be some right-brain-left brain kind of thing going on there." Genie grinned. "About last night. I thought the taxidermist was kinda sweet."

Rachel's fingers stumbled on the keyboard. She deleted

the jumble of letters she'd written, looked up and grimaced. "What you really mean is kinda *sick*."

"But he brought you a present made with his own two clammy hands. If he was just trying to impress a date—" Genie's eyes widened with her grin. "Think what he would do if he was serious about a woman."

Rachel's stomach roiled. "Thank God, I will never have to know." She flipped the lid of the laptop closed and gave Genie her full attention.

"Honestly, I don't think the singles page is going to work. You never know what you're going to get. I'm better off sticking with the dating service. At least, they pre-screen their clients."

Picking up the box sitting on the farthest corner of the desk, Genie opened it and stared inside. She gulped once, grimacing, then smiled craftily as she closed it and set it back down. "I don't know, Rache. Looks like Lenny made an impression on you. You didn't trash his gift."

Rachel shivered. "He was so insistent that I keep it, I took it with me when we left. I forgot all about it until I was driving to work today and smelled something funny. I just brought it in so that I could get rid of it. That thing gives me the willies. Please, just put that piece of roadkill in the garbage, will you?"

"Oh come on," Genie teased, "it was a gift of love. Picture it! Every time you lift the little squirrel's head you can tell the time and know that your honey is hard at work making more innovative jewelry just for you."

"That's what I'm afraid of. That guy gave me the creeps, and he's one of the three reasons I don't want to try another shot in the dark with an advertisement."

"Have it your way." Genie shrugged and tossed the box into the wastepaper basket next to Rachel's desk. "What makes you think the dating agency will provide you any better specimens of manhood?"

"I checked. Date-Your-Mate is certified, and they do pre-screenings which, by the way, include searches for police records."

"So, Vinnie doesn't have a rap sheet, at least not one they could find, huh? Are you going to ask for more videos?"

"No, I've decided to try dating a few of the men we've already seen. I plan on going out on a date with each one of them, starting with Vinnie, since he scored the highest."

"You're going for the Italian Noodle?" Genie grinned.

"Stop that. It's Vinnie Fetachelli," Rachel said primly, then with her lips twitching added, "of Fetachelli's Deli." They both dissolved into giggles.

Rachel took a deep breath before announcing, "Well there's no time like the present. Hand me my day planner." Opening the little book, she searched through it to find Vinnie's phone number. Putting her desk phone on speaker, she punched the numbers and waited for an answer.

"Fetachelli Deli, we slice it the way you like it. What can I get for you, today?"

Genie clapped a hand over her mouth to stifle another giggle.

"Vinnie Fetachelli, please," Rachel said in her most business-like voice.

"Ya want Vinnie?" The man sounded incredulous.

"I want to *speak* to Vinnie, please," Rachel corrected firmly.

"Hey, Vinnie, there's a chick on the phone for ya," yelled the voice from the other end of the line. Muffled conversation could be heard. "Well, whatcha know, even guys with a mug like yours can get a babe to call. What did ya have to pay her? Here, take the phone, I gotta get back to slicing salami."

"Yo! This is Vinnie."

"Vinnie, this is...uh...Rachel Taylor. You came up as a match for me from the Date-Your-Mate website, and thought I'd give you a call to see if you'd like to...," suddenly losing her nerve, Rachel stammered, "uh...go out with me." There, she'd done it.

"Rachel..." Vinnie paused. "Are you the starchy dame in the suit?"

"Yes, I'm the starchy dame... I mean, I was wearing a suit."

"What the hell. I'd consider it a challenge to go out with yooze. Might even take some of that starch out of that suit, if ya know what I mean."

"Well...yes...uh..." Her huge vocabulary failing her, Rachel mouthed the words *Now what?* to Genie.

Pointing at her watch, Genie indicated that Rachel should set a time.

"What time?" she blurted.

"How's six o'clock on Friday?" Vinnie offered.

"That sounds..."

Genie was motioning again, holding up four fingers.

"Four?" Rachel asked Genie.

Vinnie replied, "Well, if four is better for you, I guess it's okay wit me."

Genie shook her head and held both of her hands up with two fingers on each, then put them together.

"Two?" Rachel asked.

"Two?" Vinnie sounded confused. "Make up your mind, and I'll be there."

Genie finally leaned down and whispered into Rachel's ear, "Double date."

"Double date?"

Suddenly comprehending, Rachel gathered her wits. "I'm sorry, Vinnie. I meant I would like for you to join me on a double date with a couple of friends of mine, and six o'clock on Friday would be just fine."

"Rachel, I'll handle the eats. You and your friends just meet me here at Fetachelli Deli, and I'll take care of dinner, capeesh?"

"Capeesh. I mean, yes, I understand."

Rachel hung up the phone and collapsed against the back of her chair.

"I think this may be an interesting evening," Genie chortled.

"I hope I don't choke on a meatball," Rachel groaned.

"GENIE, what am I going to do? I've never been on a blind date. How should I act? And what do I wear to an Italian Deli, for chrissakes?" Rachel threw her hands in the air. "This is why I haven't dated in…in…"

"Forever?" Genie grinned. "Calm down. He's just a guy. Sheeze."

Rachel—the normally unflappable of the pair of friends —darted between the bedroom and the bathroom in her underwear.

So far she' decided on panties and a camisole. From there she hadn't a clue what to wear. Genie had helped Rachel apply her makeup since Rachel normally settled for a smear of lipstick before heading out to work in the morning.

Genie chuckled. "I can't remember the last time you

were on a date. It does my heart good to see you so out of control."

Rachel and Genie had so little in common it never ceased to amaze her that they had been friends for so many years. Their friendship went all the way back to high school.

Genie had been outgoing and vivacious, never lacking for boyfriends.

Rachel, on the other hand, had hidden behind books. The influence of her elderly, stodgy parents had made her mature beyond her years, and naive beyond comprehension. High school boys had been hard for Rachel to understand.

Rachel stopped in front of Genie, wringing her hands together. "I know nothing about his man. What if I don't recognize him when we meet."

Genie shook her head. "You know what Vinnie looks like, and you've already heard him in action."

When Rachel spun away, her gut knotted so tightly she felt like doubling over. "I should call and cancel. He could be an axe murderer for all we know." She riffled through blouses that hung in precision in her closet, organized by color and style. Yeah, she was a card-carrying control freak.

"Chill, girl. It's just a date," Genie insisted. "Besides, he lives with his parents. Just where do you think he'd hide the bodies?"

"He works in a deli, doesn't he? I'm sure he could hide a little thing like that with all the meat they have hanging around in the freezers."

Genie wrinkled her nose. "Gross, Rachel, you're coming unglued. How about a drink to calm your nerves?"

"I don't have time for a drink. I'm not even dressed."

She shoved aside hanger after hanger. "Sure, I'm nervous, but you don't understand. I have to do this. Finding a man is all key to my plan." Rachel walked to her dresser, picked up her day planner and flipped it open. When she found what she was looking for, she stabbed her finger on it and pushed it under Genie's nose.

"What's this?" Genie stared down at the page indicated.

"In order for me to have a baby before I turn thirty-one, I have to start now. Look, I have it all planned out. We go on our first date tonight. If he seems right to me, next weekend we get more affectionate. By the end of the month, I'm sure to have him in bed. That would give me a good chance to be pregnant before summer."

Genie's eyebrows shot up. "Rachel, Rachel, Rachel. These things can't be controlled by a timeline. They have to happen naturally."

"Nature can be helped," Rachel said. "I'm a very determined woman, and when I go to the trouble of making a plan, I intend to stick with it."

Genie shook her head. "You really need to reconsider this so-called plan. Don't you think it is a little unfair to the sperm donor? After all, he would be the unwitting father of a baby."

Rachel huffed. "I'm not going to feel guilty about this."

"Yeah, right. The look on your face says something entirely different." Genie touched her arm.

Rachel raised her hand in self-defense. "I'm determined to have a baby and, in this case, the end justifies the means."

Shrugging, Genie smiled. "I had to give it a shot. You're my best friend, and I would consider it an injustice to let you go without a motherly lecture."

"Okay, enough with the lectures. Help me find something to wear." Rachel bounced in place on the balls of her feet and looked hopelessly at the racks of beautifully tailored business suits in her closet.

Genie joined her in front of the closet. "Rachel, honey, I don't think you own anything casual. How about this silk pantsuit? It comes about as close as you'll get. And don't wear panty hose underneath."

"Fine." Grabbing the hanger from Genie, she stripped the smoky blue pants from the hanger and slid into them. "Now, what about a blouse?"

"Yup, that's a good idea. Unless you want to make a great first impression on the Italian Noodle. How about that silver silk shell?"

Genie helped Rachel pull the shirt over the mass of curlers in her hair.

"Do you think these rollers have cooled enough? I only have five more minutes until your date arrives."

"Yes, come with me, and I'll take them out."

Genie had volunteered to help her get ready for the date, knowing Rachel was fairly inexperienced in the art of attracting a man. Choosing the right eye shadow, blush and perfume was right up her alley, having dated since she was an early blooming fifteen-year-old.

The contrast between the women was not only in their personalities, but also in their shapes. Where Rachel was an average height and boyishly slim with firm, but average-sized breasts, and barely a hint of curvature at the hips, Genie was petite and buxom.

The peal of the doorbell startled the two women.

"Ohmigod. I'm not ready. You answer it." Rachel pushed Genie toward the front of the house.

Glancing at her watch, Genie raised her eyebrows.

"Loverboy's early...must be a little anxious. I'll gladly get the door. You finish dressing."

Rachel glanced in the mirror at her reflection, alarmed at the amount of poof the curlers had given her normally straight hair.

Genie's voice drifted through from the other room. "Whoooeeee, look at you, cowboy."

Cowboy? Since when had Genie been dating a cowboy? They shared everything. How had she missed telling Rachel about this new development? Or had Rachel been too caught up in her own plans?

"Rachel's not ready yet, but we can wait in the living room and get to know each other better."

A deep, strangely familiar voice answered, "I'd like that."

Rachel slipped on a pair of sandals, frowning. She'd been so nervous about meeting Vinnie, she hadn't bothered to ask Genie who she was bringing on their double date. Now her curiosity was piqued.

GENIE SHIVERED as the sound of his smooth country drawl washed over her. *Geez, Rachel, if you don't notice this man who's crazy about you, I'm going to jump his bones, myself. He's delicious!*

Divine inspiration had led her to invite Jesse along as her date. She considered it her duty in life to help Rachel get a life. If it meant taking matters into her own hands, well she'd just give Mother Nature a little nudge.

She hadn't been in the least surprised at how quickly he'd leapt to accept the invitation, and she knew, with only a twinge of envy, it had nothing to do with her. The best part of the plan was that Rachel had been in such a dither over her own date she hadn't bothered to ask Genie who she was bringing.

Genie smiled a little feline smile. Rachel was in for a surprise. And she might be a little pissed, but then, what were best friends for? "Oh by the way, I hope you like Italian. Rachel's date owns a deli."

Jesse didn't comment. His gaze was glued to the slowly opening bedroom door.

Rachel stepped through, pausing on the threshold. She wore the jacket to the smoky blue pantsuit, giving the outfit an appearance of an executive heading for work, instead of a woman going on date.

As she stood behind Jesse, Genie pulled at the shoulders of her shirt and mouthed the words, *Lose the jacket.*

Rachel never saw her. She only had eyes for the sexy man standing in the middle of her living room.

About time she noticed. Genie attempted to draw their attention. "Well, I guess we should be leaving," she said, heading for the door. "Yoohoo. We need to go. It's getting late. I'll be waiting in the truck when you guys put your eyes back in your heads." She shrugged in mild disgust.

Yep, with a little feminine intervention, this evening had possibilities.

CHAPTER 6

Rachel was still reeling from the startling effect of seeing Jesse standing in her apartment. The combination of seeing him out of the context of her work environment, and standing in her personal space, had left her off balance. She tried hard not to stare as he drove, but her gaze kept returning to his golden hair and strongly chiseled profile.

He'd made her feel utterly feminine from the little chivalrous courtesies he had shown her. The small of her back was still warm from the hand that had guided her into the back seat of his white pickup truck. Never mind, he had shown the same courtesies to his date.

Genie sat in front of Rachel in the passenger seat.

With his back to her, Jesse wouldn't notice Rachel studying him. He was incredibly sexy in his light blue shirt and neatly pressed trousers, and his eyes were alight with laughter each time he glanced at Genie.

Envious of their easy banter, Rachel observed their body language.

Several times, Genie leaned over and touched his arm, causing the hackles to rise on the back of Rachel's neck.

The logical side of her brain said this was what Genie did all the time with everyone she talked to. The emotional side of Rachel's brain wanted to scream for her friend to stop touching him. She had to catch herself and bite her lip several times during the short ride to the deli. Who was she to tell Genie not to touch her own date? Rachel was going out with Vinnie, not Jesse. Her relationship with him could never be anything but business. It was a rule that had served her well, and she meant to stand by it.

Finally arriving at the Fetachelli Deli, the threesome climbed out of the truck and stared at the building with skepticism. It looked small, a little ramshackle, and very ordinary, but if the number of cars parked in the parking lot was any indication, the food inside must be good.

Holding the door for the two ladies, Jesse entered the establishment behind them.

A waitress greeted them. "How many in your party?"

"Three, but we're here to meet Vinnie Fetachelli," Rachel said.

"Oh!" The waitress' eyes grew wide, and she quickly looked Rachel up and down. "Don't go nowhere." Turning, she stood on her toes and looked around the room until she spotted someone. "Hey, Viinnnnie!" she screeched so loudly Rachel jumped. "She's here!"

She came down off her toes and practically launched herself at Rachel. Rachel stepped back in alarm, but wasn't fast enough to avoid an exuberant hug.

"Hi, I'm Carla, Vinnie's sister. Nice to meetcha."

"It's very nice to meet you too, uh...Carla."

Genie giggled behind her, and Rachel leveled a killing glare her way. When Rachel turned back she saw Vinnie weaving his way through the tables toward them. He was larger than he'd looked on the video. Dressed in dark slacks and a white polo shirt, which contrasted nicely against his dark olive complexion, he wasn't bad to look at. His ruddy complexion was becoming redder the nearer he drew to them.

If she hadn't already seen Vinnie's video, the number of dark-haired, dark-eyed people who also answered Carla's shrill call might have confused her. Vinnie gave a look of exasperation over his shoulder to the gathering throng. He reached her first and stood surrounded by an ever-increasing crowd forming a semi-circle around him. They were different sizes, shapes and ages, but all remarkably resembled Vinnie.

"I'm Vinnie," he said, holding out his hand. "You must be Rachel."

"Hello, Vinnie." Hesitantly, Rachel held out her hand to the dark Italian. Taking it, he quickly shook it and dropped it, as if embarrassed.

Shoving a meaty fist out to Jesse, Vinnie introduced himself. "Name's Vinnie...Vinnie Fetachelli."

"Jesse Jordan. Glad to meet you."

A rather large woman pushed past Vinnie, brushed by Rachel, and moved toward Genie with a joyous smile. "Vinnie, I like what I see. Your Rachel is *perfetta*."

Arms extended, Genie's head almost disappeared in the ample arms and bosom of the older woman. She hugged her so tightly, Genie's eyes crossed.

"She's not too skinny, like your usual girlfriends. She's got just the right meat on her bones. And oh, that red hair." Crossing herself, she smiled and hugged Genie close again.

"Excuse me, but I'm Rachel, ma'am. You're hugging Genie O'Connor," Rachel interrupted, already feeling like a disappointment to this happy woman.

Vinnie's mama withdrew her arms from Genie, finally

noticing Rachel hovering awkwardly beside her son. "*Scusilo, scusi.* I didn't mean to upset you. It's just that my Vinnie hasn't brought a ladyfriend home since we moved from New York."

She moved to Rachel and flung out her arms. In desperation, Rachel grabbed her hands before she was enveloped in that bone-crunching hug. She lightly squeezed as a form of introduction.

"Vinnie, who'd you bring to see us?" said a gray-haired little man with a big mustache.

"Pappa, come meet Rachel."

"Rachel, Rachel, Rachel, you are *bellissima*," he sang as he ignored her attempt to hold out a hand for him to shake. He wrapped his skinny arms around her and squeezed hard enough to lift her off the ground. "What, you no like to hug? Whatsa matta wit Americans? I just can't get enougha hugs, ask Mama."

Moving back to stand next to his wife, he put an arm around her ample girth and squeezed affectionately. "I could spend all day hugging Mama. With Mama, you hug and chalk and hug again, until you get all da way around her. Right, Mama?"

Batting half-heartedly at him, she smiled and grabbed his face, kissing him loudly in front of everybody.

Vinnie rolled his eyes, and then grinned at the astonished newcomers. "Welcome to Fetachelli Deli." He ushered everyone into a large room in the rear of the establishment.

A long table was decorated in a bright red-checkered tablecloth, with candles and bistro-style chairs—enough to seat thirty people. Rachel watched in amazement as all thirty chairs filled quickly.

"Vinnie, are all these people family?" Genie asked.

Shrugging, Vinnie smiled at her as he pulled a chair out for Rachel across from Mama and Pappa. "We're Italian, what can I say?"

Jesse pulled out another chair, two down from Rachel, and seated Genie before seating himself between the two women.

"Such a shame," Mama shook her head sadly. "Halfa da family is still in New York. Vinnie's brother, Alfonzo, runs the old deli. Vinnie brought me to Texas for my health." Reaching over, Mama pinched Vinnie's cheek, following the pinch with a pat. "My Vinnie is a good boy, he is."

"Mama, stop it, you're embarrassing me." Vinnie's cheeks stained crimson. Even though Vinnie pushed Mama's hand away from his face, you could see his love for her in his eyes.

Rachel could admire a man who loved his mother enough to move halfway across the country for her health. That was a good character trait she would want in her child. She'd have to remember to make a note of that in her spreadsheet.

Two dark-haired, dark-eyed young women set large serving bowls filled with pasta and tomato sauce on the table. Another brought out a huge tray of bruschetta, the savory toast covered with chopped tomatoes, pesto and cheese. The conversation continued until all the food had been placed on the table along with several bottles of rich red wine. The young ladies took their seats at the table, and the entire family bowed their heads for the blessing.

While everyone listened to Pappa thanking the Lord for all the good food and family, Rachel sneaked a peak around the table. Vinnie's family was large and apparently believed in doing things as a family. Having grown up as an only child, Rachel felt a little overwhelmed at the mass of humanity sitting at one table to share a meal. She was not quite sure how to feel about all of it.

This group of people looked like a tight-knit community of family members looking out for each other. How would they feel about her if they knew why she was there? They wouldn't take lightly to her procreating with their darling Vinnie and absconding with one of their own bambinos. *They'd probably send me packing, or worse,* Rachel gulped, *send cousin Guido after me.*

The prayer ended, and the noise resumed immediately as dishes were passed around the table. Without realizing it, Rachel let out a soft sigh. Suddenly, she felt a hand patting her knee beneath the table. Her immediate reaction was to jerk away. She glanced sharply at the man to her left.

Jesse raised his hands in mock surrender and leaned toward her. "Sorry, I didn't mean to startle you," he said quietly into her ear so that he could be heard over the rising voices of the boisterous family. "I just wondered, why the big sigh?"

"I always wished I was a part of a large family." Rachel gazed around the table wistfully.

"It's a bit of a culture shock if you're not used to it, isn't it?" Jesse smiled warmly. "I grew up in a large family too, and I wouldn't trade it for the world."

The dishes arrived in front of her, and she helped herself to familiar favorites, spaghetti with marinara sauce, thick golden slices of bruschetta, a large vegetable-filled salad. She swirled the pasta on her fork and brought it to her mouth. Her taste buds exploded. Moaning, Rachel closed her eyes. When she opened them, she blushed as she realized several pairs of eyes were watching her reaction with interest.

"Oh, this is so good!" She smiled at Vinnie.

"Of course, it is. It's Mama's recipe."

Mama acknowledged the compliment with a nod, and then stared pointedly across the table at her. "Rachel, tell me about your family?"

Rachel slurped a troublesome noodle inelegantly to free her mouth to speak. "I don't have any. My parents died several years ago."

"But what about the rest of your family?"

"I have none. I guess you could say that Genie is the closest thing I have to a sister."

Mama's mouth pursed in disapproval. "No family, that's too bad. Did you hear that Vinnie? Rachel's got no family."

Vinnie grimaced and lifted his shoulders, but didn't rise to the bait she had thrown his way.

Turning to Genie, Mama smiled warmly. She definitely liked this one. Rachel suppressed a smile of her own, glad to have Genie in the hot seat with the irascible old woman.

"Genie, what about you? Do you have family?"

"Oh lord, yes. My parents are Irish Catholic. They believe in large families. I have five brothers and sisters. I was a middle child, but I can still remember changing diapers for my little brother and sister. And the noise! There was never a dull meal in our family. This gathering feels like home to me."

"The girl who gets my Vinnie will have more family than she knows what to do with. Isn't that right, Vinnie?" Mama crossed her arms over her chest.

"Mama, be quiet. You're embarrassing me. This is our first date. Next thing, you'll be talking about weddings and babies."

"And what pretty babies you'd make, huh? Only I don't

know how Rachel could feed them with those little boobies."

Rachel choked on her spaghetti.

Jesse pounded her back, his lips twitching.

If he smiled, Rachel would stomp his foot beneath the table.

"Mama, leave Rachel's boobies alone," Vinnie roared, then dug the hole deeper. "She has pretty boobies."

Rachel was finally able to breathe, but her cheeks burned with embarrassment. She felt Jesse shaking beside her and turned to see his hand clapped over his mouth to suppress the laughter bubbling up.

Vinnie looked around the table and caught sight of Jesse's expression. "What? Did I say something wrong?"

"Nothing, Vinnie. I agree with you," Jesse grimaced when Rachel slammed her shoe into his shin, but he bravely finished the sentence. "Rachel's boobies are just fine."

Genie and Jesse burst out laughing and were joined by the rest of the people at the table. Rachel was mortified that her attributes, or lack thereof, were being discussed so openly.

"So Rachel, do you work?" Mama continued her cross-examination.

"Yes, ma'am. I'm an executive at an advertising firm."

Her face lighting up at this piece of news, Mama smiled with more interest at Rachel. "Vinnie, you finally find a girl who is useful. Maybe you can get her to advertise for the Fetachelli Deli, no?"

"We'll see, Mama." Vinnie shrugged, and gave Rachel an apologetic smile.

Mama's eagle eye turned to Genie. "Genie, what do you do for a living?"

"I'm a physical therapist."

"What's that?" Mama asked.

"I use massage therapy, exercises and manipulation to help patients manage pain."

Mama's eyebrows drew together. "Are you like one of those girls who work in the massage parlors?"

"Mama, would you be quiet, already? She's legit. She does massages for doctors," Vinnie explained.

"She only does doctors? I guess they must pay better."

"That's right Mama, I'm a professional," Genie grinned, taking it all in stride.

Vinnie gave her an approving look. "Finally, someone who can stand toe to toe with Mama."

"So, Jesse," Mama's eyes narrowed, shrewdly, sizing him up. "What do you do?"

Genie jumped in, grinning, before Jesse had a chance to respond. "He's a model."

"A model? What kinda job is that for a man?" Mama demanded.

"Thank you Genie, I'll take it from here," Jesse's voice dripped with sarcasm. "I own a chain of ranching supply stores."

"And he models," Genie repeated.

"With or without your clothes?" Mama wanted to know.

Rachel burst out laughing, barely avoiding spraying wine out her nose. In revenge, Jesse smacked her sharply on the back as she sputtered and coughed.

"Is Mama always so outspoken?" Jesse asked Vinnie, with a smile aimed at Mama.

Vinnie raised his hands, palms up, and shrugged, "We're Italian, what can I say?"

. . .

JESSE HELD open the door to his truck as Rachel crawled into the back seat and Genie climbed into the front. Closing the door, he walked around to the driver's seat. Vinnie was already sitting in the back. Jesse slid into the driver's seat and set the truck in motion.

"Jesse, aren't you going to tell us where we're going for our entertainment?" Genie asked.

"Nope, the entertainment was up to me, and I want it to be a surprise."

They had driven for nearly thirty minutes, and Rachel still had no idea where he was taking them or where she was. Jesse had said it was a surprise, and Rachel had never liked surprises. They had a tendency to make her feel off balance and out of control.

After a half hour of listening to Jesse's casual southern charm aimed at Genie, Rachel was ready to head home. For some reason, Jesse's open flirtation with her best friend was getting on her nerves. She gave up all attempts at engaging Vinnie in a conversation. He seemed to be just as intent on eavesdropping on Jesse and Genie's dialogue. Rachel didn't mind his interest. She felt no spark of attraction for the handsome Italian. Her tastes ran in the direction of blue-eyed blonds.

All through dinner at the deli, Rachel had felt like the odd woman out. Genie and Jesse fit right in, sharing the banter and conversation as if they were already part of the extended family. Having been an only child, Rachel wasn't familiar with the way everyone picked on each other. She had a hard time telling whether they were serious or just poking fun.

Dinner at her house, growing up, had been an entirely different affair. Her parents talked quietly about their work and asked her questions about her day at school.

Since her school days were anything but exciting, the conversation was short, and she quickly excused herself from the table. She preferred to find the latest book she was reading to escape into a fantasy much more interesting than her life.

Her love of books and learning kept her going through school. But looking back, she realized how much she'd missed by not establishing relationships with her schoolmates. Now, she lacked the ability to socialize naturally.

She could see how Jesse would be more attracted to Genie. With her ability to talk about everything or nothing and make it all sound interesting, Genie was much more lively. She had lived and done exciting things, whereas Rachel had only read about them. She had lived her young life vicariously through experiences she had only read about. How could she share those experiences when they weren't even hers to share?

Rachel sat back against her seat and stared out the window, watching the sides of the road illuminated by the headlights. Maybe Genie was right. Maybe she should get a life. Maybe the baby idea was only part of it. Thinking back on her upbringing, Rachel wondered whether she really had what it took to raise a child. It wasn't just the loving and caring, it was sharing experiences and spreading your wings, willing yourself to take a chance and encouraging that in your child.

Finally, the pickup slowed and turned off the country highway and into a gravel parking lot in front of what looked like a large old barn. If there had ever been paint on the barn, it was long gone, and the boards were gray and weathered. The roof was rusting tin, with a patchwork of shinier pieces here and there, from past repairs. On the side of the barn facing the road, was a large faded sign announcing KENDALIA DANCE HALL.

Jesse climbed out of the pickup and came around to open the passenger doors to let the ladies out. As he handed Genie then Rachel out of the truck, Rachel heard the loud and lively music blasting from inside the barn.

Genie looked at him questioningly. "How on earth did you find this place?"

He laughed and draped an arm around her shoulders. "Let's just say I stumbled onto this place in my wilder days."

Rachel hesitated as the group moved toward the door. Vinnie grabbed her elbow and started to usher her toward the entrance, past a long line of Harley Davidson Motorcycles.

"Jesse, are you sure it's safe?" Rachel hesitated to move around the bikes as if the inanimate objects were poised to attack.

Pulling the screen door open, he smiled back at her reassuringly. "Yes, I'm sure it is. The folks that come here even bring their families."

As soon as she stepped through the door, she felt like she'd stepped onto another planet. A very loud and lively planet.

What appeared to be a biker sat at a small, wobbly table next to the door.

As Jesse paid the cover charge, Rachel eyed the man curiously.

He wore black leather from the neck down, including a spiked collar around his massive neck. A Grateful Dead T-shirt peeked out from beneath his leather jacket, and his long stringy gray hair curled below the red bandana tied around the top of his head. The lower half of his face was covered in a grizzled gray beard

The biker's beard parted in a smile revealing a bright gold tooth. "Hey, Jesse, long time no see, dude."

Rachel frowned.

The biker knew Jesse.

Just how much did she know about this man who owned his own chain of ranch supply stores? Determined to keep him at a professional distance, she'd refused to satisfy her curiosity. Yeah, he was sexy as hell, but beyond that, what else did she know about the man?

Since the evening began, she'd learned more about him than she wanted to know. And what she'd learned wasn't helping in her effort to keep the man at arm's length.

He was from a big family—something Rachel had only ever dreamed of. He knew where to go for a casual night out with friends, and he was more chivalrous than any man she'd ever met.

Rachel glanced at Jesse's hand on Genie's arm as he leaned into her in a protective way.

Vinnie cupped Rachel's elbow and stood beside her as Jesse greeted his biker friend.

Despite her vow to keep her clients on a professional level, Rachel had the odd feeling she was with the wrong man.

CHAPTER 7

JESSE and the biker clasped hands in what Rachel assumed was a friendly greeting. As the handshake continued, both men strained and leaned into their clasped hands, their smiles turning into grimaces.

"Nice to see you too, Bubba," Jesse gritted out the words, and finally yanked his hand from the big man's clutches.

Bubba laughed and pounded Jesse on the back.

Wincing, Rachel backed up a step, afraid he would pound her with equal force and send her sprawling across the room.

"Who've you got with you?" Bubba asked.

"Bubba, this is Genie O'Connor, and my friends Rachel Taylor and Vinnie Fetachelli," Jesse shouted over the music. "Everyone, this is Hubert Rausch, but everybody calls him Bubba."

Bubba shook Vinnie's hand then Genie's.

Rachel waited for them to grimace or cry out in pain. When it came her turn, she timidly offered her hand in greeting, fearing the bone-crunching squeeze she'd witnessed a moment before when he'd shaken hands with Jesse. The big man's hand engulfed her own, and he shook it gently.

Relieved, Rachel raised her voice over the music, "It's very nice to meet you, Mr. Rausch."

"The pleasure's mine, ma'am. Hey, y'all are in for some foot-stomping entertainment tonight. We got the Swamp Rats, all the way from the Louisiana bayous."

Hoping that was something good, Rachel nodded to the big man then followed the rest as they made their way through the crowd. As Jesse led the small group into the darkened interior of the dance hall, Rachel observed the bar's occupants. It was an interesting mix of bikers and cowboys. All ages, including children, grandparents and young people, were present and attired in varying colors and styles of clothing. The commonality among them all was they seemed to know each other, and they were having a good time.

The room had a surprisingly large open area for dancing on the concrete floor. It was lined with long wooden tables with plank benches pushed up to them for seating. Christmas lights were strung loosely along the ceiling.

Leading them to an empty table, Jesse helped Genie, then Rachel, climb over the plank bench to sit. Vinnie sat next to Rachel looking around the room with undisguised interest.

Music blared from the huge speakers resting on the edge of the wooden stage. A man, wearing a red bandana on his head and a leather outfit similar in style to the biker at the door, played the base guitar and sang. The lead guitarist wore a graying white t-shirt and faded blue jeans exposing his bony knees and his boxer shorts through strategically shredded holes. His hair was an uncombed streaky blond, and he had a week's worth of stubble accumulated on his chin. The drummer was all but hidden from view, but what you couldn't see, you could certainly hear.

Shouting over the sound of the music, Jesse asked the group, "What would you like to drink?"

"What do they have?" shouted Genie.

Jesse grinned. "Any kind of beer or whiskey you could possibly want."

"Why doesn't that surprise me?" Genie smiled. "I guess, beer it is."

Rachel and Vinnie nodded their agreement and Jesse waived to a passing waitress to order four beers. When the waitress returned, she plunked four long-necked bottles of beer in front of them. Rachel thought the waitress had forgotten the glasses until she noticed Jesse drinking straight from the bottle. Shrugging, she lifted her own and took a long swallow.

It was hard to carry on a conversation over the noise, so they sat listening to the music and drinking their beer until the song ended and another fast-paced tune began.

Grabbing Genie's hand, Jesse pulled her out onto the floor and gave her a brief dancing lesson on the Texas Two-Step. After two or three attempts, Genie mastered the steps, and the couple began to make wide circles around the dance floor. They laughed and danced along with everyone else.

Rachel and Vinnie sat watching, occasionally looking over at each other and smiling awkwardly. They both finished their beers, and Vinnie motioned for the waitress to bring another round. She knew she should try to converse, but she couldn't think of anything interesting enough to make her want to shout it over the music. So, she sat like a stump, waiting for her date to make the next move.

As Genie and Jesse rounded the dance floor once more, they swung close to the two sitting on the sidelines. Their heads leaned together in conversation, and the next thing Rachel knew, Jesse was pulling her out onto the dance floor, and Genie had Vinnie in tow.

Jesse demonstrated the dance steps, and in no time Rachel was able to perform them with some semblance of grace. Craning her neck to watch the other couple, Rachel smiled to see Vinnie struggling to keep his two left feet from tripping himself and Genie all over the dance floor. Genie didn't seem to mind.

Jesse whirled Rachel around the room throughout the song, until the music ended.

Rachel stood breathless and laughing. "I'm glad you brought us here. This is fun," she said, and meant it.

His face close to hers, Jesse replied, "I'm glad you like it. I don't think I've ever seen you smile so much. You should do it more often. It makes your eyes shine."

The band eased into a soft country ballad, allowing the dancers to catch their breath.

Rachel looked around for Genie and Vinnie and noted they were already moving together to the music.

Jesse opened his arms. "Let's not waste a perfectly good song."

Rachel's heart tripped. *It's just a dance.* She took a deep breath and stepped into his embrace. She rested her hands against his chest and leaned into his body.

His lips close to her ear, he murmured, "You're beautiful."

The sound of his voice rumbled against her ear, and she melted into the warmth of his arms. Rachel didn't respond in words. Instead, she pressed closer, while his words washed over her with the music. With her cheek resting on his chest and her nose close to the open neck of his shirt, she inhaled the clean smell of cologne and spicy soap.

Her body fit perfectly against his as they swayed in unison. Closing her eyes, Rachel allowed herself to fantasize. After all, according to the gossip columnists in newspapers all over Texas, this was the man dreams were made of. He had a smile that could make a woman's knees weak. He was polite to a fault—and he was pretty pleasing to the eye. For just this dance, Rachel let herself live in the moment.

Inhibitions melted away, and she did the thing she had been aching to do for what seemed an eternity. She lifted her hands, wrapped them around his neck and plunged her fingers into the warm golden wealth of his hair.

God, she loved his hair. She loved the way it curled over his collar, and the way he ran his hands through it when he was thinking. But right now, what she loved most was the way his hair felt so silky soft underneath her hands while his hard body rubbed against hers. It sent delicious sensations racing along her nerve endings, stirring her blood more than the fast pace of the earlier song.

Too soon the ballad ended, and the music made an abrupt change to a livelier tune. She pulled her hands away from him and leaned back against his arms. But he didn't release her right away.

"Can you polka?" Jesse asked, smiling down at her.

That beer must have been pretty high octane, she thought. For when he smiled, her knees turned to liquid, and she was ready to do anything he asked. "No, but if you're willing to teach me, I'm game."

After a clumsy start, which had them both laughing, they took off once more, flying around the floor. When the dance ended, they collapsed onto the bench seat facing the dance floor, gulping from their warm bottles of beer. Rachel unbuttoned her jacket and flapped the lapels to cool off. Jesse's arm settled on the table behind her, and she leaned back against it, feeling more alive and excited than she'd ever felt. For once, she knew what it felt like to participate in life instead of just watching from the fringes.

Glancing around, she spotted Vinnie and Genie still dancing around the floor. Vinnie had finally found a dance step he could handle, and he seemed determined to dance until he dropped. Rachel smiled at their exuberance. She was truly happy Genie was getting along so well with Vinnie—and not Jesse. *Now, where did that thought come from?*

Rachel and Jesse sat in companionable silence throughout the rest of the song. When the Swamp Rats announced the next song would be a Cotton-Eyed-Joe, Jesse jumped to his feet and dragged her out on the dance floor, despite her protests. One more time, he led her through the complicated steps, and Rachel, liberated by beer and his approval, caught on quickly.

Halfway through the number, Rachel stripped her jacket off, twirling it playfully over her head before tossing it toward their table as they passed. Instead of landing on the table as intended, it landed on a large man passing by at just that moment. Peeling the jacket off his head, Rachel watched as Bubba studied it then looked out on the dance floor at Rachel.

Jesse's eyes lit with laughter as wolf calls rang out from the biker gallery.

Rachel pressed closer to the cowboy as his arm rested on the bare skin of her shoulder and they continued the dance. The tempo increased steadily, the frenzied dancers attempting to keep pace.

Suddenly, the song ended, and the dancers burst into relieved laughter and applause as they gasped for air. Jesse pulled her close for a quick hug then leaned back with his arms wrapped loosely around her waist.

"Now, tell me you're not having fun," he challenged.

"I love this place. Thank you for bringing me...us," she amended.

Looking up at him, she knew her skin was pink from exertion and her hair was wild and unruly, but she didn't care. She felt free and happy.

The first strains of the "Tennessee Waltz" began, and Jesse quirked an eyebrow in invitation.

Before Rachel could respond, Bubba appeared at her side with her jacket folded neatly over his beefy arm.

"Excuse me, Ma'am," he said, glancing at the jacket, not her. "I believe you lost something during the last dance."

"Thank you, Bubba." Rachel took the jacket and turned to lay it on the table behind her. When she spun toward the dance floor, she noticed Bubba still stood politely in front of her.

He cleared his throat once, then blurted out, "Wanna dance with me?"

Alarmed, Rachel glanced hopefully at Jesse, waiting for him to claim the dance as his. Instead, she saw a smile tugging at the corners of his mouth and knew he wasn't going to do any such thing. The rat!

To avoid looking snobbish, and determined to show

Jesse she had gumption, Rachel replied, "I'd be happy to, Bubba."

Without a backward glance at the traitor, Rachel slipped her hand through Bubba's crooked elbow and followed him onto the dance floor.

Leading her out, like a grand duchess at a ball, Bubba turned and stood in front of her, giving her a deep bow. Then he raised his arms. Rachel stepped as close as she could get without bumping into his belly and placed one hand on his shoulder and the other in his upturned palm. She braced herself as Bubba began counting to himself.

Bubba nodded his head in rhythm with the beat. "One, two, three. One, two, three. One, two, three."

Then they were off.

Waltzing around the room, Bubba pumped his lead arm up and down like a metronome.

Rachel struggled to maintain two or three inches away from his protruding belly, embarrassed each time they bumped together.

Before long, Bubba relaxed and quit counting. The dance became more natural, and Rachel found herself smiling and talking with this big beast of a man, learning he was a mechanic at a local motorcycle dealership. His love and his life were the Harley Hawgs sitting outside. He went into great detail about their engine capabilities.

Rachel smiled, although she didn't have a clue what torque and suspension had to do with any of it. But he was certainly entertaining and passionate about his bikes.

When the dance came to an end, Rachel smiled and thanked him, returning to the table where Jesse, Genie, and Vinnie were talking animatedly. Jesse grinned from ear to ear as he stood to seat her.

"Well, how's Bubba's waltz? From what I observed, it's improved immensely."

The others smiled along with him, waiting for her response.

"Actually, he was quite good, thank you very much. Remind me to dance with him again this evening." Tossing her hair back, she added haughtily, "And I think he is a very interesting man. I think I know quite a bit about Harley Johnson motorcycles, now."

Vinnie and Jesse looked at each other and burst out laughing.

"What?" Rachel frowned, not understanding what set them off.

Genie leaned close to Rachel and said, "That's Harley *Davidson*, not Johnson."

"Right. I knew that." Rachel tried to sound flippant, but the blush spreading up into her cheeks belied her irritation. How could she be so stupid as to forget the name Harley Davidson. Being near Jesse befuddled her.

Another ballad began, and Rachel gratefully recognized Hank William's song "I'm So Lonesome I Could Cry." Her feet were beginning to ache.

Both men stood. They shared a glance, and a decision appeared to be made. Vinnie extended his hand to Genie. Rachel looked up expectantly to Jesse. With a nod to the dance floor, she gladly let him curve his arm around her back to lead her to the floor.

Dancing with Jesse was a revelation. Whether it was the beer or the uniqueness of the whole evening, Rachel felt drawn to the comfort of his embrace. *It was just a dance,* she reminded herself, because she needed reminding. She allowed herself to relax against Jesse. Her cheek rested against his chest, and she felt the strong beat of his heart.

Her arm tightened around his back, and she let her hand explore the broad expanse of his shoulders.

The man was solid, lean and...substantial.

Rachel inhaled and breathed deeply of the faint trace of cologne and the musky male scent that was Jesse.

The sad notes of the song pulled a melancholy sigh from her.

JESSE LEANED down to place a kiss against her forehead, before pulling her body snugly against his own. For whatever reason, tonight she was pliant in his arms. The evening had battered her defenses. Knowing tonight wasn't a victory, he also didn't consider it a loss. It was but a single skirmish in the long battle of wills to come, and he decided to enjoy her momentary surrender.

She burrowed closer in his arms. He rested his hand against the small of her back. They moved in a sensuous haze around the room, slowing with each turn, until they were no longer dancing but standing in the middle of the floor, swaying together. Now, their arms embraced each other, any semblance to a waltz lost to their enjoyment of each other. Other dancers continued to circle around the edges of the dance floor, ignoring the couple wrapped in a close embrace.

Jesse unlocked the hands resting at the lower curve of her spine and ran them up her sides. When his thumbs came to the swell of her breasts, he could feel the sharp intake of her breath. She didn't draw away. Encouraged, he continued his gentle exploration. Stroking the undersides of her breasts, he moved the pads of his thumbs upward and over the taut nipples.

A moan escaped from between her lips, and he bent down to capture it with his own.

Clutching at the back of his neck she wove her fingers into the curls, pulling him deeper into the kiss.

Jesse's body burned every place their bodies met. They couldn't be any closer with their clothes on. This soft and sexy Rachel was a revelation.

Moving his knee between her legs, Jesse felt her brazenly rub her center against his thigh. He danced them both in a small tight circle lifting his leg slightly higher with each step to increase the pressure. Fire spread up into his groin from the point where her feminine warmth touched his leg, causing that part of him to throb and pulse. He felt himself growing in size, pushing against the buttons of his jeans. With each bend and straightening of his leg, he rubbed against her silk-covered sex, until he was looking around frantically for an exit.

From the very first moment he'd met her, he'd been attracted to this woman with the reserved smile and melting eyes. Her sensuality simmered just below the surface, and he knew he was the man who could unleash it to its full glory. But instead of a suave and calculating seduction, he found himself losing hold of his control. He wanted to throw her down on the dance floor and bury himself inside her there in front of God and Kendalia.

Thankfully, the song's slow beat came to an end, and they reluctantly broke apart, breathless. Standing on the dance floor, hands clasped with hers, he gazed into her eyes for long seconds before the band started up another lively beat, breaking the tenuous accord he had discovered in her arms.

Jesse wanted, more than anything, to whisk Rachel away from the dancehall and make mad, passionate love to her. But he hadn't gotten so far in the business world without trusting his gut. And it was telling him to take it slow, or he'd scare her away.

This woman was well worth fighting for, and if it took a long, slow battle, so be it. He was in it for the long haul. This woman would be the one he'd grow old with, his partner in life and the mother of his children

.

CHAPTER 8

RACHEL LET JESSE lead her back to their table. They sat close together, not speaking. Her hand still rested in his, and she felt awkward. Although she wanted to pull her hand from his and put about a foot of space between them, she was also oddly reluctant to break the contact. So, she sat there quietly, while Jesse rubbed his thumb slowly over her knuckles.

The beer finally made its way to her bladder, and Rachel reluctantly excused herself, her hand cooling without the warmth of Jesse's holding it.

In the crowded restroom, she stared at the stranger in the mirror with wildly tangled hair and cheeks pink with excitement. She finger-combed her hair back into some semblance of order and splashed water over her cheeks. Her belly still thrummed with tension.

Closing her eyes, she imagined herself back in his arms, and as near to an orgasm as she'd ever come. It wasn't fair the only man who could light a fire in her was one she couldn't have. He was a client. Strictly hands off.

Rachel opened her eyes and stared down at hands that

had been all over the man's upper body. So much for hands remaining off. Still, she refused to be one of Jesse's many conquests. She had to shake this attraction. She could see no future in it.

Straightening her shoulders, Rachel pushed the door open to return to their table. After the brighter lights of the bathroom, her eyes took a moment to adjust to the darkened dance hall. Keeping gaze down to weave through the tables, chairs and guests, Rachel made her way back to their table. She didn't notice the woman draped across Jesse's lap until she nearly sat on her.

"Whoa there." The bottle-blonde steadied her with a hand, and Rachel stared at it, then at Jesse.

"Rachel, I'd like you to meet Pauline." Jesse said it so casually, Rachel's head jerked up in disbelief.

Her mouth tightened to prevent the words she really wanted to say. Rachel glared at Jesse.

The jerk had the nerve to grin back at her. She watched him place his hands under the woman's buttocks to scoot her off his lap.

That move was enough for Rachel. Turning on her heels, she found the nearest exit and walked out into the sultry night air. *I knew it! The man's a low-down womanizer. He couldn't limit himself to one woman if he tried.*

She walked the length of the parking lot, avoiding the door she'd exited on the off chance he managed to disentangle himself from the blonde octopus. Rachel didn't want to speak to him ever again, which worked well with her plan to fight her attraction to him. As far as she was concerned, the blonde drunk could have him and the horse he rode in on!

"Well, well, well...hic...whaddawehavehere?"

Rachel screeched in alarm, when an arm snaked around

her waist and pulled her into the concave chest of one of the skinniest men she'd ever seen.

"Let go of me," she demanded, pushing her hands ineffectually against him.

"Lemmejusshavealittlekiss." The thin, grizzled man closed his eyes and aimed his puckered lips at hers.

"Eeeeeuw!" Shoving hard against him, she stomped against his instep. His mouth continued downward, and she strained to lean farther back, trying to stay away from his fetid breath.

Rachel didn't doubt he was a fairly harmless old drunk, and she really didn't want to hurt him, But she wasn't about to let those lips anywhere near her person—no matter how much alcohol he had disinfected his mouth with.

"Now, Snake, you need to let the lady go," Jesse's voice cut through Rachel's distress. "Pauline's been looking for you."

"Huh? WhosPauline?"

"Your *wife*, Snake." Placing an arm loosely around his shoulder, he steered Snake, Rachel and all, around to face the dancehall. "You know, you might want to ask one of the designated drivers to give you both a ride home. Pauline's had a little too much to drink, too."

"Mywife? Hic...yesIbetterdothat." Snake let go of Rachel abruptly and tipped his non-existent hat to her. "Youhaveagoodeveningmiss."

Rachel's fascinated gaze followed him as he weaved drunkenly toward the door of the dancehall.

"Yes, sir. Snake's a medical miracle," Jesse said, with admiration in his voice.

Rachel turned to look at him questioningly.

"I'd bet his blood-alcohol level would melt a Breathalyzer if he got pulled over by the county sheriff."

Rachel smiled, until she remembered something he had just said. "Pauline is his wife? You played patty-cakes with that poor man's wife?" she asked, raising her brows.

"Now, Rachel..." His hands extended toward her shoulders, but she batted them away.

"Don't you *Now Rachel* me. I know what I saw. That woman's ass has your fingerprints all over it."

"Rachel, she had a few too many. I can't help she fell into my lap saying hello."

"Well I'm saying goodbye." She turned from him but only got one step when a firm hand on her shoulder spun her about.

"You don't really mean that." His arms came around her, trapping hers at her sides.

"Now you can read my mind?" She scowled at him. "Of all the unmitigated gall. Why can't you take no for an answer?"

"I haven't asked a question. Jesus, what burr got up under your saddle?"

"You!"

"Not yet, I haven't."

She got no more warning than that. His mouth sealed hers, cutting off any further argument. Not that she would have been able to form a coherent sentence.

His arms relaxed, though they didn't release her.

Rachel's moved of their own accord, sliding eagerly around his back to pull him closer.

Large, work-calloused hands found the curves of her backside and squeezed.

She nearly came apart. Standing on tiptoe, she couldn't get close enough.

The screech of tires as a car peeled out of the parking lot, broke through their sensual haze.

Rachel dragged her lips from his and backed away within the circle of his arms, panting. She couldn't meet his gaze, but felt his lips against her forehead in a feather-light caress.

Jesse drew in a deep breath and stepped back. He took her hand and led her back inside the dancehall to their table where they sat beside each other in silence.

Rachel didn't know what was going through his mind, but hers was scrambled.

How could she keep falling into his arms when he was nothing but a womanizer? All the tabloids said so. Every week, a new lady graced his arm, smiling up at him as he grinned down at her. How could Rachel compete with that? How did he rack up so many women?

Because he's damn good at it, that's how.

The man was gorgeous, sexy and, based on his performance in the parking lot, a knight in shining armor—not to mention a helluva kisser. What was not to like? That was the crux of the matter. Jesse made it impossible for her to hate him. Rachel felt like she was up against a wall, tussling with her conscience in a losing battle.

Genie and Vinnie gave her conscience a reprieve when they collapsed onto the opposite bench.

"Why aren't you two dancing?" Genie wiped sweat from her brow with a napkin.

"We were enjoying watching you two," Rachel said with a strained smile. Although Rachel had set out to seduce Vinnie, she really was glad to see how well Genie was getting along with him. He was very different from Genie's usual dates, but surprisingly they had a lot in common. Both were from large families, both had a blatant disregard for formality, and both seemed to enjoy each other immensely.

Rachel couldn't feel bad for the way the evening had turned out for Genie. She deserved someone special in her life. And Rachel couldn't imagine sharing sex with Vinnie, however handsome he was.

She stole a glance at Jesse while he wasn't looking. Comparing him to Vinnie, she had to admit her tastes ran to blond-haired, blue-eyed men more so than dark Italians.

Hell. Her *plan* was becoming more complicated by the minute. She was embarrassed at how wantonly she had responded to Jesse. But knowing Jesse's reputation, he likely didn't think it was anything out of the ordinary. She would just have to pretend it wasn't special to her, either.

When they finally left Kendalia Dancehall, Rachel's ears were ringing from the continuous noise.

Genie climbed into the back seat, insisting she was shorter than Rachel, and she didn't mind at all. Rachel knew her eagerness had everything to do with the fact that the handsome Italian was already back there.

Suddenly feeling shy with Jesse, Rachel allowed him to hand her into the passenger seat, but she remained stiff and aloof all the way home. It was as if the safety of numbers had been stripped from her, and her attraction to the man sitting beside her was exposed for anyone to see.

She didn't want to examine her feelings just yet. They were too new and tender to subject to close scrutiny. So, she sat in silence, her hands folded neatly in her lap, actively fighting her growing awareness of the man sitting next to her.

Since it was on their way, they dropped Vinnie at his home a couple of blocks from the family deli. Genie waved from the back seat then sat in a dreamy silence the rest of the way to their apartment building. Getting out first, Jesse held the door to the truck open for Rachel and Genie, then walked them to their apartments. Genie opened her door, and turned to wink at Jesse and Rachel.

"Don't do anything I wouldn't do," she said before closing the door behind her.

Alone with Jesse for the second time that night, Rachel fumbled with her key, hurrying to unlock her door, only to feel Jesse's hand close over hers, stilling her attempts.

"Rachel."

Refusing to look up, Rachel stared dumbly at her hand encased in his.

"Look at me, Rachel." Jesse placed his free hand under her chin and gently turned her face up to his. "I want to thank you for a magical evening," he whispered.

Rachel watched as his lips moved slowly toward hers. There were no words she could utter to stop him, when her lips longed for his. She surrendered herself to his embrace.

There was always tomorrow to strengthen her resolve and get back on track. For now, she closed her eyes, ignored her rule, forgot her plan, and lost herself in his kiss.

JESSE POPPED the tops off two longneck beers, handed one to Gage and collapsed on the sofa in his friend's living room.

"This better be good. I was about to hit the sack." Gage lounged in his leather recliner, surrounded by boxes and packing paper. He tipped his beer and downed half of it in one long gulp.

"Sorry to keep you up, but I saw the light on, and I, well,

I needed an ear to bend." Jesse drank a long swallow then leaned his head back, closing his eyes.

"I'm listening," Gage said. "Wasn't tonight your double-date with Rachel and her friend?"

"Yeah." Jesse tensed, his body humming at the memory of the kiss he'd shared with Rachel in front of her apartment.

"Based on the fact you're here and not in her bed, my guess is she wouldn't have anything to do with you." Gage took another pull at his beer, a smile tugging at his lips." He swallowed and raised his brows. "Am I right?"

Jesse shook his head, staring down at the bottle in his hand. "No."

Gage leaned forward, a frown pushing his brows lower. "No? Then why the hell are you here and not with her?"

Jesse drew in a long breath and let it out slowly. "I really should be back home under an icy cold shower. The woman has me tied in knots."

"What exactly *did* happen?" Gage drank the last of his beer and set the bottle on the end table beside him.

"Her date liked her friend better, leaving Rachel to me. I took them to the Kendalia Dancehall. We danced, had a good time and I left her at her door with just a kiss."

Gage stared at him as if he'd grown a shiny new horn. "What am I hearing? She didn't invite you in for the night? Are you losing your touch?"

"I didn't hang around long enough for her to take that step."

"Why?"

"Rachel's different than any other woman I've ever been with. She's beautiful."

"You've been with beautiful women."

"I know." Jesse shoved a hand through his hair. "She's sexy."

"You've been with sexy women," Gage pointed out.

"She's sexy in a different way. Rachel doesn't know she's sexy. She wears these business-like suits." He set his beer on the coffee table and curved his hands in the shape of Rachel's hips. "Hell, she doesn't even know how sexy she is in those damned silky skirts and pantsuits."

"Okay, you have a thing for pantsuits. So?"

"And she's smart."

"Smart enough not to go after you?"

Jesse glanced up. "That's what I'm afraid of. I don't want to push her too hard. She might run the other direction. On the other hand, I don't want her to think I'm only interested in a one-night stand."

"Do you love her?"

Jesse nodded. "I do. And I don't want to screw this up."

Gage grunted. "Then you're doing the right thing. I don't claim to know how a woman thinks. Hell, you don't see me engaged or anything. Take it slow. Wear her down by being around. Feed that Jordan charm to her a little at a time. She'll come around. They always do."

Gage was right. Jesse had to take it slow. He had to show Rachel he was serious and willing to wait until she figured it out for herself that Jesse Jordan was the only man for her.

CHAPTER 9

"WELL, THANKS A LOT, RACHEL."

Sitting across the table from Genie, Rachel gave her friend a confused look. "Thanks for what?"

Genie crossed her arms over her chest and narrowed her eyes. "For stealing my date Saturday night."

"Stealing...oh." Rachel had the grace to blush. "I'm sorry. You were having such a good time with Vinnie, I thought I would dance with Jesse to keep him out of your way."

"You call what you were doing dancing? I would call that sex to music."

At just that moment, a man walked by their table his eyebrows raised.

Genie winked at him and grinned as he passed, then continued her teasing. "Really, Rachel, it does my heart good to see you behaving with such wild abandon. I didn't think you had it in you."

"Thanks for the vote of confidence, Genie," Rachel declared flatly.

"No, really. It's about time you learned how to cut loose."

Rachel chose not to comment, instead, launching her own attack. "Speaking of stealing dates, what's up with you and Vinnie?"

"Well..uh...nothing, I guess."

It was Genie's turn to blush. This had to be the first time since they had been friends that Rachel had ever seen Genie blushing and at a loss for words.

Rachel tilted her head as she stared at her friend. "Genie, are you falling for Vinnie?"

"I don't know." Gina shrugged. "We just kinda hit it off. You know, both coming from large Catholic families and all. We actually had something in common."

Rachel reached across the table and touched her friend's hand. "Well, I think that's great."

Genie leaned forward eagerly. "You do? You mean you aren't still interested in Vinnie as a possible candidate for your plan?"

"Not in the least."

Genie released a big breath that billowed her cheeks. "That's wonderful. But what about you? Any possibilities between you and Jesse?"

Rachel paused before answering Genie. She groaned inwardly. What could she say? There was some unusual chemistry between them. If the circumstances were any different, she would say there were definite possibilities.

Her lips still burned from his kisses. She'd been mindless by the time he had peeled himself away from her.

He had twisted the key in the lock of her door and all but shoved her into her apartment, before mumbling a quick goodnight and turning on his heels to leave. Gradually coming to her senses, she was grateful he had called a halt to their lovemaking. She couldn't have.

Realizing Genie was staring at her and expecting a

response, Rachel gathered her wits and opened her day planner. Sometimes, she felt as if her day planner was her only link back to reality. It was her security blanket, and she felt naked without it. "I don't mix business with my personal life. There's no way I can get involved with Jesse. End of subject."

Genie shook her head. "Rachel, remind me again why you want a baby."

Closing her day planner, she stared out the window of the café. People passed by in the street and seconds slipped by before Rachel answered. "I want someone I can love, and who will love me back, unconditionally. Is that too much to ask?"

Turning back to Genie, Rachel tried to explain. "Too often, I've watched people marry someone because they admired certain things about them. After they were married, those things they admired before they married become the same things they want to change in them afterward."

Genie grimaced. "Tell me about it. You don't even have to be married for that to happen."

"I want the kind of love from someone who accepts you for who you are, not who they want you to be. I'm not going to change for anybody. A baby loves you from day one, no changes required." Dropping her gaze to her hands, Rachel added, "I also need someone I can love."

"Rachel, not all relationships go bad. Why do you think you can't have that kind of love with a man?"

Immediately, the image of Jesse came into Rachel's mind. What would it be like to love him and be loved by him? How long would it last? He was a beautiful, sexy man with his choice of equally beautiful, sexy women. If she let herself love him, how would she feel when it was all over?

No, it was much smarter never to risk that kind of heartbreak. "That's fairytale stuff...you know, that happily-ever-after thing. I don't believe in it."

"But Rachel, what about your parents? Their marriage lasted until the day they died."

"I know, but it just didn't seem like a very fulfilling relationship."

"What do you mean?"

"For heaven's sakes, I never once saw them kiss."

"Good grief, Rachel. They had to have had some kind of affection for each other, otherwise you wouldn't be here."

Rachel shuddered at the mental picture that came to mind. Leave it to Genie to always say it exactly like she saw it. "Logically, I know that, but I just can't picture them making love when they never even held hands in front of me. I always thought they'd just grown too comfortable with each other to divorce. They stayed together out of habit, rather than love."

"Oh, Rachel. Did you ever think that it might just be a generational thing? Like, maybe your parents just didn't believe in displaying affection in front of others—-even their own child. It could be as simple as that. And Rachel, you don't have to be like that, and you don't have to marry a man like that."

"Genie, I'm so much like my parents, I'm afraid I'll choose someone I'd only be comfortable with and not realize it until it's too late. I don't want that. Besides, I've already made up my mind." Rachel picked up her day planner and shoved it into her purse. "I don't want to get married. I want a child, and it *will* happen according to my plan. Jesse is business and, as such, off limits to me."

"I give up. Your head is as hard as a plank." Genie

heaved a huge sigh. "Okay, have it your way. Who's next on your list of possibilities?"

"Marion Hohenberger."

"The Muscle Mouse guy?" she asked, her eyes rounding.

"That's the one."

"Are you going on a date with him?"

"Not really a date." Rachel hesitated. "I've kind of arranged to meet him at his health spa tomorrow after work."

"Are you going out on a date from there?"

Rachel squirmed in her chair. "No, he wants me to work out with him."

Genie's eyebrows shot upward. "You've got to be kidding. Work out? This will be priceless. That man probably works out in his sleep. I hope you don't plan to try to keep up with him."

"No, I don't," Rachel leaned forward. "But I do need your help."

"Well, what are friends for? What do you need?"

"Clothes."

"Clothes?"

"Workout clothes. I don't have time to go shopping, and I need something that looks nice to wear to a fitness club. Do you have anything like that?"

"Boy, do I." Genie grinned. "I've got just the thing for you."

THE NEXT DAY, Rachel got out of her car and groaned. "I can't believe I let you talk me into wearing this thing. I really should have known better," Rachel lamented, pulling the strap of the thong out of the crack between the cheeks of her buttocks.

Genie rounded the vehicle form the passenger side. "Rachel, this is what they wear to these places. Trust me." She wasn't even attempting to disguise her glee at Rachel's expense. Standing outside the door to the Royal Academy Health Spa, she grinned from ear to ear at Rachel's discomfort.

"You don't have to enjoy this so much, you know," Rachel grumbled.

"Oh, but I do. Besides, you look fabulous."

She didn't feel fabulous. She felt like a sausage stuffed into a tight casing. If there was a lump to be found on her body, it would be emphasized by the shiny black bicycle pants. The matching sports bra squashed her average-sized breasts down to what appeared to be training-bra material.

The worse thing about the outfit was the bright neon green thong she wore on the outside of the bicycle pants. She still hadn't figured out what that was all about. Never having worn one in her life, Rachel was left wondering how women in exotic dance clubs could stand it. She was very uncomfortable and self-conscious about the whole thing. *I guess that's why I am an ad executive and not a stripper.*

"Don't worry, you look just fine," Genie encouraged. "Besides, I'll be showing up in a few minutes to back you up. Not that I think your muscleman would try anything in a place like this."

"It isn't that I think he'll try anything; I'd just like to have a second opinion. That's why I wanted you to come along."

"Well, I'll be there before you know it, and I am loaded with opinion, none of which you'd care to listen to right now."

Ignoring Genie's last remark, Rachel took a deep breath. "Well, here I go. Cross your fingers."

Rachel pushed through the door and marched up to the reception desk to ask for Marion Hohenberger. Much to Rachel's chagrin, the receptionist keyed a microphone and paged him over the loudspeaker. The announcement drew every eye to the embarrassed woman standing at the desk in the ridiculous outfit.

While she waited for Marion to appear, she glanced curiously around at the busy establishment.

Teal wall-to-wall carpeting, mirrored walls and rows of training apparatus—most of which Rachel could only guess at their function—filled the large open space. And the people! Tanned, oiled and firm male and female bodies moved confidently from one contraption to the next.

Rachel felt flabby, but was reassured that at least she was dressed appropriately. That helped, only slightly, to ease her tension.

Then Marion appeared on the other side of the huge room, moving toward her like a linebacker, his sheer size incredibly intimidating. His arms didn't hang at his sides, instead, they curved away from the excessive muscles around his ribcage. He wore a wife-beater tank top, which only covered a fourth of the smooth, oiled skin on his hairless chest. On the lower half of his body, he wore a pair of running shorts, which no doubt barely covered his tight ass.

Marion came to a looming halt in front of her, his gaze raking over her, traveling from head to toe before he spoke. "Welcome to the Royal Academy Health Spa. Our motto here is *We'll have you in shape in no time.*"

His high, nasal voice certainly didn't improve in person, and it didn't go with the rest of his Mr. Universe physique. It grated on Rachel's ears as much as it had when she'd seen him on the video.

Well, she wasn't here for his voice.

She stuck out her hand. "Hi, I'm Rachel Taylor. I believe we have an appointment."

He took her hand in his meaty grip. "I assume you signed up for the long-term plan by the looks of the droop of your gluteus maximus."

"What?" Rachel jerked her hand free, blushing furiously. "I'm Rachel Taylor...from the dating service."

Comprehension dawned on his face like a light coming on in a dimly lit room. "Ah, yes...Rachel." He reached for her hand again, squeezing until her knuckles popped.

As soon as he loosened his grip, she pulled it quickly from his grasp, shaking it to get the feeling back.

He continued without noticing her pained expression. "Let me start over. I'm Marion Hohenberger, but you can call me Marion. I'm sorry, I thought you were a client for a minute there. Thank you for coming here for our first meeting. I have to work tonight, but we can get to know each in between showing clients the ropes."

"Oh, I didn't realize you had to work. If you'd like, we could reschedule for a more convenient time." Rachel felt a moment's relief for the reprieve, but was immediately disappointed.

"No, really, if you don't mind hanging around, I'll get a break in an hour, and we can go to the juice bar and get to know each other."

"Well, if you're sure," she said, wishing he'd taken her up on the chance to reschedule—not that she would.

"I'm sure. Now, will you excuse me for a moment, I need to see to these customers."

Rachel was ready to strengthen her excuses and escape when Genie stepped through the door...followed by Jesse.

Rachel's breath caught in her throat, and her body

hummed to life. This was unexpected. Genie had failed to mention that she planned on bringing Jesse. It was one thing for Genie to participate in this interview, or date, or whatever you would call it, but to have Jesse there to witness Rachel's humiliation, was just too much.

Stepping to the side, Marion greeted the couple as they reached the receptionist's desk. "Hello, I'm Marion Hohen-berger. I'm the owner and general manager of the Royal Academy Health Spa. I take it that you haven't been here before. Would you like a tour of our facilities?"

Jesse smiled broadly at Rachel, who stood behind Marion glaring at them.

Why hadn't Genie told her she was bringing Jesse? Her frown deepened. His very presence irritated her in some way or another, like a persistent itch. What was Genie up to, including him on each of her dates? If her friend insisted on dragging Jesse along each time, she'd have to reconsider bringing Genie. Her mission was humiliating enough without having him as a witness.

Rachel could feel Jesse's gaze traveling over her skin. She raised her arms self-consciously to her bare midriff to shield it from his view.

"Yes, we would really like to see what you have," Genie answered with a wicked grin.

"Then please follow us," Marion said, motioning for Rachel to join them.

She was forced to go along with the tour instead of hanging back at the receptionist's desk, as she'd hoped.

She listened with only half her attention as Marion launched into a sales pitch describing the facilities, classes and professional instruction available.

Stopping in front of a piece of machinery, Marion introduced it by its technical name and explained its use.

"This particular machine is designed to strengthen the biceps, triceps and latissimus dorsi."

"Just where are the biceps, triceps and the lata-whats-it? I'm sure you know *all* that stuff." Genie smiled innocently and batted her eyes at the hulk.

Responding to the obvious flattery, Marion straightened his shoulders, pushing his massive chest out even farther, like a peacock strutting his feathers. "Miss Taylor, would you mind demonstrating?"

"Who, me?" Rachel squeaked. "I've never seen this machine before in my life. How could I possibly demonstrate how to use it?"

"It's easy. Please, take a seat, and I'll walk you through the steps."

Already self-conscious about her attire, sitting in front of Marion and Jesse didn't make Rachel feel any better. Straddling the cushioned seat, she sat facing the threesome, refusing to meet their gazes. "Now what?" she said, with little enthusiasm.

"Raise your arms parallel with the ground and place them behind the cushioned arms of the machine, holding the handles like so."

Marion moved her hands to the handgrips on the apparatus. "The latissimus dorsi are the muscles over the upper ribcage." Marion touched Rachel's side, frowning when she jerked her arm downward in reaction. He replaced her hand on the handgrip and pointed to the top of her upper arm, this time not actually touching her. "This is the bicep." Moving his hand below her arm, he flicked the skin under it and watched as it barely swayed back and forth. "That is the tricep. This machine will help to tighten the...for lack of a technical term...jiggly stuff," he said, winking at Genie.

Blushing furiously, Rachel's lips tightened, but she held her tongue.

Unaware of any injury to Rachel's pride, Marion continued the demonstration. "Now, I will set the weights to give just the right amount of resistance for her current ability. We don't want to overdo it on the first visit, do we?"

Leaning down, he adjusted the weight settings to the least number of pounds it would carry. "There. Now, push your arms together in front of your face."

Marion made the desired motion with his arms to show her how.

Rachel strained against the cushioned levers.

"That's right, only do it slowly. Now you've got it. You'll need to start with ten repetitions per set. As you increase your strength, you will increase the number of sets and the number of repetitions per set."

As RACHEL PUSHED her arms in, then let the machine swing them back out, Jesse watched her breasts squeeze together, then relax. Squeeze together, then relax. Squeeze together, then relax. Good grief, just watching Rachel exercise was turning him on. He shifted to stand behind Genie to hide his growing arousal. He began sweating as he watched Rachel complete her ten repetitions.

"Is that it?" Rachel asked, a fine sheen of moisture beginning to gather on her forehead.

"That's all for this machine," he said, patting it as if it were a favorite pet. "Let's move on to the next one."

"Yes, please, I want to see more," Jesse agreed enthusiastically, although unsure of how much more he could take.

Marion already had his back to her and was walking to

the next machine. They followed, Genie behind Marion, Rachel behind Genie, and Jesse behind Rachel. And what a behind she had. Jesse enjoyed watching her hips sway side to side, emphasized by the tight black bicycle pants and the neon green thong. Imagining the same hips swaying, with only the little green instrument of torture, almost made him turn around to leave before he really embarrassed himself.

"Rachel, please stand here next to the apparatus. This machine is designed to strengthen and tone the muscles of the calf...," Marion gestured toward Rachel's calf, "...thigh...," he pointed to her thigh, "...and the gluteus maximus..." With one large hand, he grabbed the closest cheek of her buttocks and patted it firmly. Rachel's jaw fell, her eyes grew wide and her face flamed in embarrassment.

Jesse took a step forward ready to challenge Marion's hand on Rachel's bottom. Before he could say anything, Marion had gone on with his monologue, once again unaware of any insult inflicted.

"We can't have our backsides continuing to jiggle when we have stopped, now can we?" He looked at Rachel pointedly, then turned to smile at his clients.

"No we can't, can we, dear?" Genie played her part to the hilt, amusement dancing in her eyes. "Such a shame to let oneself get in such bad shape. Tsk, tsk."

Jesse watched the fire burn in Rachel's eyes, as she glared at Genie.

"I must agree with you. It goes along with that pay me now, pay later saying, if you know what I mean," Rachel gritted out, with a saccharine-sweet smile, placing emphasis on the *pay later* part.

"Oh, please, Mr. Muscle Man," Genie walked up to

Marion, "Can I touch them?" Her hand hovered over his chest.

Marion frowned. "What?"

"Your gorgeous muscles, silly." Genie smiled up at him, batting her eyelashes again.

Curving his arms inward and bunching his fists, he struck one of those muscleman contest poses and encouraged Genie to touch. "Go ahead, they won't break."

"Ooooo, they look so smooth and soft, but they're as hard as a rock," Genie cooed.

Jesse watched Genie with amusement, turning just in time to catch Rachel rolling her eyes in disgust. When he grinned at her, she shrugged and smiled back. God, she looked good in that little thing she wore—every curve exposed. Of course, all he really wanted to do was to tear it off and see the rest of her delectable skin. But he knew he still had his work cut out for him, if he was going to convince her to go out with him.

Genie had told him she refused to date her clients. If he hadn't already contracted for advertising through her firm, he would have backed out of the deal. He was stuck with it and had to figure out a way to talk her into breaking one of her own rules.

The demonstration continued to each and every piece of equipment to include the exercise bicycle, cross-country ski machine and treadmill. Rachel was a good sport and in fairly good condition, but Jesse could tell she wasn't used to all the different forms of exercise. By the time Marion completed his tour, she was looking somewhat wilted and moving stiffly.

"Well, Marion, thank you for the grand tour of the spa. I was very impressed by your facility and especially by your personal attention to our needs," Genie gushed.

"Would you care to join us at O'Malley's for a nightcap?"

Jesse invited both Rachel and Marion.

"No, thank you. I don't drink alcoholic beverages," Marion quickly refused.

"Well, I do." Rachel jumped on the invitation as an excuse to escape. "Thank you for a lovely evening, Marion." Rachel shook his hand vigorously. "I'll call you."

"But, I thought you were going to join me for a veggie drink..." Marion whined in his mousy voice.

"Maybe another time. But thanks for the workout. I'll never forget it." She rolled her shoulders and winced.

Rachel followed Jesse and Genie as they exited the Royal Academy Health Spa. Just outside the door, Genie and Jesse stopped and turned toward Rachel.

"Well? Are you coming with us to O'Malley's?" Jesse asked, fully expecting a negative reply.

"You weren't kidding?" Rachel's shoulders sagged.

"Oh, Rachel, you go on home. You look all worn out." Then hooking her arm in Jesse's, she smiled and goaded, "I'll catch a ride home with Jesse."

Jesse watched as Rachel appeared to hesitate. Looking from him to Genie and back to him again, she squared her shoulders and took a deep breath.

"I'll go, too," she answered resolutely.

"Oh no, really Rachel, you shouldn't feel like you have to tag along. It'll give me some time alone with Jesse." Genie leaned into Jesse's side and smiled up at him. "Right, Jesse?"

A little slow on the uptake, Jesse finally caught on and smiled down into Genie's eyes. "That's right, Genie." Then looking over to Rachel. "You look a little worse for wear, Rachel. You should go home and get some rest."

Rachel's lips thinned into a straight line. "I'm fine. Just fine. But if you two would rather be alone, I can take the hint." Spinning on her heel, she marched to her car and spun out of the parking lot like a horse with a burr under its saddle.

"Think she might be just a little bit jealous?" Jesse asked hopefully, continuing to watch as Rachel's car drove out of sight.

Reaching behind him, Genie swatted his butt and smiled. "You bet your gluteus maximus, cowboy."

CHAPTER 10

WHAT A DISASTER! Rachel sat at her kitchen table with her head in her hands. It was bad enough she'd been used as a human guinea pig to demonstrate the use of all that exercise equipment. Having Jesse there to gloat over her humiliation had been the worse part. She needed to have a talk with Genie. Bringing him along had been a lousy trick to play on your so-called best friend.

Tired and depressed, Rachel had arrived home the previous evening not feeling too bad for all the unusual exercise. It wasn't until about halfway through the next day at work that her muscles began to stiffen, and it was all she could do to get home.

Now, she sat at her kitchen table reviewing notes in her day planner, wondering if she shouldn't just give up the whole idea of selecting her own sperm donor. Hell, she should go ahead and give up all thoughts of having a baby for that matter. The way she felt after last night's exercise, she couldn't imagine having enough energy to keep up with a little one. How did mothers do it?

Gingerly stretching her arms above her head, Rachel

groaned. She had never realized how many muscles she had in her body. Now, she could tell where each and every one was, not just because of the anatomy lessons given by Muscle Man Marion last night, but more so because they all hurt.

Glancing again at her day planner, she noted her dwindling list of dating service candidates. Scratch Vinnie— Genie seemed to like him better than she did. Scratch Marion the Muscle Man. Rachel didn't have the energy and desire to try to keep up with that man. She couldn't imagine what sort of sexual gymnastics he would expect. That left Plug Man.

The more she thought about Genie's comments about uprooting his hair, the more Rachel had to admit she would have a hard time looking him square in the eyes without busting out laughing. Scratch Plug Man.

Drawing a line through the name of the last candidate on her list, Rachel made a note on the next day in her calendar. *Find a sperm donor.* She would just have to play Russian Roulette at the sperm bank and hope for the best. She didn't have the time to personally find the perfect donor for her baby.

Taking out the yellow pages, she flipped through it until she found the section listing physicians and specialists. Finding an entire page dedicated to fertility specialists, she circled a few and jotted the numbers down in her notebook. She would make those calls tomorrow to locate a fertility specialist and ultimately a sperm bank.

Unbidden images of Jesse popped into her head. What pretty babies he would make. He was from a large family, so chances were he would be potent, too. If only she didn't like him so much. Jesse's interest in her was apparent, and she knew she could entice him into an intimate relationship. But it would end. She admitted to herself she wasn't sure she would come away whole when he eventually moved on to the next flavor of the month.

And she wouldn't feel right tricking him into giving her a baby. As a matter of fact, she was having second thoughts about doing that to anyone. She had just been fooling herself into thinking she was the type to love 'em and leave 'em after she had what she wanted. It wasn't in her nature.

Discouraged, Rachel rose stiffly from her chair. She found pain relievers and washed them down with water, hoping for a little relief. Maybe a hot bath would help to ease the ache in her muscles.

Too tired to care about the mess, she left a trail of clothing as she headed for the bathroom. She filled the tub with water as hot as she could stand it and added a little bubble bath. Stepping gingerly into the tub, she eased her abused body into the piping-hot water, laid back and closed her eyes.

"Ahhhhh...I've died and gone to heaven."

The hot water soaked into her tired muscles helping Rachel relax. She grabbed a bottle of scented bath salts and sprinkled them liberally into the water around her, filling the air with the scent of jasmine.

As her muscles relaxed, her mind drifted. The first thing her roving thoughts focused on were images of Jesse. Jesse at the photo studio. Jesse surrounded by Italians at the Fetachelli Deli. Jesse holding her close at the Kendalia Dancehall. Her breasts tingled remembering the feel of his chest against hers as they danced.

Raising her hand, she brushed the tips of her breasts, imagining him rubbing them roughly with his calloused fingertips as he had while they'd danced. Her pulse quickened and desire surged through her veins, causing an ache that went deeper than the soreness in her muscles, and was sure to last much longer.

What was she going to do about him? Every time she tried to move forward with her plan, he showed up, distracting her from her course. And what a distraction. Oy!

She wondered what it would be like to make love with him. Not that she should consider it for even a moment. Would he be rough or gentle? Jack-hammer fast or sensuously slow?

Her body ached for an entirely different reason. She had to remind herself that rules were important. Rules kept away the chaos. A relationship with Jesse simply would not do. But her traitorous mind couldn't help wishing for just one night.

He certainly wouldn't do for her plan. Jesse didn't strike her as someone who would love 'em and leave 'em, if that meant leaving 'em pregnant. But if she were to get pregnant with Jesse's child, what a beautiful child it would be, with those blond curls and gorgeous blue eyes. It was too bad she knew him and liked him. It would have been much easier if she could have picked him out of a catalog at a sperm bank. She needed to remain unemotional and detached from the prospective donor to ensure there would be no hard feelings and no strings attached to her child.

Enough of Jesse, already! Logic kept slipping to the side of her thoughts as she pictured Jesse in the soft lights of the dancehall, his leg rising between hers and his hand resting on the curve of her rear. Groaning, she slid her head beneath the water, hoping to cleanse her hair and her thoughts with the water.

"Rachel!"

Lunging into a sitting position, water splashing over the edge of the tub, Rachel sputtered and gasped, her heart beating at ninety-to-nothing against her ribcage until she recognized Genie as the person standing in the bathroom.

"Genie! Don't do that! You scared the bejeezus out of me!"

"Not nearly as much as you scared them out of me." Genie looked equally as stunned as Rachel, a hand pressed to her chest. "I came over to bum a razorblade off you, and I find you drowning yourself in your bath tub. Let me tell you, girl, you scared a year off my life."

Rachel ducked down to make sure her body was covered in bubbles and glared. "Did you ever hear of knocking?"

"I did. You never answered, so I let myself in with my spare key. I figured if you were out, you wouldn't mind if I stole a disposable razor."

"You know I don't mind. Look in the cabinet under the sink."

Searching in the cabinet, Genie found what she was looking for and straightened. Her gaze returned to study Rachel's face. "So, what's with the drowning scene? Let me tell you, no man is worth that. I've already thought of it and discarded it as a waste of my time."

Blushing, Rachel tried to think of a good reason for her actions, besides the truth. "I wasn't trying to drown myself. I was...uh...washing my hair."

"Wrong. You might as well fess up. You're a terrible liar, Rachel. What's really on your mind?"

Shrugging and sinking lower in the water, she gave Genie a sheepish look. "Would you believe I was trying to wash a man right out of my hair?"

Genie's mouth stretched into a small smile. "Now, that

sounds like a plausible excuse or a really old song." Closing the lid to the toilet, Genie sat down on it, making herself comfortable. "Let me guess, it wouldn't have been one sexy cowboy, would it?"

The heat searing Rachel's cheeks and neck had to be a dead giveaway.

"Now, why would you want to do that?" Genie asked. "The man is so delicious you could eat him."

"I told you—"

"You don't mix your business with personal life," Genie finished for her. "I have a much better motto you should adopt—*Rules are meant to be broken.* Especially when the rule has to do with someone as gorgeous as Jesse. Rachel, if you don't go for it, you're a fool."

"Thanks for the vote of confidence. I just can't do it, though. Jesse is too nice a guy for me to use in my plan."

"Really, Rachel, you should scrap this plan and come up with a new one. One that includes the usual trappings of having children. One that starts with wedding vows to love, honor and cherish, until death us do part."

Rachel lifted her chin and shook her head. "We've been over this before, Genie. My mind is made up. Jesse is out of the question. Besides, Jesse may be good baby-making material, but he's not husband material."

"Says who? Sometimes you can be so hard-headed." Standing, Genie moved toward the door of the bathroom, stopping as she stood in its frame to glance back at Rachel, still immersed in the tub. "Well, I better get going, at least one of us has an honest-to-gosh date."

"You do? With whom?"

Genie wrinkled her nose. "The Italian Noodle, of all people."

Rachel chuckled. "Really? You and Vinnie?"

"I know, I know. Who would have ever thought I'd end up going out with a guy from a dating service? Nobody would believe it."

"I'm glad. I think Vinnie's nice."

"Well, thanks for the razor. Don't get up. I'll let myself out."

"See you later, Genie."

Lying back against the edge of the bathtub, Rachel tried to regain her previous state of relaxation. Only the water had cooled, and her mind had become restless. Rising from the water, she wrapped a towel around her body.

"Hello?"

Standing stock still in water up to her calves with only a towel covering her nakedness, Rachel held her breath.

"Rachel, are you in here?"

Her core rocked, aching all over again. Talk about conjuring up an image. That voice belonged to the object of her thoughts.

Jesse.

JESSE HAD THOUGHT of nothing but Rachel all day long. The image of her wearing those tight exercise pants and the little green teaser crept into every waking moment and every dream he'd had the night before. The fantasy of her wearing nothing but the thong made him hard, and he'd been in that condition for most of the day.

Before he'd realized where his thoughts had taken him, he'd found himself standing outside the door to her apartment, trying to come up with one good reason for her to let him in.

Genie had told him Rachel didn't want to go out with him because he was a client, but that had not stopped his obsessing about her. He had to find a way to make her break her own rule.

He wondered what it was about this one woman that was driving him nuts. He didn't like to think too much regarding his relationships with women. But, this one was different. She pushed him away with her words, but her kisses told another story.

Curling his fist with resolve, he reached up to knock on the hardwood door. With hand in mid-air, he practically fell through the door when it had suddenly opened. Genie's startled expression turned to wicked pleasure when she realized who was standing in front of her.

"Well hello, stranger," she purred, letting her glance slide up and down his body. "I don't suppose you were looking for me, now were you?"

"As fascinating as you are...no, I can't say I was," Jesse replied with a genuine smile.

Genie feigned a regretful sigh, then her gaze slid slyly to the interior of Rachel's home. "Then you must be looking for the lady of the house. She'll be out in a minute if you'd like to wait."

"Do you think she'd mind?"

"Mind? Oh, no, I don't think so. In fact, I'd bet my last cent she'll be excited to see you." Winking, Genie squeezed through the door to exit, purposely rubbing her breasts against his muscular chest as he entered the apartment.

Closing the door quietly behind him, Jesse looked around for Rachel. It had been a stroke of luck, running into Genie outside the door to Rachel's apartment, but Jesse didn't know just how much luck it would lead to. He felt a little awkward that Genie had let him in without announcing his presence, but he was inside now. The only problem was, where was Rachel?

"Hello?" he called. When no one responded, he called louder, "Rachel, are you here?"

Again, no answer. Jesse moved farther into the room, his gaze roaming the interior with curiosity. He hadn't had an opportunity to look at her place the last time he was there. Soft brown eyes had captured his full attention. Without the distraction of her presence, he explored.

It was a room designed for comfort. Large, plump cushions, in predominantly navy and cream tapestry patterns, adorned a navy sectional sofa. They were an invitation to nap.

Jesse's eyebrows rose when he spotted the brown silk skirt tossed carelessly over the back of the sofa. She wasn't as meticulous at home as she was in the office. Rounding the sofa, he found a trail of deliciously feminine apparel ending at the door of her bedroom. Jesse backed away, certain Rachel would prefer he not know she favored scarlet silk underwear. He filed that little bit of information away to savor later.

A collection of photos of Rachel and Genie and an older couple on a table were interspersed with objects appearing to have sentimental meaning rather than monetary value.

He found a photo of Rachel on graduation day, diploma clutched tightly in her hand, standing beside the couple he assumed were her mother and father. Rachel's features were a blend of her parents'. The shape of her mother's eyes was the same, but the expression wasn't--they lacked Rachel's sparkle. They also shared the same delicate structure and height. From her father, she inherited the slender, aquiline nose and her slightly square chin. But there was something odd about the pose.

Then it struck him. Her parents stood to either side of

her, with reserved smiles, neither placing an arm around their daughter. Graduations were joyous and jubilant occasions, but they all stood apart with guarded expressions.

He left the photos and walked toward the kitchen, a surprisingly feminine room. The cabinets were painted in white with bright chrome handles. White and gray marble counters, with a backsplash area tiled in gray-blue glass tiles, were completely free of any evidence of the normal small appliances a kitchen might hold. Only tall canisters in a cobalt blue lined its surface. Bistro chairs with yellow upholstered cushions surrounded a glass table already set with yellow and blue plaid place mats. A silk arrangement of yellow roses filled the vase at the center of the table.

On the table lay a phonebook open to the yellow pages. Large red circles were drawn on the open page. Out of curiosity, he walked closer to see what advertisements had caught Rachel's eye. He frowned when he caught a brief glimpse of one of the ads. Fertility specialist? *Huh?*

All thoughts of the phone book flew from his mind when he saw a movement out of the corner of his eye.

He turned to see Rachel standing in front of the doorway to her bedroom with a towel wrapped around her body, her hands clutching the fabric closed, hair dripping onto the carpet.

Jesse's mouth went completely dry, and his tongue was temporarily useless. He stood and gawked like a virgin schoolboy seeing a naked woman for the first time.

Rachel was beautiful standing there in nothing but the towel. Long, well-defined legs glistened with a sheen of moisture. Her face, still flushed from her bath, reddened further with the heat of his scrutiny. Gone was the starchy, buttoned-up executive. This Rachel looked younger, more feminine and imminently kissable.

"What are you doing here?" she asked.

Jesse raised his hand, displaying a tube of cream as if offering it up as a sacrifice to the gods ruling his tongue. "I brought this," were his imbecilic words. He felt the hot color of embarrassment creep up the back of his neck.

Staring blankly at the tube in his hand, Rachel remained where she stood, frozen. "What is it?"

"It's for sore muscles." Once again, he sounded stupid. Where was the smooth-talking cowboy when he needed him? His mind was befuddled by all the possibilities that were presented to him in the form of a gorgeous woman wrapped in one simple towel. He had to think more coherently if he were to take advantage of this situation. And, boy, how he wanted to take advantage of every inch of this situation.

"Oh," was her equally inept response.

Good. She was as much at a loss for words as he was. This lent courage to his lagging confidence. She hadn't run screaming, and she hadn't ordered him out of her apartment yet. He reminded himself he mustn't move too quickly, or he'd spook her.

Moving slowly, he crossed the floor toward her, holding her gaze. He willed her to retain eye contact, as if it would keep her from noticing he was now standing right in front of her with only one damp square of fabric between her skin and his intentions. "I thought you might need this after yesterday's workout at the fitness center," he spoke softly.

"What? Oh yes, I do." Again, she blushed, and her gaze slid away from his. Rachel shook her head as if to clear the cobwebs. It didn't help, she still sounded confused with her next comment. "Won't you come in?"

Jesse smiled slowly at her unconscious invitation. *Not yet...soon.* "I am in."

"Oh, yes...I see...you are," she stammered nervously. Raising one hand to her wet hair, she licked her lips, staring at his mouth all the while.

"Would you like me to rub it in for you?" He mentally kicked himself. *Not smooth.*

Her breath caught, and her eyes widened. He wondered if she realized the towel was beginning to slip from her fingers. The fabric hugged the curve of her breast. A merciful god would let it slide just a fraction lower...

She exhaled, blowing shakily between her lips. "Yes, please. Rub it in."

Jesse schooled his face to an impassive mask. He hoped she wouldn't notice he was starting to sweat. If she could see the desire raging through him, she'd definitely run screaming.

Unscrewing the cap from the tube of lotion, he squeezed a dab onto his palm, capped the tube and put it in his pocket. After rubbing his hands together, he moved behind her.

"Lift your hair," he requested huskily.

She reached a forearm behind her and slid it beneath her hair, raising it. The scent of apples and some fragrant flower rose from her skin and hair.

He inhaled and let his eyes fall closed for a moment. Then summoning fortitude, he opened his eyes and immediately decided the delicate back of her neck was every bit as sexy as the long legs quivering below. His mouth watered, and he longed to press a kiss against her bare neck or bite at the skin stretched across her creamy shoulders.

She smoothed her hair forward over her shoulder, and let the arm drop to her side.

He exhaled gustily and reached out to smooth the lotion into Rachel's white shoulders, kneading and caressing his way down her arms.

He rubbed until the ointment began to gently burn. Jesse knew the moment Rachel relaxed beneath his hands, for her breathing slowed and deepened.

Her head tipped back, and she moaned softly.

He couldn't resist standing closer to her, breathing in her fragrance. His hands caressed her shoulders deeply. Then he rubbed the lotion into skin at the base of her neck, smoothing his work-roughened hands across the creamy expanse, his fingers dipping over her shoulders to trace deepening circles along the tops of her breasts.

Her head fell back against his chest.

"If you'll lay down, I can do a much better job," he whispered in her ear.

Rolling her head toward him, she opened passion-dazed eyes and looked at him for a long moment. Without a word, she led him into her bedroom.

CHAPTER 11

JESSE FOLLOWED CLOSE BEHIND HER. The bulge in the front of his trousers pressed insistently against his jeans as his heart hammered a loud tattoo. She paused for a moment beside the bed, uncertainty clearly written on her face.

Jesse drew a deep breath. As much as he wanted to take advantage of the situation, he had to consider his ultimate goal. Pouncing on her wouldn't win her trust. *I need to take this slowly.*

He walked up beside her, and she looked away, her alarm apparent in the rapidly increasing rise and fall of her chest. Touching a finger to her cheek, he turned her face toward him. "Look at me." He deepened his voice, but kept it soft, not wanting her afraid, but needing her to submit.

Rachel met his gaze and pulled her bottom lip between her teeth.

Jesse brushed the back of his hand along her jaw. "I'll rub your back, and whatever else hurts, but I won't go any farther than that without your permission."

Her gaze locked with his for a long, charged moment. Then she climbed onto the bed, pushed the pillow aside and lay down on her stomach. After a moment, she loosened the towel beneath her and reached behind to push the edge lower down her back. Finally, Rachel faced away from him, waiting.

She looked small and sexy, stretched out on the bed.

His hands shook as he bent to remove his boots, their loud thuds causing Rachel to gasp. But she remained where she was. Loosening the buttons at the neck of his shirt, he swiped his forearm across his sweat-dampened forehead, before he rolled back his sleeves. Then climbing onto the bed, he lifted one leg over her still form before gently allowing his weight to press down against her buttocks.

Her hands clenched the bedspread, causing him to smile.

Taking the tube from his pocket, he squeezed a more liberal amount of the ointment into his palm. He tried to ignore the soft swell of her bottom, or what part of his anatomy pressed against it, and began to work the warm lotion into the muscles of her back. Cupping her shoulders, he rolled them back in a circular motion, raising a soft groan.

Tension gradually left her muscles.

Jesse let his hands wander freely down her spine, pushing and kneading. His fingers splayed across her smooth back. The contrast of his sun-darkened skin against her creamy white flesh brought up some primitive exultation. She was warm and pliant beneath him now.

Pushing her arms above her head, he trailed his fingers along the side of her arms, until he reached the tender hollow of her underarm.

She shifted restlessly beneath him.

Jesse traced a line from her underarm to the soft flesh at the side of her breasts.

Rachel shivered.

He heaved himself off her and climbed off the mattress. Walking to the end of the bed, he picked up one of her delicate feet in his hand, and pressed his thumbs against the sole, squeezing gently. He bent and placed a feather-light kiss against the tender instep.

Her toes curled at his touch.

He moved his hands upward kneading her calves. She flexed the muscle in response, and he pulled her leg straight, sliding his hands up her thigh. He placed a knee on the bed, between her outstretched legs, and followed with the other knee, pushing her open to him. Frustratingly, her towel still cloaked her feminine center.

She gasped as he opened her, but didn't protest. Her head briefly lifted, only to fall, her forehead cradled against her arms. Her breathing came in ragged hitches.

He turned his attention to her other leg and began the slow journey upward once more. As he reached the bottom edge of the towel draped across the crease dividing leg from creamy cheek, he paused. He'd come to deepen their connection, to provide her relief. She'd allowed so much more by inviting him into her bedroom. He didn't want to push for more than she was ready for, but she was aroused. She trembled beneath him. And the scent of her excitement was there every time he drew a deep breath.

With his hands still on her flesh, he fought himself for control. Should he give them what they both appeared to want? "Rachel, do you want me to stop?"

Breathing rapidly now, she moaned and whispered, "Jesse, please..."

He leaned forward, bit lightly through the towel at her

rump then laid his head against her there. "Tell me, Rachel. Tell me what you want," he said, his voice hoarse with his desire.

"Please, please come inside me...now," she wailed. Tremors coursed through her.

Relief and exultation shot through him. Sitting back on his bent legs, he pulled the towel from her slowly, dragging it across her skin. His heart pounded faster as he stared at what was now revealed.

The slender indent of her waist flared outward to feminine, rounded hips. He placed his hands on her lower back and leaned forward, continuing his massage, circling and squeezing, lower and lower, until he kneaded the soft flesh of her bottom.

She writhed, gasping his name.

Jesse picked up the pillow she had pushed aside earlier. Sliding an arm beneath her belly, he lifted her and placed the pillow beneath her hips.

"Jesse, no." She tried to move off the pillow, but he pressed her back down with his body stretched over hers.

"Let me do this," he soothed, pressing kisses to the back of her neck. "Don't be embarrassed, honey...shhhh."

He licked a trail down her spine, feeling her surrender as she once more sank her forehead against her arms. He took a moment to wipe his fingers on the towel to be sure all traces of the analgesic cream were gone. Then he let his finger trace the crease separating the cheeks of her buttocks and rounded the gentle curve to brush against the soft curls guarding the place he longed to sink himself into. He slid two fingers into her and circled.

A warm, fragrant response greeted him. He groaned, and leaned forward to reward her with nips and kisses to her bottom. Circling, pushing deeper, he felt a further gush of liquid and the tightening of her inner muscles. She moaned again.

"Oh yes, baby. I'll give you more. You're so tight, so wet. Wait for me." He pressed wet, openmouthed kisses along her spine while slowly withdrawing his fingers.

On her elbows now, hips rising higher, Rachel reared up in protest, moaning a ragged, "No, Jesse, Christ don't stop now."

He pressed his lower body, fully clothed against her, once...twice...in imitation of the act he was desperate to begin.

Then suddenly clothing was too tight, and he couldn't breathe. He rolled off the mattress and tore at the buttons of his shirt and shrugged out of it, flinging it across the room. His hands shook as he opened his pants and pushed them down, freeing his legs and the aching part of himself. *Lord, let this last.* He climbed back onto the bed behind her.

With the fingers of one hand opening her, he dipped inside to wet them, then smoothed the creamy liquid along the warm soft folds of her feminine flesh. With the other hand curved around his own hard flesh, he made a circle around her wet rim before guiding himself to her entrance. Closing his eyes, he eased himself slowly, into her warm, wet channel.

He sighed. This was where he wanted to be. Where he'd longed to be since he'd met this incredible woman.

RACHEL FELT THE LONG, thick glide of him and fought another moan. He was *soooo* deep...*soooo* hot. She gave into the impulse to surge backward against him, bringing him further into her.

"Sweet Jesus," he gasped, his mouth close to her ear as he leaned over her.

He paused for a moment, and she squeezed her inner muscles to hold him there. She gloried in the feel of his body, large and warm, blanketing her, and the other part of him so deep she felt him pulse all the way to her heart. His arms snaked beneath her belly to hug her closely. Resting his chin in the curve of her shoulder, his breath rasped in her ear.

A wet, warm tongue laved the shell of her ear, and a shuddering groan escaped her. She felt her inner muscles stretching and contracting to accommodate the length and girth of him, and he groaned in answer.

"Rachel, come with me," his voice whispered harshly.

Strong hands held her firmly against him, never breaking the connection, as he raised their bodies to their knees. Her chest remained on the bed, and her nipples, pointed and peaked, abraded erotically against the coarser fabric of the bedspread.

Lifting her head, she raised her upper body on her arms, and wadded the bedspread in her fists, waiting for the storm to erupt.

Jesse straightened behind her, and she felt cool air lick at the perspiration on her back. His hands slid to her hips, and he gripped her almost bruisingly before pulling himself out of her, until just the tip of him remained inside.

Every muscle in her body tensed, waiting for the moment, and then suddenly he slammed into her, then withdrew, only to repeat the long thrust again and again.

"Oooooh." She released a long moan, which ended in a sob as she reared back to meet his push. He was almost too much to take.

Growing breathless, everything around her faded. She

forgot why she shouldn't be doing *this* with *him*. Forgot why she'd felt trepidation at having him behind her while she was vulnerable and exposed. All she knew at this moment was the rasp of his breath and the firm grip of his hands guiding her backward to meet each sleek, long glide of him—pounding harder and harder against her womb—skin slapping loudly against skin.

Just as she felt the muscles at her core convulse in the first hot spasm of fulfillment, he abruptly withdrew. She held herself there, quivering and panting from exertion, wondering why he'd stopped. Then his hands turned her, and his body nudged her to her back. He came down over her, and her legs opened to him automatically.

Holding his body above her, he leaned his weight on his elbows, and his gaze raked over her nakedness, pausing at the open juncture of her thighs. She tried to close her legs to his scrutiny, but his body was there, blocking her attempt. She placed a hand over herself, and glanced away, suddenly uncertain.

"Don't," he said softly. One of his large hands drew hers away. "You're beautiful."

Turning her face back to his, she searched it, wondering what he was thinking. *Was this as special and frightening to him as it was to her?*

Finally, he lay down over her, his weight settling against her skin, his shaft resting against her open cleft. Surely now, he would begin the ascent again.

Instead, his hands framed her face and smoothed back her damp hair. His lips met hers in a wet openmouthed kiss, tongue gliding against hers, then sliding to lick and suckle at her full bottom lip. She moved restlessly against him, urging him to enter her once more.

He shifted, moving further down her body and laughed

—a single, soft, groaning sound. Continuing to torment her, he bit softly at her neck.

She closed her eyes and rolled her head, exposing her neck to give him better access to the sensitive skin.

Sliding further down to nuzzle against her breast, his mouth hovered over a peak, his breath teasing.

Rachel arched her back to bring her nipple to his lips.

His teeth settled around it, nipping lightly, his tongue offering comfort, flicking at the nubbin, before drawing it deeper into the cavern of his mouth. Releasing it, he looked up to snare her gaze, before rubbing the sensitized point with the soft bristles of his mustache.

"Oh God, Jesse, please now...please." Her feet dug deeply into the mattress, and she bucked beneath him, desperate now for him to fill her.

Jesse sat back on his knees, then pushed her hands to her breasts, his hands showing hers how to continue the gentle assault against her nipples.

His fingers combed through the nest of curls over her sex and tugged gently. Bucking upwards, her thighs trembled with excitement, inviting him nearer her core. He parted her folds and pushed a single finger into her, wetting the tip with her juices, then withdrew to rub it over the swollen knot at the top of her sex.

Her heels dug into the mattress, and she writhed against the comforter. She was wild with excitement. Her head tossed from side to side, a litany of pleas escaping her. Her fingers squeezed greedily around her breasts. Anything to increase the sensations. She was beyond shame, beyond herself. She knew only a painful need for him to end this torture and join his body with hers.

Hooking his forearms beneath her knees, Jesse raised her bottom from the bed and positioned himself once more at her slick cleft. He closed his eyes, and with a look of fierce concentration on his sharply drawn features, rammed home.

Rachel screamed as wave after wave of intense sensations washed over her. His strong, steady thrusts prolonged the sweet convulsions pulsing deep inside her. She sobbed openly now, each ragged breath a prayer for completion. At the last, she opened her eyes to watch as Jesse flung his head back in triumph, shouting her name loudly, riding the storm with her to the end.

JESSE CRACKED ONE EYELID OPEN. Sunlight was edged around the sides of the curtains in the window. He didn't remember falling asleep, but wasn't surprised he'd slept so soundly when he did. Between work and chaperoning Rachel's "dates", he'd worn himself out. Lifting his head, he grinned. Rachel's body was glued to his side, her hand nestled against his chest and her leg draping over his. A cloud of soft brown hair spread across his chest, and his smile broadened. At least in her sleep, she knew where she belonged.

He laid his head down and savored the intimate moment. He didn't for a minute believe being here meant Rachel had thrown in the towel. But this was definitely progress.

Yup! Women were like horses. First you just let them get used to the sight and smell of you. Then you lead them gently around the corral. Soon soft words and soothing hands gentle them to your touch and they hardly notice when you slip the halter over their head and slide the bit in their mouth.

Yup! Rachel was gentled, haltered and all that remained

was the branding. She didn't know it yet, but Texas's most eligible bachelor was bound and determined to ride her until she was broke to the saddle.

Slipping from her bed, he gathered his clothing quietly. She stirred and turned to her back, and his good intentions almost bit the dust. Her pale, rose-tipped breasts made his mouth water, and he longed to slide right back inside her and surprise her with another run for the roses.

But he was beginning to understand what made Rachel... Rachel. He figured he could probably have her going before she was even fully awake, but once the bloom of their lovemaking ended, she would come back to her senses and pull in all her defenses. And she was going to be pretty mad. Probably more at herself than him.

No, he'd give her a little space and time to remember what had happened between them. Besides he had a few loose ends to tie up himself.

Closing her bedroom door softly behind him, he dressed in the living room and, with his hat in his hand, walked thoughtfully out of her apartment.

Jesse headed straight for his office since it would take too long to drive all the way out to his ranch and back, just for a change of clothes. He could pick up a plain denim shirt off the shelf of the ranch supply store his office was attached to.

Sliding through the front door of the store, Jesse made a beeline for the shirts, grabbing one off the shelf and hurrying to his office. Mentally congratulating himself over escaping the notice of his staff, he opened the door to his office and found his office manager already hard at work. *So much for avoiding questions.*

"Hey, if it ain't Billboard Bob gracing our humble presence." Cleatus Martin, otherwise known as Marty, rounded the corner of the desk and stuck his hand out. "Would you shake my hand? I would be ever so grateful. Why you're practically a celebrity."

"Hi, Marty." Ignoring his outstretched hand, Jesse fumbled with the pins and buttons on the shirt. "What are you talking about?"

"What am I talking about?" Marty turned as if speaking to another person in the otherwise empty room. "He asked me what I'm talking about." Opening the blinds shading the window, Marty stood to the side. "Are you blind, hot shot?"

Baffled at Marty's behavior, Jesse stepped toward the window and looked out. "What am I supposed to be looking at?"

"For Pete's sake, it's bigger than a barn. How could you miss it?" Marty waved at the huge billboard high above the ranch supply store sporting a larger than life image of Jesse.

Jesse's cheeks burned. "Somehow, I didn't think the photos would be *that* big." Starring at his likeness, he cringed. "Kind of embarrassing, ain't it?"

Marty pounded him on the back then walked around to the desk again. "Embarrassing, yes, but damned effective." Picking up a pile of papers, he waved them in the air. "Sales have practically doubled since the new wave of advertising began. And most of the sales have been to women."

"Huh?" Jesse stopped in the middle of slipping out of his favorite date-night cowboy shirt to stare at Marty. "What do you mean most of the sales have been to women?"

"They come into the stores hoping to catch a glimpse of Billboard Bob. That's what I mean."

"Jeez, and I thought I was modeling for jeans and ranch supplies." Jesse pulled the shirt off and tossed it on the back of a chair. Standing bare-chested, he was wrestling with the buttons on the cuffs of the denim shirt when the door to the office opened.

"Oh, excuse me," came a sultry feminine voice. "I thought this was an office, not a boudoir."

Standing in the doorway was a tall, beautiful woman with straight blond hair, raised eyebrows and an amused smile on her face.

"Oh, hi, Adele." Jesse managed to get the buttons to release and slid the shirt over his shoulders. "Come on in." He struggled to secure the buttons up the front of his shirt when slim, manicured fingers took over and completed the job for him.

"There, now you're dressed like a proper store owner," she said, letting her fingers linger at his collar. "Although, I must admit, I liked you better without the shirt."

Jesse grabbed her hands from around his neck, leaned over and kissed the side of her smooth, tanned cheek. "How's my favorite neighbor?"

The woman pouted, caught his cheeks between her palms and kissed him soundly on the lips. Afterwards, she brushed her thumb across his mouth to rub at the lipstick.

"I take it that means you're fine?" Jesse pulled his hand-kerchief out of his back pocket to erase the remaining lipstick from his lips. He glared at Marty who was trying to smother a laugh.

"Yes, that means I'm fine. And you?"

Stepping out of her range, Jesse strode to the desk to put wood and distance between them. Lately, Adele's startling familiarities had begun to make him uncomfortable. Having grown up together on neighboring ranches, he felt she was practically his sister. He squashed the thought that they were more like kissing cousins—he preferred to forget the few times she'd found her way into his bed.

"I'm fine. What brings you to the store so early? Don't you have cases to try and depositions to take?"

"Yes, but a certain cowboy wasn't to be found last night, and I needed to talk to him." The whole time she spoke, Adele moved in on the desk. She perched her ass on the edge and crossed slim legs beneath the short, tailored skirt.

Jesse glanced at the legs then at Marty who was strangely quiet.

One glance at his manager and Jesse knew why. The man's tongue and eyes were hanging out of his head as he drooled over the pair of legs so brazenly displayed.

"I went out last night," Jesse offered in as much of an explanation as he wanted to get in to.

"Oh?" Adele's gaze traveled from the shirt on the back of the chair to the new, creased shirt he was wearing. "And you're just getting in?"

"Yes." Jesse made a pretense of shuffling papers, unwilling to subject himself to a cross examination from the woman sitting on his desk, especially in front of his curious manager.

"Is she anyone I know?" Adele fished for answers.

"No." Jesse looked up, schooling his expression into a blank mask. "What was it you wanted to talk to me about?"

Swinging her legs off the desk, Adele stood and walked to the window.

"I came to tell you that I set up the meeting with the other sponsors for the charity cattle drive. They've all agreed to come out this Saturday."

"That's great." Jesse's smile was genuine. The charity cattle drive was the culmination of the efforts of a lot of people, and his heart was warmed by the level of support he received from others in positions of influence. "Thanks for setting it up. It wouldn't have happened without your help."

"Anything for you, Jesse. Anything." Adele smiled and flipped her hair behind her ears. "Now, I really must go. Stop by the house later, and we can go over the legal papers for the project. That is, if you have time…"

Her raised eyebrows and a pointed look garnered a sheepish grin from him, and he rose from his chair to come around the desk. "I will, Adele. Again, thank you for all your help." Taking her in his arms, he gave her an affectionate hug. "I'll be by later so we can talk."

"I'll be waiting, so don't let me down," she said, reaching up to kiss his lips before he could back away. With that, she left the office and a couple of quiet men, each deep in their own thoughts.

Marty was first to break the silence. "Got yourself a situation there, don't you, bossman?"

Rubbing the lipstick off his lips with his handkerchief, Jesse stared at the closed door and shook his head. "Yup! No doubt about it."

"Looks to me like you're burning the candle at both ends, what with Adele and whoever you spent the night with last night."

Jesse shot an irritated glance at his manager. "Who said I spent the night with anyone last night?"

"Nobody, but how do you explain the need to dress in the inventory, if you didn't stay in town last night?"

Jesse frowned. "Marty, you're too nosey for you own good."

"Yup, I reckon so. You've also got the problem of all the other women clamoring to meet you."

"What other...oh yeah...the advertisement." Man, this was getting to be more than he wanted to grapple with after a fairly sleepless night.

"Although, most of what I know about women could fill the cap of a beer bottle, I do know one thing." Marty's lips twitched.

"Yeah, and what's that?"

"They don't like to share their men with other women." Marty headed for the door. "They're kinda funny that way. Well, I better go earn my paycheck before the boss fires me for being a slacker. Have a nice day." Marty left the office.

Jesse settled into his desk chair and swiveled around to look out the window. Where the sameness of the view usually calmed his nerves, it didn't have that effect today. Not with the huge picture of himself staring back. It was as if he was looking at his inflated ego, and it was mocking him and his way of life.

Perhaps it was time to clean up his life and think about not only the future of his business, but his personal future as well.

His thoughts returned to the bedroom he'd left earlier that morning. Had it only been that morning? It seemed much longer since he'd left Rachel. He suddenly had the overpowering urge to see her again. Slamming his hand against the arm of his chair, he thought, *why the hell not?*

Jesse pushed to his feet, slapped his hat on his head and left his office, work untouched.

CHAPTER 12

Standing in the lobby waiting for the elevator, Jesse whistled off-key as he twirled a single rose between his palms. Knowing he was about to see Rachel again put him in a remarkably good mood. Last night had been so absolutely unbelievable he felt like shouting out loud, or beating his chest like a gorilla on the prowl for a she-gorilla. Instead, he put the rose between his teeth and raised his hands above his head, snapping his fingers and clicking his heels on the granite-tiled floors.

He heard laughter around him, and realized he wasn't alone. Heat rising into his cheeks, he lowered his hands and took the rose out of his mouth, but continued grinning like a fool at anyone who passed.

He still couldn't believe what had happened. Beneath her stiff and business-like exterior, Rachel had burned in his arms last night. He felt himself thicken as he remembered the feel of her silken thighs wrapped around his waist. Nonchalantly, he positioned his hands over his crotch like fig leaves in an attempt to hide his growing arousal.

The longer he'd stayed away from Rachel, the more time he had to contemplate how she might be feeling by now. Would she be regretting their night of shared passion? Probably.

Self-doubt began to set in. Not about how good they'd been together. That had been one hundred percent natural and beautiful. He worried that maybe it had been too fast for her.

Rachel didn't seem to be the type of woman who would casually accept a man into her bed. Remembering her reactions to their sex play, he'd lay odds she'd never known an orgasm before last night. And her inexperience went along with the reserve she wore like a cloak.

He might have scared her off by pushing past her armor, especially if she wasn't sure she even liked him yet. No, Rachel would prefer a slow courtship, a chance to know the man before she agreed to the intimacies.

He surprised himself with that observation. Maybe he was getting smarter and more perceptive in his almost middle age. That, or the women he'd known had failed to challenge his intellect because they'd been just as eager to jump right between the bed sheets. Somehow sex with them was a less intimate act than having a conversation with Rachel.

The elevator door finally slid open, and he stepped in behind a little old lady, stooped with age.

Her hair stood out in front but was flattened in the back. As the doors closed, he reached for the button to Rachel's floor, but the old lady crowded in front of the control panel and looked at him as if he was trying to steal her purse.

"What floor?" she demanded in a thin crackled voice.

"Sex," Jesse replied without thinking.

"Trying to get kinky with me, young man?" Hefting her purse up in front of her, she patted it knowingly. "I got protection against perverts like you, sonny, so don't try anything."

Realizing that she was threatening him, he tried to remember if he had said anything to offend the old lady. At a loss for her reason, he shrugged. "Did I say something to offend you, ma'am?"

"You know darn well what you said, and if you come any closer, I'll let you have it."

Backing into the corner, she moved far enough away from the control panel for Jesse to reach over and punch the number six. As his finger made contact with the button, he heard a sharp hissing sound, and he jerked back, his eyes burning as if they were on fire. "What the hell?"

Blinded, he clutched at his eyes, desperately trying to wipe the spray out. As tears streamed down his face, he was vaguely aware of the elevator doors opening.

The little old lady thumped out as fast as her cane would take her. "That'll teach you to try to have sex with a senior citizen. Humph, I ought to call the elevator police on you!"

The door to the elevator closed as Jesse struggled to open his eyes. Each time he opened one, the air hit it and the burning sensation intensified. Squeezing both eyes shut, he waited for the elevator door to open on the sixth floor.

Ding! The doors slid open. Jesse quickly opened one teary eye to get his bearings and slammed it shut again, wincing with the pain. Stepping through the open doors of the elevator and out into the hall, he walked what he guessed was the right number of steps to the opposite wall, then bumped into it with his outstretched hand.

Opening the other eye, he focused quickly on the door to Rachel's office and gauged the distance before closing them both again and setting off. Feeling his way, he counted the doorframes until he reached the office. He twisted the knob and nearly fell inside as the door was opened from the inside.

"Jesse, what are you doing standing out there?" a familiar voice asked.

"Mildred, is that you?" he croaked.

"Of course it's me, who else would I be?"

"I was attacked in the elevator. You've got to help me."

"Attacked? I'm calling security, right now."

"*No!* No, Mildred, just help me get this stuff out of my eyes." God, could the situation get worse? Security would call the police, and he'd be hauled away to jail because of a misunderstanding with an old woman in the elevator. Images of reporters shoving microphones into his face made Jesse's knees go weak.

"Are you sure you don't want me to call security?"

"Quite. Now, will you help me, or do I have to call for an ambulance?"

"Did someone punch you in the eye?"

"No, that would be too easy. I think I was maced."

"Mace? He sprayed mace in your eyes?"

"Not he...she."

"You mean you were attacked by a woman?"

"Yes, I mean no. It was all a big miscommunication."

"Come over to the water fountain and let me flush out your eyes."

Mildred lead him by the hand to the fountain in the hallway.

He leaned over the water with his head tipped sideways and allowed Mildred to poor blessedly cool water over each eye with a Dixie cup, until the burning lessened, and he could open his eyes for more than five seconds at a time.

Once he was reasonably certain he wouldn't go blind, he straightened and followed Mildred back into the office and collapsed onto the edge of her desk.

"Here." She pressed several tissues into his hand.

Jesse dried his face and was finally able to look at his old friend. "That's better. Thank you, Mildred. You're a lifesaver."

Mildred stood before him, her arms crossed over her chest, the look on her face accusing. "So, what did you say to that poor woman to scared her enough to use mace?"

Jesse stared at one of his oldest friends as if she'd lost her mind. "Poor woman? She almost put my eyes out."

"Yes, poor woman. Now, what did you say?"

"She asked me what floor I wanted, and all I told her was six."

Narrowing her eyes, she glared at him then nodded sagely. "That must have been it."

"What?"

She waved her hand, her lips tilting upward. "Never mind. What are you doing here?"

"I came by to give this to Rachel."

Jesse held a crumpled red rose out for Mildred's inspection.

"Oh, boy. I see you're trying to sweep the girl off her feet with that." Mildred's words dripped with sarcasm.

"What? Not enough?"

"Depends on your purpose."

"What do you mean?"

"Men give women flowers based on the purpose they hope to achieve."

"I'm a little foggy here. Can you give me a for instance?" His head ached, and he really wasn't in the mood for one of Mildred's long, drawn-out lessons.

"When a man wants a woman to know he's interested in a long-term relationship, he sends a modest but sincere bouquet of red or pink roses."

He wondered what possible difference the color of the rose made. "He does?"

"Yes. When he's in the doghouse, he sends a huge bouquet—usually two dozen or more—of yellow or red roses, hoping she'll forgive him and take him back."

Jesse was a little uneducated in the nuances of roses, but he was a fast learner. "And where does this puny excuse for a flower fit in."

"When he's feeling cocky and self-assured, thinking he has her in the palm of his hand, he brings her a single red rose. Sometimes going so far as to place it between his teeth to present it to her."

Feeling the color rise in his cheeks, he shook his head in amazement at how intuitive Mildred was. Even when he was a child, she'd always been able to read him like a book. "Mildred, are you some kind of witch or psychic?"

"No, just observant." Her brows rose. "So what are you and Rachel not telling me?"

"Telling you? I don't know what you mean?" Jesse tried to evade the question, but Mildred would have none of that.

Her gaze narrowed. "You know exactly what I mean. Waltzing in here to see Rachel with a single rose and a blush to boot."

He hedged, refusing to look the woman in the eye. "What has Rachel told you?"

She tapped her toe. "Nothing so much in words as actions."

"What do you mean?"

"She was late." Mildred's lips thinned.

"So, what's wrong with that?"

"She's never late," she said. "I went in just a few minutes ago, and she practically bit my head off and told me she didn't want any visitors."

Jesse almost smiled. Just as he'd predicted, she was pulling in her defenses. He was starting to understand Rachel. "So, maybe she had some bad news over the phone or in the mail," he said, shrugging nonchalantly. No way was he going to admit to the old tartar he was the source of Rachel's grumpiness.

"She won't take any calls, and I haven't delivered the mail, yet." Mildred looked at him expectantly, one eyebrow rising.

"Why are you looking at me? I wasn't even here."

"There's something going on between you two, and I mean to find out what."

Tempted to cross his fingers behind his back as he had when he was a child, he assumed a neutral expression. "There's nothing going on. Really."

"Horsefeathers! Jesse Jordan, I'm going to tell your mother you lied to me."

"Now, Mildred. Be reasonable. Rachel and I are grown up people. There are some things you just don't discuss with sixty-year-old women."

"Tell that to the lady who got you with the mace. I might have known you two had sex."

"Mildred!" Jesse stood straighter, though he couldn't stop the heat rising up his neck. The old battle-axe didn't pull any punches.

"Don't bother denying it. Rachel is already showing all the signs of full-scale denial."

His chest tightened. "She is?"

"Yes." Mildred moved to stand directly in front of him and poked her finger at his chest. "And it's all your fault."

"Why mine?"

"Amateur." She snorted. "It was too soon."

Jesse slid off the end of her desk and paced the room. "Don't you think I've been thinking the same thoughts? I don't know how it happened..." He heard Mildred snort again. "It just did."

"Did you use any protection?"

"No," he admitted, heat making its way into his cheeks. "It all happened so fast, I didn't even think of it at the time."

"Well, there can be consequences associated when you don't take precautions," she said, wagging a finger.

"You mean she could be pregnant?" Surprisingly, the thought didn't have him breaking into a four-alarm panic. After all, Rachel was the woman he wanted to bear his children.

Mildred's arms crossed her chest again. "I guess you'll need to hang around her long enough to find out, now won't you?"

The enormity of his carelessness hit him like a punch in the stomach. A picture of Rachel growing large with his child struck him physically. He wanted her in his life, wanted a family with her, but he didn't want to do it by trapping her.

"Do you want me to leave you two alone?" Mildred asked.

Disoriented, Jesse swung toward Rachel's door and back to Mildred. "Huh?"

Mildred rolled her eyes. "I'm referring to you and your conscience."

"Oh. No, but I would really like to see Rachel."

"I'm not sure now is a good time."

"Why?"

"She said she didn't want to see anyone."

Jesse stepped toward Rachel's door. "But I have to."

Mildred darted in front of him, pressing her palm to his chest. "You'll just have to wait until she's ready."

For a moment, Jesse considered pushing past Mildred, but everything she'd said hit too close to his own thoughts. Finally, he sighed and stepped back. "Then I'll wait." Jesse pulled up a straight-backed chair and straddled it.

Mildred's brows descended. "I meant wait, as in days."

Jesse shook his head. "I won't go barging in, if that's what you're worried about."

Mildred shook her head. "You're thick-headed, Jesse."

"Not at all. I'll wait, like you said." He grinned. "I'll wait until Rachel comes out on her own."

Her lips pressed into a thin line, Mildred sat behind her desk and made a show of going through the stacks of mail in her inbox.

Minutes ticked by with Jesse silently watching the door to Rachel's office.

Exasperated, Mildred threw down her letter opener and propping her elbows on the desk, rested her chin on her folded hands.

Jesse grimaced. Obviously, Mildred had something more to say.

"Rachel is not the playing-around type of girl, Jesse. You can't expect her to get involved with someone who's not willing to go the whole nine yards."

"What do you mean?" he asked wearily, his head throbbing in earnest.

"She won't settle for less than a ring and a promise."

"What are you talking about?"

"Did your mother raise a fool? Do I have to spell it out?"

"No to your first question, and yes to the second."

"Marriage, Jesse. Marriage."

"Oh."

Mildred studied his expression, a frown forming between her eyes. "Do you love her?"

Avoiding her eyes, Jesse stood and began pacing. "Yes. I think so." He ran his hand through his hair. "We haven't really spent all that much time alone together. We've only been out on two dates, and she wasn't even my date, either time."

"Then tell me why you can't seem to leave her alone?"

Jesse frowned, trying to understand, and then come up with the right words to voice his feelings. "There's something about how proper she is...and then when I look into those soulful brown eyes, I'm lost." He glanced up at Mildred. "Does that sound like love?"

Mildred's eyes narrowed, and she leaned forward. "What about the preacher's daughter you met in high school? You thought you were in love with her. When she started hinting about diamonds and place settings, you ran like a scalded cat."

"That was puppy love, Mildred, and you know it. At nineteen, I wasn't ready to settle down and play house with any woman."

"Well then, what about that lawyer lady your Mama says you're going to marry some day? Are you in love with her?"

His shoulders slumped. "That is a problem. You know

Adele's ranch is next to ours. We were practically raised together, and our parents have always thought it would be a good idea for the two of us to marry, eventually. I used to think the same thing. I know it's a lousy thing to say, but she was convenient."

"Does she think there's going to be a wedding, too?"

He sighed. "I don't know. We've never really talked about it." Jesse shook his head. "But it wouldn't work. We have a lot in common...maybe too much. We've...you know...fooled around enough for me to know it was kind of like kissing my sister."

"Sounds like you have some loose ends to tie up."

"Yeah," he raked his hand through his hair again. "I need to talk to Adele. I don't think she'll be terribly hurt. She's more interested in raising my horses than raising my children. That was always kinda hard on my ego, but not my heart."

"I'll bet she's interested in more than that," Mildred disagreed. "But seriously, what Rachel needs is a man and babies of her own. Are you willing to provide her all that?"

Jesse resumed pacing. That was his plan. He knew Rachel wasn't one of those women you played with and discarded when you got bored. She was gutsy and beautiful, deserving of more than just a one-night stand.

So, what are you waiting for?

Stopping halfway across the room, he paused. His plan was good. He was thirty-five years old and not getting any younger. He would like to have a family and children to come home to. The thought of waking up to see Rachel beside him each day made him smile.

"Why not?" Jesse said out loud, his back to Mildred.

"Why not, what?" Mildred asked him.

Turning toward Mildred, he grinned from ear to ear.

"Why shouldn't I be the guy to give Rachel all that?"

"Now, you're talking. I just knew you'd be the one for my Rachel." Clapping her hands together, she rubbed them with relish. "So what's your game plan?"

"Game plan?"

"You have to have a game plan, or you won't win the game. Come on, Jesse, get with the program."

Jesse stared at Mildred's avid glance. She thought he had a plan. He cleared his throat. "What do you suggest?"

Mildred rolled her eyes and sighed. "You need to spend more time together, for one."

"That would be nice—if I could get her to agree to go out with me. But, if she's shoring up defenses, she won't even consider it."

"Then you have to think of another way to spend time with her." Mildred got up from behind her desk and began to pace behind Jesse. They made a pair, heads down, marching in step, thinking.

When Jesse stopped suddenly, Mildred slammed into his back.

"Warn me next time, will ya?" she grumbled.

"Sorry." Jesse turned. "What about continuing to double-date with Genie?"

"That might work for a start, but you need to find a way to get her on her own, so you can use the Jordan Charm to woo her."

"I know I need to get her alone," Jesse grumbled and started pacing again.

Mildred fell in step behind him, giving him a little more space in case of sudden stops. They made several passes in front of her desk, without any ideas springing forth.

"I've got it," Jesse blurted, stopping suddenly again.

"What do you have?" Mildred snapped.

"You know that cattle drive coming up in a couple of weeks? I could use that as my front."

"How?"

"Think, Mildred. Rachel's an advertising executive—the cattle drive needs to be advertised. It's perfect."

"She's already working for you. How's this going to be any different?"

"She'll have to come out to the ranch to understand what she's advertising. I can get her alone out there. You know, long rides on horseback, just her and me."

"Great idea, Jesse, except for one thing. Rachel hasn't a clue about ranches. She hasn't ever ridden a horse to my knowledge."

"Even better." Jesse was practically rubbing his hands together in glee. He could already picture Rachel out in the Texas Hill Country, sitting on his front porch watching the sunset and letting nature take its course.

"Excuse me, but is this the office of Ms. Rachel Taylor?" A delivery boy stood in the hall doorway with a beautiful and sincere bouquet of a dozen pink roses with a hummingbird perched among them as if sipping nectar from the fragrant petals.

Mildred moved forward to intercept the delivery boy. "This is the office of Rachel Taylor."

"Could you sign here, please?" The delivery man held out a clipboard and a pen.

Taking the clipboard from the boy's hands, she scrawled her name on the document and handed it back to him. Placing the bouquet into her outstretched hands, he disappeared from the direction in which he had come.

"A dozen pink roses." Mildred looked over the bouquet with a pointed look at Jesse. "Looks like you've got competition."

He tossed the single rose bud into the waste bin by her desk and shrugged. "Can't compete with that. Who's the admirer?"

Mildred's lips twisted. "It's none of our business."

"Oh, come on, Mildred. I'd like to know who the competition is."

"Never you mind. It'll do you some good to have a little competition. Now, if you'll excuse me, I'll just deliver these delightful roses to Rachel. Maybe it'll put her in a better mood."

CHAPTER 13

RACHEL LOOKED BLEARILY at her computer screen and read the column of numbers again, without comprehending a single thing she saw. Groaning, she pushed her laptop away from her and let her head hit the desk with a dull thunk.

Stupid! Thunk! *I'm so stupid!* Thunk!

She rested her abused forehead on the cool surface of her desk. She'd overslept that morning, having forgotten to set an alarm the evening before. Because of her tardy awakening, she'd rushed to dress, skipped her breakfast, and had still arrived late to work, for the first time in her life.

Mildred had raised her eyebrows in stern disapproval and clucked, but otherwise let her be all morning. Rachel was hiding out in her office, wishing the day would end soon, so she could slink back to her apartment, bar the door, and come to grips with the horrible mistake she'd made.

Rachel thumped her head on her desk again. *What was I thinking?* After Jesse had left her apartment in the early

159

morning, Rachel had drifted into a deep, satisfying sleep only to awaken with a full-blown attack of guilty conscience.

I made hot, passionate love with the most notorious playboy in Texas. He was probably gloating, wearing a "cat that ate the canary" grin on his handsome face. All he'd had to do was wave a tube of Ben Gay in the air, and she'd melted like a puddle at his feet.

She tried not to think about the sexy, wonderful things he had done to her body. His hypnotic, soothing hands had seduced her. The man was altogether too smooth. He'd had plenty of practice too, if the accounts of all his conquests were even a quarter accurate. The most exciting sexual encounter of her life was just another notch in his belt.

She'd never be able to look him in the eyes again and maintain a semblance of a professional relationship with him. And worse, she'd have to transfer his accounts to another exec. How would she explain?

Coming to work had not helped to erase the feeling of having made a big mistake. She'd broken one of her cardinal rules by mixing business with pleasure.

Unbidden thoughts of the night's passion had slipped into her consciousness all morning, causing her to lose concentration on the job at hand. Just an hour ago, she had talked with a client on the phone, hung up and asked Mildred to place a call to the very same client. What must Mildred think of her lack of focus?

She probably thinks you've gone off the deep end or got laid. Geez! That's all she needed was for word to get out that she was having a relationship with a client.

Thunk. Thunk. Thunk. Rachel moaned as her head responded to the abuse and began to throb. She needed to call Genie and chew her out for letting Jesse into her apartment last night. That's how the whole thing had started.

Perking up at finding someone else to blame, she sat up straighter and reached for the phone just as it began to ring. Rachel jumped as if the inanimate object had suddenly come to life and read her thoughts. She lifted the receiver and answered automatically before Mildred could respond from the other room.

"Hello."

"Rachel? Is that you? How come you're answering the phone and not Mildred? Is she sick or something?"

"Hi, Genie. No, Mildred is not sick, I was just reaching for the phone to call you."

"Really? It's as if we were on the same wave length, or something," she said cheerfully.

"I seriously doubt it," Rachel replied flatly. "Hey, what was the big idea, letting Jesse into my apartment last night while I was in the bath?"

"Oh, so you noticed, did you?"

Rachel could hear Genie laughing on the other end of the line. "Don't get coy with me. That was a rotten trick to play."

"Only if the results backfired. So, what happened?" Genie asked in a breathless rush.

"Nothing." Rachel wasn't ready to discuss her transgressions with Genie.

"Nothing-nothing or something-nothing?"

"Nothing, and it's none of your business, anyway."

Rachel's ear was blasted by the sound of Genie squealing excitedly. "You did it, didn't you?"

"*Noooo.*" Rachel may as well have yelled into a screaming jet engine. Genie was carrying on like an excited schoolgirl and just wasn't listening to her.

"Wow, Rachel, that's terrific. So, tell me, is he as good as he looks?"

Rachel gave up trying to pretend nothing had happened. "Yes...I mean, no." Rachel leaned an elbow on the desk and sighed into the phone. "Oh, what's the use? It was the most exciting experience I've ever had."

"That's great."

Rachel wished she could be as excited about it as Genie, and would have if it weren't breaking all her rules, and if the man wasn't Jesse Jordan, notorious bachelor—and if he hadn't snuck out of her bed without so much as a kiss goodbye. "No, it's terrible."

"Why? He's perfect. Just think of the beautiful babies he could help you make."

"It's all wrong, Genie. Last night was the biggest mistake of my life."

"Oh, for heaven's sake, why?" Genie sounded exasperated.

"He's nothing but a flirt, and he's a client. Need I say more?"

"Yes. So far, I haven't heard one real reason that will hold water. They're pretty lame, if you ask me."

"For the record, I'm not asking you. What I am asking is that you don't let him in my apartment again without my knowledge and consent."

"But he's gorgeous, and the situation was too much to resist."

Rachel sniffed. "I don't care. Do I have your promise?"

"And he has the cutest ass I've seen on a guy."

"Promise me, Genie." Rachel's voice was firm, uncompromising.

"Oh, all right, if you insist," Genie grumbled. "Really, Rachel, you need to learn to lighten up."

"Thanks for the unsolicited advice. See ya later."

"Later? But I want all the gory details," Genie wailed.

"No way."

"But, I'm your best friend. You're supposed to share all the deets with me," Genie whined. "Well, then at least tell me one thing…"

Rachel made a face at the receiver then placed it against her ear again. "What's that?"

"Are you going to see him again?"

"No," Rachel stated flatly.

"Why not?"

"Oh, no, you don't. You've had your one question. I have to get back to work. I'll see you tonight."

"But Rachel…"

Click. Firmly placing the receiver on the rest, Rachel covered her face with her hands. Try as she might, she couldn't get the image of Jesse out of her mind. She needed to resurrect the wall she'd so carefully built around her emotions, but how?

She had to think of something she didn't like about him and concentrate on that the next time she saw him. That way, she could remain focused and avoid being seduced by his charms.

Thinking about the way he'd left her was as good a place as any to start.

A light tapping on the door to Rachel's office pulled her out of her musings. Mildred entered, carrying a bouquet of pink roses, but Rachel barely saw the roses, because she only had eyes for the man following Mildred.

"Some flowers arrived for you, Ms. Taylor," Mildred said.

Rachel blushed. An annoyingly gooey feeling returned full blast. "Really, Jesse, you shouldn't have."

His lips stretched into a thin line. "Don't worry. I didn't."

"Oh?" Her racing heart lurched to a halt. "Then who are they from?"

"There's a card in here somewhere." Fishing among the flowers, Mildred found a small card, which she proffered to Rachel.

Taking it, Rachel absently looked at the envelope then handed it back to Mildred.

"Oh, Mildred, you read it. I'm having a hard time concentrating today." Then she blushed, knowing Jesse would rightly guess he was the reason.

Opening the envelope, Mildred read out loud. "Dear Rachel, I enjoyed meeting you the other day, and remembered what you said about not liking animals against your skin. The hummingbird in the arrangement is one of my 're-creations', so to speak. Don't worry, it was already dead when I found it. I just put it on my water heater to dry. It looks as bright and vibrant as when it was alive. I hope you enjoy the arrangement and will agree to see me again. Your humble servant, Lenny Lindeman."

Locating the offensive bird amongst the beautiful roses, Rachel shuddered. "Eeeeuw! Gross. Take them away."

"What, after a nice gentleman has taken the trouble and expense of giving you this wonderful arrangement of roses?" Mildred shook her head. "Are you crazy? Why, I would give my left arm for a man to give me roses again."

"The roses are fine, it's the dead bird that gives me the willies. If you like them so much, put them on your desk. Please, just take them out of here."

Jesse stepped forward with a grin, examining the hummingbird. "But Rachel, Lenny did a great job. This is real artistry. It looks like it's still alive...well, almost."

Leaning forward, he made a pretense at sniffing the fragrance of the roses. "Only problem is the smell of the roses doesn't quite mask the smell of dead bird. But if you don't get too close, you won't even notice."

Jesse was standing entirely too close for Rachel's comfort. She could smell his musky male scent, which sent her imagination drifting with her hand running over the smooth muscles of his shoulders and down his back to his firm and delicious buttocks. Remembering just what he'd done to her buttocks had her heart galloping again.

She shook her head and stared at him critically, trying to find some physical fault to latch onto. Not the hair, it was windswept with just the right amount of curl to make a woman want to run her hands through it to watch it spring back into place.

Forcing herself back to the conversation, she insisted, "I don't think I could stomach having a dead animal or bird sitting on my desk. It's so...morbid! Lenny is a very sick man."

Jesse grinned. "The man's lovesick, Rachel. Put him out of his misery." Then he winked at her.

Reaching blindly behind her, Rachel found her chair and sat down before her melting knees buckled, and she disgraced herself by falling in a puddle at Jesse's feet. Really, this was getting ridiculous.

She desperately searched for something about him she didn't like. His face was too perfect, with high cheekbones, full, extremely kissable lips, and blue eyes that can see right into her soul. She was doomed.

Rachel realized she'd been staring at Jesse stupidly for a long time because his smile was growing cockier by the minute.

"So, does that...kill...my competition?" he said, tongue in cheek.

"Competition? I don't know what you mean." Rachel stalled, unwilling to admit to any relationship between them, despite the something that had occurred last night.

But Jesse wasn't going to let her get off so lightly. "I guess a dead hummingbird is not my idea of romance. I go more for candlelight and a stimulating *massage*."

Rachel's face flamed as the image of Jesse smoothing lotion into her skin flashed into her mind. Her defensive reaction to her own physical response was to snap back at him. "I'm sure you've had plenty of opportunities to practice those techniques, too," she replied sharply.

"Reeerrrrr pffft...," Mildred muttered, as she eased toward the door and exited the room, leaving them alone.

Rachel pushed out of her chair, weak knees and all, and walked over to the window overlooking the city. The man was entirely too good-looking for her own good. She would just have to avoid looking at him altogether and maintain her distance. On the verge of telling him to get lost, she had to forcibly remind herself she shouldn't because he was her client. Maybe he was here on business. Dear, sweet Jesus. What a tangled web she'd let herself get caught up in.

JESSE STOOD in the middle of the room drinking in the sight of her silhouetted against the light of the window. Her hair, normally upswept and screwed into a tight bun, was loose, spilling down to the middle of her back. The cut of her suit emphasized the gentle curve of her waist and hips. Closing his eyes, he took a deep breath, concentrating on maintaining his control. It was as he had guessed. She was having second thoughts.

"Hey, gorgeous," Jesse called softly.

In profile, her chin shot up. "Is there something you'd like to discuss, Mr. Jordan?"

It was worse than he'd thought, she was closing down on him. He wouldn't have taken back last night if he could, but he did wish the timing had been a little better. Rachel wasn't ready to commit to a relationship with him. Now, he would have to scale the wall she'd erected around herself, again. Only this time it would be even higher. "Rachel, about last night..."

Her back stiffened, and she hesitated before responding to his gentle insistence. "Mr. Jordan, I don't wish to discuss last night."

He'd have to try another tack, a little reverse psychology. "I just wanted to apologize for taking advantage of you last night. I blame myself one hundred percent for what occurred. I had no right to force my attentions on you."

Pausing, he allowed her to digest that bit of information and waited to see what she would say.

Her chin dipped toward her chest. "My actions were also inexcusable. It was a huge error in judgment, and I insist on taking at least half of the blame." Still, she didn't look his way, and she stood ramrod straight.

Realizing he wasn't getting the response he wanted, Jesse shifted tactics and launched his second assault, donning a business-like attitude and a serious expression. "I really came to you today on a business matter, Ms. Taylor."

Looking startled by his announcement, Rachel spun around. "Business?" She almost looked disappointed.

Schooling his expression into a polite mask, he said, "Yes, business."

"What kind of business? Were you dissatisfied with the ads we developed for you?"

"No, on the contrary, I have another proposition for you." Seeing the color rush into her cheeks he quickly added, "Excuse the pun, please."

"Excused," she said, breathlessly.

"I need your help with some kids."

"Kids?"

Curiously, Rachel's face blanched at his statement. "Yes. To be more specific, I need your help with a little project I have in mind to develop a summer camp for kids."

Rachel shook her head and gave him a confused look.

Jesse walked around the desk and wrapped his hand around her elbow. She flinched as if his hand burned through the jacket of her suit. In truth, Jesse could almost feel the silkiness of her skin as he had the previous night.

Instead of pulling her into his arms, as was his inclination, he guided her to her chair and pushed her gently into it. Striding back around the desk, he put distance between them to allow her to gather her wits. He paced back and forth before the desk as he formulated his thoughts. "As you know, I have a large ranch out in the Hill Country. It's a beautiful place, full of wide open spaces, sunshine and fresh air." Turning, he paused to see if she was listening.

Although wary, her gaze glinted with interest. "I'm listening, go on."

Jesse resumed his pacing, not because he was nervous, but because it kept him from drooling all over Rachel. "About three years ago, the son of one of my employees was diagnosed with leukemia. The boy was only seven years old. They gave his parents no hope he would survive the disease, and they told them to make him as happy and comfortable as possible."

"How awful." Rachel's eyes brimmed with tears.

"In an effort to cram as many happy moments into his few remaining months, they asked him what he wanted to do most. What do you suppose his answer was?"

"I have no idea."

"He wanted to ride a horse."

Her eyebrows rose. "A horse?"

Jesse moved to the window and stared out, not at the real estate in front of him, but on the scene conjured in his memory. "Yes, a horse. When I got wind of his wish, I took him out to my ranch for several weeks and taught him how to ride, to throw a rope around a fence post, and even toast marshmallows over an open fire.

Jesse turned to Rachel. "Don't you see? These were things he'd never done, living in a city—and never would have, if I hadn't taken him into my home and shown him how."

"That was very kind of you," she whispered, tears welling in her eyes.

Striding away from the window and to the center of her office, he turned angrily toward her. "The point is not that I want someone's gratitude. I was moved by the smile on a little boy's face and how happy he was for the short time while he fought a terrible disease."

Crossing the room and coming around the desk, he grabbed Rachel's hands and pulled her up from her seat. "I want to build a camp for kids with terminal diseases, so they have a chance to play and be happy, and do things they wouldn't have the opportunity to do otherwise."

Rachel shrugged. "Then do it. You have the money."

"I could build it all by myself, but I want the community

to have stake in it. Whatever they donate, I'll match. And I'll donate the land for the camp itself."

With her hands in his, Jesse's brow puckered with the intensity of his emotions as he willed her to understand and agree to help him fulfill his dream.

She drew a slightly ragged breath. "What do you want me to do?"

Relieved, he let a small smile curve his mouth. He pulled her close for a hug. "I knew I could count on you, Rachel." Leaning back, ever so slightly, he dropped a kiss on her forehead, and then set her away from him. No use tipping his hand too early. The plan was to get her out to the ranch before he seduced her again. He didn't feel a moment's remorse for using his cause to gain her cooperation. Both efforts were equally important to him.

"I'm planning a charity cattle drive for next month on the ranch. It'll help raise money to build cabins and facilities for the camp. I want you to help me pull it off. I've been working with local officials, charity organizers and various businesses around the city to sponsor and donate time and money to the cause."

Dropping her gaze, Rachel smoothed a lock of hair behind her ear. "Sounds like you have all the help you need."

"No, I need someone like you to help advertise the big event in just the right way to generate the kind of funds a place like this is going to need."

Her chest rose around a deep breath, but she gave him a little nod. "I'd be glad to organize the advertising. Just let me have all the details, and I'll get someone on it right away."

Jesse shook his head. "Rachel, everyone who is helping with this venture has pledged to participate to show their support. That means they're all going to be at the cattle drive, riding horses and the whole bit. Your presence as the owner of this agency, showing your personal support, will be required."

"Whoa!" Looking alarmed, Rachel raised her hands. "I'll help, but I'm keeping my feet on the ground. I don't know the first thing about horses, and I don't intend to find out."

"But Rachel, it is all part of the event. All the supporters will participate to show their dedication to the children."

"Jesse, I have never ridden a horse in my entire life. I'd kill myself." Twin patches of red stained her cheeks, and her eyes grew rounder.

"Now, don't you worry about it," he soothed her. "There's a whole month before the cattle drive to learn."

"I don't know about this. I'm more than willing to help any way I can, but I don't understand why I have to go on the cattle drive."

He could hear her wavering. Triumph scorched his veins. He continued to press his advantage. "It's no worse than falling off your bicycle."

"I haven't ridden a bicycle in ten years and, for the record, I never fell off. I refused to."

"Well, I'll make sure you have the best riding instructor in the county to teach you all you need to know."

"And where will I take these riding lessons?"

"At my ranch, of course," he said, suppressing a triumphant grin.

Her eyes narrowed. "And let me guess...you're the best riding instructor in the county?"

He waggled his eyebrows. "Bingo."

"Somehow, I feel like I'm being shanghaied," she said with a glimmer of wry humor.

"Think of it like this...those kids go through a lot more

challenges than learning to ride a horse. Think of it as your personal challenge to overcome for the kids."

She wrinkled her nose. "You play dirty, you know that?"

"Maybe. But you gotta love me for it," he said with a smile designed to melt even the iciest shell.

CHAPTER 14

I CAN'T BELIEVE I let him talk me into this.

It had been a week since Rachel had seen Jesse, but she hadn't thought about anything else but Jesse for the entire time. Now, instead of continuing to avoid him, she was headed out to see him in the wilds of the Hill Country. She must be crazy to think she could be alone with him and keep him at arm's length. There was something about his smile that turned her backbone into a limp soggy noodle. It was truly disgusting. *I'll bet all the women he flirts with feel the same.*

That's what hurt the most. Knowing he turned that same smile on every woman didn't make her feel special. The knowledge made her feel like one of Jesse's infatuated groupies, hanging on every word.

Rachel followed the directions Jesse had given her, but she felt like she had been driving forever and still wasn't at the ranch. Wishing Genie had come with her, she took a quick look at the folded paper with Jesse's handwriting on it.

"Turn left at the old school house and follow the road until you see a huge oak tree shading the lane."

Great, I hope the oak tree wasn't struck by lightning in the last week.

Talking to herself made Rachel feel almost as if someone else was in the car with her to share this adventure. Genie should have come, but she had a date with Vinnie and his mother to learn how to make meatballs.

Ah-hah! There's the tree, just like the note says. Thank God. She'd begun to think this was turning out to be a wild goose chase.

Following the country lane up a rise, Rachel knew she was almost there. The ranch should be coming into view any minute. At the top of a gentle slope, Rachel gasped at the vista spread before her. She brought her car to a stop and stared at the beautiful countryside kissed by the mid-morning sunlight.

In the valley below, fields of knee-deep grass looked like lush, green carpet, decorated with the gnarled beauty of the live oak trees native to south-central Texas. To the west, there was a small creek-fed lake gleaming in the sunlight. The water was so still it reflected the cypress trees growing from its banks.

On the hill opposite from her, beyond the lake and fields, nestled on a plateau rising above the valley floor, was a sprawling ranch house, surrounded by matching outbuildings. From her location, Rachel could tell one of the outbuildings was a barn, with corrals and fences separating a couple dozen grazing horses.

Setting her car into motion, Rachel followed the road into the valley. It wound around the open fields and crossed a stone bridge over the creek that fed the lake. Pulling up in front of the ranch house, she parked her car next to a dozen others. *Thank God we won't be alone.* She had half believed that his invitation to learn to ride a horse was his version of, *Do you want to see my etchings?* Rachel breathed a heavy sigh of relief and sat staring, drinking in the beauty of it all.

The house was built of white limestone, trimmed in forest green. A wide porch graced the front of the house along with square columns of roughly hewn cedar. Porch swings on either end dangled from the eaves, an invitation to sit and enjoy the view. Which was precisely what several people were doing at that very moment.

Rachel frowned, wondering at the many people gathered at the ranch house. She had assumed she would be meeting with Jesse to discuss the coming cattle drive. After checking her face in her rearview mirror, she glanced down at her casual attire, purchased just for the occasion. The chemically-faded, brushed-cotton jeans and light blue chambray shirt were just the thing for a ranch, or so Genie had convinced her. The outfit made her feel like a gangly teenager instead of a polished professional woman. She had drawn the line at buying boots to complete the ensemble, opting instead for light tan, leather loafers and twisting her hair into a French knot at the nape of her neck. She would feel like a fraud marching up to his house dressed like some cowgirl from an old western movie.

With a sigh, she stepped out of her car and smoothed the wrinkles from her jeans. She strode up to the front porch hoping she wouldn't trip and make a fool of herself in front of the people gathered there. She felt like she was in high school again, trying to make herself invisible to avoid attention of any kind.

Squaring her shoulders and tucking in a few stray tendrils of hair behind her ear, she reminded herself to act the adult, and remember any one of the people she met were potential clients for the firm. *For god's sake, grow a backbone.*

As she approached the steps to the porch, Rachel was greeted by an older woman with soft blue eyes and a smile very much like Jesse's. "Hi, I'm Margaret Jordan, Jesse's mother, but you can call me Margie, everyone does. You must be Rachel Taylor from the ad agency. I'd recognize you anywhere by Jesse's description. Come on up and join the fun."

"Thank you...Margie," Rachel said tentatively, then smiled. Rachel took pride in her ability to judge a person's character based on their first impression. Her gut feel on this one was that Margie was a warm and caring individual who would do anything for her family and friends. "I'm sorry I'm late. I didn't know how long to give myself to get out here."

Margie waved a hand. "Fiddlesticks. We were about to give everyone a tour of the house and outbuildings, so you're just in time."

Looking around at the people sipping lemonade on the front porch, Rachel didn't see Jesse among them.

"Jesse's out at the corral, saddling his horse for a riding demonstration," Margie said, as if she had read Rachel's mind. "Here, have a glass of lemonade to wet your whistle."

Pressing a cool glass in her hand, Margie turned to hand a similar glass to another guest. Working her way through the gathered crowd, Rachel smiled and chatted. She began to relax when she realized that several of the people she met were city folk as well.

Finding an unoccupied corner of the porch, Rachel leaned against the rail and studied the people standing around in small groups talking excitedly about the coming cattle drive. The mood was positive, and the cause was worthy. Apparently, everyone was here to help with the cattle drive and children's camp in one way or another—either by helping with the organization, providing funds or participating in the drive itself.

Margie appeared after a few minutes and took Rachel by the hand. "Rachel, honey, you probably don't know a soul here. Let me introduce you around."

Pulling her along behind her, Margie marched across the porch to a couple sitting on the porch swing a few steps away. Appearing to be in their mid-forties, they were both dressed casually in khaki slacks and polo shirts. The woman wore glasses, and her graying, blond hair was cut to just below her ears in a bob. The man had dark hair peppered with gray, and he sat dangling a pair of sunglasses in his fingers.

"Rachel Taylor, I'm pleased to introduce you to the Doctors Oglethorpe, this is Olivia and this is Stan. Yes, they are both doctors, and they are married to one another. They're the kind folks who've been helping Jesse understand the medical needs of young cancer and terminally ill patients."

"It's nice to meet you. Do you both practice medicine in the field of oncology?" Rachel asked as she shook their hands.

"Yes, we do," they answered in unison and smiled at each other.

Olivia continued, "We're very excited about Jesse's plan to build a camp for the children. They've seen so much pain and suffering in their young lives, it would be nice to give them a little hope and happiness."

"Rachel will be doing the PR work for the cattle drive," Margie offered.

"That sounds like a very interesting line of business. You must meet a lot of fascinating people," said Olivia.

Rachel smiled. "It is fun, and I do meet a lot of people, but I can't help but feel like my contribution to this event is not nearly as important or worthy as yours. I admire you two for the work you do."

"Thank you, but you mustn't feel your efforts are unworthy. After all, in order to raise the money we need to make this camp a reality, the event must be well publicized. We need to grab people's heartstrings so they'll be willing to reach deeper into their pockets to support this organization. Your job's critical to our success."

"I never thought of it that way, but I guess you are right. The entire agency is donating their time and efforts to pulling it off."

"That's wonderful," Margie interrupted. "Now if you'll excuse us, I wanted Rachel to meet the DeWinneys." Grabbing Rachel's hand again, Margie moved among the guests until she came to an older couple standing with an attractive younger woman.

"Rachel Taylor, I would like you to meet my dear friends and neighbors, the DeWinneys."

"Hi, I'm Winnifred, but you can call me Freddie," Mrs. DeWinney held out her hand to Rachel. She must have been somewhere in her early sixties with graying hair and a welcoming smile.

Rachel gave her an answering smile. "Nice to meet you, Freddie."

"My name's Charles, but you can call me any darned thing you like," her husband said with a wicked waggle of his bushy eyebrows. "As long as you don't call me late for dinner." He laughed at his own joke.

"Now, Charles, quit flirting with the pretty girls. I

swear, I can't take you anywhere." Freddie batted at her husband playfully, smiling despite her rebuke. Then as if remembering the other woman standing in their group, Freddie turned to her.

"Rachel, this is our daughter, Adele."

"Nice to meet you, Adele," Rachel said as she held her hand out for the customary shake.

Adele ran her appraising gaze down the length of Rachel's factory-faded jeans to her leather loafers as if she found her wanting. With regal insolence, she extended her hand.

Reluctantly, Rachel took it as if it were a snake, coiled to strike.

"Charmed," was Adele's cryptic reply.

"I'll bet you two have a lot in common, both living in the city and all," infused Margie, trying to get a conversation started.

"I'm sure we don't," Adele answered.

Freddie frowned at Adele, but turned to Rachel to elaborate where Adele hadn't.

"Adele is an attorney for the Sandifer and Raynovich Law Firm. We live on the ranch next door. Adele and Jesse practically grew up together." Freddie and Charles smiled as another couple approached, leaving Adele and Rachel eyeing each other cautiously.

Beginning to feel perhaps they did have more in common than she'd originally thought, Rachel studied Adele DeWinney a little more closely. The other woman was everything Rachel was not.

Where Rachel was average height and pale-skinned, Adele was tall and beautifully tanned. While Rachel's hair was dark, wavy and unfashionably long, Adele's was a sandy blonde and lay straight to her shoulders. Her figure was displayed to full advantage in slim-fitting black jeans and a low cut, western-style midriff blouse, which exposed ample amounts of her full bosoms.

Adele was model material for a western clothing advertisement, Rachel thought in chagrin. Another woman's basic nightmare for competition, not that she was in competition with this woman.

"I suppose you and Jesse are very close." Rachel offered as a statement, not a question.

"Close is an understatement," she said with a small confident smile. "We expect to marry someday."

CHAPTER 15

RACHEL'S EYES widened and her heart plunged at Adele's bit of news. It shouldn't have bothered her, considering she wasn't interested in pursuing Jesse to further their relationship. This just confirmed what she already knew.

"If you're so sure you're going to marry, why haven't you already?" Rachel couldn't believe the words had escaped her mouth, and wished she could recall them as soon as they were said. She cringed inwardly waiting for the model-lawyer to respond.

"I want to make sure he's through sowing all his wild oats before he comes home to me."

Suddenly feeling sick to her stomach, Rachel's face paled. Adele watched her with curiosity. "Based on your reaction, I'd assume you're one of his so-called oats?"

A fiery blush colored Rachel's pale cheeks, giving her away without having affirmed or denied a word. Wishing the floor would open up and swallow her, Rachel was relieved when Margie called for everyone to gather around.

"Thank you all for coming. It means so much to us that

you've agreed to help in this exciting venture to provide some special children a chance to be happy. Jesse asked me to give you a tour of the ranch house, first. Then he wants us to join him out at the corral. So, if you would follow me..."

Margie led the crowd of people through the rambling ranch house pointing out all its features and amenities. The high, open-beamed ceilings and the interior rock and wooden walls gave the house depth and character.

Bringing up the rear of the tour group, Rachel stepped through the front door and, turning to close it, noticed the windows overlooking the valley. They stretched from the floor to the top of the two-story ceiling. The view was breathtaking. She could imagine living out here and waking up to that view. Of course, model-lawyer Adele would have the pleasure of this view each day. Somehow, Rachel didn't think she would even notice.

Glancing around Rachel didn't see Adele, and she wondered where she'd slithered. The blonde was nowhere to be seen. She probably knew the house as if it were already her own. That thought bothered Rachel. The green demon of jealousy sat squarely on her shoulder. She shrugged, hoping to dislodge it from its perch.

Falling behind the rest of the group, Rachel was just going into the master bedroom as everyone else was leaving. It allowed her to view the room without feeling self-conscious about her curiosity. Like the living room, this room was located at the front of the house, overlooking the same spectacular view. Here too, the ceilings were high, giving the room cavernous proportions. In the center of the room was a huge four-poster bed, smothered in richly textured fabrics.

Staring at the bed, Rachel visualized a naked Jesse

sprawled in the middle with a wicked grin and a come hither look in his eyes. Her breath quickened and a rush of desire heated her body.

The thought was immediately followed by one of Adele lying in the bed beside him. The image had the same effect as a bucket of ice water being thrown over her head. Suddenly feeling ill, Rachel hurried from the room to join the rest of the group heading out the back door. It irritated Rachel to no end that she couldn't distance herself from this situation. *It's not like I'm in love with the man,* she silently insisted, although the thought rang hollow.

By the time she caught up with the rest of the group, they were gathered around a corral, staring at a horse and rider. As Rachel drew closer, she could see it was Jesse mounted on a spirited horse demonstrating turns, stops and other riding techniques.

"He's beautiful," she whispered aloud, before realizing the words had actually come out of her mouth. Looking for a way to cover her blunder, she focused on the horse. "That is the most beautiful tan and black horse I've ever seen."

"It's called a buckskin," offered a man dressed in jeans and a straw cowboy hat. "Hi, I'm John Jordan, Jesse's dad. Don't believe we've met. I'd remember a pretty little filly like you." He stuck out his hand and shook hers gently. "You can call me JJ."

"Nice to meet you JJ. I'm Rachel Taylor."

"I take it you haven't been around horses much."

She shook her head. "Not at all."

"There's really not much to them. Four legs, two eyes, a tail—pretty much a big dog, if you look at it that way."

Rachel laughed, relaxing in the man's company. "It's the big part that scares me."

"Nothing to be scared of. Most of the horses on the ranch are well-trained and wouldn't harm a fly."

"When and if I learn to ride, I want a horse who knows what to do. Basically, I want one that will train *me*."

JJ laughed and slapped his knee. "I gotta admire a woman who knows what she wants. You should have no problem learning to ride. Jesse is a good teacher. And if you don't like the way he teaches, you just call on old JJ, here. I taught the boy to ride when he was only three years old."

"I appreciate the offer, Mr. Jordan."

"JJ," he insisted.

"JJ," she responded with a grin. Jesse came by his rascally charm honestly.

They turned their attention back toward the pen just in time to catch Jesse smiling in their direction. Heart in her throat, Rachel looked around, trying to see who he was aiming the smile at when she noticed Adele was only a few bodies away, leaning against the rails of the fence. Her heart settled back into her stomach like a ton of lead. The beauty of the man and horse working together as one creature lost some of its appeal.

Pulling the animal up to the rails where everyone was standing, Jesse swung lithely from the saddle and held the reins out to Adele.

"Would you like to show them how it's done, Adele?"

"Really, Jesse, you were doing just fine without me," Rachel heard her say in a voice so falsely sweet it made Rachel's teeth ache.

"But I'm sure they would rather see a lovely lady show them the ropes versus a dusty old cowboy."

"Well, if you insist." Like a graceful cat, she climbed the

fence and dropped to the ground beside Jesse, near enough to rub against his body.

Rachel's blood boiled at the smile Jesse bestowed on the woman. He had a lot of nerve hosting two of his women at the same function. She was itching to tell him a thing or two, but kept her opinions quiet, reminding herself she had no strings attached to Jesse Jordan, and therefore no right to tell him who he could or couldn't invite to his place.

Helping Adele adjust the stirrups to fit her length, Jesse gave her a boost up into the saddle. It was apparent Adele was every bit as accomplished a rider as Jesse. Rachel envied her skill and confidence. The horse knew exactly who was boss and obeyed each command, quickly and efficiently. Rachel found herself wishing the woman would fall off the horse, and she immediately chastised herself for having such uncharitable thoughts. Was there anything Adele couldn't do?

"There's not much Adele can't do," Jesse said proudly, as if reading her mind. He moved to stand on the inside of the fence in front of Rachel and JJ.

"I wish she'd fall in horse poop," muttered Rachel beneath her breath.

"What was that?" Jesse asked, turning his full attention and brilliant smile on Rachel.

Blushing, she scrambled for a reply. "That horse looks really tall," she said, almost wiping her brow in relief when he turned back to the center of the corral.

"Jake's sixteen hands. He's one of the horses from my breeding program."

Searching for a way to impress Jesse with her newfound knowledge she blurted, "He's a beautiful doeskin horse."

Jesse frowned and gave her a confused glance.

JJ leaned close to her ear and corrected her. "Buckskin," he whispered. "The horse is a buckskin."

Blushing for the second time in front of Jesse, Rachel found herself babbling. "Doeskin, buckskin, they're all deer, what's the difference?"

Staring at her as if she had lost a few marbles, Jesse's smile lifted at the corners of his mouth, and he burst out laughing, drawing the attention of the crowd away from Adele.

Too embarrassed to look Jesse in the eye, Rachel caught the narrow-eyed glare Adele aimed right at her.

The blond didn't look too happy at having her show ignored.

Rachel couldn't help herself. She smiled a little feline smile and waggled her fingers in a taunting little wave at the other woman.

Sliding to the ground, Adele handed the reins to Jesse and stalked over to Margie. "Do you think we've had enough of this show? Is it time for lunch, yet?" she prompted Margie.

Glancing at her watch, Margie's hand flew to her face. "Oh my, look at the time. If y'all would just head on back to the house, the catering service will have lunch on the table in ten minutes."

Handing the reins to a ranch hand, Jesse climbed the rails and jumped to the ground next to Rachel. "Ready to go?"

"Yes, I am, Jesse." Adele suddenly appeared, hooking her arm through his and pulling him in the direction of the house. Which left Rachel standing by the corral.

Rachel looked to JJ.

She read speculation in his expression as he watched

the couple depart. He offered his arm. "If you don't mind a crusty old geezer, I'd be proud to show you the way back to the house." He winked at his wife, heading their direction and added, "...as long as you don't mind sharing me with the missus."

"I don't mind if she doesn't," Rachel added loud enough for Margie to hear and join in the teasing.

"Lord you can have him—nothing but trouble, he is. Always flirting with the young girls. I guess that's where Jesse gets it." Margie grinned and waved a hand. "Don't pay him no mind. He's all talk."

Reaching around her, JJ gave Margie a squeeze and a kiss on her cheek. "Course, you always saw right through me. Must be why I love you so much."

Rachel smiled at the light banter and open affection she witnessed between Jesse's parents. If it hadn't looked so natural, she would have been embarrassed.

Her parents had restrained from any show of affection in front of her. What a difference between philosophies in child rearing. Instead of being embarrassed by the older couple, she admired them. Their love was a palpable thing, extending to all who surrounded them. Rachel felt warmed by it.

With a soft smile curling her lips, Rachel followed JJ and Margie to the front of the house and out onto the lawn where tables had been set for the guests.

Jesse was leaning over Adele at one of the long tables. When he spotted his parents, he motioned them forward, inviting them to sit at his table. Rachel followed to keep from being left standing alone.

As they approached, Adele placed a hand on Jesse's arm. "I'll save this seat for you, Jesse," she purred up at him, her eyes fluttering seductively.

"Oh...okay, Adele."

Noting that all the seats around Adele and Jesse were taken, Rachel followed JJ and Margie around to the other side. They ended up sitting directly across from Jesse and the blonde lawyer-equestrian.

Adele glared straight at Rachel accusingly, as if she had planned on the seating working out that way.

Determined to keep Adele's hostility from getting to her, Rachel ignored her, flicking her napkin open and sliding it onto her lap.

Once everyone was seated, the catering service went into action, laying plates of food and glasses of iced tea in front of each of the guests. The conversation flowed with the cattle drive as the central topic.

Throughout the meal, Adele kept Jesse entertained with anecdotes from their childhood.

Attempting to ignore the couple across the table from her, Rachel made a half-hearted effort at conversation with JJ and Margie, pushing the food around on her plate instead of eating.

"So Adele, when is the happy occasion?" a woman asked, breaking through Rachel's blue funk, and bringing her undivided attention to Jesse's face.

Adele smiled at Jesse then turned her smile to encompass the guests at the table, pausing for effect. "In two months."

"That's wonderful, congratulations," exclaimed one of the guests.

"I'll bet you're excited."

"Yes, as a matter of fact, I am. I thought it would never happen, then one day it just did. I couldn't be happier."

The man sitting next to Jesse, pounded him on the back.

"Congratulations, man."

Jesse smiled, graciously accepting the congratulatory words from the guests around the table.

Smiling though her heart squeezed hard in her chest, Rachel added her congratulations to the rest. Adele had been telling the truth.

I guess I was his last oat to be sown.

As the thought sank in, she felt her blood pressure rising. How dare he make love to her one week and ask another woman to be his wife the next?

"We'll be sure to let you know when the big day arrives," Jesse said. "But for now, I want to show you my dream. I've arranged your transportation, if you don't mind an old-fashioned hay-ride."

As if on cue, a flatbed wagon filled with bales of hay, was pulled into the yard by a huge pair of matched reddish-brown horses with glorious black manes. Jesse disappeared around the side of the house as the laughing guests climbed onto the wagon. The elder male Jordan climbed into the driver's seat, and with a click of his tongue and snap of his wrist, JJ set the wagon in motion. Jesse reappeared around the corner of the house, mounted on his buckskin horse, reining it into a trot beside the wagon.

The hayride was a huge success, for most of the guests. Margie led the group in singing songs like Old McDonald, Bingo and Home on the Range.

Rachel made a half-hearted attempt to join in, sitting amid the itchy hay in her light-colored jeans, accumulating grass stains and getting angrier by the minute. If looks could kill, Jesse would be six feet under.

Each time Adele addressed Jesse with a comment displaying her familiarity with the land and horses, Rachel wanted to jump up and scream. The woman had a way of flaunting her relationship with Jesse that made Rachel madder than a disturbed hornets' nest.

After twenty minutes of riding and singing until Rachel's face felt stiff, she was relieved when the wagon pulled to a stop at the edge of a wooded area close to a lake.

As they climbed out, everyone marveled at the beauty of the location.

Jesse slid off his horse and strode up to the group.

"What do you think about this for the location of the camp?" he asked the group in general.

"It's a wonderful spot. The children would love it," exclaimed Olivia Oglethorpe.

He directed their attention to the stand of trees. "I see the camp cottages here among the oaks to keep them cool during the hot part of the day."

Nods of assent followed his statement.

"I envision the barn and pens at the west end of the camp with a dock built out into the lake for the kids to fish and swim from. We'll offer canoeing, horseback riding, hiking and games. And each of the cabins will be equipped with the necessary medical equipment to help these kids in case of emergencies."

Caught up in the passion for the cause, Stan Oglethorpe jumped in to add to the list of amenities and services. "I've begun organizing volunteers to man the camp, with nurses and doctors willing to volunteer their time to make the camp safe and worry-free for the parents. The air rescue units will be made familiar with the location in case they have to make an emergency visit to pick up one of our patients."

"I've negotiated donations of lumber and building

materials from all the local lumber yards," said a man Rachel had met earlier, who had identified himself as the owner of a wholesale lumber supply store.

Freddie DeWinney added her contribution. "We've organized the local ranchers to provide horses for the cattle drive and labor to help build the cabins and buildings needed for the camp."

Others added to the growing list of volunteered supplies, services and workers, until it was apparent to everyone this idea would come to fruition.

It was with a sense of purpose and hope that everyone climbed back aboard the hay wagon to make the return trip to the ranch house. The singing was louder, the crowd more boisterous and spirits were high...except for Rachel's.

She had been impressed with the location for the camp and the level of support the organizers of the drive were promising. What she had a hard time dealing with was Adele draped all over Jesse, acting as if she hung on his every word. The woman who had been so cold to her sizzled with Jesse.

Rachel couldn't wait to get away from them. Seeing the couple together, and knowing they were engaged to be married, made her want to lose her lunch. As far as she was concerned, Miss I'm-better-than-you deserved Mr. Flirt-with-every-skirt. She didn't want any part of Jesse Jordan.

When they arrived back at the ranch, Rachel found JJ and Margie Jordan and thanked them for their hospitality, assuring them she would come through on some very inspirational advertisements for the cattle drive. Having thanked her hosts, she turned toward her car and was about to make good her escape when a voice behind her halted her in her tracks.

"Rachel, I'd like you stay after everyone leaves. I need you to help me with something."

"Can't you get your girlfriend to lend a hand?" she snapped without turning around.

A warm chuckle rumbled behind her. "Do I detect a note of jealousy?"

Hearing him chuckle, she turned around to see he was grinning. That infuriated her even more. "No, not in the least. As far as I'm concerned, you and Adele deserve each other."

"Nevertheless, I do need you to stick around."

She didn't lower her chin even when he added a soulful look and the simple entreaty. "Please?"

She hated herself for falling of his charm, yet again. But she did. "Okay. But make it quick. I don't have all day."

AFTER SEEING all the guests off and, finally, getting Adele to leave, Jesse turned and strode toward Rachel where she leaned against the hood of her car, impatiently tapping her fingernails against the metal behind her.

He could tell she was mad for being kept waiting, so he donned his most endearing smile as he drew closer to her. "I'm so glad you waited," he said in his deepest, sexiest voice, hoping to soften her up and douse her ire.

"Well, I'm here, what do you want me to do?"

Make love to me. I want you to rip my clothes from my body and yours and make mad passionate love to me.

Damn, she was beautiful when she was mad. With her hair twisted into a knot behind her head, curling tendrils floating loosely around her ears, and her eyes alight with fire—she was a sight to behold. The casual outfit she wore made her appear more like a wild thing than a female executive. "Would you please follow me and I'll show you."

A frown puckered her brow, and she hesitated.

Jesse held his breath, not certain Rachel would comply with his request.

Finally, she shrugged and pushed away from the car. "Well, let's get this over with so you can get back to your girlfriend."

Jesse's eyes narrowed. Leading the way around the house, and out of the sight of others, Jesse turned suddenly. "Alright, before we go any further, what are you talking about? What girlfriend?"

She backed up a step, frowning. "Oh, give me a break. Don't try to deny it. I was there during lunch, I know what I heard."

"I don't know what you're talking about. Whatever you thought you heard—it wasn't true." He turned abruptly, angry because she was being so unreasonable. Nearing the corral where he had performed the demonstration earlier, he glanced her way again.

She was still glaring at him.

Irritated, Jesse snapped, "What?"

"What, yourself," Rachel flung back at him. "Why did you bring me here?"

"I wanted to give you your first riding lesson," he said gritting his teeth in irritation. "That's all."

Standing outside the corral with reins looped around the fence rails was a large horse, fully saddled and ready to ride.

Backing up, Rachel's face changed from anger to fear. "You want me to get on that huge creature? Are you out of your mind? Don't you have a smaller one?"

"Come on, Rachel, this horse wouldn't hurt a fly. He is

the gentlest horse in the entire herd. I picked him out especially with you in mind."

"But he's so...so...tall! If I should fall, it's a long way down. I'd break my neck."

"Now, don't start talking about falling, when you haven't even tried to get up on him first. Here, let me show you how."

Walking to the left side of the horse and grabbing the saddle horn, Jesse placed his left foot in the stirrup and swung his right leg slowly over the top of the horse, settling into the saddle in one fluid movement. Reversing the motion, he was on the ground next to her in half the time.

"Now, let me help you up." Jesse moved close and took her hand to lead her toward the horse.

She pulled back, her eyes wide, her fingers twisting together.

"Still afraid? I showed you how easy it is. I can show you again."

"No, if I'm going to do this, I'll do it myself. I don't need your help."

He raised his hands in surrender. "Okay, have it your way."

Standing back, he crossed his arms and smiled smugly as he watched Rachel approach the horse from the wrong side. She stood several minutes studying the saddle and stirrups, before she stretched up to grasp the saddle horn. The horse was so tall, it was all she could do to get her hands around it. Pressing closely to the horse to keep hold of the saddle horn, she couldn't see where the stirrups were. He chuckled when she brought her right foot up, searching with the toe of her shoe until she accidentally bumped into the stirrup. Placing the toe of her leather loafer into the stirrup, she swung her left leg over the top of the horse.

As her left leg left the ground, the horse sidled to left, and her fingers lost their grip on the saddle horn.

Jesse lunged for her as her arms flailed in the air, and she let out a squeak of surprise. Unfortunately, he didn't get to her in time.

Rachel landed with a thud on her backside in the dirt.

Holding his hand out to her, Jesse tried to help her to her feet.

"I can do this myself, thank you very much." Pushing herself up from the ground, Rachel stood beside the horse once more.

"Ahem. Let me give you a hint, the horse is used to being mounted from the left side," Jesse prompted gently.

Instead of thanking him, Rachel glared, raised her chin and made a wide circle around the horse. Her nose was so high in the air she didn't see the pile of horse dung until too late. *Squish.* "Oooooo...what the hell?"

"That's the primary reason we wear boots on the ranch," Jesse said, his lips twitching as he fought the smile threatening to overtake his mouth.

Rachel lifted her foot gingerly out of the fragrantly steaming horse droppings. Any deeper and it would have oozed over and into her loafers. She walked to the corral fence and scraped the smelly green goo from her shoe on the bottom rail before turning to approach the horse.

This time, she grasped the sides of the saddle, since the horn was so high. Placing her left foot into the correct side of the stirrup she attempted to heave herself up into the saddle. Unfortunately, the horse shifted on its hooves once more, startling her, and she let go of the saddle.

Catching her under the arms, Jesse broke her fall with

his body, but the momentum sent them both tumbling to the ground.

With Rachel lying on top of him, Jesse lay still and breathless—not from her weight, but rather from the full body contact. With his hands still beneath her arms, his fingers lightly brushed the swell of her breasts, and he felt her body jerk. When she didn't automatically scramble off him, he took it as a sign of encouragement.

His body reacted instantly, his cock pressing against the soft derriere that rode the rigid length of him. He heard her gasp and, before he could stop to think, his hands moved farther around her to cup each breast. Thumbs and forefingers sought the hardened points of her breasts and rolled them, pinching slightly.

Nuzzling the soft skin at the nape of her neck, he whispered wryly into her ear, "Bravo, Rachel. You have me where you want me now, but all you had to do was ask. I'm more than willing."

CHAPTER 16

Rachel's body went still at his words then, in a burst of motion, she was on her feet and fuming.

"Of all the self-centered, egotistical, flirts, you top them all, Jesse Jordan. For God's sake, you're engaged. How could you do this to me, and what about your fiancée?"

Picking himself up off the ground, Jesse stood directly in front of Rachel, staring at her as if she had sprung horns or alien antennas. "What the hell are you talking about? I'm not engaged. And I don't have a girlfriend."

"Good lord, you don't even have the decency to acknowledge your fiancée. You are as low as they come. I'd be ashamed of myself if I were you. I suppose you plan to play the field even after you're married to her?"

"Will you quit yelling so I can sort this out?"

"I'll quit yelling, because I'm leaving." Rachel moved to go around him and headed for her car, but he blocked her path.

Jesse grabbed her arms and backed her up to the rails of the corral. Then he picked her up and plunked her onto the top rail. "You aren't going anywhere until you listen to me, Rachel Taylor," he said in a dangerous tone.

Trying to keep her balance on the slim rail of the fence, Rachel was forced to rest her hands on Jesse's shoulders. He stood between her knees with his hands planted on the rails beside her, his face inches from hers.

"Let's get a few things straight," he began. "I don't know where you got your information, but I am not engaged, and I have every right to pay attention to whomever I want. You've had a burr under your saddle since you got here. You need to get over it. I'm here to teach you how to ride a horse and that's all."

"But what about your girlfriend? Don't you even..."

Jesse closed the distance between them by crushing her lips beneath his in a desperate attempt to shut her up. He was tired of arguing when all he wanted to do was carry her back to his house and make love to her into the wee hours of the morning. He didn't know what she was talking about, but he was sure it was all a misunderstanding they could sort out later. For now, he was content to ravage her lips and run his hands over the body he'd recalled in every waking moment since the time they'd made love over a week ago.

When he finally broke off the kiss, he picked her up and plunked her into the saddle, climbing up to sit behind her. Nudging the horse in the direction of the lake, Jesse guided the horse out of the yard, leaving the house behind.

As the distance increased from the house, Rachel's stiff back relaxed, and she leaned against him.

Resting his chin on the top of her hair, he inhaled the fragrance of her shampoo and sighed. "Feel better?" he whispered. He regretted breaking the mood with his words when he felt her sit up straight and lean away from him.

"Let me down," she demanded and made as if to slide down.

Jesse reined the horse to a stop and swung down from behind Rachel.

Refusing his hand, she slid off the saddle and stood facing him with her hands planted firmly on her hips. "I want to get something perfectly clear. I am not one of your horses that needs to be gentled, and I have no intention of becoming one of your harem."

"Woman, you aren't making any sense." He scrubbed a hand through his hair. "What do you mean by that?"

"You already have another girlfriend, and I refuse to be another notch on your bedpost."

"What girlfriend?"

"Please, don't play dumb. The blonde lawyer who was hanging on you all day long."

"Adele?"

"Yes, Adele."

He shook his head. "But I'm not interested in Adele."

"Well, that's news to her."

"What are you talking about, she's only interested in my stud."

"Your what?"

"My stud, for which she pays a fee."

"You charge a fee?"

"Of course, you don't think I'd let her have it for free, do you?"

"If you are that mercenary, *I'll* pay you for it."

"Huh? What the hell are you talking about? You don't even own a horse."

Jesse noted the confused look on her face, feeling as if his expression must match hers.

"You were talking about your horse?" she asked in a small voice.

"Of course, what else would I have been talking about?"

As Jesse watched, her face burned a fiery red. Confused by her embarrassment, it was several seconds before Jesse realized what she had been thinking.

"You thought *I* was the stud?" he asked incredulously. When the ridiculous thought hit home, he chuckled softly, and stopped. Then exploding with laughter, he bent over with his arms wrapped around his middle in pain from laughing so hard. When he finally regained control, he wiped the tears from his eyes and looked around for Rachel, only to see her striding toward her car in the distance.

"Rachel, wait. I could give you a good deal," he said, clutching his sides again as he rolled over, hitting the ground, laughing until his muscles hurt.

A WEEK LATER, Jesse stood outside Rachel's apartment door with a modest bouquet of flowers and a spare cowboy hat. He raised his hand, but hesitated to knock.

One week had passed since he'd seen her, and they had not parted on the best of terms. In fact, he wasn't sure she would even answer the door if she knew it was him knocking. She hadn't returned any of his calls, and Mildred said she got all his messages. It served him right for being so unfeeling.

His lips twitched as he recalled her misunderstanding about the stud fee. That wouldn't do. She was probably still mad he'd laughed so hard at her embarrassment. If he stepped into her apartment and started laughing all over again, she would toss him out faster than a muddy cat.

What confused him most was Rachel's comment about paying his stud fee. It was apparent she'd thought it was him, not his horse. Well, for what it was worth, she could have all his studliness for free, no charge. The thought of "servicing" her had his studly part snapping to attention, ready to serve at a moment's notice.

It was still fairly early. Rachel might not even be up. Having second thoughts, he turned to leave and come back at a later hour.

Before he could take a step away from her door, the door across the hall opened and a sleepy Genie poked her head out, crouching to snatch the newspaper from the floor. Straightening, her gaze landed on Jesse.

One dark eyebrow rose. "Having second thoughts?"

Genie had read his mind. "Uh, no. I just thought she may want to sleep in late on Saturday morning, and I didn't want to disturb her."

"Rachel, sleep in late? Not a chance. Go ahead and knock. I'm sure she'd be happy to see you."

"I don't know about that. Last time we saw each other, I'm afraid I embarrassed her."

"That's not hard to do with Rachel. She likes everything orderly and precise. When things don't go according to plan, it confuses her."

"That's pretty deep for someone standing in fuzzy slippers and a baby-doll nightgown." Jesse smiled as his gaze traveled appreciatively down her form. His mouth turned downward into a frown. "I'm having a hard time reading her myself. Any insight you can give me?"

"First, tell me, what's your interest in Rachel?" Genie asked.

Contemplating the hat he twirled in his hand, he gave her question some thought before answering. "She's beautiful, and a bit starchy, but beneath all that stiffness is a core of fire. I sensed it the moment I met her. It's as if she keeps that side of herself well hidden and refuses to acknowledge it. I think she's afraid to let fun and passion into her life."

"Bingo. I tend to think it's because fun and passion are too messy. She might be out of control, and that makes her uncomfortable. But it doesn't really answer my original question."

"It doesn't?"

"Not really. Where are you going with this relationship?"

Not willing to voice to Rachel's best friend exactly where his hopes were leading, he said, "I'm not sure, but I know I spend my every waking moment thinking about her. I've never felt this way about any of the women I've dated in the past."

"Well, that's a start." Genie shifted in her fuzzy slippers and glanced down as if remembering her state of undress. "How about we meet for lunch on Monday to discuss your plan of action?"

"Plan of action?"

Genie shook her head. "You have to have a plan to win the battle, my dear Jesse."

"Do all women see romance as a battleground?" he groused, and then sighed. "Okay, I'll agree to go to lunch with you on one condition."

"What's that?"

"You don't wear those fuzzy slippers."

"I promise I won't wear my fuzzy slippers."

"Monday at the deli across from Rachel's office building?"

She nodded. "It's a date. Now, you've wasted enough

time. If you stand here much longer those roses will wilt. Get on over there and knock."

"Thanks, Genie."

"Good luck, Jesse."

Jesse waited until Genie closed her door then turned to address Rachel's door as if it were a great wall to be torn down. Straightening his shoulders, he bucked up his courage and raised his hand to knock on the door.

As if on cue, the door opened before he could knock. This was becoming a habit. But instead of Genie opening it this time, Rachel stood there barefoot in a satiny bathrobe, her hair in wild disarray as if she had just woken up.

"Jesse," she exclaimed, her eyes widening. "What are you doing here?"

Trying to force carnal thoughts from his head and words into his mouth, Jesse stood staring at the woman in front of him. His first inclination was to toss the flowers and hat to the floor and gather her into his arms. He wanted to part the satiny robe and slide his hands beneath it to feel the silk of her skin.

"Well?" she said, a frown denting her brow.

Apparently, he had stood long enough without an answer. Lifting his arms, he presented the flowers first. "Beautiful flowers that cannot outshine the beauty of the woman standing before me. Please accept the flowers and my apology for my ungentlemanly behavior last weekend." Jesse let out a deep breath, glad he'd gotten through his rehearsed apology, then added with honest regret, "I shouldn't have laughed at you."

Gathering the bouquet into her arms, she leaned over them to inhale their fragrance, hiding her blush amongst the red of the roses. "Apology accepted. Would you like to come in for some coffee?" she asked, and moved away from the doorway to allow him entry.

"That would be nice," he said with relief, and stepped through the doorway, recalling the last time he'd been in her apartment. He didn't know if he could sit down, right now. He couldn't seem to control his rising passion. Using the spare cowboy hat, he covered his zipper and eased onto the couch in the living room as Rachel perched on a chair nearby.

"Since when do cowboys wear two hats?"

"Huh?" Jesse blushed sheepishly, realizing he was still wearing his hat while carrying another. Reluctantly, he pulled the hat away from him and passed it to her. "Actually, this one is for you."

"For me? What would I need a hat for?"

"To go out riding with me, today." His tone was matter-of-fact, giving her no leeway to argue.

"Today?" Rachel glanced around the room as if hoping for an excuse not to go.

Jesse jumped in before she found one.

"I insist. Our last riding lesson was just the beginning. You need quite a few more before the cattle drive."

"Do I really have to ride at the cattle drive? Couldn't I just drive a jeep or something?"

"No, Rachel, everyone contributing will be participating. That includes you. Besides, I want you to get the feel of the land and have a chance to look for photographic opportunities for the advertising."

"I don't know about this." She stood with one hand pressed against her belly and the other closing the top of her robe.

Eyeing her defensive pose, he pivoted to another tactic. "If you don't do it for yourself, then do it for those kids who are depending on you. Show your support. Remember they're facing tougher challenges than riding a horse."

Rachel narrowed her eyes and raised one eyebrow in his direction. "I wish you would quit playing on my emotions for the kids. Okay, okay, I give up. I'll go. What time?"

"Now."

"Now?" she squeaked.

"Yes, I have a full day planned. Go put on a pair of jeans and some sturdy shoes you don't mind getting dirty. I'll wait."

Rachel rose from the chair and marched off muttering, "What's with men, anyway? They think a woman can just throw on clothes and rush out the door at a moment's notice."

The door to the bedroom closed, but Jesse could still hear her talking to herself about men not bothering to understand the ways of women.

Despite her grumbling, Rachel was back out in the living room fifteen minutes later, wearing the faded jeans and chambray shirt she'd worn the previous weekend. Her hair was pulled back in a loose ponytail at the nape of her neck. Without her stuffy clothes and very little makeup, she looked like a teenager.

Plunking the cowboy hat on her head, Jesse put a finger under her chin and lifted her face to his. His gaze on her lips, he almost leaned forward to capture them with his. But he pulled himself up short and tapped her nose with his finger. "The outfit makes you look dangerous," he said, raising an eyebrow.

"Dangerous? How so?"

"Dangerous in a good way, but dangerous none-the-less," he replied, unwilling to admit to her that she was dangerous to his heart. He turned away and opened the door to her apartment and made a grand sweeping motion with his hat. "Your chariot awaits, my lady."

Jesse made it a point to be entertaining and not too personal on the ride to the ranch. Rachel seemed to relax and respond the farther they got away from the city. They talked about the different activities that would accompany the cattle drive and the people who were sponsoring each event.

The miles passed quickly, and before he knew it, they were pulling up in the driveway to the ranch.

"You must love it out here," Rachel said with a sigh.

"I do," he responded.

Trying to view it through her eyes, he had to admit, city slicker or country bumpkin, this place appealed to everyone. He always felt a sense of coming home each time he drove down the driveway and up to the house.

One day, he'd like to see children playing in the yard or riding up the path on a horse to greet him when he came home. Glancing over at Rachel sitting beside him in his truck, he could picture her on the front porch with a baby on her hip. The vision brought a smile to his face. Rachel caught him smiling, and he turned the smile into a wink. "Ready for lesson number two?" he asked.

"Not really," she said and sighed again. "But I'll do it for the kids."

"Good girl."

Jesse dropped down from the truck, and rounded the front to hand Rachel down.

By the time he reached her door, she'd already slipped out and stood staring at the pen with the horses, a frown marring her lovely face.

"Do you want to pick the horse, today?" he asked.

"No, I'll let you have the pleasure. I trust you'll get the slowest and best behaved."

"That would be Little Joe, the horse you had the other day. Come on, let's saddle up."

Inside the barn, Jesse grabbed a couple of lead ropes and a few sugar cubes from a stash kept on a ledge inside the doorway. Armed with the bribe, he rejoined Rachel.

Together they headed for the gate to the horse pen.

Rachel looked out at the horses grazing nearby. "How do you catch them?"

"They'll come to us." Jesse took her hand in his and laid a square sugar cube in her palm. "All you have to do is show them that sugar cube."

As he predicted, as soon as she held out her hand, the horses perked up and trotted toward her outstretched hand.

The closer they got, the rounder Rachel's eyes grew. She backed toward the gate, appearing ready to make a quick escape if the horses should decide not to stop and run her over instead.

"They will stop, won't they?" she asked, her voice shaking.

He chuckled. "On a dime...for a sugar cube."

"My, but they are so big." Her voice faded to a whisper as some of the horses grazing farther out, raced toward her.

Jesse stepped forward with a cube of his own. The horses stopped right in front of him. The first one there nibbled the cube from his palm.

"Now, you try," he encouraged, holding his hand out to capture hers and bring her toward the horses.

She strained against his hold. "How do you know they won't bite?"

"I don't, but you just hold out your hand flat, and they'll take the cube from your palm without using their teeth."

Rachel drew in a deep breath, closed her eyes and stuck out her palm in the direction of the horses. She almost dropped the cube when the thick soft mouth of a horse snuffled at the treat. Her eyes opened just as the cube and the horse's mouth left her hand.

The horse munching on the sugar cube was a dark, brownish red with a black mane and tail and white stocking feet. Sporting a white blaze down the middle of his forehead, he was magnificent. It stood two feet taller than Rachel with his head held high.

Jesse was reminded of how small she was in comparison and felt an overwhelming need to protect her wash over him. "Let me formally introduce you. This is Little Joe, the horse you and I rode the last time you were here."

Reaching her hand out to stroke the horse's velvety soft muzzle, Rachel spoke gently. "Hi, Little Joe. I hope you don't mind, but I'm going to ride you today. Do me a favor and show me how."

Jesse smiled at the tremor in her voice. Determined to introduce Rachel to the joys of horseback riding, he hooked the lead rope onto the halter and led the horse through the gate.

"Hold the rope with your hand close to the horse's head. If you give the horse too much lead, he might misbehave."

Her hand paused halfway to the lead rope, and she pulled it back. "Misbehave?"

"Head-tossing and, on occasion, rearing back. Don't worry, Little Joe's a pussycat." He guided her hand up the rope, close to the horse's head. Rachel stood stock-still, her bottom lip caught between her teeth.

With the other lead rope in his hand, Jesse reentered the pen and snapped the lead on the halter of the buckskin he'd ridden in the demonstration for the cattle drive sponsors.

"We aren't riding together?" Rachel asked.

"Much as I'd love to, I think it would be better if you learned to ride alone first," he responded. "Come on, let's go saddle up."

Jesse walked toward the barn leading the buckskin gelding. He turned to watch Rachel's progress only to note she and the horse were still standing in the same spot.

Rachel shrugged and gave him a sheepish grin. "How do you make him go?"

"Click your tongue and tug on the rope at the same time, he'll come like a dog on a leash."

Clicking her tongue, Rachel tugged on the lead rope, and the horse stepped out quickly, almost leaving her behind.

Jesse shook his head, a smile spreading across his face. Rachel had a long way to go.

He led his horse to a hitching post outside the barn and looped the lead to the post, tying it snuggly.

Rachel watched and performed the same procedure with her horse, then stepped around the hitching post and followed him inside.

The interior of the barn was dark, and it took them several moments for their eyes to adjust to the limited lighting. Moving toward a row of saddles mounted on halved barrels, Jesse selected one, hefted it over his shoulder and grabbed a saddle blanket. He headed outside again.

Rachel followed. Jesse noted with satisfaction how she carefully watched everything he did.

Tossing the saddle blanket then the saddle on top of Little Joe, Jesse turned to teach Rachel how to cinch the girth.

"See that long strap hanging down the other side of the horse? That's the girth. It's what holds the saddle on the horse. It is very important to tighten it securely, otherwise you'll find your saddle slipping to the side as you ride. Reach under the horse's belly and grab the girth."

"Me?" she squeaked.

"Yes, you. Part of learning to ride is learning how to use the tack. When you're out on the cattle drive, you'll remove the saddle at night and put it back on the next day. Better to learn now than wait until you're out on the drive. I don't know if I'll be around to help you when you need it."

Nodding her understanding, Rachel moved slowly toward the horse and bent to reach for the girth hanging on the other side of the large animal.

"I can't...quite...reach it. There. I got it." Straightening back up with the end of the girth in her hand, she smiled triumphantly. "Now what do I do with it?"

Jesse looped the leather strap hanging from the near side of the saddle through the ring on the girth and back up to the saddle, looping it through the saddle and back through the girth a couple of times, then pulled the girth snug against the horse's belly.

"Even when you tighten the girth before you ride, you may need to stop and adjust during your ride. Sometimes, while cinching the girth, the horse will blow out its belly, making you think you got it tight, but he's just fooling you. You'll know by the feel of sitting in the saddle when the girth is loose. Immediately dismount and readjust."

"Don't worry, I'll remember."

Ducking back into the barn, Jesse returned with his saddle and a couple of bridles.

"This can be tricky. Most horses put up a little resistance to the bridle." Jesse looped the bridle over the top of Little Joe's head and brought the bit in front of his mouth. "Come on, Little Joe, be a good boy and take the bit."

Little Joe clamped his teeth tight and tossed his head.

"As I was saying, most horses resist. Put your thumb in the corner of his mouth like so, back behind his teeth. Pull back, and he'll open his mouth."

The horse opened his mouth, and Jesse slid the bridle between his teeth and looped the straps over his ears, then turned to smile at Rachel. "Easy."

"Yeah, sure," she said skeptically. "I thought cars were complicated. Horses are worse, and they have an added personality factor that'll take some getting used to."

Jesse slipped a bridle on his horse, removed the lead ropes on both and left them hanging on the hitching post for their return. With both horses ready, Jesse came around to stand beside Rachel.

"It's show time. Let me give you a boost up," he said, raising his hand to squelch any argument. "I insist."

Cupping his hands, he leaned forward. Rachel placed her shoe in his cupped hands and held tight to the saddle horn as he lifted her high enough to swing her leg over the top.

Landing with a hard thump in the seat, she maintained her death grip on the saddle horn.

"You can hold the saddle horn as long as you hold the reins as well. The horse won't know where to go if you don't steer him. That's what the reins are for."

"Are you sure we have to ride separate horses?" she asked.

"Absolutely. It's the only way to learn."

"Okay, could you give me the reins, please?"

Handing her the reins, he showed her how to hold them evenly and how to turn the horse by pulling the left or right. Jesse finally climbed into his saddle, and they moved the horses toward the house.

"I need to step into the house to pick up something." Jesse studied the woman sitting stiffly in her saddle. "Are you going to be alright?"

"I'll be fine as long as the horse doesn't decide to take off."

At the back porch, Jesse swung out of his saddle and trotted up the steps into the house. He returned with a saddlebag looped over his arm and a secretive grin on his face.

"What's in the bag?" Rachel asked.

"A surprise," was his only answer.

They set off across the yard and down toward the lake, riding side by side and at a steady plod. After ten minutes in companionable silence, Jesse noted that Rachel was loosening her grip on the saddle horn and actually looking around at the scenery. He smiled reassuringly when she looked in his direction.

"You look like a natural, Rachel."

Her lips pressed together. "Stop patronizing me, Jesse."

"No, really. With your hair pulled back and the cowboy hat, you look like you belong out here."

She snorted softly. "Ah, but looks can be deceiving."

"If that's the case, keep on deceiving me." He smiled. "I think you're sexy."

She stood in the stirrups. "Do these saddles come with padding?"

"I take it you are getting a little saddle sore. If you can

hold out for just a few more minutes, there's a special place I want you to see."

"I suppose I can."

Continuing in silence, they rounded a bend in the shoreline of the lake. There before them lay a cool shady spot where the lake was shallow and the grass was soft and green.

Jesse reined his horse to a stop.

Little Joe stopped beside him, with little direction from Rachel.

Jesse slid from his saddle and came around to help Rachel down from her horse. Once she was safely on the ground, he removed the saddle bag from the back of his horse. From the bag, he pulled a thin blanket from one pocket, a paper bag and a wine bottle from the other and held them up for her to see. "Voila! Instant picnic."

"How nice. I was just thinking how lovely it would be to have a picnic here in the shade by the lake."

Between the two of them, they had the blanket spread and the sandwiches out in short order. Jesse fished a Swiss army knife from his pocket, and used the corkscrew to open the bottle of wine. "We'll have to share. I couldn't figure out how to fit two wine glasses in the saddle bag."

"I don't mind," she said lifting the bottle to her lips to drink.

Jesse watched as a small trickle ran down the side of her face. He reached over and stopped it with his finger, raising it to his lips to taste.

Rachel's gaze followed his finger, and her tongue darted out to lick her lips as his wine-covered finger entered his mouth.

She gulped and passed the wine bottle to Jesse. Then she lay back on the blanket, closed her eyes and inhaled deeply. "I don't think I've ever felt this relaxed. It's a strange feeling to be content to let time go by. No schedules, no planning, just existing."

Jesse stuffed the cork in the bottle and set it aside, then slowly stretched out next to Rachel, almost afraid to destroy her philosophical mood. When she didn't protest, he propped up on one elbow and stared down at her upturned face. "I think it's important to keep things in perspective. Sure, if you work, you have to keep to the schedule necessary to perform tasks assigned. That's alright when you're at work, but there has to be time in your life for relaxing and living life outside the boundaries of rules and a schedule."

Rachel opened her eyes and stared up into his face, her gaze shifting form his eyes to his lips as he spoke. "For instance?" she prompted softly.

"Have you ever gone walking in the woods and listened to nature going on around you?" Jesse asked, fighting the urge to kiss her.

"No."

"Have you ever gone fishing with a cane pole and a can of worms?"

"No."

"There are so many things I want to show you, Rachel."

She sighed. "Jesse?"

When she said his name like that, his insides tensed, and he clenched his fists to keep from reaching for her. "Yes, ma'am?"

"Shut up and kiss me."

CHAPTER 17

ALTHOUGH SURPRISED AT HER COMMAND, it didn't take him long to comply. The whole time they'd been talking, he'd wanted nothing more than to sink himself deep within her. Tongue, fingers, everything—in every way his imagination had fantasized during the past sleepless nights.

He planted a hand on either side of her head and leaned over her, feeling his body harden to granite instantly at the sight of her licking her lips in anticipation of his kiss.

He was beyond gentle, and light years beyond civilized. He prayed for just a minute more of control to bring her to just a fraction of the excitement he felt, or he feared he'd scare her silly. He opened his lips over hers and pulled at her mouth with an open, sucking kiss. Drawing her tongue into his mouth, he raked it with his teeth, before coming up for air.

Her eyes were wide, her nostrils flaring and her breath every bit as ragged as his. Abruptly, he sat up and straddled her hips. Reaching for the buttons of her shirt, he freed the first couple before giving up and impatiently peeling it over her head. Her bra was gone in a flash.

Rachel raised her hands to cover her breasts.

Jesse shook his head, and raised her arms straight above her head as he nuzzled her nipples, brushing his lips over the swollen peaks again and again until she writhed beneath him.

"Please Jesse...I need you inside me, now."

He reared off of her and began to tear at his own clothing. She also worked with trembling fingers to shove off her shoes and tug down her jeans.

Once they were both naked, they faced each other on the blanket.

Rachel blushed, closed her eyes and leaned against Jesse, rubbing just the tips of her breasts in the curling hair on his chest. When she opened her eyes, she stared down to the place where their bodies touched.

Jesse clenched his hands against his thighs as he struggled to maintain control.

Rachel sat up and pushed to her knees.

A moment of panic seized him. She couldn't stop now. Not when she had him so wound up he felt as though he'd explode.

Then she turned toward him and straddled his hips. "Am I doing this right?" she asked.

"Oh, darlin', yes." He gripped her hips and settled her over his length without driving into her.

As her damp sex rubbed against the length of his manhood, her eyes widened. She arched her spine and leaned back her head, her ponytail sliding down the middle of her back.

Jesse surged against her, so ready to plunge into her, but equally aware of how great this gift was. He couldn't imagine Rachel taking the lead in a sexual encounter very often. In fact, he suspected this was a first for her.

She grasped his shoulders and raised herself.

The sensitive tip of his cock pressed against the wet, passion-slicked folds of her entrance. Poised to ram upward, he held back.

Rachel moaned and ran her hands up her sides to her breasts, squeezing and rubbing the tips.

Her motions teased Jesse into a frenzy of lust. He clutched at her hips, and centered himself at her opening.

In the back of his mind, he could hear Mildred asking if he'd used protection their first time. On the edge of losing control, he closed his eyes and gritted his teeth. "Wait."

Rachel's brows descended, and she braced her hands on his shoulders. "What did you say?"

"Wait." He reached out his hand, patting the blanket beside him, searching for his jeans and the wallet inside. "We need protection."

She drew in a deep, shaky breath and let it out slowly. "I'm glad one of us thought of it." She lifted the jeans, slipped the wallet from his back pocket and handed it to him.

Jesse fished the spare condom from inside and tore it open, flinging his wallet to the side.

Rachel took the rubber from his hands and slipped backward, perching on his thighs. Then she rolled the condom over his erection, taking her sweet time. She glanced up, her lips curving in a teasing smile that set Jesse's blood on fire.

When she finished, he grasped her hips and positioned her over his cock. "Just say no, and it stops here," he whispered fiercely.

"Seriously?" She shook her head. "Don't be a tease." She lowered herself over him, taking in his length until he was completely sheathed inside her.

Her chest pushed out, and her eyelids sank. "Oh, sweet Jesus," she murmured. She dragged in another breath and rose on her knees. The movement impossibly slow.

Then, staring into his eyes, she sank as he rose against her. Her breath caught, and he felt a moan rise from his lips as their bodies crashed together.

Jesse pumped, his hips moving in opposition to hers. When they came together, the slapping sound of skin meeting skin only made him hotter. Again, and again, they met, until the tension stretched so tightly, Jesse was sure he'd lose control before Rachel reached her climax.

Then Jesse felt the first tremors of his release. He was so close to losing it, when she pulled him tightly against her to still their movement.

"Stop!" she gasped.

"Jesus," Jesse fought to breathe, struggling to regain control. "What do you want? Tell me." His hands moved in urgent, rough circles against her back, smoothing and squeezing her flesh.

A shudder racked her body, and she leaned up on her arms. "I want more."

He laughed, the tone more desperate than humorous. "Holy, hell, woman. What more do you want?"

She stared down at him, her eyelids sinking to half-mast. Her tongue swept across her full, luscious lips. "I want you so deep inside me I don't know where you end and I begin."

"Sweet Jesus," he ground out. He cupped her buttocks and lifted her off of him. Cradling her in his arms, he guided her backwards until she lay with her back on the blanket. Then he spread her knees wide and back, opening her to the sunshine and his gaze. "Look at us, Rachel," he commanded.

She lifted her head, her gaze going to his shaft.

One large hand palmed the length of his staff in two long strokes. He reached with his other hand to finger the opening to her sex, sliding one...then two...and finally three digits up into her. Hot musky liquid coated his fingers as he dipped them in and out. With his thumb, he teased the nub of her desire until she writhed against the blanket.

"Now, Jesse," Rachel cried. "I can't wait a moment longer."

He fit his cock against her, wetting the tip. Leaning forward, he placed her legs over his shoulders and slowly pressed into her warmth.

"Watch us, Rachel," he gritted out. And in the small space between their bodies, they both watched as he slid in and out of her, harshly, at times jerkily, grinding the apex of their thighs together until the explosions began, shooting them both over the edge.

A long while later, he pulled out of her, urging her legs to slide down alongside his. Resting on one forearm, Jesse cupped her cheek and kissed her tenderly. Then he smoothed the loose hair back from her face and moved to release her hair from the elastic band holding it in place. He took her lips again, drowning in the intensity of the kiss.

Jesse rolled to his side and stared at her lovely body so naturally exposed with her pale, smooth skin dappled by the shadows from the overhanging trees. Beauty surrounded by the beauty of nature. This was how it was meant to be. He gave her a crooked grin. "I feel like beating my chest and yelling like Tarzan. You excite me in a very primitive way," he said, as he bent down to take a nipple gently between his teeth, tugging gently until she moved restlessly against him. Raising his head, he stared at the darkened, turgid peak.

"The other one feels neglected," she complained softly.

"Can't have that, now, can we?" He flicked the tip of his tongue against the neglected one, and felt the soft skin of the aureole pucker and draw tightly around the peak. He plumped the breast with his hand, kneading and squeezing, while he plied the tip with gentle tongue lashings and fierce nibbles. He simply could not get enough of her, and he suspected he never would.

RACHEL HAD NEVER IMAGINED how sensitive her breasts could be. They puckered hard and tight under his ministrations. Heat curled inside her, and her hips began to dance in frustration. One orgasm just wasn't enough with Jesse.

Abruptly, the man cursed.

Rachel felt a moment's alarm as he rolled her onto her stomach. Alarm turned to intense satisfaction as Jesse probed her from behind. She raised herself to her knees, sinking her shoulders toward the ground. Rough hands kneaded her rump, as he found her and drove hard into her folds.

This round of lovemaking was as ungentle as the last— fast, furious, hot and hard. At the very moment her womb clenched in its first spasm of climax, he pulled her up so that her buttocks rested in his lap.

He encouraged her to bounce against him as one hand sought to roughly tweak the globes of her breast, and the other found the passion hardened nubbin of flesh between her legs.

Rachel gasped and her breath caught for one long

moment as she poised on the edge of a passionate precipice.

She emitted one long cry, followed by a series of shudders, her channel clasping his sex in a rhythmic glove of sensation. She felt the pulsing throbs of Jesse's release inside her.

He tilted her head back and claimed her lips in a tender kiss. Jesse held her in his lap, arms wrapped tightly around her, rocking them both gently, his head resting against her shoulder.

When her breathing returned to normal, Rachel stirred against him. Pressing her lips to his shoulder, she tongued his skin then sucked gently.

Jesse slid out of her.

Rachel collapsed on the blanket.

He joined her, stripped off the condom and stretched out beside her.

As a breeze brushed across her bare skin, Rachel reached for Jesse's hand. She'd never felt so uninhibited, lying there as naked as the day she was born, letting the sun gently dry the sweat from her body.

As she stared up at the leaves of the trees, all Rachel could think was that her heart was in deep, deep trouble.

JESSE MUST HAVE DOZED, for when he awoke he still lay on the blanket, but Rachel rested on her knees, her legs straddled over his hips.

"I wondered if I would have to go this alone," she teased.

He drank in the sight of her firm breasts so tantalizingly close, nipples hardened to peaks, ripe for the touch, which he did. He cupped her breasts as she leaned into his palms.

Rachel threw back her head, closed her eyes and rocked her hips gently over his, pressing against that part of him he had thought would remain catatonic after their earlier bout.

He stiffened beneath her, his flagging staff shooting to attention at just the slightest touch from her.

Rachel rose up and down on her knees, allowing him the opportunity to slide his lengthening shaft into her channel.

He dipped into her opening, basking in her juices. Then he was out, his penis standing erect and throbbing in the warm breeze.

Jesse lifted his head, curious as to why Rachel had dismounted and surprised when she moved between his legs and wrapped her soft hands around him.

The juices he'd gathered on entry allowed her hands to glide smoothly up and down his shaft. Her hands rode him firmly and deeply, twisting slightly until he teetered at the brink.

He grabbed her arms and lifted her far enough up his body to grasp a breast in his mouth and suckle, pulling hard enough to make her gasp. He released the nipple with a pop and cupped her ass, positioning her over the tip of his impatient sex.

Once he found her entrance, he slammed her hips downward, feeling her sheath him deeply. He lifted and shoved her down again, gathering momentum and establishing a rhythm until spasms shook their bodies. At the last second before he shot, he lifted her away, his come shooting out over his belly.

Rachel lay by his side and pressed a kiss to his neck.

Jesse gathered in his arms and breathed in the fresh scent of her hair intermingled with the musk of their lovemaking.

They drifted off into a contented sleep, awakening to the afternoon sun headed toward the horizon. Jesse gazed into Rachel's eyes.

She looked away first. Her cheeks flushed a rosy pink, and she raised her hands to cover her breasts.

Delighting in her shyness after all they'd shared, Jesse smacked her bare bottom and jumped to his feet, pulling her up with him.

"I'll bet you've never been skinny dipping, have you?"

"No, Jesse, I haven't, but shouldn't we be going?"

"Not until you've been skinny dipping," he said with a grin, dragging her toward the edge of the lake. Rachel planted her heels in the ground.

"But the water might be cold."

"Have it your way." He released her hand. When she turned to find her clothes, he scooped her naked body up in his arms and carried her to the lake, walking in up to his hips before pausing.

"Jesse, don't you dare throw me..." Rachel started, but he wasn't listening. He tossed her into the water then dove in beside her as she came up sputtering and pushing wet hair from her eyes.

He surfaced behind her, sliding his body up hers. He cupped each breast in his palms, tightening his hold until her wet body fit snugly against his. "Much as I'd like to make love to you in the lake, I think we need to head back before dark. So, don't even try to change my mind," he said as he massaged her breasts and pressed his groin against her backside.

Rachel turned in his arms, smiling wickedly. She

rubbed her breasts against the hair on his chest and reached down to slide her hands around his awakening cock, pressing it against the curling hairs of her sex. "I wouldn't dream of changing your mind," she purred.

"You're going to kill me woman," he growled and lifted her to wrap her legs around him as he moved deeper into the water to balance her weight as he slid inside her. He was surprised the cool water didn't boil at the heat they generated between them.

"WELL, cowboy, how'd it go out at the ranch on Saturday?" Genie got right to the point, as she slid into the seat across the little bistro table from Jesse.

The café was one of her favorites. She often met Rachel here for lunch as it was close to both of their jobs and it offered a nice variety of items on its menu.

Jesse glanced away, refusing to meet her curious gaze. "Why don't you order first, before we talk?"

The comment made Genie close her menu and really look at Jesse. "What happened? Did she fall trying to get up on her horse, again?" Genie racked her brain trying to remember if she'd seen Rachel since Friday night. Nope, she'd been too busy helping Vinnie out at the Fetachelli Deli to notice whether or not Rachel was okay. Some friend she was.

"As a matter of fact, it couldn't have gone better," Jesse said, as he stared down into his coffee cup.

Genie sighed, releasing the breath she'd been holding. "Thank god. For a moment there, you had me going." Noticing that she wasn't getting any eye contact, Genie sat forward again, "So why so glum?"

"Oh, I don't know," the normally self-confidant Jesse

appeared confused and dejected. "I guess things went just too perfectly."

"Whoa, wait a minute. Let me get this straight. You're all depressed because you had a perfect day with Rachel?" Genie rolled her eyes and waved her hand in front of Jesse's face. "Helllloo? Wasn't that what you wanted?"

"Exactly, only now, I'm convinced I want it to last forever."

"You mean, like marriage and the happily-ever-after stuff?" Genie said excitedly. When he nodded, she practically bounced in her seat clapping her hands delightedly. "That's wonderful."

"I wish it were that simple."

"What do you mean?"

"Well, you know Rachel better than I do. How do you think she'll react, if I pop the question?"

The smile slid from Genie's face. "I see your dilemma." Her brows puckered into a frown as she contemplated his words. "Let me think."

Silence stretched for a few long moments. Genie drummed her fingers on the table, trying to guess what Rachel's reaction would be. "I hate to say it, but I really don't know how she'll react. Every time I discuss marriage with her, she's convinced it just won't work for her. I'm not sure if she'd turn you down flat and run screaming or fling herself into your arms."

"Exactly what I was thinking." Jesse heaved a long sigh. "One thing's for certain..."

"What's that?"

"I'm determined to marry her...but it's too soon to ask."

"Agreed. What we have to do is think of a way to make her just as determined to have you as you are to have her."

"Right," he said, pounding his fist on the table and

rattling their dishes. Then looking over at Genie he asked, "Got any great ideas on how to make her want me bad enough to take the plunge?"

Genie steepled her fingers and rested her chin on the tips. What she needed was divine guidance. What would make Rachel give up her hair-brained scheme of finding a sperm donor and go for the real thing, instead? "I've got it," Genie said triumphantly.

"What have you got?"

"What makes an animal run faster?"

"Huh?"

"Humor me, will ya? What makes any animal run faster?"

"If something is chasing it with the intention of eating it?"

"Right."

Jesse shook his head. "Right, what? I'm sorry Genie, but I don't get where you're going with this."

"If you chase her, she'll run, because she feels threatened. Don't you see?" Genie spoke slowly and clearly as if Jesse were a not-so-clever child. "You shouldn't chase her. You have to make her chase you."

"Now, I know you've gone off the deep end. How is not chasing Rachel going to get her to marry me?"

"You need to play hard to get, maybe even make her jealous."

Jesse frowned. "I don't know, sounds dishonest to me," he said, his voice deepening into a sexy growl. "I prefer being straightforward with my future wife."

Ignoring his misgivings, Genie searched in her mind for someone he could flirt with in front of Rachel. As she sat staring out the window, racking her brain, she saw Rachel striding toward the café in a hurry to get lunch.

Without thinking, Genie sprang from her chair and launched herself into Jesse's lap. She wrapped her arms around his neck and planted a big kiss on his surprised lips at the exact moment Rachel passed close enough to the window to see everything.

Genie peeked over Jesse's shoulder and had the satisfaction of catching the expression on Rachel's face. It was one of shock, followed immediately by anguish. Without going into the restaurant, Rachel spun on her heel and marched back toward her office building, her back ramrod straight.

Genie leaped from Jesse's lap, flew to the window and watched until Rachel was out of sight. She turned with a big grin.

The cowboy was still shaking his head with a frown between his brows over her sudden attack. "What the hell was that all about?" he demanded.

"My dear Jesse, the wheels are in motion," Genie said triumphantly. "Rachel just witnessed our kiss."

"What!" Jesse lurched to his feet and turned toward the door, only to be stopped by Genie's hand on his arm.

"Remember," Genie warned, "don't chase her."

"But she'll misunderstand."

"Don't you see?" Genie squeezed his arm. "That's exactly what we want."

"We do?" Jesse asked, running his hands through his hair. "Why?"

"She needs to decide whether or not she really wants you, and if she's willing to fight for you."

Jesse stared out the window. "But what if she doesn't, and she isn't?"

Genie let go of his arms and lifted her chin. "Then it wasn't meant to be."

Jesse jammed his hands in his pockets, balancing on the balls of his feet, ready to chase after Rachel to get her back.

Genie patted his arm. "I know you want to chase after her, but you do see the truth in what I've said, don't you?"

"Yes, I guess I do. I don't want to force her into a relationship. I want her to come to me because she loves and wants me."

"Now, you're talking."

"I don't know about this," Jesse said. "Seems like a back-assward way of doing things."

FLOATING on cloud nine for all of Sunday and half of Monday, Rachel decided she needed to get out of the office for some fresh air to help her regain some emotional balance. The city was alive with people, and it was only a short walk to a nearby café where she could pick up lunch for herself and Mildred.

She really was getting ridiculous. Focus was impossible with images of Jesse lying naked on the blanket by the lake popping into her mind almost as often as she took a breath. Her well-ordered life was topsy-turvy where her thoughts were jumbled with what-if situations.

She had dreams of walking down a long aisle in a white dress, with Jesse standing at the end in a white tuxedo with a matching white cowboy hat. His image was that of the shining hero in white, waiting to rescue her from the rut she was in as a lonely, pathetic single female.

Who was she kidding? Pushing Jesse out of her thoughts was hopeless. If she was honest with herself, she'd admit that she was head over heels in love with him, and it was definitely clouding her judgment.

Jesse just wasn't husband material. In fact, she hadn't

met a man yet, who was. That was the whole reason for her original idea of finding a sperm donor.

How could she even entertain the idea of throwing her lot to chance and pursuing happiness with such a flirt? Flirting was as natural as breathing to Jesse. He was outgoing, fun-loving and gorgeous, a dangerous combination for anyone interested in long-term stability. There wasn't a future with him. Was there?

What had started out as a stroll for fresh air was turning into a power walk, with Rachel arguing with herself the entire time.

What was the real reason she was afraid to commit? Was it really the many divorces she had witnessed among her acquaintances or was it something more? When she got right down to it, Rachel had to admit, it was because she hadn't found the man who melted her insides by just looking at her...until now.

The electricity they generated when they were together could light up a city. But was Jesse that way with all women, or was it just with her? That was the crux of the matter. As much as Jesse liked to flirt and play the field, would he be happy to settle for one woman *until death us do part*?

If Rachel threw in her towel and succumbed to Jesse's gentle persuasions, sort of like she had already, would she regret it in the long run? While she would be giving him both body and soul, would he commit the same to her?

Before she realized it, she had arrived at the café, glancing casually through the window to see how crowded it was inside. It was then she saw the subject of her thoughts with her best friend sitting in his lap, and they were kissing!

Rachel ceased to breathe. She swayed, all the blood

rushing from her face as she stared in shock at the cozy scene in front of her. She felt as if her heart had been ripped out and stomped into the gutter at the side of the street.

Her first instinct was to storm into the café and scream at them, but her ever-practical side won out. She turned on her heel and marched back the way she had come, letting her feet guide her, because she couldn't see through the veil of tears shimmering in her eyes.

It felt like it took forever before she was walking through her front office, head bent to avoid Mildred's eagle eye and curiosity. She almost made it through the door of her office when Mildred spoke.

"Was the café closed? Didn't you bring lunch?"

Pausing at the threshold, Rachel managed to respond. "No. Oh, Mildred, I'm sorry. I forgot all about bringing you lunch." That's when she lost it, and tears streamed down her cheeks.

Unable to say more, she dove through her office door and slammed it behind her. The tears continued to flow as she found her way to her desk and sat. Burying her head in her hands, she tried to cry quietly, but couldn't. The sobs shook her so hard, she couldn't shut them down.

When the tears slowed, she looked around the once safe haven of her office, hoping to find comfort and solace in the work she loved, only to see little reminders of her ruined pursuit of happiness.

Rachel gathered all the pictures of baby cribs and layettes scattered amongst the papers on her desk and jammed them into the waste can. She kicked the can for good measure, then burst into tears again as she injured her toe in the process. She sank back into her chair and wallowed as another wave of self-pity washed over her.

"What the hell is going on in here?"

Trust Mildred to be blunt.

Rachel raised her tear-streaked face to see her friend standing there with her hands on her hips, ready to do battle for her boss.

"Oh, Mildred. I'm such an idiot." She covered her face with her hands as more tears slid down her cheeks.

Mildred crossed the room and handed her a tissue. "Blow."

Rachel scrubbed her face of her tears and blew noisily before tossing the spent tissue into the trash.

"There, now that you have a grip, let's talk." She took the seat across the desk from Rachel and waited.

Mildred was like a drill sergeant. There was no arguing with her when she wore that determined expression. Rachel felt like she had to fess up or do pushups. At that moment, pushups sounded easier, though she hadn't done any since high school. Knowing there was no one else she could talk to, now that her friend had betrayed her, she gave up and launched into her problem.

"I've made a huge mistake."

"Work or personal life?" Mildred prompted.

"Jesse," Rachel explained in one word.

Mildred nodded. "And what mistake would that be?"

"I fell in love with him." Rachel dropped her face into her hands and groaned. "God, I'm such a fool."

"I don't understand," Mildred said. "Why would falling in love with Jesse make you a fool?"

"I just saw him with my best friend, Genie."

"So?"

"They were kissing," she wailed, her heart breaking all over again.

"Oh." Mildred paused. "What kind of kiss was it? A friends in passing kiss or a lover's tryst kiss?"

"She was sitting in his lap and all over him, there was no mistaking it. I'm such an idiot."

Mildred tilted her head, her eyes narrowing. "Seems like you do have a problem. Let me think about this." The older woman paced in front of Rachel's desk, her finger tapping against the side of her cheek. At one point, she stopped and she faced Rachel. "Has Jesse shown any interest in you?"

"I thought he had." Rachel blushed as she recalled their lovemaking by the lake.

"In what way?" Mildred demanded.

"Really, Mildred, that's personal."

Mildred studied Rachel's face, which by now was a fiery red. "Never mind, I understand." Resuming her pacing, she formulated her thoughts out loud. "It seems as though Jesse might be a little confused. He's shown definite interest in you, but this Genie thing is throwing him off track." Mildred turned to Rachel and asked point blank, "How much do you love him?"

Rachel pressed a hand to her aching chest. "It must be a lot, considering how much it hurts."

"Enough to make a commitment to Jesse?"

"I don't know," she said, drawing a ragged breath. "How can I be sure he won't leave me for another woman? After what I saw, I'm not sure Jesse even cares about me."

"Do you care?"

Lowering her eyes, she knew she did—too much for her own comfort. She was in over her head and drowning in emotions. "Yes."

"Then quit wallowing in self-pity and fight for your man."

"Huh?" Rachel stared at Mildred as if she'd grown horns.

Mildred's fisted her hands on her hips. "You heard me. If you want something bad enough, you have to fight for it."

"You want me to go beat up my former best friend? Won't I get thrown in jail for assault?"

The older woman crossed her arms over her chest. "If that's what it takes, do it."

"I can't physically assault someone, I don't even know how."

"Then think of another way to fight back. You have to make him want you more than any other woman alive."

"How do I do that?"

"You're a woman. Use your feminine wiles."

Rachel didn't have a clue what the woman was suggesting. She'd never used feminine wiles. How did one acquire them? "Can you at least give me a 'for instance'?"

"Wear perfume, something sexy—flirt, for heaven's sakes. But don't just sit there and give up. You've got more pride and backbone than that."

"But I've never flirted a day in my life. I don't know how," Rachel wailed.

"Well, boss lady, it's about time you learned."

CHAPTER 18

RACHEL TOOK off the rest of the day to go shopping with Mildred. Had she stayed at work, she would have been wasting her time in the office, anyway. Her heart wasn't into her assignments.

"You'll need clothing designed to entice a man's libido," was Mildred's sage advice. "Executive suits tend to wilt their passions, if you know what I mean."

Rachel blushed, wondering just how her crusty old secretary knew so much about what would appeal to a man. That was food for thought. But she had to admit, Mildred found some daring but classy outfits to spice up her wardrobe. She included some casual clothes suitable to wear at the ranch, as well.

When Rachel suggested cutting her hair, Mildred shook her head emphatically. She declared Rachel's long, wavy hair was her greatest asset. Men loved women with long hair when it was flattering. Mildred insisted she wear it loose whenever possible around Jesse, so he could envision burying his hands in it.

"But that's so impractical," Rachel argued.

"Since when has being a woman been practical? Are tight jeans and high heels any more practical than leaving your hair hanging loose?" Again, Mildred planted fists on her hips, squaring off with Rachel. "No. So get used to it."

The afternoon achieved its desired effect. Under Mildred's dogged guidance and drill sergeant firmness, Rachel's self-confidence returned. Her purpose was clear. She would fight for her man.

Throughout the day, she wrestled with whether or not she was a fool to love Jesse or a fool not to. She was finally ready to admit she'd rather take the chance on Jesse than to risk living a life without him.

Laden with packages, Rachel stood outside her apartment, fumbling for her key. A door opened behind her, and she spun, dropping her handbag and half of the plastic bags dangling from her fingertips. Genie rushed from the doorway to her apartment to help Rachel gather her belongings.

"No. I can get them myself." Rachel stopped Genie with her curt words.

"Are you sure? You look like you have more than you can handle," Genie said, her brows furrowing.

"I can handle everything just fine without your help, thank you very much." Rachel unlocked her door and started slinging bags over the threshold, one at a time, until they were all safely inside, and she could follow suit. Without another word, she entered her apartment and turned to close the door behind her only to find Genie blocking it.

"Mind if I come in?" Genie smiled innocently.

"Yes, as a matter of fact I do."

Ignoring Rachel's rejection, Genie sauntered in and gathered the bags from the floor. "Hey, you've been shopping. Why didn't you call? I would love to have gone. I could use a new outfit for a special date." Genie shot Rachel a glance, a smile tugging at the corner of her mouth.

Rachel was not amused, and she wasn't going to encourage Genie to enlighten her about her date. She could guess who the date was with, and she didn't want to hear about it.

Genie had other plans. "Guess who I saw at lunch?"

"I'm not interested," Rachel stated flatly, "and, I'm extremely tired. Do you mind?"

As if Genie hadn't heard a word Rachel had just said, she continued, "I had lunch with Jesse Jordan."

"Whoopee. I'm thrilled." Rachel emptied the bags onto the kitchen table, one at a time.

"I figured since you're obviously not interested in him, why not go for it?" Genie said flippantly, and then frowned. "You aren't interested, are you?"

Slamming the last bag down on the table, Rachel rounded on her friend, ready to do battle. "Genie, I thought you were my friend. Did you even bother to ask me if I cared? Did you?" Rachel turned away, taking deep breaths to calm herself.

"Gee Rachel, if I'd known you were interested, I wouldn't have had lunch with him without you there."

Rachel rounded on her furiously. "I have it tough enough vying for his attention with all the unmarried women in Texas—and some of the married ones— throwing themselves at him, without having to compete with my best friend as well. Thanks a lot."

Genie rose from the couch and walked toward Rachel a jubilant look on her face. "Whoa, Rachel, are you saying what I think you're saying?"

Rachel pulled herself up short and lifted her chin. "What do you think I'm saying?"

"Are you falling for the big guy?"

Rachel plopped into the nearest chair and buried her face in her hands. "Yes. Damn it, I am—and against all my better judgment." She scowled, not ready to let go of the anger just yet. She'd worked herself into a fine temper, and she deserved to wallow in it!

"Yee haw! You go for him, cowgirl." Genie perched on the arm of Rachel's chair and pounded her on the back.

Rachel frowned. "Huh? I thought you said you were interested in him? Why would you encourage me if you're interested?"

"I'm not really. I just wanted to see if you would confess your interest, and it worked."

"But what about lunch?"

"What about it?"

"I saw you and Jesse at lunch."

"So?"

"I saw you and Jesse *kissing* at lunch. *You* on his *lap*—*kissing* at lunch." Rachel crossed her arms over her chest. "Explain."

"Oh, so you did see us. I thought maybe you had." Genie looked pleased with herself.

Rachel's temper flared a notch or two higher. "What do you mean?"

"If you had looked closely, you would have seen *me* kissing Jesse."

"I did."

"No, you don't get it. *I* kissed Jesse—*he* didn't kiss me. It was all part of my plan."

Frowning, Rachel glared at Genie suspiciously. "Oh lord, someone else with a plan? What plan?"

"The plan to make you jealous enough to realize you really are interested in our cowboy friend. And, voila! My plan worked."

"Genie, I could kill you for that." Rachel's words were belied by the smile growing slowly from the corners of her mouth. "So, it was all just a joke?"

"Of course," Genie replied smugly.

"Does Jesse know that?"

Genie paused, frowning as if thinking about her answer before giving it. "Uh...actually, I don't know."

"You don't know? But Genie, Jesse may think you really like him."

Genie shrugged. "I do like Jesse."

"But you just said you were just playing a joke on me."

"I did, and I do like Jesse, but as a friend not a lover."

"Genie," Rachel said, drawing out her friend's name. "Don't you see?"

"See what?"

"Jesse may not know you were joking with me, and think you're ready to join his stable."

Genie's eyebrows rose. "Wow, I didn't think about that. You're right, that could happen. So, what are you going to do about it?" Genie gave Rachel a smug smile.

"Me?" Rachel's eyes widened. "You should be telling him you're not interested."

"No, that wouldn't do. If you want him for yourself, you'll have to get his attention. If he starts to show interest in me, you'll just have to divert his attraction for me and make him fall for you instead."

Rachel fell back into the chair and pinched the bridge of her nose to ward off the headache that was quickly gaining ground. "Now, you're starting to sound like Mildred."

"Mildred? What has Mildred got to do with Jesse?"

"She's who I went shopping with this afternoon to buy clothes suitable to trap a certain cowboy."

"She did that?" Genie rummaged through Rachel's purchases with renewed interest. "Wow, for an old lady, she has a great sense of current fashions. Oooo, you'll have to let me borrow this little number," she said, holding up a short black strapless dress, cut in a V-shape down to the waist in the back with slim straps crisscrossing the middle of the back. "Holy hell, if this doesn't get his attention, he's either blind or dead."

"I just hope I didn't waste one and a half paychecks on clothes, when the man may be ready to move on to a new conquest," Rachel said as she stared accusingly at her friend.

"Rachel, he'd be a fool if he passed you over for another woman, even if she's me." Laying the dress across the back of the couch, Genie planted her hands on her hips. "Besides, why shouldn't he be more interested in you? You're beautiful, smart and classy."

"Have you seen all the choices he has out there? There's the photographer at the photo shoot—"

"She's happily married."

"There's her assistant who acted like a groupie—"

"Too young, too obvious. It turns guys off."

"Then, there's that blonde bimbo-lawyer who would love to sink her claws into him...and his *stud* services—"

"He's lived next to her all his life. If he hasn't married her by now, he never will."

"And now, I have to worry about you!" Rachel shook her head. "I don't stand a chance. I'll be lost in the crowd of Jesse Jordan groupies." Rachel flung her arms in the air. "It's no use. I just wasted an entire afternoon shopping for clothes I'll probably never get the chance to wear."

Genie glared. "Rachel Taylor, are you afraid of a challenge?"

"Well, yes." Rachel admitted.

"You, the woman who graduated valedictorian of her high school, completed her degree in marketing in three years and clawed her way to the top of her advertising firm in record time? Who now owns said firm? Are afraid to fight for one little ol' cowboy?"

"Yes!" She spun away and paced across the room.

"But why?" Genie asked softly.

Rachel tried to think of the right words to articulate the way she felt. Each thought that came into her mind was discarded and replaced by another, until she decided there was no way to express her fears other than to just blurt them out. "Never in my life have I felt I had anything to lose. Grades were easy—all I had to do was read books and apply knowledge. It was pretty cut and dried, no chance of error if you knew the material."

Genie snorted, "Easy for you to say, I was a 'C' student. Grades were hard for me."

Rachel continued as if Genie had not interrupted. "Working my way up in the firm was easy because I studied and applied my knowledge again. The partners recognized my abilities, and the rest is history."

Genie rolled her eyes. "How about if I campaign for you to be president? You can't lose. So, what's so different about the cowboy challenge?"

Rachel's shoulders slumped. "That's where the rules change. Now, I'm dealing with emotions. You know me...I've never been good at love."

"Horse feathers!"

"No, really, Genie, I'm practically an old maid."

"Hey, watch who you're calling old."

"Well maybe not an old maid, but still single. The point is, I have no control over the cards in this deck. This is not like studying to take a test. I can't *make* Jesse fall in love with me. If it happens, it happens. If it doesn't..." she wilted at the distressing thought, "Jesse goes away with another woman, and I end up with a broken heart."

Genie sat in silence for a few moments before she responded to Rachel's confession. Then her eyes narrowed and her face flushed with anger. "Rachel, I appreciate that you just opened your heart to me and expressed your deepest fears, but you know, I can't feel a bit sorry for you."

"Huh?" Rachel's eyes widened as her friend turned on her.

"That's right, you heard me. You need to quit whining and learn to live in the real world." Warming to her tirade, Genie flung her arms out wide and continued before Rachel could interrupt. "Life is not some orderly schedule you can jot down in your day planner. It's living, breathing and morphing into something different every day. You can't stack it neatly on a shelf, because it's messy and hard to get your hands around. It would be like trying to nail Jello to the wall." Her scowl faded. Now, her gaze softened. "But, if you choose to join the rest of us in the living world, it can be completely, utterly, unbelievably beautiful. You just have to let it happen."

Rachel grinned. "Genie, I've never heard you be so philosophic."

"Damn right! And you better not make me do it again," she said and stomped out of Rachel's apartment, slamming the door behind her.

. . .

AFTER A LOT of soul-searching and the old tried-and-true therapy of trying on new clothes, Rachel decided to take Genie and Mildred's advice and try to capture and hold Jesse's attention. What better way than to invite him out to dinner? It sounded simple, but when she tried to get through to him at his home and work, she got secretaries and answering machines. No Jesse.

A week went by, and Rachel still couldn't get through to Jesse. Growing desperate, she decided to go to the store closest to her and hang out on the off chance he would pay a visit so she could accidentally on purpose 'bump into' him.

Saturday morning, bright and early, she climbed into her car and drove to the outskirts of the city to the Jordan Ranch Supply store located there. She parked her car in the large parking area, noting that she wasn't early compared to the twenty or more trucks already there.

Her little economy car looked outgunned surrounded by monster ranching trucks, with their reinforced bumpers and deer-squashing grills making them look all that much bigger. Feeling slightly intimidated, Rachel squared her shoulders, climbed out of her little car and walked into the store.

Even though she had advertised for his store, she had never paid a visit to one. It was like no other store she was familiar with. She supposed a rancher would feel like a kid in a candy store. There was every kind of equipment imaginable for use on a farm or ranch.

Wandering around the store, Rachel idly picked up a tool, held it up and tried to figure out its purpose.

"May I help you, ma'am?" A sales clerk asked. The young man looked to be no more than a teenager with smooth cheeks, shortly cropped hair and a sweet southern drawl. He wore dark blue jeans, cowboy boots and a white cotton shirt with the store name printed above the pocket.

Rachel's first inclination was to ask him if the boss was in, but she discarded the notion as too obvious. Grasping for something to say, she looked at the tool in her hand. "I think I need one of these."

"Uh, ma'am, have you ever used one?" he asked blushing slightly.

"No, but I'm sure I need one."

"Are you working with calves, kids or lambs?"

"Uh, kids."

"Well, ma'am, there is another tool you could use that is a little easier to manage."

Reaching into the bin next to the one she'd pulled her tool out of, the clerk grasped a shiny metal tool that looked very much like a pair of pliers. Then reaching into the box above, he removed a package of small fat rubber bands.

"If you put these rubber bands on the end of this tool and stretch them like so," he demonstrated with one of the rubber bands, "you can slip it over the animal's...uh...you know. It cuts off the circulation and it falls off after a couple of weeks, effectively castrating the animal without all the blood."

Blanching, then immediately turning bright red, Rachel finally understood what the boy was demonstrating. "You mean this is what ranchers use to castrate their livestock?"

The boy blushed a deeper red. "Why sure, ma'am. Castration is important—it cuts down on inbreeding and fighting in the herds."

Letting the tool she held in her hand drop back into the bin from which it had come, Rachel stepped away quickly. "On second thought, I don't think it's the tool I need."

Looking around again in hopes of seeing Jesse, she was surprised the boy hadn't left.

"Is there something else I can help you find?"

"Do you carry jeans and cowboy boots?"

"Yes, ma'am. If you follow me, I'll show you to the clothing section and the dressing rooms." He led her to a wall of shelves, stacked with every size, shape and color of denim.

"Thank you." Rachel selected several pairs of faded blue jeans and retreated to the dressing room.

Halfway through trying on the stack of jeans, she heard one of the female sales clerks talking to someone else outside the dressing room.

"Hi, Mr. Jordan. It's great to see you."

Gulping, Rachel held her breath, listening for the response.

"Hello, Susan, it's good to see you, too. How's that old man of yours?"

Rachel leaned against the wall and tried to think of what to do. She couldn't just jump out of the dressing room in her underwear. Quickly sliding into her tailored slacks and shoes, she glanced into the full-length mirror hanging on the wall. She smoothed her long hair over her shoulders and rubbed her lips together to make sure her lipstick was evenly distributed.

With her hand on the door, she listened again. She could no longer hear the voices. Opening the door a crack, she peeked out. The sales lady was there, but Jesse wasn't. Grabbing her purse, Rachel rushed out of the room and down the aisle in what she hoped, was the direction Jesse had gone. Near the front of the store, she could hear several people calling loudly to someone exiting through the front door.

"See ya later, Mr. Jordan."

"Have fun on your trip."

Reaching the front of the store a few moments later, Rachel saw a white pickup pulling out of the parking lot and recognized the back of Jesse's head as he drove away.

"Damn."

So much for her plan to bump into him. Shoulders drooping, Rachel returned to the back of the store. Selecting two pairs of jeans, she sat down to try on boots.

The sales lady Jesse had been talking with came to assist her with the sizing and fit of the boots. Rachel couldn't help herself, she had to ask.

"Was that *the* Mr. Jordan of Jordan Ranch Supply who just left?"

"Yes, ma'am. And I'll be danged if he isn't one of the nicest men I know."

"How so?"

"He makes it a point to visit each one of his stores at least once a week and talk with every employee. He knows all our names and a little about our families. He really cares about his employees and their welfare."

"Sounds like a saint, not an employer."

The sales lady looked off in the direction in which Jesse had disappeared. "Sometimes I think he is. If I weren't already happily married, I'd set my sights on that one. He's a keeper."

"With looks like his, hasn't every other female working for him had the same thoughts?"

"I'm sure they have, but he's never dated any of his staff that I know of, not that they haven't tried. Can't say's I blame them, he has a smile that could melt ice caps."

Staring off in the same direction as the sales lady, Rachel found herself nodding her agreement. Not only was he gorgeous to look at, he had a kiss that made her swoon, and hands that could work magic on her body.

Her thoughts transported her back to the edge of the lake on Jesse's ranch, where she could see herself lying naked next to him in the shade of the oak trees.

"Are you alright?"

Rachel pulled herself back to the present. "Yes, thank you. I think this pair fits just fine. I'll take them and the two pairs of jeans. I also need a couple of work shirts to wear outside."

Working with the sales lady, Rachel gathered the things she needed for the cattle drive, paid for her purchases and headed home. She was discouraged at having missed Jesse, but even more determined to see him than before. It was interesting that he appeared to have his own self-imposed rule about staying away from the help.

Even, if she didn't get to see him this coming week, she would see him at the cattle drive the following weekend. Then she'd be with him for two whole days, and she could flirt and tease him to her heart's delight and, dammit, he was going to notice her!

CHAPTER 19

RACHEL PARKED her sensible sub-compact car amid a sea of Texas-sized Suburbans and crew-cab pickup trucks at the Jordan family ranch. Even before she and Genie stepped out of the car, she felt the circus-like excitement that permeated the air.

Taking their bedrolls from the trunk, they made their way toward the tables that were set up beneath colorful event banners. They signed their medical waivers and received their briefing concerning the day's activities.

Rachel had hoped to arrive early enough to avoid the rush. But already, radio and television news crews were busy setting up to record the official ceremony marking the start of the drive and the dedication of the camp for kids with cancer and terminal illnesses.

Garbed in her new jeans, boots, and chambray shirt, Rachel wore the hat Jesse had given her the last time she'd been with him. She felt a bit like a fraud, wearing the cowboy clothes since she had spent the sum total of maybe ten hours on a ranch over her entire life. That didn't qualify her for the status of cowgirl or ranch hand, but she did feel as though she fit in when she saw that many of the other new arrivals were dressed in their equally new jeans and boots.

Once she was registered and wearing her official wrangler's badge, she turned to Genie. She had to smile at her friend's choice of western wear. Never one to understate, Genie wore bright red, skin-tight jeans and a red and black, western-cut shirt, which she had tied in a knot at her waist, exposing a generous slice of her midriff. She had also left several pearl-covered buttons open to display a hint of her ample breasts.

"Really, Genie, can you even sit in those jeans?" Rachel asked.

"Honey, whoever said a woman was supposed to be comfortable? The point is to always be lookin' like you stepped out of the centerfold."

"Again, you sound like Mildred."

"I like that woman more and more each day." Genie raised her arms and face to the sky and inhaled deeply. "Gee, Rachel, isn't it great to be alive?"

"Yeah, it is," she said, and meant it. The sky couldn't have been bluer. "What a day for a cattle drive."

And it was. The air was clear and soft with morning dew glistening off the trees and grass. Horses and cattle corralled behind rope barriers to the far side of the spectators' bleachers stamped their feet impatiently as if caught up in the excitement of the humans surrounding them.

Craning her neck to see over the gathering crowd, Rachel searched for Jesse's familiar face. With so many people wearing cowboy hats, it was difficult to distinguish one cowboy from the next. Still, Rachel searched for a hint of his fair hair and blue eyes.

"Oh, my god, Rachel, will you look at that." Genie

grabbed her arm and turned her in the direction she was looking. An old-style chuck wagon lumbered into the clearing. Fresh white canvas was stretched over the top with a restaurant logo printed on the sides in large red and black letters.

As the wagon turned, Rachel laughed as she read the words out loud. "Fetachelli Deli for Kids. I didn't know Vinnie was going to provide the catering for the drive."

"It's a surprise to me, too. No wonder he's been so smug —the sneak." Genie grinned. "I was beginning to think he didn't like me anymore. Every time I called him he was too busy at the Deli to talk. I thought he was giving me the brush-off. I guess, this explains it all."

Vinnie waved at them from his seat atop the chuck wagon. The man sitting next to him pulled back on the reins and brought the wagon to a halt next to the women. Vinnie's dark face split into a huge smile. "Yo, Genie, Rachel, you twos look like regular cowgirls."

He turned in his seat and swept his arm toward the canvas wagon cover and its advertisement. "What do ya think of my new wheels?" Then, standing carefully, he held out his arms. "And get a load of these threads."

Wearing a candy-apple red, white and black western shirt, black jeans and black and red alligator-skin cowboy boots with sharply pointed toes, Vinnie cut a dashing figure.

"Vinnie, you look good enough to eat," Genie teased. "I'll have to carry a big stick with me all weekend to beat off all the girls."

"Yeah, great outfit Vinnie. But, I thought Brady's Bar-B-Que was handling the food. What happened?" Rachel asked.

Vinnie smiled. "I got a call a couple of weeks ago from

Jesse. Said old man Brady backed out due to a death in the family. He asked me if I was interested, and the rest is history. It took some doin' to get this wagon cover designed and printed, but they delivered it late yesterday evening. Looks good, huh?"

"It looks great. But I can't believe you kept this a secret for so long." Genie smiled up at the dark-haired Italian.

"I wanted ta surprise you." He directed a bashful smile to Genie. "We got room for one more up here. Would one of yooze like a ride, or are ya more interested in riding a horse?"

Genie smiled at Rachel apologetically. "Looks like you're on your own today, girlfriend. Give me wheels any day. Besides four-legged beasts tend to have a mind of their own. Will you be okay?"

Rachel pushed her toward the wagon, "Go on, Genie. I don't need baby-sitting today. Have fun."

She watched as Vinnie took Genie's sleeping bag from her arms, then leaned down to grab her hand and haul her up to the seat beside him.

Genie smiled down at Rachel. "Good luck with your cowboy. I'll see you at lunch."

"I'll catch up with you two later. I'm going to see if I can find my horse." Rachel hurried toward the corral where a herd of already saddled horses was slowly dwindling as "wranglers" claimed their mounts. Nearing the corral, she saw John Jordan hailing her from his position in front of the gate.

"Sure glad I found you. Jesse gave me strict instructions on which horse you were to have."

"He did?" she said, her heart thumping.

JJ nodded. "Sure 'nough."

Suddenly, Rachel's two weeks of worry fell away. Jesse

had given special instructions for her. He hadn't forgotten her. Her mouth stretched into a happy smile.

Jesse's father gave a soft whistle. "You sure are a pretty filly. If I were forty years younger..."

Rachel grinned. "Why thank you, Mr. Jordan...I mean, JJ. Which horse did he want me to have?"

"He told me you were to have Little Joe, seeing as how you've had a couple of riding lessons on him already. He also told me to give you this."

Fishing in his pocket, he unearthed a sugar cube. "I guess that's to sweeten his disposition—not that Little Joe needs sweetening. Gentlest horse we got. Can be a little stubborn when he knows he can get away with it, so be sure you let him know who's boss."

"Yes, sir." Like she had any clue how to do that.

After letting Mr. Jordan tie her bedroll to the saddle, Rachel took the reins and led the horse toward the wagon carrying Vinnie and Genie. There was still no sign of Jesse. She assumed he was busy with last minute preparations and getting the horses and cattle ready for the day ahead.

"Hey, that's Bob Felton." Genie pointed at a tall man with a full head of artificially black hair, standing with a much younger looking woman draped on his arm.

Rachel's eyebrows rose. "Bob Felton of Felton Automotives? The biggest automotive supply guy in this half of the state?"

"Yeah, and that's wife number five on his arm."

"Man's got the right idea," Vinnie murmured. "About the time the relationship loses its new smell and starts requiring additional maintenance, trade 'em in for a new model."

Genie jabbed her elbow into Vinnie's ribs.

"Umph!" Vinnie grabbed his ribs over the sore spot. "Hey, I promise—I was only jokin'."

Genie leveled a killer stare at him. "I don't consider that the least bit funny."

Vinnie raised his hands in surrender and then rubbed his ribs again, smiling admiringly. "You're a tough little girl. You know you'll always be a new car to me, Genie." Vinnie puffed out his chest, looking proud of himself for having said it. "There, how's that for romance?"

Rachel and Genie burst out laughing at the sincere expression on Vinnie's face.

"What?" His eyes narrowed. "It was a compliment."

"I know, and all the cuter the way you put it," Genie said, patting Vinnie's knee. "Rachel, who's the blonde bombshell on the horse coming this way?"

Glancing in the direction Genie was indicating with a nod of her head, Rachel caught sight of Adele, making her way through the throng, riding a black and white horse. Everything about her was color coordinated from her black jeans, black cowboy boots, white blouse opened to expose a substantial amount of cleavage and her hair topped with a black cowboy hat tilted at a stylish angle.

"That's Adele DeWinney, the lawyer-witch I told you about," Rachel replied, her tone flat.

"Wow, talk about color coordination. I'll bet she even picked her horse to match her outfit." Genie laughed. "I can see why you were so concerned. I would be too, if Vinnie were interested in blondes, but he's not, are you Vinnie?"

Eyeing the woman in question appreciatively, Vinnie teased, "Yo, I could be converted with that one. She's real easy on the eye, if ya know what I mean. Umph! Hey, knock it off, or I'll make you ride in the back."

"First take it back about the blonde," Genie demanded.

Rachel admired how fearlessly petite Genie handled the big Italian. He easily outweighed her by a hundred pounds, but she was feisty and unwilling to back down a single inch.

"Okay, okay, you win. I take it back. I'd even go so far as to say she probably gets that blonde color out of a bottle."

Smiling approvingly, Genie patted Vinnie's hand. "That's more like it."

Despite her amusement at their antics, Rachel's gaze returned to Adele as she approached their little group.

Deciding to make the best of things, Rachel extended her smile to the beautiful blonde. "Hello, Miss DeWinney. It's nice to see you again."

Adele gave Rachel a regal nod as her only sign of acknowledgment and raised her eyebrows at Genie and Vinnie. "Who are your little friends?"

Rachel shot a warning glance at Genie who was already halfway out of her seat. "Adele, these are my dear friends, Genie O'Connor and Vinnie Fetachelli."

With a disdainful nod, Adele turned her attention back to Rachel. "I see Jesse gave you Little Joe. They always give him to the children, since he's so easy to ride." As if on cue, her high-spirited horse pranced to the side.

The show-off!

Adele easily calmed the fractious animal, patting its neck reassuringly. A smirk tipped the corner of her mouth. "Do you want me to find a ranch hand to help you to mount him?" she asked, her voice saccharine sweet.

"No, thank you," Rachel said with a saccharine smile. "As you said, even a child could ride this horse. I'm sure I'll have no trouble." Then to prove it, she dropped the reins to the ground, grabbed hold of the saddle horn, and raised her foot up to the stirrup. Concentrating and praying, she pulled herself up, swinging her leg over the top, landing neatly in the saddle.

"Bravo, Rachel! That's showing her." From her seat on the wagon, Genie clapped her approval.

Smirk still in place, Adele cocked her head a little to one side raising her eyebrows again. "Well done, but aren't you forgetting something?"

Looking around quickly to see that her feet were placed in the stirrups, then jiggling in the saddle to make sure the saddle was tight enough, Rachel smiled confidently. "No, I don't think so."

"How do you plan to tell the horse which direction you want to go—unless of course, you plan to have someone else lead it?"

With that parting shot, Adele swung her horse around with a flourish and trotted away. The blood rushed into Rachel's face when she realized she'd left the reins hanging to the ground.

Angry for allowing the woman to goad her into making a fool of herself, Rachel dismounted and gathered the reins. Once again, she mounted without mishap, but the damage was done. She had lost this round with Adele. So far, the score was Adele one, Rachel zip.

An amplified voice rang out above the noise of the crowd, calling attention to the raised stage, specially prepared for the welcoming ceremony. People on foot, gathered close, while everyone on horseback or in wagons remained where they were, able to see from their positions above the ground.

"Howdy folks, for those who may not know me, and probably didn't vote for me, I'm Senator Richard Lancaster. Jesse Jordan asked me to kick off this worthy event. So, without further ado, I'd like you to meet a friend of mine. Katie, would you come here, please? It's all right, these people are here to help make some of your dreams come true."

A small child with big brown eyes and a cherubic face stepped forward, holding tightly to her mother's hand.

The senator dropped to one knee, mic in hand, to be on eye level with the little girl. "Thank you for coming Katie. It's very brave of you."

The senator took Katie's free hand and straightened. Then, as if speaking to each person in the crowd, he delivered his speech. "Today, we are gathered to enjoy a good old-fashioned cattle drive. But more than that, we've been brought together with one goal. Without the strength of our numbers, this common cause will never see fruition. The goal is to build a camp for children suffering from the tragic effects of cancer. Little ones, like Katie here, must fight the battle to live every day of their lives."

Reaching up, Rachel dashed a tear from her cheek as she listened along with everyone else. From the corner of her eye, she spotted Jesse, sitting astride his buckskin, surrounded by three other men wearing cowboy hats and sitting naturally in the saddle.

Rachel only had eyes for Jesse, and he was looking straight at her. He smiled his hello then turned his attention back to the speaker. Her heart drank in the sight of him before she too turned her attention back to the stage.

"Today, we accept the challenge of driving cattle across country to demonstrate our determination to bring happiness into the lives of our children afflicted with this deadly disease. Thank you for your time and support to ensure this camp becomes a reality, so that little Katie can learn to ride a horse and swim in the lake like she has only dreamed of in her very short life."

Gently lifting Katie into his arms, he raised her up for everyone to see. "For the children!" he shouted into the microphone.

"For the children," roared the crowd.

Handing the microphone to Margie Jordan, and Katie to her mother, he stepped off the stage and mounted his horse.

"Hi, I'm Margie. I'm not one to waste words, so be careful, have fun and...let the drive begin!"

Hats flew into the air, and horses danced excitedly as people raced for their mounts, shouting "Yee-haw!" and "Yippee!" like children on the last day of school before summer vacation.

Little Joe took it all in stride, awaiting Rachel's command, patiently standing and occasionally shifting from one foot to the other.

From her vantage point near the chuck wagon, Rachel watched as Jesse and his three cowboy counterparts organized the riders into groups to take turns guiding the cattle across the open pastures to their destination at a neighboring ranch. Jesse's regular ranch hands would do all the real work of keeping strays from getting separated from the herd, but the participants would get a good feel for what it must have been like in the old days when long cattle drives were necessary to deliver beef to faraway markets.

Rachel was content to tag along for the trail ride, but not particularly thrilled to add herding cattle to her repertoire of riding skills just yet. She preferred to build her confidence slowly before venturing near the cattle. But more than likely, that's where she would find Jesse. If she wanted to talk with him, she'd have to go to him.

With news crews crowding along the sidelines to

capture the start of the cattle drive, the animals were herded out of the corral and across the pastures accompanied by a chorus of hooting and hollering.

Cowboys with bright colored bandanas around their necks, pulled their hats off their heads and waved them at the herd, encouraging the animals to move out.

The novice "wranglers" traveled alongside the cattle, with the wagons following a short distance behind the moving herd. It was a media event that would be played out for the public to see and experience for the two days it would take to reach their destination.

Rachel was pleased with the enthusiasm many of the local stations had shown. She'd arranged for the media coverage as part of the advertising.

Several anchors were among the riders participating in the drive, their cameramen shouldering mini-cams as they too followed the herd on horseback. The more coverage the event received, the more donations they hoped to collect to help fund the construction and operation of the camp.

Riding alongside the Fetachelli Deli Wagon for the first hour, Rachel enjoyed the sight of cowboys herding cattle, and didn't mind the natural, pungent odor that also accompanied the herd. Little Joe ambled along at a not too bone-jarring gait, and she thought she might actually be getting the hang of "driving" this old hoss. Despite her faux pas with Adele, Rachel's day was off to good start.

She didn't see Jesse until he pulled his horse alongside hers. His nearness caused her heart to skip a beat, and her face to suffuse with heat. Last time she'd seen him, she'd seen *all* of him. The image was burned into her heart and memory. Being this close in public, she was afraid her face would expose her feelings to anyone who might be watching.

"Hello, Rachel," he said.

His voice was as smooth as velvet, sliding over her like a sensuous caress. "Hi, Jesse." Her mind was a blank, and her mouth felt like cotton.

"I'm sorry I haven't been by to see you, but the final preparations for this drive sucked up all my spare time." His face mirrored the concern in his voice. "I'd much rather have spent it with you."

"I'm sure you were doing much more important things. I understand." Rachel bit her lip as soon as the words were out, second-guessing how he would interpret them. To her own ears, she sounded petulant and whiny.

Jesse grinned. "Did you miss me?"

"No, not a bit," she replied flippantly, unwilling to admit, even to herself, that she'd counted the minutes, hours then days they were apart.

"Well, I missed you for thirteen days, eighteen hours and twenty-four minutes, but who's counting," he said with a straight face.

"I got thirteen days, eighteen hours and forty-five minutes."

They laughed together at their joke, smiling into each other's eyes.

"Would you like to share the joke? Or is it too personal?" While they had been talking, Adele had managed to find them and ease up beside Jesse.

"It was personal," Jesse responded with a smile of apology to Rachel. "Hello, Adele. I thought you were riding with the herd."

"Obviously," she retorted, frowning at Rachel. "Do you

think you could tear yourself away? I wanted you to see a cow I think might be in trouble."

"Of course, I'll be right with you." All business, now, Jesse turned to Rachel and shrugged. "Duty calls. I'll be back to check on you in a little while." Kicking his horse into a slow gallop, Jesse rode off toward the herd.

Smirking with a satisfied look on her face, Adele nudged her horse's flanks, setting off after Jesse.

The chuck wagon rambled up beside her as Rachel's gaze followed Jesse's departing figure.

"I believe Adele just won round two, Rachel. What are we going to do to even the score?" Genie wanted to know.

"Not that I'm keeping score, but just who did Jesse seek out?" Rachel asked. "I'll give you one hint: it wasn't Adele."

"Meow and touché. You definitely have a point. Vinnie, remind me to serve her cream for dinner. Our little Rachel has unsheathed her claws."

CHAPTER 20

YEAH, I unsheathed my claws, but it's my tail that hurts. Two hours later, found Rachel still in the saddle, lagging behind the wagon, her jeans chafing the insides of her thighs, her boots pinching her toes, and her bottom feeling bruised to the bone.

What made it worse, Jesse hadn't returned to check on her since Adele took off with him. All in all, Rachel was feeling pretty sorry for herself.

Standing up in the stirrups, she eased her backside and strained to see the herd in the distance, knowing Jesse was working the cattle.

Several times she'd seen him riding toward her, but each time another rider on a black and white paint horse intercepted him and turned him back toward the herd. Even an inexperienced cowgirl like Rachel could see Adele was one of the best of the wranglers out there. Only difference between her and the others was that she was wrangling a man, not cattle.

Having grown accustomed to the rocking motion of the horse, Rachel relaxed her grip on the reins. Little Joe seemed content to follow behind the wagon, but he lagged farther and farther behind.

Concerned over the distance she had drifted from the others, Rachel lightly tapped her heels on the horse's flanks. She'd seen Jesse and Adele tap their horses' flanks, and their horses had taken off at a gallop.

Since Little Joe ignored Rachel's gentle tap, perhaps she hadn't applied enough pressure to get his attention.

She nudged him a little harder this time.

Nothing.

Putting a little oomph behind her heel, she gave the animal a swift kick.

Little Joe's ears laid back, and he tossed his head. But that was the extent of his reaction, and he resumed his plodding.

Frustrated but determined, Rachel lifted her feet in their stirrups as far as she could reach, then brought them in quick and hard, digging her heels into his sides.

Little Joe went from practically standing still to a bone-rattling trot in less than a second, nearly unseating Rachel in the process.

Rachel's bottom pounded painfully against her saddle, her teeth rattled in her head. In an attempt to gain control of the runaway horse, Rachel pulled at the reins, unfortunately unevenly, sending Little Joe veering to the right of the rest of the group.

Three hundred yards later, she finally managed to bring Little Joe to a halt. Pulling the horse's head around to face the other riders, Rachel gripped the saddle horn and kicked again, this time not too hard but not too soft.

Little Joe bent his head and bit into a clump of grass, contentedly munching.

As the herd grew more distant, Rachel became alarmed.

"Come on, Little Joe, you old candidate for the glue factory."

Several more unproductive digs at Little Joe's sides had Rachel angry enough to spit. Apparently, Little Joe wanted a mid-morning snack. Desperate to return to the group before anyone noticed the novice rider stuck out in the middle of the field with a cantankerous horse, Rachel dismounted. She'd just have to lead the horse away from his lunch.

Riding was hard on the leg and butt muscles, but she immediately discovered that standing again after three hours in the saddle was almost as painful. Rachel slumped against the side of the horse, holding onto the stirrup for support until she got her land legs back.

"Now, I understand why cowboys are bowlegged."

With the reins in her hands, Rachel tugged, hoping Little Joe would follow.

He ignored her and continued to graze.

Putting her back into it, Rachel leaned all her weight on the reins and tried again.

This time, Little Joe took a step, then another until he was walking steadily beside her.

Confident the horse was now willing to move, Rachel stopped, tossed the reins over his neck, then holding on to the reins and saddle horn, placed her foot in the stirrup.

Before she could swing her leg up over the horse, he moved forward, apparently impatient now to rejoin the rest of the horses.

Hopping along with one foot stretched high in the stirrup the other barely touching the ground, Rachel held tightly to the saddle.

"Whoa, horse! Whoa!" she called out.

Realizing he was not going to stop, Rachel pulled with

all her might and hefted her leg over the top of the horse, managing to land in the saddle.

"I did it!" she shouted triumphantly.

Rachel remembered everyone else was far ahead, where they were supposed to be, while she would have to ride faster than she was comfortable just to catch up. At least Little Joe was trotting willingly, having temporarily satisfied his hunger.

Bouncing along in the saddle as the horse trotted back to the group, Rachel wished over and over that she would've had the foresight to bring a pillow to cushion her bruised backside. How anyone could enjoy riding on a trotting horse was beyond her. Riding must be an acquired taste, only enjoyed after calluses were in place. It was a funny thing, she had heard of calluses on hands and feet, but she had never heard of calluses on butts.

Still wary of riding close to the cattle, Rachel hesitated to go find Jesse. Her resolve to fight for her man was flagging. How could she compete on horseback? Adele was a very accomplished rider, while Rachel still didn't know who was boss, herself or the horse.

"Hey, Rachel, where'd you go?" Genie asked as Rachel rode up beside the slow-moving wagon.

Unwilling to admit her horse had gotten the better of her, she answered vaguely, "Little Joe and I went out for a snack."

"Huh?"

"Never mind," Rachel said. "When do you suppose they'll stop for lunch?"

"I don't know, but this wooden seat is doing a number on my backside. How are you holding up?"

Rachel grimaced. "About the same."

"Somehow, I pictured the life of a cowboy to be a lot

more glamorous than this. You know, carousing at saloons, lying under a shade tree, singing to the doggies."

"I think we're just a couple of pampered city girls."

"Thank, God," Genie said with enthusiasm.

"You can say that again." Rachel looked out in the distance again, hoping to catch site of Jesse.

"So where's the lone stranger?" Genie asked as if reading her mind.

"Out punching doggies, I suppose." Rachel shrugged and sighed. This fighting for your man thing wasn't working out the way she'd hoped. She couldn't even get close enough to throw the first swing.

"I'm sure I would rather be out punching blonde lawyers about now, if I were you."

"Oh, Genie, I think I'm way out of my league here."

"Know what ya mean," Genie said, rubbing her backside.

"How can I compete with someone who grew up out here?"

"Who said you had to compete with her? Just be yourself."

Rachel gave a very unladylike snort, which was totally out of character for her. Must be the fresh country air. "But what will that help, if I can't get close enough to him to get his attention?"

"We have to stop for lunch sometime. Make your move then."

"What move?"

"I don't know, do a belly dance and strip naked in front of him. That should get his attention."

"It'd get mine," Vinnie murmured.

Rachel shook her head. "Be serious, Genie."

"Why don't you just talk to him?" Vinnie threw his two

cents worth in. "Guys don't like a babe to fake him out, pretendin' to be something she ain't."

Turning to Vinnie, Genie's eyes rounded in surprise. "Vinnie, I didn't know you were a philosopher." Genie grinned and patted his leg affectionately.

"I'm not. I just been around people all my life in the restaurant business. I call it the way I see it, if ya know what I mean."

Digesting, Vinnie's sage advice, Rachel rode on in silence. It wasn't until they closed the gap with the riders in front of them, that she realized they were stopping to give the cattle a rest and eat lunch.

The driver of the wagon pulled the team to a halt, set the brake and climbed down to stretch his legs. Genie and Vinnie hurried to the rear of the wagon to unearth the boxes of sack lunches prepared early that morning by Vinnie's family at the deli. Genie and Rachel assembled the serving table, and Vinnie and the driver set the large drink containers on the edge, with empty cups set beside them.

The lunch boxes were distributed quickly. Everyone was settled in eating lunch when Jesse came to stand next to Rachel.

"Don't you want to sit down and rest for a while, Rachel?"

She narrowed her gaze. "Not on your life. I'm standing for a reason, if you must know. In fact, I don't think I'll ever sit again."

Grinning, Jesse reached into his lunch box, but before he could pull his sandwich out, Adele appeared.

"Jesse, would you mind looking at my horse? I think his shoe is loose."

"I'll look after I eat."

"But Jesse, he's limping. Couldn't you tear yourself

away long enough to look at my lame horse?" she asked petulantly.

Looking around at the people standing around or sitting on anything they could find, Jesse's search ceased when he spotted who he was apparently looking for. "Hey, Roy!"

A leathery old man, a little over five feet tall and skinny as a rail, looked up. He wore a continual frown imprinted on his forehead and a lump of tobacco was jammed in between his bottom lip and teeth.

Already finished with his meal, the weathered old man, ambled over to where Adele stood, impatiently tapping her boot-clad foot. Stopping next to her, he turned to the side and spat a dark stream of tobacco, narrowly missing her agitated toe.

Rachel grimaced and looked away from the slimy ick.

"Yeah, Jesse, what can I do you out of?"

Jesse cocked his head in Adele's direction. "Mind looking at Adele's horse? She thinks he might be throwing a shoe."

"Guess I could," he grumbled. "Women ain't got a right to ride a good piece of horseflesh if they cain't tell whether a shoe's a fixin' to go, no how."

"But Jesse, I wanted *you* to look at him," Adele complained.

"Roy's been shoeing horses longer than you've been alive," Jesse said impatiently. "I think I'll leave it to the professional, if you don't mind."

Pursing her lips, Adele shot a venomous look in Rachel's direction, then turned to show Roy where her horse was tethered.

Quickly taking a bite of her sandwich, Rachel hid a

little smile at Jesse's treatment of Adele. The score stood at Adele's two to Rachel's one—thanks to Jesse.

"So, how *have* you been, Jesse? I haven't seen nor heard from you in while." As soon as the words were out of her mouth, Rachel realized she sounded just as petulant and possessive as Adele. It was not a good start to attracting him, so she smiled to soften her words.

Lowering his sandwich, he raised an eyebrow. "Did you miss me that much?"

"No. Just stating facts," she said, kicking the ground at her feet, careful not to step in the chewed tobacco.

With his half-eaten sandwich in one hand, Jesse took Rachel's hand with the other, toying with her fingers. "I would rather have been with you during the two weeks, but there were so many arrangements to be made to finalize this cattle drive, I just didn't have enough time to come by and see you, too." He lifted her hand to his lips and pressed a gentle kiss to her knuckles. "Do you forgive me for neglecting you?"

Rachel concentrated on not melting into a messy puddle of feminine goo. Instead she grasped at a thought that had nagged her for almost the entire two weeks. "Too busy for me, but not too busy for other women?"

His head came up, and his eyes narrowed in confused surprise. "What do you mean, other women?"

"The Monday after I came out to your ranch, I saw you having...lunch with another woman."

His furrowed brow smoothed, and he smiled. "Oh yeah, I ran into Genie at a little restaurant close to your office. If you saw us, why didn't you come in and have lunch with us?"

"Looked to me like you had as much...ahem...lunch as you could handle, already," she muttered.

Jesse's face turned a bright red, and he shot an accusing glance in Genie's direction.

The redhead returned his look with a wicked grin and a shrug.

Rachel knew it had been Genie's idea to kiss Jesse, but watching his discomfort, she had to fight back a smile. He deserved to squirm a little after ignoring her for two whole weeks.

"It wasn't what it looked like."

"What else would you assume if you saw a woman sitting in a man's lap, kissing him as if it were her last day on earth?"

"Well, I wasn't kissing back," he grumbled. He leaned close to her ear, his breath feathering across her cheek. "In fact, I was thinking I would rather be kissing you."

Her body immediately reacted to his whisper, sending blood rushing through her veins and causing her muscles to tense in anticipation of his caress. But, instead of kissing her neck, he straightened and lifted his sandwich to his mouth, taking a huge bite and chewing with a smug look on his incredibly handsome face.

Pulling her hat from her head, Rachel fanned her cheeks until they cooled.

Damn! The man could turn her on by just whispering in her ear. He had entirely too much power over her. That couldn't be good.

Oh, but it was, she recalled. Images of a naked Jesse in the lake water, had her throbbing in a place ladies just didn't mention over lunch in public, and it wasn't her saddle-sore tush.

As he polished his sandwich, Jesse gazed toward three men headed his direction. "Rachel, I'd like you to meet some friends of mine."

Rachel turned toward the three men who'd started the drive that morning with Jesse. They all appeared to be about the same age as Jesse and were tall, handsome and carried themselves with confidence, even the one wearing a brightly colored Hawaiian shirt.

"Rachel, this is Gage, Tanner and Rip, friends of mine since our college days."

She shook hands with all three, pausing at Tanner. "You look familiar."

He grinned.

Rip backhanded him in the gut. "You might have seen him in the Peschke Motors commercials."

Rachel grinned. "That's it. You're Tanner Peschke. You and your partner, Janine, had all of Austin anxiously waiting for the next Peschke Motors commercial. I never laughed so hard." She shook his hand again. "Those commercials were a great ad campaign. Wish I'd thought of it. It's nice to meet you."

"Pleasure's mine." Tanner grinned at Jesse. "She's as pretty as you told us."

The man Jesse had identified as Rip wore the Hawaiian shirt. He was next to greet her. He took her hand and raked her from head to toe with an assessing glance. "Yup! She's a looker. If I didn't have Casey…" He shot a sly glance at Jesse.

Jesse glared at the man. "Hands off, buddy."

Rip raised his hands. "No worries, man. I'm a happily engaged man." He winked at Rachel. "But if I weren't…"

Heat filled Rachel's cheeks. She tilted her head to the side. "Rip." Her eyes widened. "Not Rip O'Rourke from K-YAK radio station?"

Rip gave her a mock bow. "The one and only. I take it you've heard our show 'Something to Talk About'?"

Rachel nodded and shot a glance toward Jesse. "You didn't tell me you were friends with our local celebrities."

"Maybe he didn't want to share you with us," Gage said.

"Yeah," Jesse bumped his shoulder into Gage's. "Especially you. Rip and Tanner have their women. It's just Gage and I who are still single in this group."

"Hopefully, not for long," Tanner muttered.

"Much as I'd love to stay and chat, I have to get back to the herd." Jesse took her hands in his. "Are you sure you're okay?"

Rachel nodded. Even though her ass was sore, she felt warm and cared for. Not only had Jesse shared her with his parents, he'd introduced her to the men Rachel suspected were his closest friends.

Perhaps he really did have a thing for her. Hope surged and spread through her chest, making her happier than she could remember.

Jesse excused himself and took off with his three friends to check with the real wranglers prior to moving the herd. The rest of the cattle drive participants finished their lunches in a leisurely fashion, enjoying the company and conversation of friends and new acquaintances.

"Saddle up!" came the cry from Jesse's ranch foreman.

While everyone else quickly located their horses and climbed aboard, Rachel stood in front of Little Joe, setting him straight for the ride ahead. "You are to stay with the main group, no wandering off for between-meal snacks. Oh, yeah, and stand still while I climb up."

Rachel fished the lump of sugar she had commandeered from the chuck wagon out of her pocket and held it out to the horse as a peace offering. While he snuffled her hand for the treat, she scratched him behind the ears.

"See? You and I are going to be the best of friends. If

you're good for the rest of the day, I'll give you another lump of sugar just like that one."

"Well, isn't this quaint? A city girl talking to a country horse."

Rachel looked up to see Adele mounted on her horse, staring down her haughty nose at her. The woman might be beautiful, a brilliant equestrian and lawyer, but she had terrible manners. Tired of putting up with her bitchy attitude, Rachel confronted her. "Is something bothering you, Miss DeWinney?"

"As a matter of fact, yes."

"Let me guess..." Rachel tapped her finger to her temple and rolled her eyes upward. "Could it be Jesse's not paying attention to you?"

Rachel watched as Adele's lips pulled into a tight line, and her face flushed with anger. "Look, city girl, he may be having a fling with you now, but he always comes back to me. So, enjoy it while it lasts. I'll have him for the duration."

"Over my dead body." Rachel congratulated herself on standing up for her man.

Her eyes narrowing to a dangerous slit, Adele looked like an evil temptress. "Don't tempt me."

With those parting words, Adele jerked her reins, spun her horse around and galloped off toward the cattle.

"Oooo, Rachel, that was telling her." Gina congratulated her, pounding her on the back.

Adrenaline coursing through her veins, Rachel felt like bouncing on her toes and shadow boxing, ready for any fight. More confident in herself, she swung into the saddle like a pro and set off in search of Jesse, determined to ride with him for this leg of the journey.

She caught up with him as he coaxed the cattle to start

moving. Rachel stayed close enough for him to see her, yet far enough away so she wouldn't interfere with their efforts. When the beasts were moving at a steady pace, Jesse left them and rode over to Rachel.

In her best attempt to appear natural and relaxed as the horse bumped along in a trot, Rachel smiled, though she was sure it more resembled a grimace.

Jesse didn't miss the difference. "Are you alright? You look a little frazzled."

So much for looking relaxed and at ease on a horse. She shrugged her shoulders and gave him a lopsided smile as her head bobbed up and down.

"You know, we didn't get to move on to your next riding lesson," he said.

She twisted her lips into a wry grin. "Oh really? I thought getting into the saddle was a pretty major accomplishment."

He shook his head. "The next lesson would have taught you how to ride without jarring all your teeth out of your head and bruising your tailbone."

Her eyes bugged. "Well, what are you waiting for? Teach me, before I'm a toothless old fool with hamburger ham hocks."

Grinning at her analogy, he exaggerated his own riding motion to demonstrate how it was done. "It can be a little tricky, but if you stand a little in your stirrups and meet the saddle with your bottom every other bump, you'll find it saves a lot of wear and tear on your rear."

On her first attempt, her timing was off and she met the saddle hard, jarring her spine, pain reverberating up to the base of her skull. Refusing to give up, she tried again, this time anticipating the motion of the horse and moving smoothly to his innate rhythm.

"Wow, this is much better." Then, frowning, she pursed her lips. "You should have shown me this technique a couple of hours ago. My rump already feels like ground meat."

"I consider it my duty to offer to rub it for you with some soothing lotion. How about later tonight?"

Heat suffused her face at his reference to the last time he'd rubbed lotion into her sore muscles. Shooting a glance around to see if anyone had heard him, she answered a little more sharply than she had intended. "No, thank you." Softening her response, she added, "Besides, there are too many people around for any privacy."

Jesse heaved a heavy sigh. "We could wander away in the dark and find a quiet little spot after everyone else is asleep," he suggested, a charming smile making his proposal tempting.

"I don't know. Sounds kind of dangerous. Aren't there wild animals out here?"

"I suppose I could find someone more interested and less afraid," he said, sliding a sly glance in her direction.

Rachel's lips pinched together as she glared at Jesse, wishing she had something to throw at him. Instead, she refused to rise to his bait and continued to ride in silence, staring at the scenery as if it were far more interesting than the gorgeously, infuriating man at her side.

The scenery was beautiful here in the Texas Hill Country. Landscape varied from lush and green to harsh and rocky. The live oak trees were bent and gnarled from years of fighting the harsh summers and drought. Scattered among the green and brown vegetation were bright spots of colorful wildflowers adorning the fields.

Farther ahead, Rachel could see the sparkle of the sun reflecting off the surface of a large pond. As they moved closer to the pond, the cattle picked up the pace, anxious to quench their thirst on the dusty trail. Little Joe increased his speed to keep pace with the cows, also in a hurry to get a cool drink of water.

Holding on to the saddle horn, Rachel concentrated on maintaining her rhythm, riding a lot more comfortably than earlier. As the pond loomed nearer, Little Joe neither slowed his pace nor responded to her insistent tugging on the reins.

"Whoa!"

Riding along behind her, Jesse, didn't realize she was out of control until Little Joe entered the water.

"Rachel, pull back on the reins," he shouted, but the horse was intent on going in. At least he slowed his pace to a walk as the water came up to his belly. Rachel lifted her boots out of the stirrups holding her feet out of the water.

"Jesse, how do I get this horse out of the water?"

"First of all, you put your boots back in the stirrups."

"But they'll get all wet and they're brand new."

"If you don't you'll..."

Before he completed his sentence, Little Joe half reared in the water, sending Rachel sliding off the back of the horse into the water.

Surfacing, she gagged and spit the muddy stock pond water out of her mouth. As she wrung the nasty water out of her hair, she looked down at her blouse. What had once been crisply ironed, was now drenched and filthy from the dirty water.

Rachel looked up as Jesse nudged his horse to enter the water and edge close to her bedraggled form. So much for making an impression on him. And it didn't help when Jesse's face broke out in a huge grin as he reached a hand down with the intention of pulling her up onto his horse.

When she noted his grin, she refused his hand and planted hers on her hips, glaring up at his handsome face. "Jesse, somehow, I just know this is all your fault. You could at least have the decency not to laugh at me."

"I'm sorry, Rachel, but you're just darling standing there all wet in your see-through shirt."

Rachel's eyes rounded in surprise as she looked down at the front of her shirt. Sure enough, her lightweight chambray shirt revealed far more than she wanted to reveal to a herd of cows.

"Oh, my gosh." Wrapping her arms around her chest, she shot daggers at him with her eyes. "Well, don't just sit there laughing, help me out of this mess," she demanded.

What started as a chuckle, turned into full-fledged laughter as Jesse clutched his side with one hand and reached down to her with the other. Rachel grabbed his hand and, instead of pulling herself up behind him, she leaned all her weight backward, pulling a startled Jesse out of his saddle. With a loud splash, he landed in the water beside Rachel, sitting up and coughing and spewing water.

"What the heck was that for?" he asked, glaring.

"I just wanted to see what was so funny, and now I do," she said bursting into a fit of the giggles, which grew into gut-wrenching laughter. Grabbing her sides, she bent double with the effort to contain her mirth and tipped over into the water, landing in Jesse's lap.

Together, they laughed until tears rolled down their cheeks and they could laugh no more. Finally quieting, Jesse, placed his hands on each side of Rachel's face and kissed her soundly on the lips.

"My, my, I didn't know we were swimming on this cattle drive. Now, aren't we chummy?" Adele sat stiffly in her saddle at the side of the pond, observing the cozy little scene between Jesse and Rachel.

Playtime was over, thanks to Adele. It was time to hit the trail. Rachel couldn't help but feel a little elated. She'd gotten a kiss out of Jesse, and the score was now even with Adele. Not bad for a day's work.

CHAPTER 21

Rachel scrambled to stand up in the mucky stock pond. She slung the soggy mess of her hair over her shoulder, nearly unbalancing herself due to the slime-covered bottom of the pond.

Ignoring the still pristine and fuming Adele, Rachel grabbed Little Joe's reins and tugged until he followed her out of the water.

After a quick glance to make sure Jesse was okay, Rachel led her horse across an open field to the relative privacy of a stand of oaks and scrub brush. All the while, Rachel plucked the material away from her skin to keep the areolas of her breasts from showing through blouse and bra. Unprepared for the advent of being drenched from hat to boot, Rachel was destined to remain in her wet jeans and boots for the rest of the day.

Untying her sleeping bag from the back of her saddle, she unrolled it to reveal its contents. Inside, she had the basics necessary for a single night out. Pushing aside her toothbrush, hairbrush, washcloth and soap, she pulled her spare blouse out and shook it in an attempt to dislodge the wrinkles. It was hopeless. The blouse was one hundred percent cotton and had been rolled into a tight wad for the last five hours; the wrinkles were there to stay. She would just have to make do with a wrinkled shirt, wet boots, soggy jeans and underwear.

Quickly removing her blouse, she decided her bra would only make her blouse wet, so she removed it too. After rinsing her hair with bottled water, and squeezing as much water out of it as she could, she combed it and left it hanging loose around her shoulders to dry. She put on the clean blouse, then rolled her dry gear back in her sleeping bag and tied it once more to her saddle. Resigned to leaving her bra and blouse hanging from the saddle to dry, she knew she'd done as much as she could to improve her appearance. It was time to catch up with the rest.

"Sorry, Little Joe, but you'll have to play the role of clothes line as well as pack mule, today." Pausing to consider what she'd just said, she frowned. "Wait a minute. Why am I apologizing to you? You're the one who got me into this mess."

Standing with his head lowered, Little Joe looked almost ashamed of himself. Taking pity on the poor beast, Rachel scratched him behind the ears and rubbed the blaze on his forehead.

"I guess it wasn't so bad as all that," she murmured softly to the horse, remembering the kiss Jesse had given her while she sat in his lap in the stock pond. Her lips curved in a smile as she pictured the light of humor in his beautiful blue eyes. Filled with an overwhelming urge to see Jesse again, she led the horse from behind the bushes and out into the open.

"Come on, we need to catch up with the others."

Looping the reins around his neck, Rachel pulled

herself up into the saddle and turned the horse in the right direction, urging him into a trot. This wasn't so hard once you got the hang of it.

Falling in with the rest of the group, she traveled another hour and a half before the trail boss, Jesse's father, called a halt at the predetermined campsite for the night. Rachel helped Vinnie and Genie setting up the grills to barbecue hamburgers and hotdogs for the hungry guests. By the time everyone had been fed and the cooking equipment was made ready for the next morning's meal, Rachel was exhausted.

A fire had been built in the center of the camp, and a cowboy with a guitar started a sing-along. It was almost dark when Rachel found a spot on the ground where she could ease down onto her sore bottom and take advantage of the warmth of the fire and the beauty of the music.

This was the cowboy life she'd romanticized about. The colors of the sunset were fading into the deep black sky now filling with all the stars in the heavens. Closing her eyes, she wrapped her arms around her knees and listened as a soulful song lulled the cattle and the people into a state of contentment.

"Hello, darlin'." His softened voice blended into the notes from the guitar, yet it had the opposite effect on Rachel. Her heart skipped several beats before hammering against her ribs. She opened her eyes and craned her neck around to see the cowboy whose voice could melt butter.

Rachel smiled as she spotted Jesse standing behind her in the shadows cast by the firelight. The smile slid off her face as she realized his back was to her, and he was talking to Adele. Curiosity made her watch their exchange.

Adele was speaking so softly, Rachel couldn't catch her

words, but whatever she said to Jesse caused him to throw back his head in laughter.

Smiling up into his eyes, Adele spoke again in a pleading tone. Seeming to hesitate, Jesse finally nodded his head. Flinging her arms around his neck, Adele planted a kiss on his lips as Jesse wrapped his arms around her and squeezed, lifting her off her feet.

Turning back to the fire, Rachel's eyes filled with angry tears. How could he hold her in his arms and kiss her one minute, only to turn around a couple hours later and kiss another? She should have known. Who did she think she was, setting her cap at this outrageous flirt? What good would it do her to "catch" him? He couldn't stick to just one woman. It wasn't in his nature. Pursuing him would only lead her to heartbreak.

"Mind if I join you?" Jesse said.

Startled from her mental flogging, Rachel refused to look up and let him see the tears of anger trembling on her lashes. "Suit yourself, I'm going to sleep."

Pulling off her now-dry boots and socks, she crawled into her sleeping bag and wrestled off her jeans. She folded them to use as a pillow, zipped her bag up to her chin, and closed her eyes to feign sleep—something she knew would be a long time coming that night.

As THE FIRST light of day chased away the night, Jesse stretched and threw open his sleeping bag. He was determined to discover what had made Rachel snub him by turning her back on him and going to sleep last night without speaking more than two words. Just when he thought he understood her, she had him scratching his head all over again.

Looking over at Rachel's still form wrapped in her sleeping bag, he expected to see her still fast asleep. Instead, her eyes were huge and round, staring straight at him. Looking down at his shirt, he couldn't see anything wrong with him, so he looked back at Rachel.

"What's wrong?" he asked.

Rachel didn't respond. She frowned and looked down to her sleeping bag, mouthing a word.

"Did you lose your voice?"

Her response was the very barest of motions with her head indicating the answer was no.

Starting to get frustrated with her miniscule clues to the mystery, Jesse thought out loud. "Are we going to play twenty questions? I know you're riled about something, and I mean to have an answer, Rachel."

Her expression grew exasperated, and he let go a sigh of frustration. "Alright, have it your way. Well, let's see, there's something wrong, but it's not that you've lost your voice, even though you're not talking. This could take a long time if you're not going to speak to me."

He started to move closer to her, but her eyes grew wider, so he sat back on his haunches taking the hint that she didn't want him near her.

"How about I ask questions and you respond with one blink for yes and two blinks for no. Okay?"

Rachel blinked once.

"Good, now maybe we can make some progress."

Rubbing his hands together, he thought about his next question. "Are you not feeling well?"

Two blinks.

"No? Are you doing this because of something I did?"

Again, she blinked twice. She didn't look mad...she

looked scared. That got him to thinking this wasn't a game she was playing.

"Rachel, is something wrong with your sleeping bag?"

One blink.

His heart began to pound a little faster. "Yes. Okay, what could be wrong with a sleeping bag that would make you not want to talk?" When Rachel frowned, Jesse quickly added, "I'm sorry, I was just thinking out loud. Let me see, is there something in your sleeping bag?"

One blink and eyes wide with fear.

"Must be something bad to make you too scared to talk." Tapping his finger to his chin, he thought. "Is it a bug?"

Two blinks.

"No. Hmmm." He thought to himself again, then, "Is it an animal?"

One blink.

"Alright now we're getting somewhere. Let me see, what kind of animal would crawl into a sleeping bag on a cool night?"

As he watched, Rachel rolled her eyes in exasperation.

"Honey, is it a snake?"

One blink and a single tear rolled out of the corner of her eye.

"You're kidding, right?" he asked in disbelief.

Two blinks and more tears escaped her eyes.

Seeing her distress, Jesse jumped to his feet. He wanted to take immediate action to protect her, but he didn't dare come close enough to disturb the snake in her sleeping bag.

"Stay calm, sweetheart. Don't worry. We'll think of something."

Jesse's brows furrowed as he looked around for inspiration, finding none. His mind went through the list of snakes he knew could be found in this area, snakes he'd played with as a kid and those poisonous snakes he'd killed or steered a wide path around.

This could be a bad situation, depending on the species. Rattlesnakes, copperheads and coral snakes lived in this part of the country.

Rattlesnakes and copperheads injected venom into the blood stream and could make a person very sick. Most people didn't die from rattlesnake and copperhead bites, if they got to a hospital quickly for anti-venom treatment. They were a long way from a hospital, and it would take time for a helicopter to arrive, should they use the radio to request one.

What worried him most was the thought of a coral snake injecting venom into her. Their venom was more deadly because it went to work on the nervous system. He might not be able to get her out in time to save her life.

As that thought crossed his mind, he broke out in a sweat and raked his hand through his hair in frustration.

He couldn't rip the sleeping bag off her without disturbing the snake and risking the chance of it biting her. He basically couldn't do a thing. Glancing down at Rachel, her eyes flooded with tears, he knew he couldn't let her see his fear for her. "Well, I think we have a little problem."

Blinking once in response, more tears squeezed between her eyelids and rolled down her cheeks.

"I know you aren't going to want to hear this, but the only thing we can do is to wait until it starts to warm up. That snake went into your bag to snuggle up against your warm body. When it gets hot enough he'll come out on his own."

Her eyes widened, and then she frowned, blinking twice.

"I'm sorry Rachel, but it's too risky to try to move it. We don't know what kind of snake it is. If it's a poisonous snake and it feels threatened, it may strike. I'm not willing to risk that. We'll just stay here until it comes out."

Her tears slowed, and she closed her eyes in apparent resignation.

"Rachel honey, you just need to stay very still. I'm not going anywhere. We'll wait this out together."

Her eyes opened, and she looked at him, trust reflected in their depths. Making himself comfortable on the ground, he sat a few feet from her. The rest of the camp was rising and moving around, the smell of food being prepared filled the air and his stomach grumbled loudly. He saw a little smile on her lips.

Relieved that she didn't look quite so panicked anymore, he said, "You heard that, too? I'm so hungry I could eat my boots right now."

"Good mornin', y'all," Genie drawled as she ambled up to them. "Good morning Jesse." Then, turning to Rachel she noticed her still in her sleeping bag. "Rise and shine, sleepyhead. Aren't you going to help us get these people fed this morning?"

Before, Genie could walk any closer to Rachel, Jesse shot his arm out, halting her in her tracks. "Don't get too close to her."

"Huh? What's going on?"

"Rachel has a visitor in her sleeping bag."

"Visitor? What do you mean?" Genie asked, concern written on her face.

"A snake decided to spend the cool hours of the night in a warm place—namely, Rachel's sleeping bag."

"What?"

Enunciating each word slowly and clearly, Jesse repeated, "There's a snake in Rachel's sleeping bag."

Clapping her hand to her cheek, Genie's horrified expression spoke volumes. "Well don't just stand there, do something."

Keeping his voice calm, Jesse tried to reassure Genie and Rachel. "The only thing we can do is wait and let it come out on its own."

"You've got to be kidding! You can't let her stay in the sleeping bag with a snake."

Genie's voice carried across the camp, alerting others to the problem. It wasn't long before everyone gathered several feet away from Rachel, gawking and sympathizing with her dilemma.

Jesse waited until everyone was listening, then he explained his plan. "There's no need for everyone to sit around and wait on us. There's not much we can do until the snake decides to come out of the sleeping bag. That will be maybe an hour or two depending on how quickly it warms up out here."

"Can't we call 911 or something?" someone asked from the crowd of onlookers.

"In case you hadn't noticed, there's no phone service out here, and other than radioing for a helicopter we might not need, there's not much else we can do."

"Okay, come on let's get moving. The day isn't over until the cattle are back in their home pastures." John Jordan, herded the crowd toward the chuck wagon, where Vinnie had breakfast ready and waiting. The talk was hushed and everyone kept peering over at Rachel in her sleeping bag, shaking their heads in sympathy for her plight.

While the others ate, John returned with one of the walkie-talkie radios they had brought along on the cattle drive as a safety precaution. "Son, I'll leave this with you. We'll be within range all morning. If you end up needing medical help, you holler and I'll have a helicopter on its way, lickety-split." He turned to Rachel and gave her an encouraging smile. "I'm leaving you in good hands. Don't give him too hard a time, you hear?"

When breakfast was complete and the horses were saddled, her fellow "wranglers" filed by wishing Rachel good luck—everyone that is, except Adele. Then, the riders and cattle moved on down the trail. Vinnie and Genie pulled up in the wagon, hesitant to leave.

"Don't you want us to stay and make sure you're okay?" Genie asked with a worried frown on her face.

Two blinks.

"Rachel says no. Really, we'll be all right. If anything goes wrong, I have a first aid kit in my saddlebag and the radio. Besides, my horse is the fastest one out here. Now, go on."

"I just don't feel right about leaving her here. Promise me you won't let anything happen to her," Genie implored.

Vinnie patted her hands. "Come on, Genie. Jesse has things under control. Rachel's in good hands. We better get going, or we won't be caught up before lunch, and there'll be some grouchy, hungry people waitin' to lynch us. Oh, I saved some breakfast for you." Reaching behind the seat, he produced a foil-covered paper plate and handed it down to Jesse.

"I'm much obliged," Jesse said. "We'll see you later."

The driver flicked the lines, and the wagon lurched forward, rumbling away, leaving Rachel and Jesse alone on the prairie.

CHAPTER 22

Smiling gently at Rachel, Jesse settled on the ground close to her. "Well, you finally got me alone. But, I must say, all you had to do was ask. Putting a snake in your sleeping bag is going a little bit too far, don't you think?" Jesse joked, trying to ease her tension.

Crossing his arms across his chest, he gave her a stern look. "Actually, I'm kinda jealous. You didn't invite *me* into your sleeping bag. Women are a fickle bunch. Just when you think you know how they tick, they pull a stunt that puts you back at square one."

Jesse continued his monologue for the best part of an hour trying to keep Rachel's mind on things other than her bedmate. He was sure he was making absolutely no sense with his one-sided conversation. He didn't want to give her too much quiet to allow her time to think of all the things that could happen.

The sun made its slow climb up the sky, warming the air around them. Winding down on a tale of childhood pranks he and his brothers pulled on his sisters, Jesse glanced over at Rachel to see how she was faring.

Her eyes were round and her body tense.

"Is it moving?" He jumped to his feet, watching the edge of her sleeping bag for any sign of movement.

One blink.

"Good, I'll bet he's getting hot or hungry and is making his way out. Be very still."

Rachel rolled her eyes.

A few agonizing minutes went by before Jesse saw the snake's head peek out of the bag. Testing the air with its tongue, it hesitated, before slithering out and heading toward the tall grass, disappearing out of sight.

Releasing the breath he'd held the entire time, Jesse crouched and jerked the zipper of the sleeping bag down, allowing Rachel to escape.

"Oh, thank God!" Leaping free of the bag, Rachel flung her arms around Jesse and buried her face in his shirt.

Jesse stroked the back of her head, murmuring soothing words as her body shook with the force of her sobs. When her tears quit flowing, Jesse placed a finger under her chin and lifted her face to his.

"I'll bet your life wasn't near as exciting before you met me, huh?" he whispered, then kissed the tip of her nose.

"Yeah, and I hope I never have that kind of excitement again. Now, if you'll excuse me..."

Wiping the tears from her eyes, she turned away grabbed up her jeans from her sleeping bag and ran for a bush.

"Where are you going?"

"I've had to pee since before sunup," she shouted over her shoulder.

Chuckling, Jesse waited for her return, then handed her the plate of food, Genie and Vinnie had left behind. Tucking in with gusto, Rachel consumed it with no attempt at conversation. Scraping the last bit of scrambled eggs off the bottom of the plate, she sighed and looked up. "I was so afraid my stomach rumbling would cause the snake to bite me."

"It wouldn't have been so bad, it was only a common garter snake."

"Is it poisonous?"

"Nope."

"You mean, after all that worry, and having to remain perfectly still for over an hour, it was just a silly garter snake?"

"Yup," Jesse grinned. "Sorry to disappoint you."

Her expression was filled with disgust. "I don't mean to be ungrateful, it just seems so anticlimactic after lying there for so long. I couldn't even scratch my nose," she groused.

"Well, I'd be proud to scratch your nose for you." Jesse pulled her paper plate out of her hands and, setting it aside, circled his hand around the back of her neck, pulling her face close to his, their lips only a whisper apart. "...or anything else you have that might itch."

As his face dipped toward hers, she put a hand against his chest, holding him back. On her face was a scowl that brooked no argument. He sat back, perplexed. "What's wrong now? Are you still upset about the snake?"

"No. I just don't like being one of a harem of females you bestow your favors on, Mr. Jordan."

"Huh?" His forehead pulled into a frown as he tried to think of a reason for her comment.

"Don't play dumb. I saw you and Adele last night, getting cozy. I don't care who you kiss, but I'm not going to be one of many."

Jesse's face cleared, and his mouth started to twitch into

a smile, which he quickly reined in. With his eyes twinkling, he crossed his arms across his chest, contemplating her words with a serious expression. "So, what you're saying is you don't share?"

"As you would so aptly put it...yup!"

"And it bothers you to see Adele kissing me?"

Rachel squirmed, refusing to answer.

Jesse squelched the urge to grin, maintaining a poker face, though it cost him.

Rachel tossed her head and looked off into the distance, not meeting his eyes. "It's none of my business who you kiss. Like I said, I just don't want to be one of many."

"You're not jealous, are you, Rachel?" he pressed.

"Of course not." Her frown told the lie.

Shrugging, Jesse turned to pack his things into his saddlebag. "I guess, then, I don't need to explain what you saw," he said, slyly sneaking a peek at her face from underneath the brim of his hat.

Her emotions battled across her face and gnawed on her bottom lip.

Relenting, he turned toward Rachel. "Well, just to set the record straight, Adele was kissing me. I was not kissing her."

"And I suppose those weren't your arms wrapped around her?"

"Oh yes, undoubtedly they were. It was a hug exchanged between friends. I had just agreed to put my prized Arabian stallion up for stud, and I gave her first shot at it. She's wanted to breed her five-year-old Arabian mare to him for several years. She was showing her appreciation." Watching her expression turn from mistrust to chagrin, he hid a smile by turning away and settling his saddlebag on his horse.

"I'm sorry, Jesse, I didn't realize."

Hearing how contrite her voice was, he turned and took her in his arms. "I'd much rather kiss a certain starchy business woman than an old childhood friend." He brushed his lips across hers and pulled away, staring into her eyes.

Rachel leaned into him, passion lowering her eyelids, her gaze dropping to his mouth. When she ran her tongue across her top lip, he lost his control.

He couldn't resist. He crushed his lips to hers, putting all his earlier fear for her, and the frustration her stubborn reserve had caused him, into the kiss. His arms tightened just as the rest of his body did in anticipation of this mating.

Tongues darted out, one twisting and sliding against the other, tasting, drinking the passion.

Her hands found the buttons on his shirt, deftly loosening them one at a time until she reached the waistband of his jeans. She seemed to be in a hurry to see all of him. Rachel finished unbuttoning his shirt and moved on to the metal buttons of his jeans, giving a frenzied tug at the offending buttons.

Impatient, Jesse grabbed the top of his jeans and in one fluid motion, ripped the buttons open. She looked up at him as if surprised none of the buttons flew off. Grinning down into her face, he explained. "Thank God, they make the jeans with quick escape buttons."

Jesse reached for her, tugging her shirt from the waistband of her jeans. He ran his hands up under her shirt along her sides, cupping her soft, bare breasts with his work-roughened fingers.

When she placed her hands over his, he gazed into her eyes.

She answered with a smile. "Allow me."

Jesse stretched out on the sleeping bag, with the fly to his jeans hanging open, his erection exposed. He watched as Rachel slowly worked her hands down the front of her blouse, loosening each button with deliberation. When all the buttons were undone, the shirt hung open, teasing him with a view of the curve of her breasts and her softly rounded abdomen.

Her hands continued downward, unbuttoning the top of her jeans, and slowly tugging the zipper down. She closed her eyes and slid a hand down the front of her panties and up again. A soft moan rose from her throat.

Jesse nearly came then. If she didn't let him take charge soon, he'd likely embarrass himself.

WHEN RACHEL OPENED her eyes again, she stared into Jesse's.

His face had hardened, and a red flush stained his cheeks as his gaze followed her hand as it disappeared into her panties.

Her heartbeat stuttered, and her pulse raced. If a simple thing like fondling herself had him so entranced... Sweet Jesus, she couldn't wait to see his expression when she bared herself.

She slipped her thumbs inside her waistband and slowly pushed until the jeans cleared her hips and slid down her legs, pooling around her ankles. Stepping out of them, she hooked her thumbs in the elastic of her bikini panties, hesitating until his gaze rose to meet hers. She smiled, feeling purely feminine and incredibly powerful, then she let the panties follow the jeans.

Rachel stood above him with her shirt hanging from

her shoulders, almost naked, feeling as wild as the Texas landscape and incredibly sexy.

Jesse pulled off his boots and leapt to his feet, shrugging out of his shirt, to stand bare-chested before her.

When he made a movement to pull her into his arms, she placed a hand on his chest, holding him back. She stepped in front of him and slid her hands into the waistband of his jeans and underwear, tugging them down his legs.

She dropped to her knees and followed his jeans to the ground.

Jesse stepped out of the garment and drew in a deep breath, waiting for her to make the next move.

Still on her knees, her face only inches from his groin, she ran her hands up the sides of his muscled thighs to his hips. Smoothing her hands around to his buttocks, she looked up at him once to see his jaw tense and his fists clench at his sides.

Encouraged, she tentatively ran her tongue along the smooth flesh cloaking his rigid shaft until she reached its pulsing tip. Her eyes sought his before she settled her lips around him. Then pulling his hips forward, she took him into her mouth, alternatively sucking strongly and then teasing him with her darting tongue.

She'd heard this drove a man insane with passion. And at that moment, she wanted him as insane as he was making her.

His fingers wove into her hair as he thrust into her mouth.

Her own body tensed, her passion shooting fire through her veins. Giving him pleasure made her own experience ever more titillating.

Once again, the man had taught her more about life and living it to the fullest.

Reminding himself to breathe, Jesse dragged in air, then buried his hands in her hair and held her still. His penis was deep within her mouth and he feared he would come then and there.

Her gaze on his face, she swirled her tongue along his length, then sucked, her cheeks pulling inward with the action.

He groaned. By letting her take the lead, this joining was guaranteed to be short and fierce.

Rachel pushed his hips backward, allowing him to glide past her lips, until he was almost completely out. Her fingers dug into his buttocks, bringing him to a stop with her teeth at the ridge of flesh surrounding the head of his staff.

Jesse couldn't move, couldn't breathe and feared his heart had stopped beating.

Bringing her hands in front of him, Rachel fondled the heavy sac below. Then wrapping both her hands around his shaft, she tongued and sucked at the tip while sliding and twisting her hands down and up, down and up, until he was at the edge.

He pulled free of her greedy hands, and tugged her to her feet, finally assuming command. Now, she would feel the delicious torture she'd inflicted on him, to reach the edge of sanity at his touch.

He started by pushing the shirt off her shoulders, letting it slide slowly down her arms until she stood naked before him.

Jesse stepped back and stared at her, taking in the

beauty of her hair falling over her shoulders, brushing against the tips of her breasts. His gaze traveled down the pearly white skin of her soft abdomen to the triangle of curly dark hair covering her sex.

God, he couldn't get enough of her! He closed the distance between them and crushed her breasts against his chest, feeling the taught nipples poke against his skin. Sliding a hand behind her knees, he lifted her in one smooth motion, capturing her lips at the same time in a breath-stealing kiss.

When he came up for air, he laid her gently on the sleeping bag, knelt beside her and removed her arms from around his neck. Then, he bent to the joy of wringing delight out of every inch of her body.

Jesse straddled her hips and initiated his assault at her earlobes, nuzzling and licking, until she squirmed beneath him.

She wrapped her hands around his neck again.

"Uh-uh. It's my turn." He stopped long enough to position her wrists above her head. "Don't touch."

Moving down to her collarbone, he left a wet trail with his tongue and kisses, searing a path to her breasts. He captured one thrusting nipple in his mouth, sucking and biting softly until she bucked beneath him. He sampled the other, tasting and teasing until she writhed and lifted her hips to rub her belly against his sex.

Jesse slid down her body. His lips followed the path his hands blazed, stopping to dip in the indentation of her navel. As his tongue and teeth teased the sensitive flesh of her belly, he slipped hands further south and found his way to her inner thighs. A nudge with his knee opened her legs to his next invasion.

He skimmed his fingers along the silky skin of her

inner thighs as his lips moved toward the dark triangle of curls hiding her sex.

His fingers opened her and pushed back the hood of flesh guarding the distended button of nerve endings. He blew air softly against it and felt her fingers sink into his hair.

With his calloused finger, he stroked the nubbin of her desire, a thrill of desire arrowing straight to his cock when he heard her sharply indrawn breath. Jesse sank one finger into her warm, wet entrance then rubbed the nubbin again with his slick finger.

Rachel dug her fingers into his scalp and pulled his face closer. A silent plea for more.

He combed his fingers through her dark curly hairs and tugged, a gentle admonition for her to be patient. Once more, he spread the pink folds of her throbbing sex, before touching his tongue where his finger had been.

She raised her hips to meet every glide and flicker of his tongue. Rachel urged him to rotate his body.

Giving into his own desire to feel her hands upon him, he turned to plant his knees on either side of her head.

Her soft hand slid up the inside of his thigh, searching for his rigid, pulsing flesh.

He tongued her clit, laving the sensitized flesh with a determination to set her on fire.

"Sweet heaven, that feels so good," she moaned.

Her fingers closed around his cock, and she clutched him tightly in her fist, as her other hand continued to press his face down to her. She bucked beneath him, her hips keeping rhythm with the hand sliding along his sex, faster and faster, until she arched her back and her pussy spasmed against his mouth.

"Oh, sweet Jesse," she keened.

As her body continued to pulse in climax, Rachel pushed his body around until his face hovered above hers. She lifted her head and kissed him deeply, while she wriggled to position the tip of his shaft at her throbbing core.

He held himself poised against her, every muscle along his arms and shoulders straining. "Rachel, I can't take any more," he gritted out between clenched teeth.

She wrapped her legs tightly around his waist, then slammed upwards, impaling herself on his flesh.

It was more than he could handle. All thoughts of controlling his release flew from his head as he slammed in and out of her. She met him thrust for thrust, until he grabbed her hips and held himself deep inside her, his body jerking with his climax.

He collapsed over her, his muscles like jelly. Laying his forehead against her shoulder, he waited for his heart to quit galloping and his breathing to return to normal.

Her hand slid up and down his back and downward to cup his ass.

Jesse smiled against her. *What a woman!*

After a long recuperating moment, he rolled to his side to keep from crushing her. He was pleased when she followed him, without breaking their intimate connection.

"I could lay like this forever," she said dreamily, with her head resting on his arm, her fingers trailing lightly over his hip.

"I wish we could. You're an amazing woman, Rachel Taylor." Jesse kissed the tip of her nose then patted her rump. "Unfortunately, we can't stay here forever, or someone will come riding back to see what's taking us so long. Much as I enjoy staring at your naked body, I'm not willing to share that delight with others."

Gently pulling out of her body, he pushed up into a sitting position to stare down at her pouting mouth.

"Sure you don't want to go for round two?" she said, raising her arm seductively over her head and pushing her breasts out enticingly. She slid her foot along his calf and let her knee fall to the side, laying herself open to him. One hand fondled her breast before moving downward to slide enticingly along the swollen opening of her sex.

Boy, was he tempted. His mouth suddenly dry at the sight of her teasing him, Jesse was torn. Finally, he lay down on top of her and kissed her senseless. Then he rose in one fluid movement, and he stood above her, hands on his hips. "Woman, I am not a horse to be ridden whenever the hell you like," he said sternly. Then he grinned. "Besides, I won't be able to ride *my* horse, if we continue this." He grabbed her hand and pulled her to her feet and into his arms. "Now, kiss me and saddle up."

CHAPTER 23

JESSE CHECKED his appearance in the rearview mirror of his truck for the twentieth time as he pulled into the parking lot of Rachel's apartment complex. Not normally vain, he wanted to look his best. Tonight was the night. He was going to pop the question.

The last time he'd seen her was from a distance as the cattle drive came to an end. He had been surrounded by the triumphant riders and reporters congratulating him on the event's success and promising continued contributions to the cause. All the time he stood shaking hands and smiling, he wanted nothing more than to be alone with Rachel.

When the dust settled and most of the people had piled tiredly into their cars to head home, he'd looked around, hoping Rachel had stayed behind. There was no sign of her or Genie, and he had to assume they'd decided to head back to the city before it got too late. Disappointed, but not deterred, he'd resigned himself to her absence. He needed to set a few wheels in motion before he saw her again.

As he stood in front of her apartment door, he swallowed hard at the nervous lump forming in his throat. It wasn't everyday he made an offer of marriage to a woman. He guessed a few jitters were natural. Loosening the tie, which seemed to have tightened on his way here, he straightened his suit jacket, raised his hand and wrapped loudly on her door.

The several seconds it took for her to answer stretched interminably long. He should have called and made sure she was going to be home and wanted to go out with him. After their lovemaking on the drive, Jesse had assumed Rachel would be willing, and had even made reservations at a local French restaurant with a reputation of being classy and private. The setting had to be just right—if she wasn't already in love with him she would be by the time he got around to asking her the one question burning in his heart.

The door opened, and Rachel stood framed in it, wearing a wrinkled pair of jogging shorts and a baggy t-shirt with her hair pulled up loosely in a large clip. She was...sloppy...and mouth-wateringly beautiful. Jesse smiled and held out the dozen red roses. "These roses pale in comparison to your beauty."

Rachel stared down at her casual attire and snorted in a very unladylike fashion. With a single raised eyebrow, she stared at him, looking him up and down, taking in his suit and neatly combed hair. "Thank you for the roses, Jesse. Please come in." She stepped aside, allowing him to enter the living room of her apartment. "Did I forget something?" she asked with a perplexed look on her face.

"No, I thought I'd surprise you."

"Well, I'm surprised," she said, striding to the kitchen. She rummaged in a cabinet and withdrew a large glass vase. "So what's the occasion?" Rachel shot him a questioning glance as she set the vase in the sink and arranged the roses inside.

"I want to take the prettiest girl I know out. So why don't you go jump into your fanciest dress and let me take you out for a special dinner."

She looked up, her hand on the faucet. "Now?"

"Well, yes, unless you want to feed me dinner in your apartment, dressed in this monkey suit." He entered the kitchen, wrapped his arms around her waist and pulled her close, nuzzling the lobe of her ear, whispering softly, "Come on, Rachel, be a good girl and go get changed."

She melted against him. "I'll follow you anywhere as long as you whisper in my ear," she responded breathlessly.

"Then, hurry. We have reservations at seven."

"Seven?" she squealed. "That only gives me twenty minutes to get ready."

"Exactly, so get moving." He slapped her firm rump and gave her a nudge toward her bedroom.

"You've got to be kidding," she said as she flew through the door and ran for her closet.

"You're beautiful just the way you are, but the restaurant might have issue with the shorts. Just throw something a little more formal on. How long could that take?"

Rachel tossed a shoe at his head. "Men!" She grabbed a dress from her closet and disappeared into the bathroom, closing the door behind her.

While he waited, Jesse wandered around her little apartment, too wound up to sit still. He picked up a photograph of Rachel riding Little Joe. Judging by the crispness of her blouse and jeans, someone must have snapped it at the beginning of the cattle drive, before her dousing in the stock pond. He grinned, thinking back to the weekend's misadventures and excitement.

Having taught Rachel the rudiments of horseback riding, he looked forward to teaching her about the rest of his ranch and business. He wanted her to share in his life, with her as his wife, and he wanted to know more about her work and desires. The sooner the better.

He entered the kitchen and rummaged through the refrigerator, hoping to find a beer, only to find grapefruit juice and an assortment of vegetables suitable for salads. He closed the door and made a mental note to make sure he stocked up on steak and potatoes so he wouldn't starve to death after they married.

After five minutes of pacing the length of her small apartment, he sat at her small kitchen table and picked up the newspaper lying folded neatly, thinking to catch up on his reading while he waited. Beneath the newspaper, Rachel's day planner lay open to today's date. Jesse set the newspaper aside, his curiosity piqued. He leafed through the pages back to the day they met to see if she had written anything in it about him.

As he flipped the pages one by one, he caught glimpses of appointments with clients during the week until he got to the weeks he and Genie had double-dated with Rachel.

Jesse's chest tightened, and he laid the small notebook on the table. Words jumped off the page at him.

Ovulation cycle begins . . . date with sperm donor candidate #1 (see notes page six) . . . date with sperm donor candidate #2 (see notes page seven).

He turned to the back of the day planner, to the section marked notes. Jesse started at page one. As he read, a lead ball settled in the lowest region of his stomach, and he felt as if the world had been ripped out from under him.

There at the top of the page were the words GOAL: BABY. Beneath the bold print was a step-by-step plan to attain the goal, including finding a sperm donor, collecting the specimen, notes on ovulation cycles, best times to perform the "procedure", length of pregnancy and, ultimately, the planned deliverable, a baby.

His heart squeezing tighter, Jesse turned to the next page and read about viewing videos from a dating service and notes about each applicant, including his newfound friend, Vinnie Fetachelli.

The next page contained detailed notes about a Dr. Milton Peebles, giving a description of his mental as well as physical health, personality, pros and cons. In the upper right-hand corner was the word REJECT.

Flipping through the pages he found one more name terribly familiar to him. On the fourth page was a description for Lenny Lindeman, taxidermist.

As he turned the pages, he was only mildly relieved his name was not listed in the notes section. It didn't make him feel any better about what he'd found out. In fact, the more he thought about it, the angrier he grew.

His sexy, vulnerable Rachel was a woman with a plan. He wondered where he fit into her plan. He shoved back his chair and stood, holding the day planner in his hand.

At that moment, the door to Rachel's bedroom opened. She smiled and posed for his approval in a beautiful black sheath, which conformed perfectly to her slim figure.

God, she was beautiful, brilliant—and calculating. His jaw hardened, and his fists clenched.

"JESSE, what's wrong? Don't you like the dress?" Rachel asked. *Please let it only be the dress.*

Something in the cold glance and his stiff body told her it wasn't the dress. Then she saw the book he held open in his hand. Her knees wobbled as she stood frozen in the doorway to her bedroom, while her world crashed around her. *He knows.*

She had laid out her planner just moments before his arrival to remove all the information concerning her "plan" to have a baby. After all of her planning, she realized she hadn't taken in the emotional factor. She could never have gone through with a plan to use a man for his sperm.

Her time with Jesse had opened her heart and her consciousness to the fact she missed having love in her life. Not just the love of a child, but that of a man. And not just any man.

Jesse.

The answer to all of her prayers was the man standing in front of her. She'd been set on destroying her carefully devised plan. She no longer wanted to have a baby without involving the father in its life. It was unfair to the baby and unfair to the unsuspecting father. She knew that now. Perhaps she'd always known it. And strangely enough, having the child was less important to her now than having the man in her life.

Unfortunately, she hadn't disposed of it soon enough. "Jesse, I can explain."

"You don't have to. Let's see how well this dumb cowboy can read, huh? It looks like you were dating all those men to find a suitable sperm donor? Is that right?"

"Yes," she replied truthfully. "But please let me explain."

"There's nothing to explain. I see it all very clearly. It's all right here in black and white, isn't it? You planned on using me to get you pregnant, didn't you, Rachel?"

"No, Jesse, that's not the way it was."

"Isn't that what you had in mind for Vinnie and Lenny and Marion? Weren't they candidates?"

"Yes, but—"

"I guess when they didn't meet your very particular specifications, that's when you turned to me. Do I have it right?"

"No, Jesse, it wasn't like that with you," she said, but he was beyond listening.

"I'm surprised you'd even consider a dumb cowboy like me for the job. Where are your standards Rachel?"

"Please stop, Jesse. It wasn't like that with you." Tears slipped down her cheeks, and her body trembled. She was losing him.

"Were you even going to tell your donor he had fathered a child? Or were you going to keep that part of your plan a secret, too?" he said, contempt dripping from every word.

Rachel bowed her head in defeated silence. Her silence damned her.

"My God, Rachel! Do you realize how devious and unfair that would be to the father?"

"Yes, that's why..." she tried desperately to cut in, to explain

Jesse wasn't finished for her. "I thought I knew you. Sweet, shy, Rachel Taylor, someone I could trust, someone I could love." Flinging the planner on the table, he stared at her with loathing. "You're nothing but a mare looking for stud service. Now, I understand your comment on being willing to pay for it."

Rachel remained in place, trying to see through the haze of tears gathering in her eyes as Jesse marched away from her.

"Jesse, will you just listen?" she tried again, choking on a sob.

"I've heard enough. You used me, Rachel." As he

reached for the door handle, he turned and aimed a killing look at her. "As far as I'm concerned, I want nothing to do with you. We're finished!"

He yanked open the door and nearly collided with Genie as he stormed out into the hall.

"Were you in on this, too?" he demanded, jerking his head toward Rachel, clearly visible through the open door. "Stupid question. As I recall, you were there at every interview, right along with Rachel. Does your conscience bother you at all?"

He left Genie standing in the doorway and stalked down the hall and out of Rachel's life.

Silence fell between the two women. A vague thought formed in Rachel's head.

This must be how it felt to be a survivor of an earthquake. For several minutes the entire world rocks and shakes, leaving devastation in its wake. Afterward, when the ground stills, the rubble of your dreams and the sounds of anguish are the horrible reminders of the devastating event.

Rachel felt like screaming in anguish, sobbing out her grief at the love she'd lost through her selfish, single-minded desire to have a baby.

Genie raised her eyebrows and shrugged. "That didn't go so well, did it?"

CHAPTER 24

TWO WEEKS LATER, Rachel stood in the aisle of the local drugstore, wringing her hands. "Genie, what if someone I know sees me?"

"What does it matter, anyway? In a few more months, someone is bound to notice," Genie said scanning the items on the rows. "Here they are."

"Good grief. There must be a dozen different kinds. How do I know which is the best?"

"We could ask the druggist."

"No!" Rachel blurted out. "I'm sure any one of these will do, just grab one and let's go."

"*I'm* not choosing. *You're* the one who'll be blowing up like a blimp in a few months." Genie stepped away from the row of home pregnancy tests.

Rachel hesitated, looked down the aisle to ensure she wasn't being watched, and then quickly scanned the selection and chose a box. She wrapped her hand over the label so a person couldn't casually read the words. "Okay, let's go."

The checkout stand was another ordeal with only one

register open and several people in line. A woman with two small children pushed her shopping cart up behind Genie and Rachel. Keeping her back to the lady, Rachel pretended to read the magazines lining the racks of the aisle.

"You know, I used one of those when I thought I was pregnant with my second child. They work pretty well. It read positive when I was only two weeks pregnant. But, I already knew. I was already starting to feel the morning sickness. How about you, are you feeling sick yet?"

Embarrassed by the loudly spoken question, Rachel replied, "I...uh...no." She picked up a magazine from the rack and pretended to read the cover, hoping the woman would leave her alone.

The lady smiled and hiked her small child up on her hip. "Is this your first?"

"Um...yes, maybe." Rachel sighed and faced her. "How could you tell?"

"You look scared, sweetie," the woman said kindly.

Tears pricked at Rachel's eyes, and she blinked rapidly. "I am," she whispered.

The last two weeks had been hell for Rachel. She'd avoided Genie, throwing herself into her work, staying late into the evening and coming home in time to jump into the shower and go to bed.

Genie had tried several times to talk with her, but each time Rachel retreated, claiming she was on a deadline.

Last weekend, Genie had found her lugging a box of clothes out of her apartment.

"Whatcha got there, Rachel?"

"Stuff I'm going to give to Goodwill," she said flatly.

"Anything I might be interested in?" Genie asked, eagerly looking into the top of the box.

"Go ahead. You can have it all, if you want it."

"Rachel! These are the new clothes you and Mildred bought only a month ago. You can't get rid of these."

"I can and I will. They're not me."

With that, she handed the entire box to Genie and went back into her apartment, closing the door firmly on her friend's concerned face.

"Only one more person in front of you," Genie said, nudging her forward in the checkout line.

Rachel was glad she had Genie with her.

Finally standing in front of the clerk, Rachel waited while the woman scanned the bar code over the reader. It beeped and a light on top of the reader turned red. She scanned it again, and it beeped again.

The clerk shook her head, reached for the phone behind her and spoke into the loud speaker. "I need a price check on E.P.T. Early Pregnancy Test. I need a price check on E.P.T. Early Pregnancy Test kit."

Rachel wished the floor would open and swallow her. Her face grew so hot she thought it might spontaneously combust.

Unaware of her crime, the clerk replaced the receiver on the hook, chewed her gum and tapped her foot, totally ignoring the customer who wanted to crawl across the counter and strangle her.

Genie snorted and choked on a giggle.

Rachel glared at her friend.

Genie clapped a hand over her mouth, but couldn't hold back the laughter. Soon, she doubled over, holding her sides as she alternated between gasping laughter and snorting.

The phone buzzed behind the clerk, and the clerk was finally able to enter the code to ring up the purchase.

Rachel shoved her money across the counter, grabbed her change and the small bag containing the test kit and dashed for the door.

Genie followed, swiping at the tears rolling down her cheeks.

Rachel slipped into the driver's seat and waited for Genie to get in before starting the engine. "That had to be the most humiliating experience of my life."

"Yes, it was," Genie agreed, not bothering to hide her glee.

"And you were no help."

"What are friends for?" Genie choked out.

"Oh, you're hopeless," Rachel said, her face softening into a smile. "What would I do without you to show me how not to take myself so seriously?"

"You'd do a lot worse than you are now. So, are you finally ready to talk?"

"Yeah, but let's get the results of this pregnancy test out of the way first, so I know what I have to look forward to. Deal?"

Genie nodded. "Deal!"

They made the rest of the ride home in silence.

When they reached Rachel's apartment, Genie followed her inside and shut the door.

With a sense of dread, Rachel dug into the bag containing the test kit and tore open the box to find the instructions.

"Well, what does it say?" Genie asked. "What do you have to do?"

"Says here, I have to urinate on the stick. If I get a plus sign, I'm pregnant. A minus sign means I'm not."

"So, what are you waiting for? Go pee, girl!" Genie pushed her gently down the hallway to the bathroom.

Rachel stopped at the door. "But what if I'm pregnant? What am I going to do?"

"You'll have your baby, Rachel. Right on schedule."

Rachel winced. "Genie, I want you to know something. I gave up on my plan when I fell in love with Jesse."

Genie touched her shoulder. "I know, honey."

"I kind of forgot about it the longer I spent time with him. And I honestly didn't think about using protection."

"I believe you Rachel. It's not me you have to convince."

Rachel hung her head. "Genie, I was really starting to believe in happily-ever-afters." A single tear escaped her lashes and slid down her cheek.

Genie gave her a hug. "Honey, it's not over yet. You both just need time."

"No, I didn't play by the rules. It's no use, Jesse never wants to see me, again."

"Have you tried to call him?"

"I've dialed his number half a dozen times and let it ring, but as soon as he picked up, I chickened out. I just don't have the nerve to ask him to come back and let me explain. I'm afraid of his answer."

"My mother always said, *Nothing ventured, nothing gained.*"

"That's good advice, but I don't think I can take any more rejection."

Genie hugged her again. "You really do love him, don't you?"

"With all my heart. I never thought I'd be happy with someone who can make me laugh one minute and mad as hell the next. I always thought all that excess emotion was...messy." Rachel swallowed the sob rising up her throat. "I'd give anything for him to come back and make me crazy again."

"Well, let's tackle one problem at a time. We won't know what other issues we must deal with until you get this test over with. Now, get in there."

Rachel's hand trembled as she held it under her stream. She laid it on the counter, refusing to look at it, and finished up. She didn't know what she felt or what she wanted the test to prove.

Genie knocked on the door. "Well?"

Rachel opened the door slowly, then turned back for the stick lying on the counter. She glanced at it quickly. Then let her gaze bounced up to her own face in the mirror. It was ashen.

Genie's gaze met hers in her reflection. "You're not pregnant, are you?" she said softly.

Rachel felt numb, hardly able to process... "Oh, Genie, what am I going to do?"

Genie gathered her into her arms, patting her back. "There, there. We'll come up with a better plan, Rachel. Only this time, you leave the details up to me."

"No, Genie, you don't understand. I'm pregnant!"

Stopping in mid pat, Genie pushed Rachel's face off her shoulder. "You're what?" she nearly screeched.

"I'm pregnant," she whispered, smiling now through her tears. Yes, she was scared, and she'd rather have Jesse at her side happily sharing her news, but...she was pregnant! A child was growing inside her. Rachel pressed a hand to her flat belly.

"Rachel, that's wonderful," Genie said, then hugged her tight. "I thought by the look on your face, you weren't. I was so disappointed I wasn't going to get a niece or nephew. This is really great."

Rachel's joy faded. "You realize what this means, don't you?"

"That we're going to have a lot of sleepless nights with a crying baby?"

"Besides that." Rachel stared down at the stick. "Any chance I had of getting Jesse to believe me is shot. He'll think I did this on purpose."

Genie arched an eyebrow. "You weren't the only one 'doing' it, Rachel. Once he calms down, he'll see that."

Rachel pictured a little Jesse running around her apartment. "Jesse would make such a wonderful father."

"You have to tell him," Genie stated in a matter-of-fact tone.

"I know, but not yet." Grabbing Genie's hands in hers, Rachel waited for Genie to look her straight in the eye. "Promise me you won't tell Jesse about the baby," she said firmly.

"Rachel, Jesse has a right to know."

"I know, but I want to tell him in my own time."

"Rachel, you need to tell him about the baby. If you wait too long, he'll think you were holding out on him—again."

"Genie, I'll tell him...I promise. I just need a plan."

CHAPTER 25

"JESSE, open the door. We need to talk." Genie stood anxiously in the doorway of his home, praying he wouldn't leave her standing there much longer. She had braved the long drive out into the middle of nowhere to talk some sense into him. She wasn't leaving until she had accomplished just that.

"Go away, Genie, I have nothing to say," he said from the other side of the door.

"Jesse, I'm not leaving until I've said what I've come to say."

"Suit yourself," Jesse fired back.

"So help me, if you don't open this door, I'll…" What could she threaten him with that was worse than opening the door? Genie grinned. "If you don't open the door, I'll sing." Hey, it had worked in *Ghost*!

"Good," Jesse responded. "I love music."

"You won't love *my* singing, Jesse. I can't carry a tune in a bucket."

"That's your problem."

"Soon to be yours," she muttered. Taking a deep breath,

Genie launched into song. "Ninety-nine bottles of beer on the wall, ninety-nine bottles of beer. Take one down, pass it around, ninety-eight bottles of beer on the wall."

Twenty minutes later, Jesse opened the door to a hoarse Genie in mid-croak at twenty-four bottles of beer on the wall.

"All right, all right, you win. Here, drink this beer. You deserve it." He shoved a beer into her hand as she fell through the door.

Without waiting, he turned and stalked toward the wooden cabinet at the corner of the huge living area. The fully-equipped bar contained bottles of every kind of hard liquor a public bar would carry, but Jesse reached into the small refrigerator under the cabinet and pulled out a beer just like the one he'd handed to Genie.

He twisted off the top and faced Genie. He raised his bottle in mock salute. "I must commend you on your stamina."

"Stamina, be damned. What burr crawled up under your saddle, Jesse Jordan?"

He snorted. "You know damned well."

"Let me guess. You're fired up about Rachel's little plan to have a baby. Is that right?"

"You bet, I'm fired up. Who does she think she is, sneaking around stealing sperm from unsuspecting men?"

So, the man was going to be pigheaded about this. Genie planted her hands on her hips. She could out-stubborn any man. "Let's set the record straight. Rachel never actually stole anything from anyone."

Seeking calm, she took a long pull from the bottle of beer. The future of Rachel and Jesse's baby rode on her ability to get them back together, no matter what. "Rachel's methods may not have been right, but she was desperate.

She wanted a child more than she wanted anything else in the world—not as a possession, but to love and cherish for all of its life."

"Well, then, why didn't she go the normal route and get married to some unsuspecting slug and have a passel of kids?"

"Rachel didn't believe that marriage would ever work for her. She thinks she inherited some gene guaranteed to ward off wedded bliss. Least, that's the way she put it."

Jesse snorted.

Genie glared at him. "To tell the truth, I think she never felt a love strong enough to convince her to take the chance on a man. She probably thought it would be better for the child to be raised by a single parent from the start, rather than suffer through an inevitable divorce."

"There are no guarantees in this life," Jesse said. "Just where would that child have been if something happened to her? He'd be orphaned and destined for foster care."

"That's the whole point, Jesse. I really don't think she had any intention of going through with her plan." Genie recalled all the angst and indecision she'd witnessed that was so unlike Rachel. "If she had intended to follow through with her plan, she would have gone to a sperm bank and been done with it."

"And that's supposed to make me feel better about her?" Jesse downed the rest of his beer and smacked the empty bottle onto the bar's surface.

"She was just scared. Her biological clock's been tickin' so loudly she can't hear herself think."

"Biological clock?" Jesse threw his hands in the air. "Women can have babies clear into their forties. Rachel's not even close to that."

"Maybe not, but a lot of women who wait until their

thirties to have children have difficulties conceiving. I think Rachel felt panicked and wanted to make sure she didn't miss her window of opportunity."

"Well, she can count me out." Jesse shook his head. "I'm not her window, and I'm not giving her the opportunity. When I father a child, I want to be around to see him grow up."

Genie almost slipped and told him, he'd already fathered a child. But she'd promised Rachel. "Problem is, Jesse, you weren't one of Rachel's candidates. What happened between you two wasn't supposed to happen. It just did."

"It doesn't erase the fact she was looking for a sperm donor, and I just happened to be convenient."

"I know for a fact she fought her attraction for you. She didn't want to fall for you."

"Now you're going to tell me she loves me?" He snorted. "Well, I'm not buying it. A woman who could trick a man into giving her a baby, couldn't possibly know what love is." Jesse turned his back to Genie, and stared out the window, his shoulders stiff, his bearing unapproachable.

Genie knew she was losing this argument, and she was running out of ways to convince him of Rachel's feelings. But she was desperate to salvage the situation for the baby's sake. "Jesse, do you, or should I say, did you love her?" she asked softly to his back.

He stood so still, and for so long, she thought he hadn't heard her.

Finally, he turned to face her. Drawing a deep breath, his face appeared haggard and defeated. "What I feel or felt for Rachel is gone, and I don't want to talk about it anymore."

"I understand you're angry. Rachel's pretty broken up

about this, too. So just one last thing, Jesse." Genie stared deeply into his eyes. "Are you willing to let her walk out of your life forever?" Holding her hand up before he could answer, she continued, "No, don't answer that. Just think about it."

With that, she walked to the door and paused on the threshold. "Jesse, you've been in business for a long time. Surely you must know, sometimes you just have to go with your gut."

With that, Genie stepped through the door and closed it quietly behind her.

LEFT STANDING in the middle of the room, Jesse continued to stare at the door, not really seeing it. Instead, an image of Rachel flashed through his mind. The one of her laughing in the shade of a live oak tree on the banks of a little lake.

"Damn!"

He grabbed the beer bottle, remembered it was empty and slammed it down on the counter. In a detached sort of way, he was vaguely surprised it didn't shatter into a thousand pieces with the force of his anger. He felt like breaking something. Instead, he reached into the refrigerator behind the bar for another beer, deciding it was about time he broke his rules about drinking alone and drinking to get drunk. Humming the tune Genie had sung, he started on his ninety-nine bottles of beer.

"Hello!" A voice shouted from the doorway.

Jesse glanced across the room as Gage, Tanner and Rip entered.

"Go away," he muttered.

Tanner nudged Gage. "I told you it was time for an intervention."

Gage shrugged. "Yeah. You're right. He doesn't look so good."

"Nah. He looks like he's been on a bender." Rip marched across the room. "I thought you had a rule about drinking alone."

Jesse snorted. "Fuck the rules."

Rip walked past Jesse. "The least you could do is offer us a beer. That way it'll solve your problem."

Nothing was going to solve his problem. "I'd rather you left," he said and slumped into a leather lounge chair. The last thing he wanted was an audience to witness him drinking himself stupid.

"Why thank you. I don't mind helping myself." Rip grabbed three longnecks, popped the tops and handed one to Rip and Tanner. Then he dropped onto the sofa and took a long pull before he spoke. "Haven't seen you in the past two weeks."

Tanner settled in the chair across from Jesse. "You didn't show up for the last meeting of the TBC, and you didn't call to say why."

Gage propped his foot on the fireplace hearth. "So, what's eating at you?"

"Nothing," he lied and tipped his bottle, downing the beer, hoping his so-called friends would get the hint and leave.

"Were you sick?" Tanner asked.

"Did you get a terminal diagnosis from your doctor?" Rip asked. "That's the only reason I could come up with for you to miss one of our meetings."

Jesse almost wished he'd gotten a diagnosis from the

doctor. At least, then, he could medicate the pain away. "I'm not sick."

"Maybe not physically sick." Tanner's eyes narrowed. "Could you be love sick?"

Well, give the man a prize. Jesse glared at Tanner. "I don't want to talk about it."

"The way you were grinning when we left the cattle drive, we thought you had Rachel in the bag," Rip noted.

"If anything, she had me in the bag," Jesse took another pull from his beer. He was going to be here a long time. Two drinks down and none of his senses had dulled.

"She seemed pretty taken with you. What did you do to screw it up?" Rip asked.

"I didn't do anything. And she wasn't all that taken. She was using me."

The other three men in the room exchanged confused glances.

Gage crossed his arms over his chest. "Enlighten us."

If he didn't, Jesse knew his friends wouldn't leave him alone until he confessed what was bothering him. Downing the rest of the beer, he set the bottle on the end table and laid back, staring up at the ceiling. Then he lifted his head and stared around at the men who'd stood by him when he was at his lowest. If he couldn't tell them, who could he tell? "She only wanted my sperm."

Gage did a double-take, Tanner gasped and Rip spewed beer across the room.

"Say again," Gage demanded.

Jesse told him what he'd learned about Rachel and her plan to get pregnant.

When he was done, his friends shook their heads.

"The one time I was ready to toss caution to the winds and commit to one woman, she turns out like all the rest.

She didn't want me for me. She wanted me for what I could give her."

Somewhat cursed since adolescence with good looks, Jesse had girls and then women throwing themselves at him. Then, when his business, and then *businesses* flourished, the women were throwing themselves at him not only for his good looks but also for the money flowing in.

This situation was somewhat the same, yet totally different. This time, instead of throwing herself at him for his money and his good looks, a woman had thrown herself at him for his sperm. What the hell was the world coming to?

The more he thought about it, the angrier he got. The angrier he became the more beer he wanted to drink. He pushed to his feet and strode to the mini-fridge and pulled out another beer, praying the alcohol would take the edge off his anger.

"Now, wait a minute," Tanner rose from his seat and paced across the floor. "If I'm not mistaken, you were the one who couldn't capture her attention. Wasn't that what you told us?"

Jesse popped the top off the beer. "Yeah, so?"

"She didn't invite you on the dates with the other guys, did she?" Rip asked. "That was all her friend's doing."

"So?"

"So, that means she wasn't looking to you for a contribution to her plan," Tanner deduced.

"Not in the beginning." Jesse shoved a hand through his hair.

Gage's eyes narrowed. "Did you ever consider she might have changed her mind about following through with her plan?"

Genie had said the same thing, and he hadn't wanted to

listen. Jesse had held onto his anger like a lifeline. Her words came back to him like a canon shot to the gut. Was he willing to let Rachel walk out of his life forever?

Rip leaned forward, all joking aside and the beer wiped from his face. "Jesse, do you love her?"

Jesse stared into Rip's face without seeing his friend. All he could see was the tears in Rachel's eyes as she tried to explain to him the meaning of the notes in her day planner. He hadn't listened.

"I was going to propose to her that night," he admitted, his voice low, almost a whisper.

Rip slapped his knee. "Damn, dude. Don't screw it up."

Tanner shot a killer glance at Rip and stopped in front of Jesse. "You must love her, if you were ready to propose."

Jesse nodded. "I'm just not sure she loves me."

"Are you afraid to ask?" Gage muttered, hitting the problem on the head. "Are you afraid she was only after your sperm and not you?"

Jesse sank back into his chair and buried his head in his hands. "I don't know what to think. I was ready to commit to a woman. To make her my wife, and then I learned she wasn't who I thought she was."

"Isn't she still the woman who learned to ride a horse because she wanted to spend time with you?"

"To get my sperm," Jesse insisted.

"Didn't she try to discourage you from chasing her?"

"Yes."

"But you persisted." Tanner shook his head. "If anything, you pushed her into something she might not have been ready for."

"And she responded by falling for you," Gage said. "I saw it in the way she looked at you."

Jesse snorted. "Like you know what love looks like? Have you ever been in love?"

Gage shook his head. "No, but Rachel only had eyes for you. She didn't even look my direction, and I'm single and a potential sperm donor."

Jesse's fists clenched.

Gage grinned and held up his hand. "Don't worry, I'm not offering."

Tanner tipped back his head and stared down at Jesse. "The real question is, are you willing to let her go?"

Jesse shoved a hand through his hair. "I don't know."

"Well, maybe you need to think about it." Tanner glanced at Rip and Gage and jerked his head toward the door. "Come on. Our man has some stewing to do."

Rip stood. "Don't be a dick. If you love her, admit it and get that ring on her finger."

Jesse didn't walk his friends to the door. He sat where they'd left him, a million thoughts rushing through his head, all of them centering on Rachel.

He rose and paced the room, unable to quiet the cacophony in his head. So, he drank another beer. And another. No amount of alcohol dulled the ache in his chest.

Was he willing to walk away from her, after finally admitting he was ready to commit to her and a life full of love and sharing? Was pride an excuse to throw away the best thing to ever happen to him? Did he want some other guy to be the father of her babies? Ah, hell no!

Torturing himself was accomplishing nothing. He didn't need a psychologist to tell him, he couldn't let go. He already knew it. He was still in love with Rachel, and he'd be damned if he was going to lose her. She may have only wanted him for stud purposes, but she was going to get a lot more than she bargained for.

He shot a glance toward the clock resting on the fireplace mantel and was shocked to realize it was three o'clock in the morning.

Today was Saturday. Rachel would be sleeping in on her day off.

Tossing the dregs of his last beer down his throat, he pulled on socks and boots and rammed his cowboy hat over his unkempt hair. He shoved his wallet into his back pocket and staggered for the door. When he nearly tripped over his own feet, he realized he was in no shape to drive all the way to the city. He needed a ride. He jerked the phone off its cradle and called Mildred.

"Hello?" said a sleepy voice on the other end of the line.

"Mildred, I need your help. Will you drive me into the city?"

"Jesse? Is that you?"

"Of course, it's me. Who else would be callin' you at..." Jesse leaned closer, trying to focus his eyes on the clock, "...three-fifteen in the morning?"

"Jesse, it's not even light out. Why can't it wait until morning?"

"Because, what I got to say can't wait until morning." He belched and leaned against the wall.

"Jesse Jordan, are you drunk?"

"What does that have to do with any damn thing?"

"You're in no condition to drive to the city," Mildred said.

"No shit. Pardon my French."

"I get it, you're so drunk you can't drive and you want me to drive?"

"Give the lady the prize," he said swinging his arm out wide and knocking his beer bottle off the side table, sending it crashing to the floor. "So, how long will it take you to get here?"

She snorted. "Assuming I decide to come?"

"If you don't come, I'll drive myself."

"You can't do that. You'll kill someone—most likely yourself."

"Mildred, you're my mom's best friend. How would you feel if I died in a fiery crash, and you coulda saved me?" Jesse made a motion with his hands as if he were reeling in a huge fish at the end of his fishing pole.

"Okay, okay," Mildred said, sighing her resignation. "I'll be there in twenty minutes. Don't go anywhere."

As she hung up the phone, Jesse puffed out his chest and let his receiver dangle from the cord like an angler holding a prize fish, posing for the camera.

With no clear plan in his head, he knew he had to see Rachel, and he was sure to catch her at home between now and seven o'clock in the morning. Pacing the floor was difficult when it kept moving on him, so he went in search of another beer and sat down to wait for Mildred.

Twenty minutes later, a horn honked outside his house. He grabbed his hat and staggered through the front door. Thankfully, he made it to Mildred's compact car without performing a complete face-plant and slid into the passenger seat, banging his knees on the dash. He adjusted the seat backward as far as it could go, but he still felt like a sardine crammed into a tin can. Oh well, it was not to be helped. Finally, he turned to Mildred. "Holy shit, Mildred! What the hell have you done to yourself?" he blurted.

He'd never seen Mildred in sponge rollers and face cream. He squinted at her in the darkness and saw that she also had her fuzzy slippers on and a faded housecoat pulled tightly over her pajamas.

She gave him the stink-eye. "Not one word from you, Jesse Jordan. Not one word. Do you hear me?" she threatened.

"Sorry," Jesse said, remorse finding its way through his alcohol-soaked brain.

She shifted into drive and headed for the highway. "So where are we going at this god-awful hour of the mornin'?" She cut a glance his way. "A rehab facility?"

He stared straight ahead. "You just get me to Rachel's."

"Hot damn!" Slamming her foot onto the accelerator, the little car roared into motion and bumped dangerously down the gravel drive.

Jesse hung on, his head spinning and his stomach roiling with each bump Mildred hit.

Once they reached the highway's smooth pavement, he could breathe again and relaxed against the seat.

"Are you going to tell me what couldn't wait until morning?" Mildred asked.

"Nope," he said, staring at the stars glowing in the night sky hazed by his foggy brain. At that moment, he couldn't form a coherent sentence, much less voice what he wanted to say to Rachel. The only message registering in his brain was, *Enough, is enough!* Something was going to get settled when he got there. What, he didn't know.

They sat in silence as the little car ate up the miles between the ranch and Rachel's apartment building.

When they pulled up in the parking lot, Jesse sat for a moment to get a grip on his spinning head. Then he turned to Mildred. "Do you mind waiting? What I've got to say won't take long."

"Sure, what else do I have to do at five in the morning?" She leaned her seat back and closed her eyes. "Don't mind me. I always sleep in strange parking lots."

Guilt settled in his belly as he stared at the older woman. "You know, Mildred, you're an amazing person."

"Yeah, yeah. Go fix things with Rachel. You left her a complete mess."

Mildred's words gave Jesse a strange feeling of hope. He still didn't know what he was going to say, he only knew he had to see Rachel.

All the lights were off in the building except the outside security lights on the corners. Jesse climbed the steps, clutching the railing to keep from reeling backward. Once inside, he staggered down the hall. When he reached Rachel's apartment, he knocked on her door loud enough to wake the neighbors.

As he waited for her to answer, his mind caught up with his body. What was he going to say to her? He was still mad, but he wasn't going to let her go. Damn, what was taking her so long to answer the door? He reached up and banged his knuckles on the door again.

This time, the door behind him opened, and a sleepy Genie peeked her head out. "Jesse, is that you?"

"Go back to bed, Genie. I've come to talk to Rachel," he answered curtly.

"Okay, Jesse," she mumbled incoherently, closing the door like an obedient child. When the door was closed and the bolt shot home, he could hear a muffled *Yes!* through the hard wood panels.

While Genie's door had been closing, Rachel's opened.

Jesse turned his attention back to the source of his drunken binge. She stood there in a pale gold, silk wrapper, her feet bare and her hair gloriously disheveled around her shoulders, a surprised look on her face.

It had been more than three weeks since he'd last seen her, and his gaze drank in the sight of her. All the anger seemed to slip away, and his first impulse was to pull her into his arms and brand her with his kiss.

"Jesse, what are you doing here?"

"We need to talk. We can do it out here, or you could invite me inside so we won't wake the neighbors."

A door opened then closed farther down the hall as if to emphasize his point.

"Too late," she murmured, a small frown creasing her brow. "I think they're awake already. But, you might as well come in before they call the police on you for disturbing the peace." Rachel moved slightly to the side, to allow him to pass next to her.

Once inside, Jesse stood in her living room and removed his hat to run his hands through his hair. Pivoting on his heel, he turned toward the door, startled to see Rachel had walked up to within a yard of him, her footsteps muffled by the soft carpet covering the floor. Disconcerted by her nearness, he blurted the first thing to come to his mind. "Why?"

"Why, what?" she asked, her frown deepening.

"Why didn't you tell me?"

He watched as her face paled to a deathly white. The dark circles around her eyes intensified, giving her an ethereal quality.

"You know?"

"Of course, I know. Why did you lie to me?"

"I never lied to you, Jesse." She pulled her robe closer as if to ward off a chill.

Jesse's anger rose as he stood before her. How could she stand there and lie to him again? He was giving her every opportunity to confess her crime. He was willing to forgive and try to forget, but she wasn't willing to tell the truth. "Excuse me. Maybe I'm just a gullible country bumpkin, but what do you call tricking me into a relationship to get you pregnant, if you don't consider it a lie?"

"Jesse, go home." She turned and walked toward the door. With her hand on the knob, she faced him. "You aren't ready to listen."

"You're damn right I'm not ready to listen. I'll never be ready to listen to another lie. Do you deny you were looking for a sperm donor to get you pregnant?"

Rachel bowed her head. "No, I don't deny it," she said, her voice barely above a whisper.

"Besides being downright immoral, isn't that illegal?" He closed the distance between them.

"I...don't know," she said, glancing up at him with a wary look. "I mean, I realized it wasn't right, but I had pretty much ditched the plan when I started seeing you." She reached out to place a hand on his arm.

Jerking back as if burned, he stared down at his arm. He fought the blinding anger that surged through him. He needed to get past it to say what he'd come to say. What was it, again? "I see only one way to settle this," his tone cold and hard, "you have to marry me."

"Are you crazy?" Her shocked and angry expression pierced his heart.

"You heard me—you're going to marry me in two weeks' time."

"I won't," she said, her eyes filling with tears. "You don't love me."

"What did love have to do with your plan?"

She shook her head, tears spilling down her cheeks. "You can't make me marry you."

"If you don't, so help me Rachel, you'll regret it."

"Jesse, please, don't do this." Rachel buried her face in her hands. "I can't take much more."

He opened the door and glanced down at her one last time. "I'll press charges if I don't get your answer by this evening."

"HE SAID WHAT?" Genie erupted, sending the kitchen chair she'd been sitting in toppling over backward as she leapt to her feet.

"He said I have to marry him, or he'd press charges, or something like that. Frankly, I was in a state of shock. He may have said something about me regretting it if I didn't marry him." Rachel stared across at her friend. "Hell, at this moment I regret ever having met the man. Can he do this?" Her chin was propped in the palms of her hands, her fingers spreading up the sides of her cheeks, ready for the next round of tears.

"Boy, he really botched that proposal, didn't he?" Genie said as she paced back and forth, her brow puckered in a frown and her finger tapping her lip.

"It wasn't a proposal, it was a threat."

"Proposal, threat, who cares? If it makes Jesse the legal father of your baby, what do you care?"

"Oh Genie, I can't," Rachel wailed. "He doesn't love me. He's only marrying me because of the baby."

As far as Genie was concerned, Jesse Jordan was the best thing to ever happen to her friend. He untied every knot in that woman's personality so effectively, she was a mess. It did her heart good to see Rachel falling apart, especially with a bonafide marriage proposal awaiting her acceptance. "Precisely! Rachel, you can no longer think only of yourself. You have to consider the child you're carrying."

Genie knew she was hitting below the belt, but she

scored. She knew Rachel's sense of obligation to her child would be the clincher. Genie wasn't above tugging on heartstrings or laying on a huge guilt trip to see her best friend married to the man of her dreams.

Setting Rachel's cell phone on the kitchen table in front of her, Genie crossed her arms and tapped her toe. "What are you waiting for? Call him."

Rachel stared at the phone. "But what will I say?"

"Tell him to name the place. You'll be there."

For a long moment, Rachel stared at the phone. Finally, she straightened her shoulders, grabbed the device and dialed Jesse. "Hello, Jesse? This is Rachel. I'll marry you."

Genie waited impatiently as Rachel listened to the other end, and then hung up without uttering another word.

"Well? Did he change his mind?" Genie demanded.

Burying her head in her hands, Rachel sobbed, "No. I'm supposed to be ready on Saturday, two weeks from today. He'll have a car sent by to pick me up, then we'll be married by the justice of the peace at the court house."

Genie clapped her hands. "Rachel, that's wonderful."

"No, it's not. He's only doing this for the baby. He doesn't love me."

"Don't let it worry you. You'll have an entire life-time with him to soften him up."

"But weddings shouldn't be sad events."

"Well, if it makes you feel better, I'll stand with you at the ceremony. After all, I am your only family."

"Will you?" Rachel looked up, her eyes filled with tears.

"I wouldn't miss it for the world, Rache."

CHAPTER 26

"I can't go through with this, Genie." Rachel stood at the mirror over her dresser, staring at her face, but not actually seeing herself. The tissue she twisted in her hand disintegrated, depositing white dust and tissue fragments on the navy-blue silk suit she wore.

"You can, and you will." Genie's voice was firm and brooked no argument. "Your baby needs a father, and Jesse is the man to do it. Now, go put some makeup on over the dark circles under your eyes. You don't want to look like death warmed over for your wedding."

Genie ushered Rachel into the small bathroom and rummaged in the drawers until she found the base makeup and a sponge applicator. Dabbing a small amount of base onto the sponge, she tapped it gently against Rachel's cool skin, trying to cover the evidence of sleepless nights and worry.

"I just can't do this," Rachel repeated mechanically.

She had adopted the phrase as her mantra for the past two weeks. Sleep had been hard to come by. Her nights were spent tossing and turning, interspersed with nightmares of losing Jesse or just falling into a dark abyss. Days had been endless, with Rachel trudging through her work with little to no enthusiasm.

Mildred ran interference on more than one occasion, anticipating her needs before she even recognized them. In fact, her executive assistant was more animated than Rachel had seen her in a long time. Being so deeply entrenched in her own problems, Rachel didn't ask what was making Mildred smile more often.

Five days before the wedding, morning sickness had set in with a vengeance as if punishing her for all her past sins. The only bright spot in her day was the fact that the ceremony was going to be at three o'clock, past the time she usually lost the contents of her stomach. At least, she wouldn't humiliate herself in front of the justice of the peace.

After brushing blush on Rachel's pale cheeks, Genie pressed a tube of lipstick into her palm.

When Rachel didn't make a move, Genie planted her hands on her hips and gave her a disgusted look. "Okay, it's your turn, put some color in those lips, or folks will think you're a zombie. Geez, Rachel, you'd think you could get a little excited about the whole thing."

"Excited?" Rachel shook her head. "Excited? I'm about to marry a man who doesn't love me. It's really hard to get excited about that."

"Well, that's one way to look at it. Or, you could look at it like you're going to marry the man *you* love and will spend the rest of your life with, raising children and growing old together."

Applying the lipstick, Rachel capped the tube, set it on the counter and trudged back into her bedroom to sit on the edge of the bed. "I know you're right, but I feel so miserable."

"Would you feel better if you called it all off?" Genie asked, sitting next to her on the bed.

"Maybe."

Genie harrumphed. "It seems to me, for someone with a logical brain, you're not thinking very logically."

"What do you mean?"

"You think you'll be miserable with him because he doesn't love you."

"Yes."

"How would you feel if you didn't go through with this marriage, and you never saw him again?"

Bowing her head, Rachel lifted a clean tissue to her eyes to keep the tears from staining her silk skirt. "Miserable," she whispered.

"Which miserable situation would be the worst?"

Rachel's heart wrenched at the thought of losing Jesse. She had always thought a child would be enough to love. After knowing Jesse, she knew it would never take his place.

"Living without him," she finally answered.

"Seems like an open and shut case, to me," Genie clapped her hands together, sharply. "So, you're getting married. Try to look a little happier. At least, you're getting your man."

Rachel couldn't help but respond to Genie's enthusiasm. A small smile crept up the corner of her lips. It wasn't much, but it was a start.

A sharp knock sounded on the door to Rachel's apartment, startling the girls out of their conversation.

One look at Rachel's frightened expression was all it took, and Genie reached over and patted her hand. "You just repair your makeup, and I'll get the door," she said as she headed for the door.

Rachel dashed back into bathroom, her heart pounding against her ribs. She stared at the frightened woman in the mirror. Her mascara was smeared, and a tear trail streaked down one cheek. She was nowhere near ready, physically nor mentally.

Grabbing a washcloth, she dabbed gently at the mascara smear and tear streak, then applied a little base to cover the damage. As she finished, Genie appeared in the doorway with a confused expression on her face and her arms loaded with two large garment boxes.

"Did you order something?" Genie asked.

Rachel stared at the boxes, shaking her head. "No."

"Some guy in a monkey suit delivered these and said they were for you. He also said he would be waiting downstairs when you were ready to go."

"Do you suppose he's our ride to the J.P.'s office?"

"It's the only thing I could think of," Genie said, starting to cave under the weight of the boxes. "Can you help me with these? They're heavy."

"Yes, of course." Rachel grabbed the large box off the top and laid it on the bed, while Genie set hers down beside it.

"What do you suppose is in them?"

"Only one way to find out. Open them."

Rachel took the big box, Genie, the smaller one, and they lifted the lids at the same time.

"Wow," Rachel whispered.

"You can say that again," Genie responded.

"Wow," she said automatically complying. "Are these what I think they are?" Rachel asked not quite believing what she saw inside the boxes.

"Yep, I believe they are." Genie lifted a pale yellow, satin and chiffon gown from the tissue and held it against her shoulders. The color set off the highlights in her fiery red hair. "This one has to be mine, the color's perfect for me." Turning to the other box, Genie nodded toward it. "That one has to be for the bride. Go ahead, see if it fits."

Rachel gently lifted the gown out, holding it up to her figure. It was perfect. "But who...?" she asked, glancing across at her friend.

"Who else, dummy? It had to be Jesse."

"But I thought..."

"Don't start looking a gift horse in the mouth. Get dressed. You don't want to be late for your own wedding."

Slipping out of their clothes, the women pulled the dresses on and helped each other button the backs, then stood looking in the mirror over Rachel's dresser.

Genie grinned from ear to ear at the stunned expression on Rachel's face.

Rachel couldn't get over her own transformation. She was as pretty as any bride should be on her wedding day. The soft ivory satin wedding dress was simple, but elegant. The sleeveless bodice dipped at the neckline to expose the shadows of her cleavage and hugged Rachel's form down to the matching V-shaped waistline. The skirt flared out over her hips, falling gracefully to the ground just an inch beyond her feet. The back of the gown dipped in a long V to the middle of her back.

"I found these in the bottom of the box," Genie handed her a pair of matching ivory satin, high-heeled shoes.

Rachel slipped into the shoes and marveled at the ensemble. They fit so perfectly, they could have been custom made.

Genie grabbed her arm and led her toward the apartment door. "Come on Rachel, our chariot awaits." Lifting the hems of their gowns, the women quickly maneuvered the stairs rushing out to the parking lot to look around for their ride.

There in the middle of the pavement, taking up five parking spaces, was a sleek white limousine. A chauffeur in a black suit stood holding the back door open as the ladies approached. As they neared the door, an impatient voice boomed from within.

"Well don't just stand there. Get in. You're letting all the air-conditioning out."

"Mildred?" Rachel leaned over to peer into the interior of the limousine. Sitting in the far corner was her executive assistant, dressed in her finest.

"Are you going to stand there gaping, or are you going to get in? It's not every day I get all gussied up, and I don't want to be this way any longer than can be helped."

Gathering their skirts, Genie and Rachel slid in next to Mildred.

The chauffeur closed the door behind them and rounded to the front of the vehicle assuming driver's seat. "Ready?" he asked.

"Just get us there before she changes her mind," Mildred commanded.

The driver set the big car in motion.

Staring around at the posh interior of the vehicle, Rachel's gaze landed on Mildred. "Did you arrange for all this?"

The older woman shrugged. "Some of it."

A little disappointment slipped into Rachel's thoughts. She had hoped Jesse had thought of this. Shaking her head, she realized that was just a dream. The last time she'd seen him was when he'd made his demanding proposal. He couldn't have forgiven her by now. Rachel wrapped her arm around Mildred's slim shoulders and hugged her. "Thank you for being so considerate."

"I'd love to take all the credit, but I was under strict orders. I just got the right sizes and picked up orders."

"Then who...?" Rachel's question was interrupted as she noticed the limousine was slowing to swing into the crowded parking lot of a church.

Cars were parked in every empty space and some lined the streets. Not a soul was to be seen outside.

"Why are we stopping here? I thought we had to be at the Justice of the Peace's office by three for the ceremony?"

Mildred grinned. "There's been a change of plans."

Rachel pressed a hand to her roiling belly. "Did he change his mind?"

"On the contrary, he's waiting inside," Mildred grinned and jerked her head toward the church.

Rachel's breath caught in her throat, and her pulse hammered hard through her veins. She stared at the church, hardly able to comprehend what was happening.

The chauffeur opened the door and handed Genie out onto the pavement, then reached in to help Rachel alight.

Mildred scrambled out and grabbed Rachel's elbow. "No time to stand around gawking, they're waiting for you," she said, pulling a dumbfounded Rachel toward the door.

"But this can't be right. I think I'm dreaming."

Mildred did the honors, pinching her arm hard enough to hurt.

"Ouch!" Rachel rubbed the red spot on her arm and frowned at Mildred. "What did you do that for?"

"Proving you're not dreaming." She grinned unapologetically. "Now, quit yammering and let's kick off this shindig."

The doors opened as if on their own, allowing the ladies to step into the darkened interior of the vestibule. Someone handed a large bouquet of yellow roses to Rachel and set a shoulder-length veil in her hair, pulling the front flap over her face, where it fell just below her chin.

A smaller version of Rachel's bouquet landed in Genie's hands as Mildred disappeared into the interior. A matronly woman stood near the doors to the interior of the church, urging a couple of cherubic little girls to take their places, while she motioned to someone inside the church.

The heavy chords of the wedding march blared from inside the large room, and the woman gently urged the little girls to start down the aisle, scattering yellow rose petals as they went.

The woman smiled at Rachel. "I'm the wedding planner. I'll make sure you get down the aisle at the right moment." She winked and turned to three other young women, dressed like Genie and carrying matching bouquets.

One of them grinned at Rachel. "We're Jesse's sisters, we've been away at college or we would have been by to meet you sooner. We'll introduce the rest of the family at the reception. Right now, we have a wedding to attend." She spun and started down the aisle after the cherubs.

The next sister followed the first, and then the third fell in line.

"Now you, Genie," the wedding planner said with a smile.

Pausing in front of Rachel, Genie wrapped her arms around her and kissed her quickly on the cheek, through veil and all. "Everything is going to be wonderful, wait and see," she whispered in Rachel's ear, then turned to begin her glide down the aisle.

The wedding planner watched as Genie moved forward, and then turned to Rachel nodding. "Now, it's your turn."

Clutching the bouquet like a lifeline, Rachel took a deep breath and stepped through the door. Before she took another step, an older gentleman stepped in beside her.

"I would be honored if you'd let me give away the bride." John Jordan looked handsome in his black tuxedo.

"The honor would be mine, thank you." Rachel swallowed hard to dislodge the lump in her throat and smiled shyly at her future father-in-law.

When she turned to face the church's interior, Rachel finally saw Jesse standing in front with his three college friends standing beside him as his groomsmen, and Vinnie Fetachelli as the fourth groomsman. They all smiled in her direction as she walked in a daze down the aisle, praying it all wasn't a dream.

Genie took her position across from the groomsmen.

Vinnie grinned and teased her with a wink.

But, Rachel had eyes only for Jesse. He was dressed in a black tuxedo with a yellow rose corsage, the only dash of color gracing his lapel. The formal attire accentuated his blond hair and blue eyes, making Rachel weak at the knees.

His face was unreadable, neither smiling nor frowning.

The knot in Rachel's stomach tightened, threatening to make her ill in the middle of the day instead of her usual morning sickness. She gulped to tamp down the rising fear and bile, afraid she would make a fool of herself in front of Jesse and his family. A quick glance around the sanctuary confirmed it was crowded, every seat filled with Jesse's friends and family.

As they drew near, the preacher motioned them to stop. "Who gives this woman in marriage?"

"I do," John Jordan answered solemnly.

He stepped back and released his hold on Rachel's arm, gently urging her to move forward and take her position beside Jesse.

"We are gathered together to join this man and this woman in holy matrimony."

As the preacher began the ceremony Rachel stole a look through her veil at the handsome man standing beside her. He looked so incredibly good she forgot to breathe, almost passing out, there at the altar. Trying to calm her shattered nerves, she took a deep breath and closed her eyes, momentarily.

"If there is any reason these two should not be joined in the holy state of matrimony, please speak now or forever hold your peace."

"I have a reason why they shouldn't be married!" came a male voice from the back of the church.

Rachel, Jesse, Vinnie and Genie turned to stare as Lenny Lindeman, the taxidermist, walked hesitantly toward the front of the church, wringing his hands and darting a nervous look at the assembled congregation.

The preacher waited, allowing Lenny time to reach the front to explain.

"You see, I love Rachel and want her to marry me," he said with a sad, lost-puppy look on his pale face.

"Oh Lenny, I can't marry you," Rachel implored, stepping down from the raised platform and holding her hands out to him. "I don't love you."

"Are you sure?" he asked, hope pouring from his eyes.

"I'm absolutely positive." She stepped back up beside Jesse, indicating her preference.

"Then I guess I don't have a reason to stop this wedding. I wish you two luck," he said. "If you should ever need my services, don't hesitate to ask. I'll give you a special discount." With that, he darted back down the aisle and left the church.

Rachel smothered a shudder as she pictured the squirrel watch in her mind. She glanced up at Jesse to see him gazing down at her, a slight smile curving the edges of his wonderful mouth.

"Uh, is there anyone else here with a reason these two should not be married?" the preacher cringed as he asked.

There was a long pause, and Rachel thought the preacher was clear to continue. As he took a deep breath, another voice erupted from the audience.

"Yes, I have a reason they shouldn't be married."

Mildred? Again, the people on the platform turned, mouths agape, this time to stare at the diminutive older woman. Why would Mildred stop the wedding?

"Step forward and explain, please," encouraged the preacher.

"This man did not propose properly to this woman. I think she has a right to demand he do it again."

"Here! Here!" shouted Genie, and Jesse's mother and sisters.

The preacher looked taken aback by the request and the response, but handled it in stride. "Rachel, do you want Jesse to propose properly?"

Blushing furiously beneath her veil, Rachel gave a slight shake of her head, indicating a negative response.

"Excuse me," Jesse interrupted, "I would like to do it even if she doesn't want me to."

The preacher nodded once and took a step back waving his hand with a flourish. "By all means, propose."

Jesse took Rachel's trembling hand, sank down on one knee, and looked up into her face.

Rachel felt a little jolt, staring into his face. He looked thinner, and there were shadows beneath his eyes. Had he been as miserable as she'd been?

"I'd like to start by asking you to forgive me for my actions over the last few weeks. The time we've spent apart made me realize how much you mean to me."

The backs of Rachel's eyes began to burn, and she fought the urge to cry. Was he doing this for her? To make sure their marriage started on the right foot, or did he really care?

"I don't want to spend the rest of my life without you. You are the sun rising in the morning, the air I breathe and the hope that shines in every star in the sky. If I were to lose you, it would be like losing my own life. Rachel Taylor, will you do me the honor of becoming my wife?"

A single tear rolled down her cheek splashing on their hands clasped together. "I love you, Jesse Jordan, with all my heart. I would be proud to be your wife."

A cheer went up from the congregation, accompanied by happy laughter and clapping hands.

The preacher cleared his throat. "Once again, is there anyone here who has any reason these two should not be married, now that the old boyfriends have been adequately disposed of and the proposal has been properly administered and happily accepted?" The preacher glared at the gathered audience, daring anyone to speak. Not a peep was emitted from the crowd.

"I have a reason," Rachel grimaced and shrugged.

"What is this? Catholic confessional?" muttered the Methodist preacher.

"Kinda," she replied with an apologetic look at the

preacher. Turning to Jesse, she lifted the veil from her face and stared into his eyes, her own begging him to understand what she was about to say. "I need to know if you love me for myself of for the baby I'm carrying."

Jesse's eyes grew wide and his mouth unhinged. "What baby?" he demanded.

"Your baby," Rachel said her brows drawing closer in confusion.

"This is the first I've heard of a baby," he said, still shaking his head.

"But the other night when you demanded I marry you, you said you knew," she said, her confusion slowly turning into happiness, because by his expression, Jesse had no clue. "You mean, you didn't propose because of the baby?"

"No. I proposed because I couldn't live without you." He stared down at her belly. "What baby?"

"You mean you want to marry me because of me?" she squeaked, still disbelieving.

"Of course, I want to marry you because of you," he said, sounding insulted. "You're going to have a baby?"

"Yes!" Throwing her arms around him, she kissed him hard.

Jesse raised his arms around her and swung her in a circle, then held her at arm's length to look down into her eyes. "You're pregnant?" he asked, wonder shining from his eyes. "I'm going to be a daddy?"

Smiling, she nodded.

Grinning from ear to ear, Jesse turned to his groomsmen. "I'm going to be a father," he stated proudly, as if they hadn't been standing there during the entire confession.

"Congratulations, man," Gage said, grinning.

The groomsmen took turns pounding Jesse on the back.

"Ahem, I hate to interrupt, but are we going to conduct this wedding before you two have grandchildren?"

Jesse grinned. "That's right, let's get this wedding moving. I'm going to be a daddy."

Continuing where he'd left off, the preacher asked once more, with a pained expression on his face, "Is there anyone *else* here with a reason these two should not be married?"

Everyone in the entire church, down to the last adult and child, answered. "No!"

The wedding continued without further interruption.

Rachel vowed to love, honor and cherish Jesse until death.

When it came time for Jesse to repeat the vows, he turned to Rachel with all his love shining from his eyes. "Rachel, I promise to love honor, cherish and be your own, personal baby maker for as long as we both shall live."

With that the preacher announced, "I now pronounce you husband and wife. You may kiss the bride...again."

And Jesse did. Then he tucked Rachel's hand through the crook of his elbow and marched past his groomsmen. When he passed Gage, he leaned over. "You're next, man. Stick with the plan. You'll be happy you did."

Rachel leaned against him. "What plan? I thought I was the one with all the plans."

He patted her hand and swept her down the aisle and on to a life filled with love and children. It didn't get any better than that.

THE END

LOVE & WAR

TEXAS BILLIONAIRES CLUB BOOK #4

Elle James & Delilah Devlin
New York Times & USA Today
Bestselling Authors

LOVE & War

TEXAS
BILLIONAIRES
CLUB

NEW YORK TIMES BESTSELLING AUTHORS

ELLE JAMES
DELILAH DEVLIN

CHAPTER 1

IT'S ALL HIS FAULT!

Sophie Keaton's boots slurped in the mud as she trudged onward while mentally listing the numerous reasons she resented the new captain. He was autocratic, judgmental, unfeeling, overbearing... The list continued as she concentrated on putting one sore foot in front of the other to keep up with the long column of shadowy figures in front of her. Her head hurt from the weight of her helmet, and her shoulders ached from carrying the fifty-pound rucksack she had slung across her back. With her hands fully occupied carrying the M4A1 rifle, she couldn't satisfy an itch that was beginning to grow under the elastic bands of her underwear. With each step, she silently repeated her mantra, *It's all his fault!*

It had rained hard enough before the sun set to wash away the last trace of mosquito repellent, and a scourge of the winged creatures hovered around her, feasting on her exposed skin. The weather was unseasonably warm—even for springtime in Texas. She could feel the steam rise from the rain-soaked grass, plastering the heavy layers of her uniform to her body, adding to her ever-increasing misery.

Her platoon's training schedule specified an afternoon road march between the rifle range and their camp. That wouldn't have been so bad, but the morning's weapons qualification firing had taken longer than expected, stretching late into the afternoon.

Sophie was reaching for the field radio to request transportation to take her soldiers back to camp, when the new Company Commander, Captain Jenkins, arrived in his government-issue, desert-camouflaged HUMMV. The vehicle had the top and doors removed in deference to the heat, which made it an easy task for him to climb out in a hurry. He leaned over to say something to his driver, then strode in Sophie's direction. Snapping to attention, Sophie executed a sharp salute, returning her arm to her side when he returned it with his more masculine, and muscular, version.

"Lieutenant Keaton, what's the hold up? You're an hour behind schedule."

What did you expect, Keaton? Sophie mentally groused. How's the weather? What's your favorite color?

"Thirty-three qualified today, Sir. We had four fail to qualify, who required retraining and retesting. We now have one hundred percent of the platoon qualified, Sir."

Sophie lifted her chin and squared her shoulders, preparing for the inevitable finding of fault. When he didn't respond immediately, she studied him from beneath the rim of her helmet.

The captain wore those infernal sunglasses, which made it impossible for Sophie to read his expression. All she could see of his eyes were the crinkles beside them as he watched the soldiers chuck their gear for a break in place.

She hated the way he spoke to her without looking at her. But she supposed she was a bit of an eyesore in her rumpled camouflaged uniform and thick black, army-issue glasses—not that she wanted to appeal to him, or could for that matter.

Perspiration ran down the side of her face, and she knew her blond hair was probably frizzy and falling from its once neat coil at the nape of her neck.

Captain Jenkins, on the other hand, looked fresh. His uniform still held its starched creases despite the humidity. His hair was completely covered by his helmet, but he had the beginning of a five-o'clock shadow sprouting dark and thick. The rim of his helmet cast a shadow over his eyes, but Sophie could see a somewhat broad nose and a full bottom lip that was...interesting. Other than the fact that he needed a shave, he looked as sharp as the day they'd left for the field. He didn't even have the decency to break a sweat. Life wasn't fair.

Sophia sucked in a deep breath and dared to break the silence. "Since we finished up late, may I have your permission to call the First Sergeant to arrange for transportation to take the platoon the rest of the way back to camp?"

He turned to look her full in the face, lifting one eyebrow over the top of his sunglasses, a corner of his mouth slanting in a poor excuse for a smile. "The training plan specified a road march, Lieutenant. Are you or your soldiers afraid of the dark?"

She could learn to hate that smirk. It made her blood boil, and her hand itched to wipe it off his face, the arrogant so-and-so. He stood so near she had to tilt back her head to look into his face.

"Of course not, Sir. I just thought since we'd finished so late..."

"You'll continue with your training schedule, Lieutenant. You need to learn to take advantage of unexpected opportunities to train. We can include a lesson in light and noise discipline during night movement, while we march back to camp."

Oh no, what did he mean by *we*? She didn't want *him* joining her platoon for the march. Things happened whenever he was near her. Her normally poised and collected body seemed to grow two left feet, and she always managed to say the stupidest things. Her mouth seemed to disconnect from her brain in his presence—she couldn't seem to help herself.

Captain Jenkins pulled a map of the training area from a pocket in his uniform and spread it over the hood of his vehicle. "We'll follow the road until we reach this hill," he said, pointing at the map, "Then we'll leave the road to go cross-country for the rest of the march."

"But Captain, it's rained every day since we arrived. The ground's pretty muddy. Shouldn't we stick to the road?"

That eyebrow shot up, and the smirk started again at the corner of his lips. Her stupid mouth had just earned Captain Jenkin's sarcasm. Instead of showing her concern for her troops, she managed to sound like she was whining. Sophie knew what was coming next.

"Why, Lieutenant, are you afraid you'll melt?"

"No, Sir. I just thought it would be nice to get a transport for the men..."

She realized her mistake as soon as the words left her lips. Too late, she'd done it again.

Those eyebrows shot up over the top of the damned sunglasses. "Nice? *Nice?* Lieutenant, maybe you haven't noticed, but this is the Army not a tea party. Next thing you know, you'll have the men knitting socks."

The blood rushed up Sophie's neck, creeping across her face and into her eyes until she saw red. "Captain Jenkins, *Sir*, you may be my superior officer, but that remark was uncalled for, and I resent it. My job is to look out for the welfare of the men under my command."

"Lieutenant, you need to remember that these are soldiers, and you're supposed to be their leader not their mother."

"Oooooo!" Sophie stamped her booted foot. "And you are not my father, or step-father, for that matter, although you're just as opinionated. I've been in charge of this unit for over three years, and these are my soldiers. I look out for them as would any officer worth his, or her, salt. You've only been in charge for two days, most of which you've only shown up two times for a few minutes. You don't know my platoon like I know them. They work hard, are dedicated and know their shit." She stopped short of saying she loved them like brothers. That would have set off the captain, yet again. Without waiting for a response, Sophie pivoted on her heel and marched toward the soldiers. "Platoon, fall in!"

THE RAIN STARTED AGAIN when they were twenty minutes further into the ruck march. The soldiers took it in stride, unfurling their waterproof ponchos to cover themselves from head to knee. Unfortunately, Sophie's hung past her feet, dipping into the mud as she slogged along, causing her to stumble. Forced to choose her steps cautiously, she fell behind.

The terrain was every bit as sodden as she'd warned the

captain, but it didn't seem to faze him. And to her chagrin, the soldiers seemed to enjoy the challenge of marching through the muck. Sophie angrily berated herself for her earlier outburst with the captain, recognizing how unprofessional and childish it must have sounded. Not exactly the image she had worked so hard to build in front of her troops.

A stinging sensation assailed her cheek, and her hand automatically swung up to smack the pesky mosquito. The sound echoed loudly in the dark. The column in front of her halted, and one shadow separated from the rest of the men to draw close to her.

"Keaton, you're supposed to lead by example. Some example. At least *try* to keep the noise down," the voice whispered harshly.

Sophie recognized the source of the sharply issued command as her nemesis, Captain Jenkins.

"Sorry, Sir," she muttered, resigning herself to the fact she just couldn't do anything right in his eyes.

The soldiers turned to continue their march. Adjusting the straps of her rucksack, Sophie shifted the weight to a slightly less agonizing position. She was beginning to think the captain had an exceedingly poor sense of direction. She felt as if they'd been walking for hours.

With little else to keep her mind busy, Sophie thought back over the past three years she'd been a part of the unit. Admittedly, she'd joined the Army National Guard, partly to rebel against her stepfather's autocratic ways. He was dead set against her going into the Guard. That had made joining even more attractive. The poster of men in uniform went a long way toward her decision as well. Sophie loved a man in uniform. There was something sexy about a man standing at attention, with every line of his body reeking patriotism and discipline.

Her first day drilling with her unit burst the man-in-uniform bubble. Most of the men in her unit were good-old-boys. A good portion of them were overweight, tobacco-spitting red-necks. After the initial shock, she'd realized they were a great bunch of guys, who, despite their slovenly appearance, knew their jobs. The best part about the group of soldiers under her command was their marvelous, if somewhat raunchy, sense of humor. Never a drill went by without some memorable practical joke.

Sophie had busted her butt trying to earn the respect of her troops through her intelligence and willingness to learn. She overlooked some of their shenanigans, and they helped her to learn the job of leadership. In the space of two days, all that work seemed to be inexorably sliding down the drain. Why should the advent of a new Company Commander have such a negative effect on her?

Captain Jenkins had been introduced as the new Company Commander in front of formation on Friday night before they'd left for their weekend bivouac on the nearby military reservation. And to think, Sophie had actually admired him at that point.

Jenkins had stood straight and tall, all his creases lining up perfectly. He could have been the poster boy for an Army National Guard advertisement. His military bearing was enough to make her catch her breath, but it was the way his rolled sleeves strained against his muscular biceps that set her heart racing. She loved to see a man who went to the trouble of keeping in good shape.

The lenses of her glasses steamed at the memory. Since she could barely see her hand in front of her face anyway, she pulled them off and stuffed them into the pocket of her uniform.

Her only regret at the moment he'd been introduced was that his eyes had been shaded by the brim of his hat. She'd imagined him with soft brown eyes that could melt her to her soul. Now that she'd experienced his derision, Sophie figured he probably had ice-blue eyes that matched the color of his heart.

Sadly, his first impression on her had been a far cry better than her first impression on him. Everywhere she'd gone that evening in preparation for their field training, Captain Jenkins had been two steps ahead of her, issuing the commands she should have given. Her initial admiration had quickly turned into irritation.

"Kinda like our new captain, do you, L.T.?" asked her crusty old platoon sergeant, Sgt. Schott.

He chuckled at her discomfort and she muttered beneath her breath, glaring daggers into the new captain's departing back.

"You know the type, fresh off active duty, new to commanding a National Guard company, trying to make a good first impression. Hang in there, we'll break him in right, you'll see. Just leave it to us Non-Coms."

So far, she hadn't seen any breaking on Captain Jenkins part, but she, on the other hand, was getting ready to run screaming through the woods with his arrogant macho bullshit.

The night was dark as pitch, but she could hear the faint sounds of the soldiers moving down a ravine. Deciding she might as well get as comfortable as possible, she stopped to remove her helmet, placed the strap of her rifle over her head, and heaved the weapon around her back. Replacing her helmet on her head, she turned to follow the sounds of the soldiers as they made their way down the pitch-black ravine.

At the top of the gully, she paused, squinted and searched for the path the others had taken. With a deep breath, she stepped off the edge and landed in a muddy hole that sucked her foot downward until she stood ankle deep, the muck covering the top of her boot. "Damn!"

All she needed was to call attention to herself once more. The captain already thought she was hopelessly inept. With the suction of the mud pulling her down, she attempted to pull her foot free, then gasped as the weight of her rucksack carried her backwards to land with a *whomp* in the deep mud.

Sophie flailed helplessly, like a turtle on its back, her hands searching for something to hold on to so she could pull herself back up. At least her trapped foot was free of the sinkhole filled with mud. Then her other foot lost traction and slipped out from under her, she let out a long screech as she slid down the rain-soaked hillside. The rifle beneath her acted as a sled, the added weight of the rucksack giving her momentum to catapult her toward the group of soldiers walking single-file near the bottom of the ravine.

Muffled curses accompanied scrambling soldiers as they tripped over each other, trying to scatter out of the way. Too late. Her hurtling form collided with the tall man standing at the rear of the column of soldiers, looking up the hill toward her speeding form.

She swept his legs out from under him, and he landed with a whoosh on top of her, knocking the wind out of both of them. Together, they continued to slide, plowing into the group of soldiers causing a domino effect, toppling one soldier after the other. Finally, they bumped to a halt amid the chaos of soldiers and equipment.

Sophie remained still for a moment, winded, certain the rock on top of her had crushed the life out of her. The instinct to survive spurred her into action. She struggled to suck the breath back into her lungs and wriggled her arms up her sides, inserting her hands between herself and the rock. With all the strength she could muster, she pushed to dislodge the heavy weight from her chest, barely budging the massive frame.

The rock moved, slowly raising its head. Even in the dark, Sophie could feel his glare burn into her eyes. Her heart stilled, and she groaned inwardly as she realized the hunk of granite on top of her was none other than Captain Jenkins.

"Lieutenant Keaton, you are a boil under my skin." He shifted his weight, pushing Sophie deeper into the mud.

Slime oozed beneath her clothing, and she wondered whether he might decide to lie there long enough to make sure she sank all the way to China. The weapon and ruck-sack underneath her back pushed her breasts against his chest, and she limply gave up any further attempt to dislodge him. Her breath came in shallow gasps, and she grew light-headed. "Captain...Sir," she wheezed. "Just...get...off!"

He placed his hands in the mud on either side of her and lifted his chest from hers, which left the lower half of his body resting heavily between her legs. His nostrils flared, and his lips tightened. Sophie felt him pause for a moment before he abruptly lifted the rest of his body, until only his feet and hands rested on the muddy ground. Crab-stepping over her, he jumped to his feet, adjusted his uniform and donned his military bearing like a cloak. "With soldiers like you, who needs enemies," he growled. And with one last look of disgust, he turned and walked away.

The other soldiers rose to their feet, grumbling and swiping at the mud clinging to their backsides. After retrieving their rucksacks and weapons from the mud, they trailed after the captain.

Sophie sat up slowly. *I guess that pretty much sums up his opinion of me.* It wasn't as though she'd crashed into him on purpose. Tears stung her eyes, but she refused to let them fall. Soldiers didn't cry. She pushed her loosened hair from her eyes and looked around for her helmet. When she found it, she plunked it on her matted hair and hurried to catch up to the column of men.

Flashlights glowed in the thick darkness. Because of her, it was a little too late to worry about light and noise discipline now.

When Sophie finally caught up with the formation at the road bordering the training area, Captain Jenkins was just replacing the mike of the radio carried on a soldier's back.

Within minutes, a large, smoke-spewing truck lumbered down the road toward them, and Sophie heaved a sigh of relief. The captain had abandoned the idea of completing the ruck march. A spit bath and a sleeping bag weren't too far away, and she was exhausted.

The vehicle pulled to a halt beside them, but Sophie hung back, waiting for the last soldier to climb aboard. Struggling to get her foot high enough to reach the metal step on the tailgate of the truck, she was suddenly lifted by a large hand placed strategically against her derriere. She didn't need to look around to know the impertinent hand belonged to Captain "Jerk." She flew up into the back of the truck and landed on her hands and knees.

Sophie scrambled to find a seat on the bench and tried to be invisible as she watched his dark frame walk around the side of the vehicle and slide into the cab next to the driver.

Being invisible was impossible with her platoon of soldiers. No sooner had she settled on the bench and the truck started rolling, then the comments started flying.

"Seems you're a hit with the new Company Commander, Lieutenant," a soldier commented in the darkness.

"Him and a few others," agreed another, rubbing his arm.

"Have to give you a ten for first impressions on your commanding officer."

"I think he likes you."

"Yeah, and what's with him helping you into the truck?" said a voice Sophie recognized as Sgt. Schott's. "Would've been last in had I known you needed a hand. I guess rank really does have its privileges."

"He didn't help *me* into the truck," boomed a deep male voice.

"'Cause you're too damned ugly, Luckadoo!"

Loud guffaws of laughter broke out among the soldiers as Sophie slumped further down on the wooden bench, praying the captain couldn't hear the jokes made at her expense. Keeping a quiet and professional facade, she did her best to pretend not to be thoroughly mortified.

She wondered what had made her think the Army National Guard might be a great place to build her confidence. Right now, her confidence level had hit rock bottom.

She calmed herself with the knowledge that tomorrow

marked the end of this disastrous weekend and a return to her sane, dry, civilian life, where others appreciated and respected her abilities and judgment. She wouldn't be in a constant struggle to earn the respect of the men with whom she worked, namely, one Captain Gage Jenkins. Thankfully, she only had to put up with him once a month.

ABOUT THE AUTHORS

ELLE JAMES also writing as MYLA JACKSON is a *New York Times* and *USA Today* Bestselling author of books including cowboys, intrigues and paranormal adventures that keep her readers on the edges of their seats. With over eighty works in a variety of sub-genres and lengths she has published with Harlequin, Samhain, Ellora's Cave, Kensington, Cleis Press, and Avon. When she's not at her computer, she's traveling, snow skiing, boating, or riding her ATV, dreaming up new stories.

Learn more about Elle James at
ElleJames.com
Website | Facebook | Twitter | GoodReads | Newsletter

Or visit her alter ego Myla Jackson at
MylaJackson.com
Website | Facebook | Twitter | Newsletter

Until recently, award-winning romance author DELILAH DEVLIN lived in South Texas at the intersection of two dry creeks, surrounded by sexy cowboys in Wranglers. These days, she's missing the wide-open skies and starry nights but loving her dark forest in Central Arkansas, with its eccentric characters and isolation—the better to feed her hungry muse!

For Delilah, the greatest sin is driving between the lines, because it's comfortable and safe. Her personal journey has taken her through one war and many countries, cultures, jobs, and relationships to bring her to the place where she is now—writing sexy adventures that hold more than a kernel of autobiography and often share a common thread of self-discovery and transformation.

Delilah Devlin is a prolific and award-winning author of erotica and erotic romance with a rapidly expanding reputation for writing deliciously edgy stories with complex characters. Whether creating dark, erotically-charged paranormal worlds or richly descriptive historical stories that ring with authenticity, Delilah Devlin *"pens in uncharted territory that will leave the readers breathless and hungering for more..." (Paranormal Reviews)* Ms. Devlin has published over 140 erotic stories in multiple genres and lengths.

She is published by Atria/Strebor, Avon, Berkley, Black Lace, Cleis Press, Ellora's Cave, Grand Central, Harlequin Spice, Kensington, Montlake Romance, Running Press, and Samhain Publishing.

DelilahDevlin.com
Facebook | Twitter | Goodreads | Newsletter

www.ellejames.com
ellejames@ellejames.com